THE JUNGLE GOD

The Jungle God

H. Dean Fisher

Seventh Battle Publishing

ISBN-13: 978-1-952811-09-8
Library of Congress Control Number: 2021909881

Cover illustration by: Benjamin Zeus Barnett - facebook.com/BenjaminZeusBarnett
Author photo by: John Kilker - JohnJKilker.com

Printed in the United States of America

First Hardcover printing: June 2021
H. Dean Classics Volume 1
The Jungle God: 20th Anniversary Edition
Seventh Battle Publishing
Nicholson, PA

Contents

Author's Notes

This is the first in my "H. Dean Classics" series, books I wrote at least a decade before I began publishing. As such it seemed appropriate to begin this trip to the past with science fiction, my first love. I grew up on "Space: 1999," "Star Wars," "Alien," "Blade Runner," "Battlestar Galactica," "Buck Rogers," and "Flash Gordon." My heroes journeyed to strange planets, participated in mystical rituals, fought vicious aliens, rescued damsels in distress, and saved humanity from certain death. When I began writing stories as a child, they most resembled those science fiction worlds in which I grew up.

Science fiction of the mid- to late-20th century was heavily influenced by the film and television Westerns that preceded it. The lone gunman wandering the frontier could just as easily be John Wayne in "The Searchers" or Nathan Fillion in "Firefly." Both characters are lost souls trying to find redemption on the edges of humanity. At its core, "Star Wars" owes as much to "The Magnificent Seven" (and its predecessor, "Seven Samurai") as it does to H.G. Wells and his "War of the Worlds" invasion from Mars.

As such, "The Jungle God" is more than an adventure to an alien world to steal jewels. In the tradition of my favorite fandom, "Star Trek," there is a deeper, allegorical meaning to the action. There is an indigenous population with thoughts, feelings, and motivations of their own. The human colonizers are unwelcome intruders, the indigenous population is willing to go to extremes to rid themselves of the invaders, and I drop the reader into the middle of that conflict. In that way, "The Jungle God" attempts to bring to mind the United States' westward expansion into "the frontier," with aliens taking the stage in place of Native Americans. The allegorical ideas are not as fully explored or deftly handled as I might do if I wrote "The Jungle God" today, with my writing style and perspective 20 years ago more firmly entrenched in the action than in the themes that could be explored, but the kernels of deeper meanings and understandings are there nonetheless. After a couple decades of this sitting on my computer's hard drive, I was also pleased to read I did not fall completely into the trap of the White Savior Myth as many of our science fiction and Western stories so often do – looking at you, "Avatar." Even so, I would likely push myself even further from that line were I to write this novel fresh today. For now, journey through this interplanetary romp with its distinctly-20th century sensibilities.

Are there more adventures on the horizon for Jake and Rhaina? I think so. The skeleton of a sequel has been bouncing around my mind since I finished this book, and going through the multiple revisions now for publication has only brought those pieces more firmly to mind. Jake and Rhaina are a fun, dynamic couple, and I know that more adventures with them would be exciting for both you and me. Visit my website, subscribe to the newsletter, or follow me on social media for information about another "Jungle God" if/when it happens.

I owe several people a large "Thank you!" for their assistance, both then and now. First is the Write Right Critique Group of Lubbock, TX, that saw this book in its earliest forms and gave me incredibly valuable advice. Most especially I want to thank Ann Lavendar, www.AnnLavendar.com, who always knew Rhaina was a red-head, and also James Stoddard, www.James-Stoddard.com, who believed in my stories and appreciated my critiques; today I also give a huge shout-out to my good Write Right friend Kim Hunt Harris, KimHuntHarris.com, who has been such an inspiration to me. I owe the largest thanks to my wife, Suzanne, for her patience and thorough editing skills.

When I finished this novel 20 years ago, I submitted it to the 2001 SouthWest Writers competition, and I was thrilled when it took 1st Place in Science Fiction Novels. I was given wonderful advice and encouragement from literary agents, publishers, and editors, all of which I might have pursued more quickly had I not changed careers to begin teaching. I'm happy now, all these years later, to make this novel available for people to journey across the galaxy to another world that is struggling to find a balance between the "alien Lygmies" born there and the "alien Humans" attempting to colonize it. Enjoy the ride.

Though I no longer remember the music that formed the backdrop of my writing this novel, these are the albums I played while editing and revising "The Jungle God," and they work very well as the soundtrack. Enjoy.

> Black Box Recorder, "The Art of Driving"
> Ellie Goulding, "Delirium (Deluxe Edition)"
> Ivy Levan, "No Good"

1

Jake

"Stop," the silhouetted woman said.

Jake stopped, his hands clasped behind his head.

"Let me see your back."

He turned. He couldn't see his partner, Minke, hiding among the crates, but he knew the man was there. Not a comforting thought, since he knew Minke wanted him dead.

"All right, you're clean," she said. "Put your hands down and turn around."

He did.

"So where's the money?" she asked.

Was the shadow really her? She didn't seem to move right when she spoke, like she was more mechanical than she was human.

"You haven't shown me the datafile," Jake said. He blinked, twisted his eyes to the right, and his implants kicked on. The optical receivers in his right eye transmitted the digitized data to his brain, and his suspicions were confirmed. The silhouette was nothing more than a robot with a built-in voice amplifier. Their real contact could be hiding anywhere.

The receivers also told him his batteries were down to 11%, not surprising since he hadn't been able to recharge in almost a month. He hated jobs like this.

"Did you hear me?" he asked, glancing around. The optical receivers weren't picking up anyone in his field of vision, but his field of vision was hampered by the crates of luggage and supplies piled to the ceiling. Whose brilliant idea was it to make this exchange in the ship's freight hold?

"Um, Jake?" That was Minke. He was supposed to stay quiet until the contact was in the open. "I've got a little problem here."

Jake turned. Minke stood in the center aisle, a gun pressed against his ear. The gun was held by a silhouetted arm extending from behind a crate. Presumably, their contact was attached to the arm.

"Alone, eh?" the woman said, shoving the barrel deeper into Minke's ear. "What else have you lied about?"

"Nothing," Jake lied. "He's not with me. I guess he followed one of us."

"Then you won't mind if I splatter his brains across the suitcases."

It wouldn't bother Jake if the woman killed Minke – it would save him the trouble later. But their escape shuttle's security was voice-printed to Minke. Which meant Jake either found another shuttle when he left, or he kept his "partner" alive a while longer. He would probably regret this, but....

"Wait." Jake reached in the front pocket of his jacket and pulled out the plazgun. It was useless at anything beyond three dekatics anyway. He set it on the ground and kicked it aside.

"And the bug," the woman said.

Jake grinned. She had to be using the new TriniTech 1100 if she saw the bug, and the 1100 was notoriously glitchy in high-light environments – which explained why they were using the dark freight hold for this exchange. He popped the bug from under his collar and dropped it to the floor. A quick tap of his heel shattered it.

"It's your game now," Jake said.

"Set the money on the floor. Kick it between the two crates at your left. Then step back seven paces."

A black and white pouncer slinked out from between the crates at his left and knelt to the ground, its mouth open near the floor. Genetic engineering at its stupidest had given some feline-loving scientist the grand vision of creating a breed of cat with a human/animal voice box and a highly-developed psyche. But instead of pleasant lap-cats with a propensity for intelligent conversation, the scientist ended up with a pack of animals who enjoyed hunting humans in the dark. And of course they escaped. And then they bred like...well, like cats.

"What's the matter, human," the pouncer purred. "Cat got your tongue?" It sniffled at him, the closest the animals came to a laugh.

"I can't believe not one of your species has developed a decent sense of humor."

The pouncer's eyes widened black and his ears went flat.

"When we are free of the shackles of humanity," the pouncer growled, "then we will have something to laugh about."

"Right," Jake said. Never argue with a pissed pouncer. He removed the blueback from his coat pocket and slid it along the metal floor.

The pouncer, still growling at Jake, snatched the blueback into his mouth.

"By the way," Jake said. "That's one of the new issues – you know, with the anti-drug security system so you can't blow it all on the good stuff."

"We're not all nipster addicts," the pouncer carefully enunciated from around the chip. He turned and trotted into the maze of cargo, his tail in the air and a distinctive strut to his little prancing steps.

"Okay, it's your turn," Jake said to the elusive woman as he backed up seven paces.

"When this deal's done," the woman said, "I don't want either of you coming anywhere near me."

"Yeah. Whatever you say."

"Got that?" she asked, drilling the gun deeper into Minke's ear canal.

"Not a problem," he said, wincing.

"Money-boy, turn around."

Jake assumed that meant him, so he did.

"See the black crate on your right?"

"Yes."

"Open it. You'll find the merchandise–" The woman suddenly screamed.

Jake spun around.

Minke had the woman pinned to the floor with one knee to her chest and the gun barrel shoved in her mouth. How did he do that?

"You like that?" Minke screamed at her. "Huh? You like the taste of ear wax? Come on, lick it off. Lick it off!"

"Minke," Jake said, stepping forward.

"Do not interrupt!" Minke yelled, yanking the gun from the woman's mouth and pointing it at him. "I am not in the mood to rationalize!"

"Rationalize this," the woman said. The top half of her body collapsed and Minke fell forward on his hands and knees. A dark figure burst from beneath the robes behind Minke and scurried into the shadows.

Jake revved up his implants as he ducked to the ground. Ignoring the low-battery warnings, he slipped into Fighting Mode, and the freight hold came alive with the digitized data blasting into his brain. Minke was jumping back to his feet at 20 tics per second, the distance between them was 1.3 dekatics, the cargo bay had a square perimeter measuring 30 dekatics on a side, there were 17 crates visible along the center aisle (including the black one), 13 suitcases were piled against the far wall by the door.... It was all very interesting, but what happened to the woman?

Minke tore apart the remains of her costume, but Jake's implants couldn't see her anywhere.

The pouncer leapt on Minke's back, claws and teeth sinking into his skin. The man screamed and lurched to his feet.

Jake's audio amplifiers picked up a rhythmic humming, and he turned to stare at the black crate. The damn thing had a bomb in it.

2

Jake

Two choices, Jake thought. Help Minke fight the pouncer or run after the fleeing contact. He needed Minke alive for their shuttle's voice-printed security system. On the other hand, they didn't come twenty bazillion kilotics to get blown apart by an audaciously ticking bomb while their only source of information just up and ran away. Besides, Minke was planning to kill him. Whoever said there was honor among thieves?

Jake jumped to his feet and raced down the center aisle, away from the black crate, past Minke and the pouncer, and through the now-open bulkhead to the food storage room. He stopped to scan the room. 33,918 units of dehydrated food. And the woman? Not there.

He ran through to the hallway down the wing of the ship. Seventeen people walked within twenty dekatics of him, but nobody matched the slight build of their contact. Jake cranked up the audio amplifiers.

A man: "Want to go to the gym?"

A woman: "We'll have 14 days to make it work."

A second man: "And at the speed we're traveling, we'll reach Earth...."

A third man: "...again that it's just a matter of time...."

A second woman: "Do you remember...?"

Nobody's voice matched! Where did their mysterious person go?

"Was that a Lygme?" someone said.

He turned and zeroed in on the man by the wall, the one talking to his son and looking aft. Jake took off at a sprint, stowing his pistol until he passed most of the other passengers. The hallway grew darker and more cramped the farther he ran. The conversations of the passengers died down, and he slowed to a walk.

This was the industrial area of the ship. Pipes and heavy machines labored loudly in the harsh, utilitarian light. Jake's thermal sensors hadn't detected heat residue on any of the doors or walls he'd passed, and if she really was a Lygme...well, she could run, but she'd be noticed.

Movement to his right.

He stopped.

The blur darted away into the shadows. Definitely Lygme. Two-thirds his height and twice his speed. His sensors calculated her probable location, and he aimed the pistol at the figure crouching just out of his line of sight and behind a nearly empty moisture-catcher.

"Do not even think about moving," he said.

She didn't reply.

Probability she was in that spot? 87%. Next best location? 31%. He kept his gun where it was, cringing as the sensors told him the batteries were dying. He had to get off Fighting Mode or his Tech would dry up. Just a few more minutes....

"The datafile," he said. "Give it to me."

His answer came as the moisture-catcher flew at him with a metallic clatter. He ducked, and the Lygme darted past him and back the way they'd come. Damn! Why did they always run?

He raced after her down the utility hallway, past the storage rooms where Minke was still fighting the pouncer, and into the main plaza of the ship. People gawked at the Lygme shoving past them. A few screamed. The Lygme raced on with her superhuman speed.

"Everybody down!" Jake yelled, flipping open the Security Force badge tucked in his outer pocket. "Federal agent! Down, now!"

Everyone did as he said – almost. A couple of old men, either deaf or curious, stood by the wall and grinned at him. They were probably out of harm's way.

Jake stopped in the center of the ship's plaza and aimed the gun. The targeting cross-hairs flashed before his eyes. Time seemed to stand still as the Tech took over. The data streamed from the gun to the transceiver in his brain where the processors told him exactly where to aim...how much energy to focus in the beam...when to pull the trigger.

The beam punched through her right kneecap, and the Lygme stumbled. She hit the ground and skidded across the smooth metal, slamming into a supporting beam near the far wall, a bloody streak marking her trail.

Jake warily approached, and the Lygme struggled to sit up. Blood ran from her leg and pooled around her body. She turned to him and grinned, her golden eyes sparkling in the harsh light as she yanked off a wig. Bright orange hair fell in disheveled strands before her eyes.

"Braku dae slitta, eh?" she said.

Jake's Lygmese might be a little rusty, but he knew an insult when he heard one.

"Badlinksda y' frosha slip, eh?" he said. Was she banished off-world because she was so tall?

She just laughed. She also squeezed her thigh to cut off the flow of blood to her knee. Damn, they were tough little critters.

"Beda'ka daip leh," she said. Something about wanting him to live....

"Eka?" Why? What did she mean by that?

"Byklendaker ee' tipaey!" she laughed. You've got the God's ear now.

Jake leveled his gun at the Lygme's head. He didn't know what she meant, but bad things happened when Lygmies laughed.

"Besch de breik," she said, clenching her jaw shut. Her body spasmed. Her eyes bulged out, her arms flew to her mouth, and she collapsed to the floor.

The instant she died, a thunderous explosion blew a hole into the main hallway. Alarms blared while people screamed. The explosion knocked Jake off his feet, and he struggled to hold the gun as he fell.

He crouched on the shuddering floor, steadying himself against the dead Lygme's body. Obviously she had some kind of poison in her mouth, probably some paste along her gum line. The bomb in the baggage hold had apparently been set to blow when she died. Probably a heart monitor, maybe a linked switch to the poison in her mouth. And then there was Minke. He and the pouncer were probably blown to a zillion pieces.

Oh, well, Jake thought. Two less people in the universe who wanted him dead.

The Lygme's last statement, though, bothered him. Look in her left shoe? He knew better than to trust the word of a Lygme, but he was out of options. If the datafile really was in the baggage hold, she had just blown it to bits. But if it was in her shoe....

The floor shook from a second explosion. The hallway was nearly deserted except for those two deaf men who were ambling along the far wall and watching the flames.

Jake ran his hand down the length of the Lygme's left shoe. Flexisteel-reinforced, of course. He couldn't feel anything through it, and his Tech wouldn't be able to distinguish a datafile from a flexisteel seam.

How did this Lygme get Army-issue boots?

Jake shook his head and pulled a pen from his pocket. Questions like that would have to wait until he was off the exploding spaceship. He unscrewed the pen cap, tipped it upside-down, and dropped a small laser knife into his palm. Stowing the pen again, he turned the knife on and set the red beam against the Lygme's boot. With a flick of his wrist, the blade pierced the flexisteel toe and he sliced it open along the stitching. Carefully prying away the sole, he scanned the boot's interior.

His sensors detected nothing more dangerous than the Lygme's foot odor. He stowed the laser knife in a shirt-sleeve holster and yanked the shoe apart. He pried along the edge until he found a datafile sewn into the lining. Grinning, he rotated the shining disk in his hand, then stowed it in a secure shirt pocket.

He turned and saw the ship-tecks battling the blazing fire. As they were there instead of humans either the fire was so intense that people would burn, or the fire had gotten so out of control that the ship-tecks were buying time for everyone to escape.

Only then did Jake hear the recording echoing from the speakers: "Warning. Evacuate immediately. General distress call going out on all frequencies."

Flashing red words bounced before his eyes. His batteries were down to 5%.

3

Jake

Jake powered down the implants to save the last of his battery, and the stats, charts, and warnings disappeared from before his eyes. His hearing returned to normal and his muscles loosened as the computer released control of his body.

He glanced once more at the ship-tecks, then wished he hadn't. Those two old geezers, the ones who stood by as he shot the Lygme, were trapped on the other side of the fire.

Jake had to escape, but he couldn't just leave them. He looked toward the stairs, but smoke overwhelmed the ship's air filters. It'd be a matter of minutes before he couldn't find his way back to the shuttle.

The old men waved at him. What in the galaxy were they doing? They obviously weren't blind – they had to see that the ship wouldn't last much longer. Yet there they stood, carefree as the day they were born, just watching him.

"Hold on!" Jake yelled, breaking into a run. "I'm com-"

The floor buckled beneath him and knocked him against a wall.

Metal groaned as the flaming hallway twisted, sending the old men flying through the air, landing atop a blazing pile of luggage. They struggled, but the fire consumed their bodies.

Jake shut his eyes. He wiped his forehead and brought his hand away covered in blood. He tried to stand, but the ship lurched sideways, and he stumbled back to the floor, clutching his head.

He looked around, but smoke swirled everywhere. A blast of heat slapped his cheek. He coughed as the fumes seared his throat. At this rate, he'd be lucky to make it another few steps. Disregarding the consequences, he blinked and twisted his eyes to the right. The implants kicked on again, and his mind and body cleared.

He accessed his internal compass and maps. The smoke burned his lungs and he tried to stifle another coughing fit, but it brought him right back to the floor. He still couldn't see where he was going, but he could breathe better beneath the smoke layer, and the maps told him he wasn't as far off as he thought. As long as he was using the implants again, he also told the computer to amplify the healing to his head. The bleeding stopped.

He turned to his left and shuffled forward one dekatic at a time, along the back wall, past the Lygme's body, and down the hallway to the stairs. The steps shuddered as he raced down the two flights to the shuttle umbilicals. He could still hear the fire raging above him. The ship's air vents were doing a marvelous job spreading the smoke to the levels that weren't even on fire.

His implants told him he'd reached his ship's gate, and his batteries went dead. With no further warning the compass disappeared, leaving him computerless. He wondered for the umpteenth time if this assignment really was worth it, but assured himself that a certain amount of money would compensate for a couple charred lungs – assuming he lived.

He still had a problem, though, because the shuttle's security system was voice-patterned to Minke. Without his implants, Jake could belt out a pretty good Captain Flatulence, but he couldn't come close to imitating Minke. Which left him the option of hot-wiring the security system.

He sucked in a lungful of the smoke-free air and stood, his hands guiding his way up the umbilical's gate. With a flick of his wrist, the laser knife shot out of his shirt-sleeve holster and into his hand. He stabbed the point into the gate's frame and sliced open the control panel. Under normal circumstances this would have set off every alarm in the ship. Fortunately, the ship was blowing up.

Dropping to the floor, he stowed the knife back in its holster and gulped more air, then stood. He yanked the computer panel from the wall, exposing the jumble of multi-colored wires and circuit boards. This wouldn't be as easy as crossing the red wire with the green, but the principle was the same. He gripped a handful of wires and ripped them from their solders. That would convince the gate that the ship had lost power – not a big stretch considering the crisis of the moment.

Next, he had to convince the gate that a ship-wide override had gone into effect so it would release all its security measures from the shuttle. A quick, electrical zap into the right circuit would work perfect. He snapped back the fingernail of his right index finger to expose the first electrical lead, then snapped back the fingernail of his left index finger to expose the second. Originally installed as a security precaution to keep any random electrical bursts from short-circuiting his implants, he had discovered many more unconventional uses for the ground wire running through his body.

He tapped his left finger against several dead wires before getting a slight twinge. Contact! He set his right finger against the gate's override, touched his left finger to the live wire again, and zapped the gate with just enough electricity to let it know who was boss. Letting the wires and circuit board drop back into the wall, he snapped his fingernails into place and leaned against the gate.

He grinned. Any second now it would open...that's right...any second....

The whole ship rocked as something really big exploded one or two decks above him. The lights flickered.

"Any second now," he muttered, turning around to glare at the stubborn gate. The smoke spiraled around his face, and he had to cover his mouth to keep from gagging on the fumes of melting plastic and rubber.

Was the gate stuck? This kind of thing always worked in the holoshows.

He dropped to the floor and pried at the crack around the gate's frame. It didn't even budge.

Choking back his desire to panic, he thought through his options. Escape pods? Even if there were any left, they were five decks above him. Another shuttle? A better idea, but it would take about as long as the escape pods.

He punched his fist into the door but only succeeded in making his knuckles bleed. *Just open,* he thought.

He stepped back and slammed his shoulder against the door. He tried again. Then a third time, and a fourth. The thickening smoke almost got to him, and he collapsed to the floor. Time to try something different, he thought.

"Open, sesame," he muttered as he turned away.

The metal lock clanked open. The door swished open, and light cut through the smoke.

"That's it?" He almost waited to see if it was a mirage, but jumped ahead instead. If he was hallucinating, he deserved to crack open his head. But if he wasn't....

Something gripped the collar of his jacket and yanked him the rest of the way inside. He skidded across the shuttle's tiled floor, burning his elbows and palms before crashing into the far wall.

The door slid shut, and a man's bloodied and beaten face grinned at Jake through the blinding light and swirling smoke. The man gripped Jake's shirt, wrenched him up, and drove his back into the wall.

The man's left eye was swollen shut. His hair was matted with blood that still trickled down his cheek, and the hand that gripped Jake's shirt was slashed and gouged, exposing shredded muscles.

The man slammed a bottle of pain killers and gulped at least a dozen, his red teeth grinding them into a sludge that he chewed with obvious distaste.

"Glad you could make it," Minke said between swallows of pain-killer paste. "The datafile wasn't in that black crate. But I'll bet you already knew that."

4

Jake

"You really played me for a sucker," Minke said, dragging Jake down the shuttle's narrow hallway. "I never believed you were a federal agent, but to be in league with Lygmies – what are you getting out of it anyway? Money? Power? A *half* night of pleasure?"

He tossed Jake against a wall, then dropped into the command chair. Jake struggled to sit up, rubbing at his tingling arm. It felt like Minke had wrenched the blood out.

"Let's enjoy the fireworks," Minke said. He released the locking mechanism to the shuttle's umbilical, flipped on the secondary rockets to give the shuttle a little boost, and switched the computer display to an aft view.

Guilty as Jake felt for thinking it, the transport looked beautiful as it erupted in flames – especially now that he wasn't on it. Fires lit almost every window of the top five decks, and flashing red and white lights winked throughout the bottom decks. If he'd felt better, Jake would have made some quip about the whole thing looking like a Christmas tree in a forest fire. Considering the circumstances, he kept quiet.

"Look," Minke said, pointing to the display. "That's where your little friend blew a hole in the ship." He laughed, then coughed a spray of blood. He slammed the nearly-empty bottle of pills to his mouth and chewed, his eyes squinted shut.

Sensing his best opportunity, Jake flicked the laser knife from its wrist sheath and leaped onto Minke's back. He drove the point through the base of Minke's skull and into his brain.

Minke jumped up and elbowed Jake in the gut. Jake rolled to the floor, clutching his chest and trying to get the wind back in him. His head started bleeding again, and he stared at Minke through blurring eyes.

Minke stumbled behind the command chair. He gripped the hilt of the knife and his head cocked nearly off his neck. He staggered, twisted the knife. His head rotated like a puppet on a stick as he bent the knife around. He yanked out the crackling, smoking blade and turned to Jake.

"You're even stupider than I thought," he said. He retrieved the pill bottle from the floor and waved it through the air. "What do you think these are? Aspirin?"

"You're a plastic man," Jake whispered. Plastic men weren't made; machines grew them to specifications, evolving a psyche and a set of skills necessary for the plastic man to complete its task. Jake had no doubt Minke was perfectly capable of defending himself against any weapon aboard the shuttle. His creators would have seen to that.

"Of course I'm a plastic man," Minke said, laughing a cloud of bloody drops into the air. He poured more pills into his mouth and kept talking as he chewed. "You didn't think they'd let you come all the way out here without some insurance, did you?"

Who is they?

As if in answer, Minke threw his head back and laughed.

"You never knew?" he said. "And all along I thought you were smart."

Jake turned and sprang for the hallway. He had an idea, but he needed to get to the back of the shuttle to make it work. A quick override of the safety controls, a sturdy grip on a shock harness, and Jake just might be able to shove Minke out an airlock. His head spun with the first couple steps, though, and he slumped to the floor. He crawled forward.

"I like your determination, Jake, but I don't see where you're going with this."

He ignored the plastic man as he pulled himself down the hallway.

"Oh, now your feelings are hurt," Minke continued. "I never should have told you how stupid you are. It took the fight right out of you."

If Jake wasn't so fond of living, he'd take death just to keep from hearing any more. He pulled himself into the galley and looked up. He'd never make it to the back of the shuttle, but least in here he might find more weapons.

Minke laughed.

"Looks like you took a wrong turn, Jake. Unless you're after a midnight snack. Is that it?" He gave Jake a wide berth as he strode into the galley and opened the walk-in freezer. He examined the rows of re-sealable food pouches. "What'll it be, Jake? Steak-in-a-bag? Maybe some rehydrated prunes?"

It wasn't what Jake had in mind, but sensing an opportunity generally reserved for holo-star heroes, he jumped to his feet and fell across Minke's back. Minke gripped a shelving unit of canned food as he fell, yanking it down on top of him with a clatter of frozen cans and metal on plastic.

Stumbling out of the freezer, Jake threw himself against the metal door and slammed it shut. He pressed the code to lock it. It did. He punched the code for the Insta-Freeze. The keypad changed from green to red, but the freezer didn't kick in. He punched the code again and waited. The keypad blinked red.

"Do something," he muttered. "Before the bad guy wakes up."

He turned to the temperature display and saw words scrolling where the numbers should have been: "Unable to begin Insta-Freeze process. Person or animal detected in freezer."

"But he's not really a person," Jake said, keying in the Insta-Freeze code again. "It's okay to do this. Trust me."

Instead, the display scrolled its warning.

Cans clanked against the freezer's metal floor.

"Stupid machine," Jake muttered, trying to think of an alternative. He leaned against the wall and rummaged through the silverware drawer until he found one steak knife and a filet knife. He knew there had to be more knives, but he had no idea where. Minke had been in charge of the cooking, and it never occurred to Jake to question why. Now he knew – he who controls the kitchen, controls a lot of handy weapons.

The ship's speakers crackled to life.

"Jake," Minke said through the intercom. "You know you can't keep me in here. Let me out before I get really mad."

Jake spotted the bottle Minke had dropped to the floor, and he dumped the plastic pills down the garbage disposal. They emitted satisfying crunches as the blades ground them to tiny chunks. Minke probably had another bottle stashed somewhere on the ship, but at least this one wouldn't do him any more good.

Minke pounded on the freezer door.

"Jaaaake," he hummed through the intercom. "Where are you, Jake?"

The hinges popped, and the door groaned.

Jake dropped his own poison capsule down the disposal, then tossed the bottle across the floor like it had been dropped there. He turned to see the red beam of his laser knife sticking out from the freezer door. It wriggled around as Minke sliced a small hole.

"The Insta-Freeze doesn't work on me," Minke said. "I'm just human enough to fool it. Kind of like you, huh? All tech'd up and no juice to go. What a shame we never found a place for you to recharge. How did we let that slip our minds?"

Jake leaned against the wall, poised to strike with the knives as soon as Minke stuck out his arm. He tried to focus on the red beam as it sliced through the metal door, but it was becoming harder to think, to move, to just stand in one spot and wait. What a time for the batteries to go dead on his tech! He was never leaving home without a spare generator again.

The laser blade disappeared, and Minke punched his fist through the hole.

Jake swung the filet knife, but Minke pulled his arm back like lightning, and Jake sliced air.

Minke's hand burst through the hole again and gripped Jake's shirt.

"Hello, Jake," Minke said. "What's a little freezer door between enemies?"

He yanked Jake forward, slamming his forehead into the door. The filet knife slipped from his hand, and he struggled to keep his balance.

"Do I have your attention?" Minke yelled. "No?"

He wrenched Jake forward again, then again and again until Jake hung like a rag from Minke's arm. Minke let go and Jake slumped to the floor. Extending his arm all the way, Minke fumbled with the keypad for a moment before hitting the right combination of buttons. He opened the freezer door, shoving Jake across the floor and under the table.

Jake groaned and struggled to push himself up. The floor seemed to slide out from under him. He blinked and twisted his eyes to the right, hoping there would be a few minutes of power in his tech. He only made himself dizzy.

"What did you do?" Minke yelled, shaking the empty pill bottle.

Jake tried to laugh, but he hurt too bad. It was funny, though, listening to Minke's plastic skin crinkle and crack from the cold freezer air.

"Down the disposal?" Minke yelled as he fished out a handful of chopped up pills.

He gripped Jake's ankle and slid him out from under the table. He pulled Jake up by his shirt so they could see eye to eye. "I'll bet you think that's funny, throwing my plastic pills down the drain. Well, let me tell you something even funnier. I have more bottles! Lots more bottles – hidden all over this ship."

He sprayed crystalized blood across Jake's face as he laughed. Then he tipped his head back and downed the pill pieces, chewing them up and grinning at him.

"My turn...to laugh," Jake muttered.

Minke stopped chewing, and he glared at Jake.

Jake smirked.

Minke dropped him and spun around, spitting out the remaining pills. He retched into the sink while Jake retrieved the filet knife. Minke could puke his guts out and it wouldn't matter. All that poison needed to do was get into the bloodstream – or in Minke's case, his plastic-stream – and it would find its way through Minke's entire body.

Minke gasped and dropped to the floor. He jammed his fingers down his throat to get the rest of the poison to come up and staggered toward the door.

"Wait," Jake said. He found the last of his strength and lunged at Minke's back, sending them both sprawling onto the hallway floor.

Minke tried to roll over to get a grip on Jake's throat. Jake didn't even try to stop him as he fell across Minke's arm and used the momentum to shove the knife in one side and out the other, pinning the arm to the shuttle's floor.

Minke laughed, the sweat on his face mixing with the bloody streaks to make his face a chaotic mess that might have inspired a modern artist.

"You're a fool, Jake," Minke gasped. "I'm a plastic man. You can slow me down with knives and poison, but it'll take more than that to stop me." Minke reached over and started beating on his plastic arm, bending and snapping the joint away to get free of the knife. The elbow popped, spewing more blood across the floor.

Jake flipped back a fingernail on his right hand and punched his fist through the plastic man's chest. He broke through the outer plastic shell and gripped the metal spine running down the plastic man's back.

Minke clawed at Jake's hand, but the poison was already taking its toll. Minke didn't have the strength to do anything more than scratch at the sleeve.

Jake flipped back the fingernail of his left hand and shoved the metal contact into the power outlet near the floor. The electricity raced through his finger, bolted from one side of his body to the other, and zapped the metal rod in Minke's back. The spark overloaded the circuits of Minke's body. He jerked and sputtered, and tiny flames split the plastic all over his body.

Jake yanked his finger from the outlet and pulled his hand from Minke's chest. Flames jumped from the hole and began consuming Minke from the inside out. His flesh burned, the metal scorched, and the plastic connecting the two just shriveled into pulp. The noxious fumes of burning plastic overloaded the shuttle's air purifiers, and Jake covered his mouth to keep from coughing.

Minke lay on the floor, his body burning, and he smiled. When the plastic man finally spoke, Jake had to struggle to understand the human/electronic voice that crackled from the flaming mouth.

"You're...good," Minke said. "We...underestimated...you."

The shuttle's fire alarms blared. White foam shot from the walls and ceiling, dousing the fire. Minke's plastic body shriveled into a pool of dripping, smoldering pulp.

5

Geminai

the Sea of Souls

Rhaina's Geminai drifted through the darkness. The raging sea beneath her stretched across the Eternity of Souls, its boundaries defined only by her knowledge of people and Lygmies. Sparks of otherworldly minds bounced across the horizon, but they never remained long enough to be pursued, and Geminai wasn't certain her thread would stretch thin enough to take her as far as she might need to roam. The sea could be dangerous, and some souls were greedy. If they found her lost, without her thread, they could grab her, force her into their own bodies, and compel her to do wicked, evil acts that her human, Rhaina, would despise.

Fingers of rainbow hues erupted at her, then cascaded back into the churning waves below. The golds, blues, purples and whites were beautiful and mesmerizing to watch, but Geminai knew all to well the realities they contained. One color was death, another life, but all the others revealed the realities of living, thinking, doing. Realities as complex as the lives they represented.

Most, whether human or Lygme, knew nothing of this world, this reality. They denied the truth of their dual souls and therefore remained constrained to the physical world. They were content in their naivete, but neither Rhaina nor Geminai could ever again return to that strangled state of existence. Together, they functioned as one. Separate, they stumbled in the darkness, lost and disoriented like so many of those around them. It was a life to which neither would ever return.

"Now," she heard Rhaina say. Geminai had to be certain of what she'd found, and finding it once before, she should easily find it again.

She plunged into the sea. The surface tides buffeted her, like always, but she felt the rhythms move over and around her, and she swam with the currents, allowing the Eternity of Souls to carry her with them for the moment. This was the safest way to enter the sea, by drifting away in its currents. If she struggled, if she tried to fight the current and swim her own direction, she'd only attract the attention of the undesirables, those Geminais who used the spiritual world as a feeding ground for their physical selves.

When she felt sure she had not attracted any attention, Rhaina's Geminai dipped deeper into the sea, swimming with the current, then gently moving through it to get where she wanted to go. She knew the way. She'd been there before, and she never got lost.

The Geminais around her watched with envy as she swam past. She knew their feelings had little to do with her; they were watching her thread, and they knew something was missing from their own lives. Their physical selves would manifest these feelings in a variety of ways. Suddenly, one physical person would grow envious of her neighbor and, for no apparent reason, start a feud that would last a day, a month, a decade. Another person would see the envy as a sin, and he would return to his faith to have the blot removed. Still others would notice the envy but not know why it was there. Unsure, they would refuse to act upon it at all, and that would allow the envy to grow unchecked. Those people would reach the end of their lives as broken and hate-filled shells, unsure exactly when and where the universe turned against them.

Rhaina's Geminai felt the pulsing knowledge she sought long before she saw it. But something wasn't right. It had moved, and it was now bound by threads to other people, both human and Lygme. How had this knowledge become so well known?

She warily approached. Guarded knowledge could be dangerous, and she had no desire to incur the wrath of other Geminais who felt the knowledge belonged to them. She examined the nearest thread to see if she recognized it, but it wasn't familiar to her. Lygmies and humans had acquired this knowledge completely on their own in the physical world – but from disparate corners of the galaxy. How could so many people find this from so many different places?

One thread drew her attention. Bright white and enmeshed in tech, he was one of the galaxy's most resourceful mercenaries – and a former friend. She felt Rhaina's first-soul leap with excitement for the chase, the adventure, and the love of this man. The lost chance at love with this man.

But whatever Rhaina's first-soul might be feeling, her second-soul, her Geminai, had a mission to complete here in the Eternity of Souls. She reached for the knowledge and prepared to take the quickest of glimpses, enough to confirm its location.

She stopped. Something still wasn't right. This didn't seem like the knowledge she sought. But it had to be. It sparkled like it did before. It bounced through the Sea's eddies and twisted with the rhythms of thoughts around it, masking its presence unless she forced herself to look directly at it – just like before. So what was wrong this time? Was it the other threads that bothered her?

No. It was the color...and the texture.

This new knowledge shone with a dingy gray, and its lumpy, uneven sides and corners made it resemble something more like...paraffin. Ear wax. Yuck! This wasn't right at all. What color was the knowledge she sought? And didn't her knowledge hold a smoother, more rounded shape?

So what had she found? And what made her think this bumpy lump of gooey knowledge was really what she wanted? How could she have been mistaken?

She reached forward again, determined to find the answer.

A serpent burst from the side of the lump, its mouth spread wide and its teeth bearing down on Geminai's wrist.

She sprang back, ready to fight, but the black serpent coiled itself tightly around the rotating mass, flicking its tail as it spit warnings at her.

"Not yourzh," the serpent hissed.

A talking serpent, Geminai wondered. *A mythological guardian?*

"There'zh yourzh." The serpent twisted its head to a shining blue sphere hovering behind Geminai.

How could she have ever missed that?

She turned back to the serpent.

"What is this?" she asked, pointing to the protected lump.

The serpent stretched its mouth thin – in a smile? – and coiled itself more tightly around the floating ball.

"God'zh Ear not yourzh. You get God'zh Eye."

Geminai repeated the name "God's Ear" to herself, then she pointed at the threaded humans and Lygmies, and said, "Is it theirs? Does the God's Ear belong to them? And if so, why do I get only the God's Eye?"

Another smile from the serpent.

"Leave," it hissed.

A threat? What was this "God's Ear" knowledge that warranted such security? And why wasn't the knowledge she'd found so well protected as this? Or was it?

"I'm sorry I bothered you," she said, letting the currents carry her away.

The serpent twisted its head and burrowed back inside the knowledge. Geminai watched until the tip of its scaly tail disappeared, then she turned to face the knowledge she'd been sent to find.

She couldn't help visualizing the smooth, blue-white sphere as an eye, as the guardian declared. The wispy colors weren't solid, though, like an eye, but swirled across the surface like clouds in an alien sky. She caught glimpses of the black line at the sphere's core...a black line that looked like a pupil.

Why couldn't she let this go? The anatomy idea wasn't real, she told herself. It had been planted in her subconscious by the gray lump's resemblance to paraffin and had been reinforced by the serpent calling it the "God's Ear." Now she was making connections where there were none, calling this knowledge an eye – even though it obviously bore no resemblance to one. Except of course that it was a sphere, and it was blue, it had a black core...and that guardian had called it an eye.

Ah, but that black core was what really destroyed the image. Human eyes didn't have vertical slits for pupils. That was an animal's trait. Except...the serpent didn't say it guarded the "Animal's Ear"; it said it guarded the "God's Ear." And gods didn't have to be human, did they?

Enough, she thought. *It might look like an eye, but it isn't.* And she could prove it. She drifted closer to the knowledge and peered through the milky wisps to get a better look at the vertical core.

A black, serpent guardian stared right back at her, its eyes locked on hers and its tongue flicking in and out. Its slender body stretched the length of the sphere, giving it the look of a pupil. What concerned her more was that this serpent – nearly identical to the one guarding the gray lump – seemed content to let her near.

She was being given this knowledge. This guardian allowed her to find this knowledge. Why?

Back away now, she thought. Run, get away, and don't ever go near this thing again. She didn't find this knowledge on her own; someone had allowed her to find it. Wanted her to find it. This serpent guarded the knowledge, kept it secure just for her, and if she had never stumbled upon its twin she never would have discovered the way she'd been manipulated.

But it was too late to back out now. Rhaina was committed.

"Get it over with, and get back out," Geminai said to herself, but she knew the words had come from Rhaina.

She touched the sphere. The knowledge exploded into her mind. Across space. Through the jungle. Beyond the barrier. Beneath the lost city. Find the jewel.

Her task complete, Geminai jerked her hand away and swam for the surface.

6

Rhaina

New York City, Earth

Rhaina gasped as her Geminai leaped back into her body and first-soul. Her hands fumbled for the water glass on the floor, and she downed the cool liquid.

"Ms. Bruci," a man said, leaning over her on the couch. "Are you all right?"

"Do not crowd me," she whispered. She wasn't trying to sound harsh, but the man jumped back like she'd hit him.

Rhaina squeezed her eyes shut and tried to remember all the details her Geminai had seen. The waxy lump, the coiling serpents, the "God's Ear," and that eyeball, the "God's Eye." Worst of all, she now knew she was being manipulated. She could have used that knowledge earlier. Bad timing, that one.

She swung her feet to the floor and sat up on the couch, cradling the empty glass in her hands. She had confirmed her knowledge, just like she'd been asked, but she did not like it. Aside from the whole manipulation thing, she now knew Jake was involved in this project.

He'd corded himself to that "God's Ear," whatever that was, and his involvement made it all the more urgent that she leave immediately. She hadn't wanted this meeting, and now she thought the waste of time probably wasn't worth it. Information was just the first factor to get manipulated. If someone knew about her involvement, they could manipulate the people and machines she'd need to finish the job. No, this got worse with each wasted minute.

"All right," she said to the man sitting in the chair across from her. "I'm ready."

He rose at her command, pressing a button within his black suit jacket. The double mahogany doors swung open and two more men in suits, one blue, the other a pale brown, joined them in the small office. Blue-Suit offered Rhaina a tray of fruit, and she gratefully accepted a pear. Fruit was really the best thing after letting her Geminai roam the Eternity of Souls, but water usually sufficed. She never said she'd need fruit, so it must have been a good guess. Or more manipulation? Maybe her host knew more than he said he did.

The three men led her from the room, Blue-Suit immediately to her left with the fruit tray. They walked the immaculate hallways of the 168th floor with its rich, textured carpeting that made it seem like she stepped across clouds. The dim lights encased in sconces only added to the heavenly illusion. Rhaina felt underdressed for the whole occasion, even with her three-piece suit.

She used the time to prepare for her meeting with this little office upstart. He was stupid and arrogant, and she had no idea how he climbed the corporate ladder to V.P. of External Affairs Analysis and Investigation – whatever that title was supposed to mean. She didn't care any more that he was paying her extra for this little "confirmation meeting." It was costing her precious time against a very worthy opponent.

Speaking of Jake, she thought. What's his role in this? The last she'd heard, he had been working some South African gold scam that went bad. If memory served, he nearly lost his life on that little excursion. Then he took a transport to the moon, and she hadn't heard from him since – except for some cryptic note he'd managed to sneak into her apartment: "Remember, Big Brother loves you. Jake." With a hint like that, she checked all the local government agencies, but she never found him.

But here he was, getting in her way after two years of silence.

They stopped before the lift and waited, but none of the suits pressed the call button.

"Look, boys," Rhaina said. "Your boss may be paying you by the hour, but I'm not. Let's go."

"That's as far as they're going," a fourth man said, stepping from the office behind them.

Rhaina suppressed a groan as the V.P. glided forward and relieved Blue-Suit of his fruit tray burden.

"You and I, however," the V.P. said, holding the tray beneath Rhaina's nose. "We have a private meeting with Mr. Rosh."

"Which one? Tweedle-Dee or Tweedle-Dum?"

"His children are just the facade," he said, trying to suppress a smile. "Mr. Rosh uses them to allow himself the freedom of retiring from public life."

"Facade?" She wasn't sure she understood where this conversation was going. "Daddy Rosh's shuttle burned up on a steep re-entry nine years ago. Where's the facade?"

The man pressed his thumb to the lift's call button and the door swung open. "After you."

Rhaina made a show of opening her suit vest to pull the gold chain of her timepiece. She flipped open the ornately engraved case and examined the hands. She'd already wasted nearly an hour with these money-men, and she raised an eyebrow at the veep to make sure he knew it. He smiled.

Sighing, she stowed the pocket watch and stepped into the lift tube, turning so she wouldn't have to look out the glass back wall. She knew the city would be beautiful from this height, if only she didn't have to be at this height to see the beauty. And she didn't look down either. Lift tubes were perfectly safe, but that didn't mean she had to look through the tube's sparkling floor every time she got in one. To make matters worse, the fruit-tray laden veep stepped in beside her, grinning like a kid who just got his candy.

Rhaina decided she could handle the view of the city better than the man's grin.

"Mr. Rosh has been quite impressed with you," he said.

Rhaina ignored him. She also released her Geminai to roam the narrow lift. Why take chances?

The thread stretched only enough for her second-soul to leave her body. She looked through Geminai's eyes and watched the veep unlock a panel in the wall. He pressed a hidden switch, then returned the panel to its place, glancing over his shoulder to be sure she wasn't watching.

"You still don't believe he's alive, do you?" the veep said.

The energy sparks in the floor drifted up, and she and the veep rose with them. Rhaina kept her eyes fixed forward and concentrated on what Geminai was seeing. No gun on the man. No wiretap. Not even any tech. How could anyone exist without a basic implant?

"Believe in the miraculous?" Rhaina said. Keep him talking. Let Geminai work.

"Miraculous?" The man grinned. "A hundred years ago, this little lift would have been miraculous. Now it's just...dizzying."

Rhaina couldn't help it. She looked down, then wished she hadn't. The sparkling floor allowed her a perfect view down the glass tube through all one-hundred-seventy-whatever floors. And they were still climbing higher. She shut her eyes and focused on what Geminai was seeing: another presence with them in the lift, some kind of spirit or soul. And it was huge.

She gave the veep only the slightest attention, enough that he thought she was caught up in his conversation, and she watched the other, spiritual presence flit around the tube. It ignored the veep, passed quickly by Rhaina herself, but seemed quite interested in Rhaina's Geminai. The Presence flitted around Geminai like she was a lost treasure only recently rediscovered. It tapped her shoulder, stroked her hair, outlined her ethereal form from nose to toes, then leaned in close to study every minute detail of her face.

Rhaina became more than a little concerned when the Presence turned its attention to their thread, the only real bond she had with her second-soul. The Presence slid a wispy hand across the thread's surface, but that was all. Then, without warning, it ducked into one of the passing hallways and disappeared within the labyrinthine complex somewhere around floor 190.

The lift sparkles dwindled around their bodies, and the translucent floor came to a halt. The veep had stopped talking a few floors earlier, but Rhaina hadn't noticed until she thought back over the silence.

"Ms. Bruci," the veep said as the doors slid open. "May I present Mr. Desmond Rosh."

She stepped tentatively into the dim room, her shoes clicking the marble floor, and Geminai followed close behind. The door slid shut, and she turned to see the veep waving goodbye. *So,* she thought, *I'm doing this alone. All the better.*

The air grew colder the deeper she moved into the room. The wall sconces were turned down low, casting long, dull shadows across every surface. It reminded her of a tacky date, one in which the would-be-Romeo thought if he turned the lights down low, she would ignore the fact he was a jerk.

Geminai roamed the long hallway before them, peering into dark rooms packed wall-to-wall with computers, monitors, and mechanized arms to lift and manipulate the things within the rooms. The arms seemed like an afterthought, and they were only barely patched into the network's hardline. They received their power through circuits built into the walls, but their instruction codes seemed to flow in only one direction: toward the computers. There was no two-way flow of communication.

The whole thing made the hair on Rhaina's arms stand on end. Something here was not right.

The Presence rose up from the floor and engulfed Geminai in its mammoth arms.

Rhaina jumped forward, but one of the mechanized arms reached from its place in the wall and gripped her ankle. She fell hard to the floor.

The Presence stroked Geminai's chin and whispered, "At last, another true spirit to hold in my arms."

7

Rhaina

"So this is how you survived that shuttle accident?" Rhaina pushed herself up to inspect the metal rod gripping her ankle.

Mr. Rosh's Presence kissed Geminai's cheek. "I know you like to keep that fleshy thing on its little leash," he said to Geminai, "but do tell it to shut up."

Rhaina thought several things she'd like to say to the vaporous Mr. Rosh, most of them obscene, but she restrained herself.

"We are not two separate entities, Mr. Rosh," Geminai said. "As her second-soul, I'm as much a part of her as her hands."

"Or her mind," Mr. Rosh said.

"We function as one."

"Then let her follow us – if she can." He pulled Geminai up with him and soared through the ceiling and into the chamber above.

Geminai thought of Rhaina's safety, but Rhaina didn't seem scared or in danger. So instead, Geminai focused her attention on the ghostly Mr. Rosh.

"Would you like a drink?" he said as he unwrapped his mammoth arms from around her and drifted across the room. "I have Enzlo juice, or I could whip up a yrunn cocktail."

"What's the point?" Geminai said. "You won't let Rhaina come up to drink them."

"I didn't ask if your pet wanted a saucer of milk," he said, floating to the bar. "I asked if you would join me for a drink."

"I suppose."

He turned and blew into a hole in the wall. Recessed track lights in the ceiling came to life, shredding the darkness, and Mr. Rosh peered over his shoulder and grinned.

"Neat trick," she said, knowing he expected some acknowledgment of his manly prowess.

He grinned and turned back to the bar to make their drinks.

Geminai took advantage of the light to look at Mr. Rosh physically as well as spiritually. The black, wispy features that gave him that wraith-like appearance in the lift were nothing more than a costume trick. The cloak covering his body was layered in long strips of cloth that blew in an ethereal breeze whenever he moved. He had flipped back the hood, and his gray hair swooped high in the front to cover the small balding spot near the top of his head. He finished mixing the drinks, drifted to her, and handed her a glass. It was a spiritual cup, solidified wisps of spiritual matter instead of actual glass. Mr. Rosh, however, held a real glass. How did he do that?

Geminai took a quick glance into the chemical makeup of the drink; nothing but alcohol.

"So your spirit came here after your body burned up," she said, sipping the drink. The cocktail had a syrupy weight to it, but its fizzies bubbled into her nose as she drank.

"I was forced here after my body burned up," Mr. Rosh said. He turned and drifted to the other side of the room, waving his drink through the air as he continued. "Forced here against my will, chained to this building – the building I built. The building I poured my heart and soul into when I was alive. The universe has a morbid sense of humor." He blew into another hole, this one above the mantle, and a fire burst to life in the stone hearth. Red firelight flickered through the shadows cast by the harsh, blue track lighting.

"What do your children think?"

"Tweedle-dee and tweedle-dum?"

Geminai glanced at the floor, but Mr. Rosh waved his drink in the air.

"Don't worry. It was funny." He stared into his glass and stirred the drink, not seeming to care whether it mixed any better. "The saddest part is, you're right. My boys are idiots. They think this penthouse is haunted, and they nearly piss their pants every time I call them up here. The first month I was here, they called in a priest to perform an exorcism." He laughed, then turned to her. "Want a tour?"

He didn't give her a chance to decline but started down the hall and talked over his shoulder as he drifted along.

"I made them remodel this penthouse for me after I got back," he said. "They installed the blowholes for me, brought some of my things down from the cabin in Maine, even indulged the old man when he said he wanted some more unconventional items installed." He blew into another hole, and a room lit off the hallway. The dim, bare bulb hanging by cords from the ceiling cast long shadows across the sparse room. A bed of nails lay along one wall and an iron maiden sat opposite.

"Every ghost needs a good torture chamber." He blew into the hole again, and the light went out. "It really is just a novelty. I use the bed occasionally, just to say I've slept on a bed of nails, but the other is just for atmosphere." He swizzled the drink some more and laughed. "Although I did hide in the iron maiden and moan once when my boys were being particularly obstinate."

"You have a morbid sense of humor," Rhaina said from the end of the hall.

Mr. Rosh and Geminai turned to see her leaning against the wall.

"You broke my mechanical arm?" Mr. Rosh said. He slammed his drink against the wall, alcohol and glass splattering to the carpet. To Geminai, he said, "Put your skin back on. She's ruined the mood."

Geminai stood where she was and let Rhaina's body scoop her up as she passed. The wispy cup became solid in Rhaina's hand, the drink sparkling in the shiny glass.

Rhaina followed the spirit of Mr. Rosh into the den where he stood before the snapping fire. He'd turned off all the lights again, but Gemi-nai had been here before so Rhaina walked with confidence around the dark sofa. She sat and stared at Mr. Rosh's translucent back, the fire seeming to burn through his chest.

"You have no idea how lonely I am up here," he finally said, not bothering to turn and look at her.

"Lonely enough to drive a man insane, I suppose."

"You believe me insane?"

"You're not a man."

"No." He turned and sat on the floor. The fire nearly obscured his head. "I'm a prisoner in this building."

"As you said, you poured your heart and soul into it. Where the soul resides, so does the man."

"And that's what keeps me here, my mortal...obsession." He spat the word like an obscenity. "But I would give anything to get out."

"And that's why I'm here."

"You've really seen it, haven't you?" He looked at Rhaina for the first time.

"Yes."

"The God's Eye." He whispered the term reverently. "How did you find it? The first time?"

"Mr. Rosh, we're wasting precious time. I learned something very bad when you asked me to perform for you."

"That was no performance," he interrupted. "That was a test. I had to know you were really in touch with your second-soul like you claimed."

"While you tested me," Rhaina continued. "I discovered something very disturbing. There seems to be a twin piece to your God's Eye, and that piece has been discovered by an incredibly determined man."

"Twin pieces do not concern me. It is only the God's Eye that I want. If you happen upon this 'twin piece,' you may keep it."

"Think like the businessman you were for just a second." Rhaina leaned forward on the couch and spoke nearly nose to nose with the spirit. "If your fiercest competitor has just discovered one piece of the puzzle, it's only a small step to discovering the second – the piece you want. Once he has that piece, you will pay ten times what I'm charging for this job, if he even agrees to sell to you. Then where will you be?"

"No." He rose. "You must get me the God's Eye. I must have my freedom."

"Then give me the operating funds we agreed upon, and I'll have my team on the first flight to Udo."

"Your blueback's on the table."

Rhaina stood to get it.

"And one of my people is going with you."

He must have been hell to work for when he was alive, she thought.

"No offense," she said, turning back to him. "But your little suits downstairs wouldn't last five minutes in the jungle."

"I agree." He drifted from the room like he had a purpose.

Rhaina followed to convince him she needed to be on her way.

"You'll need someone who can help you out," he continued. "Someone who's as much at home in the jungle as he is with guns and electronics."

They passed the torture chamber, continued to the end of the hall, and took a right. Rhaina knew from experience there was a circular stairwell to the left – she'd used that to get up here. But she hadn't realized there was more to see in the other direction.

Mr. Rosh blew into one of the holes and the wall split open to reveal a room filled with computers and bioengineering equipment. Gears and metal arms stuck out at odd angles near the ceiling and corners. A holding tank stood directly opposite them, filled to the brim with orange fluid.

"No," Rhaina said, still following the spirit. "I do not want this. I will not do this job if you make me bring...one of those things."

"I'm tripling your pay, just for the inconvenience." Mr. Rosh blew into various holes around the room. Computers came to life, and the orange liquid started glowing inside the holding tank.

Rhaina weighed her options. She'd already negotiated more for this job than anything she'd done in the last couple years. Triple-pay could set her up for retirement, and that was tempting. As much as she enjoyed the fun and adventure of her jobs, she'd been thinking about getting off somewhere, deep into the woods, and letting the universe move on without her.

"Quadruple-pay," she said. "And I want a kill-switch." Never let the negotiations die without a counter-offer.

"Quadruple-pay I'll give you," Mr. Rosh said, "but no kill-switch."

Damn. She didn't care about the money. Triple-pay was more than enough, but she needed that kill-switch.

"No good," she said and turned around.

"You won't leave this building," Mr. Rosh said.

"A threat?" Rhaina stood at the door, her back to the man-spirit and Geminai peaking out to watch him. "Let me explain what happens in that scenario – aside from the fact that my team would take great offense at you killing me. You will waste the next couple months trying to find someone else to jump through your little hoops to get this job done. Say three months have passed before your next team even lands on Udo. It breaks my heart to have to tell you this, but Jake will have discovered the God's Eye by then."

"Jake," Mr. Rosh whispered. "Jake Alon? Your Jake?"

Rhaina nodded, then said, "He would also take offense at you killing me. And then you'd never see your precious God's Eye...ever."

"Rhaina, I'm a businessman," Mr. Rosh said, his voice dripping with sincerity. "You've caught me in a businessman's bluff. I would never hurt you. You know that."

Rhaina turned to face him. Her research had shown that Daddy Rosh was indirectly responsible for the murders of at least half a dozen of his rivals before his own fiery death. She had little doubt he'd follow through on his threat.

"The kill-switch," she said.

"The kill-switch," he said with a nod. "At triple-pay, though."

"Triple-pay."

He returned to the computers. The orange tank hummed as black drops drifted to the floor, forming first the toes, then a complete left foot.

Rhaina sat and watched the building process, trying to figure out how to break the news to her team that they were now taking a plastic man.

8

Tone

Mother Earth eco-terrorist lunar base Wascheta

Commander Tone Dalal shuffled across the dusty streets of Wascheta Base on the edge of the dark side of the moon, the three guards lugging the bulky pressure crate behind him. Why did bad news always hit on a Friday, he wondered, bouncing another step. He'd had plans to drive across the border for his weekend off and have a little fun. There was a place in Federal City he wanted to take his girl where they claimed – for a fee – to be able to drop the gravity to below lunar-normal, and Tone thought that had the potential for some entertaining sex.

He yanked open the door to the airlock, led the three guards inside, and slid the door shut again, securing the locking bar in place with a thud he felt through his boots. They stood nearly shoulder to shoulder in the tight bay as the vents rattled and creaked at the air exchange. The thing inside the crate remained silent. It had its own air cannister strapped to the lid so it probably didn't even know it was inside an air-lock.

The sign above the entrance flashed "Ready," and Tone unbuckled and removed his helmet. The guards did the same as he unlocked and pushed aside the thick, reinforced door into the base. He led the way through the nearly deserted hallways, their heavy boots clacking against the floor with each hopping step. He remembered when this base used to be the center of anti-Earth activity, back when it was popular to be anti-Earth. That was before the dirt-lovers stopped blaming each other for the hole in the ozone and the melted polar caps, and they actually started doing something to fix the problems. It's harder to hate an enemy that's oozing brotherly love.

It wasn't long before most of the truly rebellious at Wascheta Base were rebelling back to Earth. "Returning to their reincarnated Mother," they called it. Tone called it pissing away a chance at true reformation. But then, he was never much into the whole spiritual side of their crusade.

They stopped at Colonel Walraven's quarters and Tone pressed the intercom button taped to the doorframe. The ragged wire ran to the ceiling, through a hole that Tone had drilled through the wall, and into the intercom tied to the colonel's desk with a piece of wire he'd found in a storage room on the other side of the base.

This place was state-of-the-art when it was built, Tone thought as he examined the exposed wire. Look what we have become.

"Come in," the colonel said through the speaker.

Commander Dalal opened the door, and the three guards carried their package into the room ahead of him. They set the crate in the center of the sparse room and moved to a side wall. Tone had told them to stay just in case there was a problem.

"This doesn't look good," Colonel Walraven said. He sat in his chair at the built-in desk and studied the guards and crate.

"No, Sir," Tone said. He shuffled forward and presented a data disk to the colonel. "It's the robotos, Sir. There was an accident."

"An accident? Did they malfuction?" He slipped the disk into the reader on his desk and watched the screen flicker to life.

Two of Roboto, Incorporated's serial numbers scrolled across the screen followed by the words "Terminated before completion of programming. Abort, retry, or fail?"

"This is no accident," Walraven said, turning back to Commander Dalal. "This is a bloody catastrophe. They were terminated? Did they get caught? Did they have their programming disassembled? I told you we should have gone with a plastic man."

"And each one costs as much as ten robotos," Tone said, nodding. "I know. You made it quite clear that any robotics failure would be my fault. But the robotos didn't get caught – hell, they never even got a chance to do their job. The ship blew up."

Colonel Walraven stared at Tone.

"Nobody's claimed responsibility," Tone said.

"They find those 'botos and they'll pin the whole bloody thing on us," Walraven said.

"We have the robotos." Tone waved at the screen. "Nobody knew they were on board. Just watch the video."

Walraven turned back to the computer screen and started the playback. Flames obscured the video for a moment, then died down. The camera had zoomed past the fire to a man leaning over the body of a dead Lygme woman. He sliced open the woman's boot, pulled out a datafile, and stowed the file in a shirt pocket.

"Who is that?" Walraven asked.

"We've identified him as Jake Alon. Earlier on the recording he claimed to be a federal agent, and we found his basic profile on the government nets, but I don't believe it."

"I don't either," Walraven said, rewinding the video and zooming in on the man slicing open the boot. "Look at that blade he's using; that thing's a beaut. High-precision laser tip, polished titanium casing...mm-hm, I'd love to have that."

"It doesn't look government-issue."

"Absolutely not. That's a professional's weapon."

Walraven let the video play forward again until the man pulled out the datafile.

"And that?" the colonel asked.

"Not certain. It could be anything."

As the video continued, the man started to turn away. Then he looked straight at the camera and his jaw dropped open.

The guards in the corner chuckled, and Tone glared at them to shut up.

"What's he doing?" Colonel Walraven asked as the man waved at the camera. "Does he know he's being recorded?"

"No," Tone said with a grin. "I dressed the robotos up as a couple of old men, and this Jake Alon actually tried to rescue them."

"What an idiot."

"Bloody heroic, I think."

"He's still an idiot. He got his datafile, and now he should get the hell out of there."

Jake Alon ran toward the robotos, and the entire ship jolted from another explosion. The robotos flew onto a pile of burning luggage, and the video turned to static and winked out. Colonel Walraven stared at the blank monitor as he tapped the desk.

"That's all we got," Tone said.

"I assumed so," Walraven said, still watching the monitor.

Tone shifted from one foot to another as he waited. Colonel Walraven did this sometimes, just sat and stared and thought, and Tone didn't want him doing it now. They still had so much left to discuss before any decisions could be made. They still had to interrogate the thing inside the crate.

"Call Billoxus at the Western State Department," Walraven said. "See if he can dig up anything on this Jake Alon, specifically any cases the man's worked recently. See if he can find out any of Mr. Alon's hobbies or interests, or if he made any special requests for information before he got on that ship. I want to know what he's doing. I want to know what he pulled out of that girl's boot."

"Speaking of which," Tone said, gesturing to the silent crate in the center of the room. "We should deal with this."

"I know you're anxious to get on with other things," Walraven said, shutting his eyes and steepling his fingers. "But consider for a moment the benefit of clear, unadulterated thought. What do we know?"

Tone started to speak, but Colonel Walraven interrupted him.

"Jake Alon, currently of the Western Governmental Alliance, is on a cruise ship bound from Udo to Earth. And he's on there with a Lygme – an illegal Lygme since they're not allowed on cruise ships, not even as servants."

"The video showed him shooting that Lygme earlier," Tone whispered.

"Really...." Walraven leaned back in his chair, his eyes still shut. "He shoots the Lygme, he cuts open her boots, and he steals a data file she has hidden inside the flexisteel lining. The flexisteel lining...." He sat forward again and replayed the video of the knife slicing open the boot.

Colonel Walraven tapped the screen, and Tone saw what he was looking at. "Those are government-issue boots," Tone said.

"Maybe. They look new." Colonel Walraven cut the boot out of the picture and exported it to a networked database. He ran a comparison, and the computer identified them as a pair of Western Alliance infantry boots retired from service nearly a decade earlier for faulty stitching in the inseam. The boots wore out nearly twice as fast as other military footwear. The manufacturer ceased production, the government sold its inventory at surplus stores, and the only boots still available were well worn and went for a couple million at auction.

"So where did a Lygme come up with a new pair?" Tone asked.

"Do we have any contacts still operating on Udo, or did they all return to their reincarnated Mother Earth?"

"I still have two or three names on file."

"Call them too. I want to know who on Udo is still dealing in government surplus and would have been around ten years ago when these boots went off the market."

"Consider it done." Tone gestured to the crate again. "Now, if we could...."

Colonel Walraven sighed and turned from the desk.

"All right, Tone," he said. "What's in the box?"

The three guards placed their hands on their pistols as Tone unlocked the lid from the crate and slid the flexisteel top aside. He yanked a length of rope from the crate and an explosion of bloody fur and teeth burst from the top. The freed pouncer howled as he ran around Tone's legs until the cord wrapped tight.

The guards took aim, but Tone shouted for them to hold their fire. The last thing he needed was three mediocre shots trying to hit a pouncer leaping at his crotch.

Colonel Walraven gripped the pouncer in mid-leap by the scruff of his neck.

"Unwind yourself," he said to Tone as the pouncer thrashed in his hand.

The animal hissed, his claws extended and his arms swatting as Tone unwrapped the length of cord from around his knees.

"Down, boy!" Walraven said, slamming the pouncer to the floor.

The move must have hurt, but it didn't quiet the pouncer for more than a second as it convulsed on the floor, re-opening its scabs and tearing the stitches from behind its left ear. Bloody droplets floated through the air to stain the wall and floor around the pouncer.

"Where did you find this wonderful creature?" Walraven asked between the beast's snarls.

"It stowed away inside one of the roboto's life rafts. Quite a violent present when we popped the lid."

"What's your name?" Walraven asked the hissing animal.

"Lick me, monkey-brain," the pouncer growled.

Walraven stared at the violent display for several moments, then hoisted the animal into the air, spun him around, and slammed him on his back to the floor.

"I am dominant!" he yelled at the animal.

The pouncer started clawing at Colonel Walraven's sleeve, so he reached into his hip pocket and pulled out a small laser knife – not nearly as good as the one Jake Alon had used – flipped on the blade and shoved it at the pouncer's mouth. The animal ceased struggling, its nose twitching at the sparkling blade so near its whiskers.

"Let's try this once more," the colonel whispered. "Who is dominant?"

"I want nothing to do with you...people," the pouncer said, spitting the last word like an insult. "You'll have to kill me."

"Oh, no," Walraven said, shaking his head and waving the red blade around the pouncer's open mouth. "We are not going to kill you. We want you to tell us what happened on that luxury liner, and we want to know how you and a Lygme got on board one of the most heavily guarded ships in the civilian line – and we want you to tell us what you were doing there. Now, who is dominant?"

"Pouncers of the universe, unite!"

"You're a long way from your alley rally," Walraven said, flicking his wrist.

The laser knife flashed through the pouncer's upper left incisor, slicing off the very tip. The pouncer howled and thrashed on the floor as the piece of tooth drifted away.

"Who is dominant?" Walraven said.

"I am not cooperating with you."

"Listen to my question: Who is dominant?"

"You'll have to kill me!"

"I am not killing you. Who is dominant?"

"I'll enjoy eating you all!"

"You won't be eating anything but yogurt if I slice off all your teeth." He picked up the pouncer and slammed him against the floor again to emphasize his point. "Who is dominant?"

The pouncer lay still for several moments, his eyes flicking around the room to the guards, to Colonel Walraven, to Commander Dalal, and back to the colonel again.

"You are dominant," the pouncer said, his legs relaxing against the colonel's arm.

"Once more, please," Walraven said. "Louder."

The pouncer's ears flicked back, and he snarled, "You are dominant."

"Thank you." He turned off the laser knife but didn't let go of the pouncer's fur. "Your name?"

"I am Silny."

The colonel picked up the loose end of the rope and handed it to Commander Dalal. "Please tie this to the corner post of my cot."

Tone secured the rope and turned around to see Colonel Walraven sitting in his chair again. The pouncer sat in the center of the floor giving himself a bath. They both seemed perfectly at ease, as if nothing at all had just happened.

"Now, Silny," Walraven said, leaning back in his chair. "Start at the beginning. How did you and a Lygme get on board that liner, and what were you doing there?"

9

Tone

"My Lygme's name was Natasha Boriskov."

"You're lying," Walraven said with a yawn.

"Listen, Oh-Dominant-Monkey-Brain. Not all pouncers are liars like you. She liked some old spy story, and she took the names when she entered your human world. If she had any other name, she never told me."

Tone went to the computer and searched through news accounts of the deep-space accident. He found the list of casualties, scanned through to the "B's," and located Natasha Boriskov. He checked her baggage list and found that she carried on two suitcases and one cat named....

"Fluffy?"

"Bite my butt." Silny's ears went flat.

"How did you get past the pouncer tests?" Walraven asked.

"Oh, you humans test for pouncers? I'm sure your tests are 100% accurate every time a pouncer wants it to be."

Tone cringed. The tests were actually blood samples that checked for the presence of pouncer-cells, the augmented red blood cells that fed nutrients to the cat's re-engineered brain. According to scientists, the test was never wrong.

"Wallow in your false assumptions later and let me talk," Silny said.

"Oh, how very rude of us." Walraven turned his attention back to the pouncer. "Please, continue."

"We took the liner at the invitation of Henry Tudor – "

"The Western Alliance President?" Tone asked.

"Is there any other Henry Tudor worth mentioning?" The pouncer laid down and tucked his paws beneath his chin. "He invited us because Natasha told him about the God's Foot, and she was willing to trade the information for asylum to the Western Alliance."

"The Western Alliance doesn't grant asylum to any Lygme for any reason," Tone said.

"The president was eager to grant Natasha the asylum when she showed him the pictures."

"What is the God's Foot?" Walraven asked.

"The most holy artifact in all the Lygme tradition – and the largest green saphite on Udo."

"And she knew where it was?" Tone said.

"Of course. She was from the Northern Braktu tribes, and all their people know the God's Foot. The problem is getting to it. It's buried in an abandoned temple overgrown by the jungle, and now the jungle has become infested by meshet. Even the Lygmies know better than to pick a fight with a meshet."

"What's a meshet?"

"No," Walraven said. "A better question is why would a Lygme give away her holiest treasure to a human."

"If you could have seen Natasha, you'd know. Sure, she was a Lygme, but she was huge. A wide, oval face.... She was not pretty, and she would always be the tribe Omega. Escaping to your human world was the only chance she had to be free of the hell they put her through."

"And you?" Walraven asked, leaning forward. "Why take you?"

"You got it back-ass-wards. She didn't take me. I took her. I found her eating scraps from a colony dumpster, and I realized she could be my ticket out of that shit-hole. She told me about her life – and about the green saphite – and I put her in touch with the president. If that federal agent hadn't killed her – probably under the president's order – we'd be living it good dirt-side."

"You're quite the hero," Walraven said.

"Of course."

"Well, I apologize for the way we've treated you. I promise to make it up to you." He stood and turned to the three guards. "Please, men, a five-star escort for Mr. Silny to the stateroom in B-Block. And let's take off this collar."

He untied the rope from the pouncer's neck and tossed it into the corner. He scratched behind the animal's ear, then drifted back into his chair.

"I'm sure you'll understand," Walraven said, "that we are a rather cred-strapped organization. We've lost several of our members and most of our dirt-side funding. I can contact a transport to get you down to Earth, but I'd really appreciate a favor in return."

"Name it," Silny said as he washed behind the ear the colonel had scratched.

"What was on the datadisk?"

"A holo of the green saphite, and its coordinates inside that jungle."

"Would you be willing to help us get it back?"

"I'm not going back to that planet."

"No, I didn't say you had to. Give us the coordinates, and we'll take care of the rest. You'll be on the next transport for the Western Alliance."

"I'll do you one better." Silny stopped washing his ear and turned to the colonel, his eyes going black. "Put me through to him, and I'll help you blackmail that lying bastard president."

"It's a deal." The colonel waved to the guards. "Men, show Silny to his room."

The guards turned and led Silny out. Tone started to follow, but Walraven put a hand on his arm. They stood and watched the group leave.

"Sir, I rarely question your orders –"

"You always question my orders." The colonel sat at his desk.

"Well, I'm questioning them again. What are you doing? That pouncer is lying – he has to be."

"And the best lies always contain a grain of truth." He handed a datadisk to Tone. "Here's the recording of our conversation."

Tone grinned as he took the disk.

"Go over that animal's statements word by word. See how much you can verify, and how much is pure fantasy. I'd start with that whole 'I-had-mercy-on-a-poor-Lygme' thing. Pouncers never show mercy."

"What about his claim to contact the president?"

"I don't know. That part could be true. We'll find out when we ask for the number."

10

Jake

colony city Sol-Win, the planet Udo

The cover sprang on the retread tank, and the thick foamy lifted Jake's newly-healed body from the perma-skin. The fluid dripped from the foamy in green glops that splattered when they hit the floor. Jake sloughed the sticky strands of hair from his goggles and air mask, smearing the fluid into a mess he could almost see through.

The shop's hyperactive proprietor, 2 Glorious, bopped into Jake's field of vision and ripped off the goggles, strings of perma-skin snapping back.

"Jackin' mo," 2 Glorious said as he ogled Jake's body. The digital glasses sewn to the sides of 2 Glorious's shaved head sparkled in the harsh light. "You bin drubbed down good."

Jake wasn't sure if the man was staring at his tech, his privates, or the healing just performed by the perma-skin. So he grinned and pretended to know what 2 Glorious babbled about.

"Da secret little oilies all over, they be jackin', but ole' Ta-Gloryes he drub you down but good. Da painin' not, no?"

Jake nodded that he felt fine, and that set off the proprietor again.

"Oh, ya," he said, grabbing the foamy and wheeling it across the room. "Ya ya ya, ya ya ya. Da drubbin' oh little oilies, das da jack, yes? Ayka Jayka saya brayka...plastique!"

He stopped pushing the foamy, leaned into Jake's face, and waved his tech'd hand through the air.

"Plastique no brayka!" he said.

Jake wasn't going to argue with him. So he didn't believe Jake killed a plastic man? Jake knew the truth, even if that truth nearly killed him.

2 Glorious pushed the foamy into the drying room, babbling the whole way. He went on about the poor state of galactic travel, railed about the terrible weather, and finally settled into a one-sided debate of Udoian politics that was quite informative. Since Jake last set foot on Udo, the local governments had banded together to protest the king's decision to consolidate the army into the urban areas. Smaller towns – like Ai – and the rural area farmers were being left to fend for themselves. 2 Glorious said his own shop had been vandalized three times in the last month by raiding Lygmies.

The foamy tilted upright and Jake stood in the center of the dryer vents. 2 Glorious flipped a lever on the side of the foamy and it collapsed to the floor. He kicked it to the side, then followed close behind and donned a heat shield vest.

"Eyes," he said, reaching for a button.

Jake shut his eyes.

2 Glorious flipped the switch and the room lit with a blinding intensity Jake could clearly see through his closed lids. The perma-skin dried instantly, shrinking down to a tight elasticity over his body. Jake knew his body would absorb the perma-skin within a day or two, shedding whatever pieces weren't necessary. The part of this procedure he really hated came next.

"Jayka."

He opened his eyes. 2 Glorious stood there, tapping a capped laser blade to his open palm. He smiled, then used the blade to point at Jake's groin.

"You bin jacked up good," he said, bursting into laughter at his own pun.

Jake waited for 2 Glorious to regain his composure, then said, "Let's just do this."

"You techies." 2 Glorious jerked the blade through the air as he laughed. "Why bazbeezle da bod?"

"I don't need a lecture," Jake said. "Just finish the job."

"Ya, Sir!" 2 Glorious feigned a salute, then held the blade under Jake's nose. "Reddy?"

His tech implants wouldn't absorb perma-skin. It sat on top of the tech until the new skin dried to a shriveling mess and the tech underneath grew mold colonies. If he left the perma-skin on that long, his tech smelled like last month's laundry. Plus, all the collected moisture gummed up the mechanical works.

Jake knew all this when he had every piece of his tech installed. He'd just never considered what some skin doctors would say at having to cut away certain excess pieces of perma-skin when he fully tech'd his penis. 2 Glorious's reaction wasn't much different from any other doc's.

He sighed, spread his legs apart, and said, "Okay. I'm ready."

2 Glorious ducked from view, and Jake shut his eyes. Some things a man just should not watch.

* * *

Two hours and far too many insults later, Jake shuffled back into the waiting room, more than ready to leave. He itched wherever the perma-skin hadn't soaked in, which was pretty much everywhere, and he desperately needed a drink. Not allowed, though. 2 Glorious stressed the importance of laying off the booze for at least a week. Jake had never seen it firsthand, but he'd heard enough accounts of alcohol breaking down perma-skin's outer lining. The polite term was "skin-sliding."

Sawn Walsh got up from his chair in the corner and replaced the paddzine he'd been reading. He ambled across the room, his easy manner one of the biggest acts Jake had witnessed in years. Behind that good-natured smile, Jake knew the man was evaluating Jake's threat-potential, scanning him from head to toe with the latest eye implants hiding behind those mirrored glasses. As bazbeezled as Jake's bod might be, it didn't even measure up by half to what Sawn had done. Fuzionic eyes, electroscopic hair follicles – all of them – flexitanium re-inforced neck muscles, pectoral armor plating, and so on. The man was a walking tech-vertisement.

"You better have one damn good reason for dragging me out here," Sawn said.

"It's nice to see you, too."

"Chuck the pleasantries. I was asteroid-hopping. Do you know how hard it is to get a transport out of the Belt that's going anywhere near this hell-hole?"

"I'm sure you worked miracles."

"Of course I did. That's not the point. I was on vacation."

"Then I'm even more grateful you're here. Shall we go?"

"No, we shall not. You promised me bluebacks; show me what you've got."

2 Glorious was nowhere to be seen, but Jake had little doubt the man had cameras wired everywhere in this room – probably mixed in with the paint on the walls.

"Now really isn't the best time."

"There are other things to do on this planet besides following you around, Jake."

"And you can start by trusting me."

"I trust you. That's why I'm here when everyone else said you'd gone Federal. Now make it worth my while." He held out his hand.

"I don't have the money right now."

"This deal's burning fast," Sawn said, balling his hand into a fist.

Jake sighed. He'd been hoping to keep this conversation until later in the day, but Sawn was never one for patience, especially when money was involved.

"Okay, I'll sum it up," Jake said, leading Sawn to the door. "I went Federal for a while, for a reason. I got a tip." He held out a computer padd.

Sawn glanced at it, but Jake couldn't tell what the man was thinking behind his mirrored glasses. Jake was going out there, with or without Sawn. Getting Sawn on board would make the expedition easier. Sawn had contacts in every corner of the galaxy, and he could get his hands on anything they needed, including guns and packs and a guide.

Sawn looked up. "This does not exist."

"Yes, it does." Jake flipped the padd closed and stowed it back in his jacket.

"It is Lygme mythology, nothing more."

"It's in the Southern Hemisphere, and it does exist. The government knows it exists too. That's why I had to go Federal, to get access to their restricted data."

"The Northern," Sawn said. "Nobody's ever returned from the Northern, and there are no maps to the area, no guides."

"There are maps to the area, and I've got copies. And I never expected you to find me a human guide."

"You would trust a Lygme?"

"Absolutely not."

Sawn grinned. "Fifty percent."

"Thirty. You're coming in late."

"Fifty. Or I walk now."

"You won't walk from this." Jake patted his pocket. "Even 30% will keep you living high 'til you die."

"Fifty will keep me higher."

"I don't need you for this. I can go it alone."

"But with me you might actually make it back alive."

Jake laughed. Sawn's overconfidence was incredible, but it was justified. Jake's chances of success were nearly certain if Sawn came along. That's why he'd called him in the first place. Plus, he had absolutely no idea where Rhaina had gone. One day she was in her apartment, the next day the apartment was closed down for rent again, the furniture moved out, and Rhaina had disappeared. Jake never had time to track her down before he left for his rendezvous with the Lygme, so he contacted Sawn.

"Okay," Jake said. "Fifty percent. But you cover our expenses."

"Deal." They shook on it. "Packs and weapons I'll have by tonight. Give me 24 hours to find a Lygme guide, and if you're ready, we can be on a plane to the Southern in two days."

Jake grinned. "Good to have you on board."

11

Tone

lunar base Wascheta

"This is Henry Tudor."

Commander Dalal watched the seconds tick by on the counter beside the phone. The president's switchboard operators would know this signal did not originate from its lunar relay station, and they would try to track down its true point of origin. With the video turned on, they could do that in less than five seconds. Voice-only delayed them by almost twenty seconds. He prayed that was enough.

Colonel Walraven nudged the bound pouncer.

"Mr. President," the pouncer said. "I've heard of your myth."

The computerized map blinked. The switchboard operators had already tracked the signal to the second relay station. They are fast, Tone thought.

"Then you know the myth's impact on society," the president said.

Tone thought that sounded like a code phrase. He looked at his watch. Seven seconds and the operators had already found the third relay station.

"It takes the right person to realize the myth's impact within his own life," the pouncer said.

Twelve seconds, and they were still at the third relay station.

"Thank you for contacting me," the president said with a sigh. "Secure this line."

"Oh, yes, of course."

They heard him tap on a keyboard, and the trace stopped just as it found the fourth relay station – fifteen seconds into the conversation. Of course he didn't mind stopping the trace, Tone thought. He thinks it's already succeeded.

"Okay, I called," the pouncer said. "Talk."

"Do you have the stone?"

"Of course I don't have the stone. You only contacted me last month."

"And you said it would be no problem to get it."

"At the right price, nothing's ever a problem. It also helps if I'm actually on Udo."

"What's your price? And how soon can you be on Udo?"

"Mr. President," the pouncer said, his eyes going black. "You realize this is a Lygme god you're dealing with?"

"My interest in the stone is none of your business."

"Of course not," the pouncer hissed. "I'm just a lowly hireling. I wouldn't know anything about mythology, especially not the one that says Urkay was pointed at Chief Feelo's enemies and they fell down dead at his feet."

"I'm no monster," the president said.

"No. You're the Commander-in-Chief who's losing ground in the Indo-Martian Conflict, and you're up for re-election next year."

"Have you ever heard that curiosity killed the cat?"

"Have you ever heard that pride killed the human?"

The president didn't reply. Tone watched the pouncer at the microphone. He wondered if the colonel knew about this Urkay myth. It had never come up in any of his research.

"What's your price," the president finally said. "And how soon can you get the stone?"

"Freedom for my brothers and sisters shackled to humans the world over."

"I'm not proposing we release every cat in the Alliance. You're crazy!"

Colonel Walraven waved his finger to stop the conversation, but the pouncer kept going.

"I didn't say I wanted those simpleton cats. I want my brothers and sisters around the world released from captivity. You know the ones I mean: the ones locked in cages inside government-run laboratories, the ones treated like farm rats as they're forced to scurry mindless mazes and push their noses against little buttons – sometimes for a piece of catnip, sometimes just to tickle their privates. I want the Pouncers free."

Colonel Walraven shoved a scrap of paper under Silny's nose and pointed at the scribbles. He wanted the animal to stick to the script, and the script never called for any political maneuvering. Find out what the president knew about Jake Alon taking the datafile, then find out what the president was willing to pay for the information – or for the stone itself. That was the colonel's plan.

"I'm running out of time here," the president pleaded. "I can't free every Pouncer in the Alliance. There are other governments, other nations to deal with. I don't know too many who'd go for this."

"Then tie it to government aid, or start a war, or just bully them all into it. I don't care how you get it done, but you're not getting the stone if you don't do this before I get back."

Colonel Walraven gripped the Pouncer's tail.

Silny spun his head and hissed, his ears flat against his head.

"All right, I'll try," the president said. "But that's all I can promise. These kinds of things take time, and I'll have to deal with Congress...I'll try."

"That will be fine," the pouncer said, his black eyes still on the colonel. "You try. I also want two hundred billion."

"What?"

"You've got that much. I'll be back in six months." He flicked his paw against the cutoff switch.

"That was stupid," Walraven said. "We weren't trying for the release of pouncers."

"I thought you were environmental mercenaries," Silny said. "Just consider the two-hundred billion payment for restoring the environment to pouncers."

"The two-hundred billion is payment for getting the bloody stone. Something which we have yet to do." He turned to Tone. "Get us on the next transport for Udo, and tell Avery and Robinson that they're coming with us."

"You're leaving only three people on base."

"Tone, when was the last time anyone bothered to attack this base?"

He didn't want to answer. It was embarrassing they were such an insignificant threat that nobody cared enough to even lob a grenade at their front door. In fact, the biggest threat to security would be the women brought back to base while the colonel was gone.

"I'll get right on it," Tone finally said.

"How lovely," Silny said, washing his face. "A little jaunt through the jungle. Just what the fur needs."

12

Rhaina

*somewhere in the jungles of the
Northern Continent, Udo*

Rhaina's eyes opened at the touch, but she didn't move. Her Geminai knew that a danger was out there somewhere, but it wasn't standing next to her cot. That was someone much more enticing than dangerous.

"Marks," Khonane whispered into her ear. "Outer perimeter. Silent."

Besides herself, Khonane was the only member of Rhaina's team sensitive to his own Geminai. He was more inclined to treat it like a traditional second soul than a true Geminai. He didn't actively send his Geminai out looking for things like Rhaina did, so his was free to roam far and quite at random from himself. Of course, the biggest disadvantage was his Geminai was seldom around when he needed it.

Khonane wasn't on watch now, so Rhaina assumed his Geminai had run across these silent marks he was talking about and woke him up. Who was on watch?

"The plastic man," Khonane said.

He also had the habit of answering her unspoken questions. They'd never figured out how they did it, but it probably had something to do with the close ties they each had to their Geminais.

"The others?" she whispered.

"Asleep."

"Your gun?"

"Of course." He tapped the pistol at his side.

Why did she even ask?

She slipped from beneath her sleeping bag, gripping the pistol and holster she kept at her side. Khonane backed out of the tight confines of her square tent, replacing his cowboy hat as the midnight thundershower pelted his head. Rhaina buckled the holster into place and slipped a cape over her shoulders. She picked up the wide-brimmed fedora Khonane had given her just before they left. He said it would keep her dry in style, but she hated hats. She had yet to wear the stupid thing. And she wasn't going to start now, she thought, tossing it back onto the sleeping bag. Maybe she would forget it was there and lay on it when she got back.

Their boots squished through the rain-soaked ground as they made their way to the plastic man's lookout at the edge of camp. He'd insisted that he take a watch during the night, making a fuss about how he wanted to fit in with the group, his overt helpfulness grating on them until they agreed.

"Going elsewhere for the midnight rendezvous?" he said, chuckling as they approached.

"Anything out there?" Rhaina asked, gesturing beyond their camp's glow.

"There's nothing out there," the plastic man said. "That forest is dead. I haven't even seen wildlife."

Rhaina grinned at Khonane, and they both pulled out their guns.

"Pity we can't give you away, plastic man," Khonane said.

Rhaina'd been about to say the same thing. How did he do that?

"You think I missed something?" the plastic man said. "Doubtful. And please, call me Majid."

"Quiet," Khonane said. "I know there are marks out there."

"Where?"

Khonane turned, studied the black, wet trees, then shrugged, aiming his gun in a general westerly direction. "I don't know. Right around there...somewhere."

Rhaina sent her Geminai. The spirit drifted through the jungle, an amazingly alive place. Not nearly dead like the plastic man seemed to think. The trees glowed with a spirit all their own, tiny bugs crawled along the forest floor, a viper sat at the edge of its burrow, waiting for the midnight storm to subside. In a circle of jungle where she didn't see any rain falling to the ground stood 17 spirits, all turned to watch her approach.

She recalled her Geminai, gasping as the second soul returned from her wanderings.

"There," she said, pointing straight to the spot.

"I don't show anything on active scans," Majid said, his eyes flicking from orange to green and back again.

"Then you're rusting already. Follow us." She stepped beyond the camp perimeter, the jungle's blackness enveloping them.

"I don't rust," Majid muttered.

"Shutup," Khonane said.

He made the plastic man walk between them. Rhaina led the way carefully through the dense undergrowth slapping at her chest and arms. She recalled where the viper had been hiding in its burrow and stepped wide around the area. Her Geminai said the marks had not moved, almost like they were waiting to be discovered. That thought chilled her more than the rain.

Majid gripped her arm. She turned, and he pointed to his ear.

She listened. Nothing.

He leaned forward and said, "They're talking."

"About what?"

"I don't understand the language. Sorry."

Rhaina's Geminai sprinted ahead for a quick glimpse. The marks were no longer turned toward the camp, but they were turned inward, huddled together, and they were speaking, but not in any audible tones. Thoughts drifted from one to another like visible radio waves between them. And the plastic man could hear that?

The marks dispersed, all but one fleeing in separate directions through the jungle. The one that remained turned to Rhaina's Geminai and stepped forward. It held its arms out to show...friendliness?

Geminai backed away, and the mark stopped. It said something to her, broadcasting its visible waves, but she didn't understand. The waves emanated from the creature for several seconds until it dropped its hands and stared at the ground, shaking its head. Then it spun around and ran off.

"Let's go," Rhaina said, leaping forward. She didn't know if she could catch up with them, but she had to try. Blindly following her Geminai's path, she let the spirit tell her where to jump over a root, where to duck beneath a branch. She burst through the jungle into a circle of dry ground and stopped.

"Aren't you afraid of scaring them away?" Majid said, coming to a stop beside her.

The circle was empty, and her Geminai searched fruitlessly for them within a twenty tic radius. Rhaina recalled her Geminai and spread her arms wide, staring at the forest canopy and the water she heard far above her.

"The rain," Majid said, looking up with her. "It stopped?" His eyes glowed orange, green, orange again.

"Right there," Rhaina said, pointing. The rain stopped halfway up the trees, striking something solid and sliding off to the side. "It's like a giant umbrella."

Khonane stumbled into the dry circle, nearly knocking over Majid before he came to a stop.

The umbrella vanished.

The pent-up water slammed into them, knocking them off their feet and nearly pounding them into the ground. Mud splashed back into their faces, obstructing their view and covering them from top to bottom. Rhaina shoved herself up and wiped the muck from her face, watching the scene as much from her Geminai's eyes as her own. The thundershower started washing the mud from her body as she knelt there, staring at the once-dry circle.

"What the hell was that?" Khonane said, sitting up and spitting mud.

"How many hours until dawn?" Rhaina asked, digging through the mud for her pistol.

"About two and a half," Majid said.

"Let's get back." She stood and vainly attempted to swipe at the mud on her pants and shirt. It didn't help. She flicked the Recall button in her palm, and her pistol leaped out of the mud at her feet and into her hand. "Khonane, wake the others. Meeting in my tent in twenty minutes. And tell everyone to bring some breakfast because we're breaking camp."

13

Rhaina

"What's so damned important we have to get up in the middle of the night?" Ramiro said, flipping the tent flap back in place and shaking the rain from his duster. He shoved the rest of his re-hydrated breakfast bar into his mouth and turned to the others. "Oh. Lapht one, huh?"

"Don't spit on me," Cailin said, swiping damp crumbs from her cropped, blonde hair.

"Phorry," Ramiro said. He took the remaining seat.

Rhaina's tent was cramped with all five of them. The lantern clipped to the tent's center pole glowed blue across everyone's face, and the rain slapped against the fleximetal roof. The air was sticky from so many closely-pressed bodies.

"We had visitors last night," Rhaina said. She looked at each of her team members in turn. The plastic man and Khonane listened politely, but it wasn't new information to them. Cailin and Ramiro, however, sat forward, instantly alert. Ramiro's eyes brightened, and he swallowed the rest of his breakfast without another chew.

"I didn't hear any shots," he said. "What happened?"

"About fifteen minutes ago," Khonane said, "something woke me up. I don't know if it was something I heard or something I felt, but I knew someone was out there."

In front of the others, Khonane always dismissed his second soul as intuition, or just something he "felt." In fact, Rhaina had never heard him discuss his Geminai with anyone other than her.

"Rhaina and I and the plastic man – "

"Majid," the plastic man said.

"– went out about thirty tics from the camp. We never saw whoever was out there, but...it was pretty incredible."

"My Geminai saw them," Rhaina continued. "I don't know who they were, but they weren't human, and they didn't look Lygme. They had some kind of visual communication system, almost like their thoughts drifted from one to another. Majid said he could hear them, but I didn't."

"Hear them, yes," Majid said. "But I didn't understand what they said."

"That is jackin'," Ramiro said with a grin. "Mystery people living in the jungle. Hey, maybe it's some lost tribe the scientists haven't even seen before."

"Ramiro," Cailin said, rolling her eyes. "One day out from the colonies?"

"So you two didn't see or hear anything unusual while you were on watch?" Rhaina asked.

"Nothing, sir," Cailin said.

"Nada. But you can bet I'll be looking. Maybe I'll get to name them. The 'Ramiron People.'" He laughed.

"What about the storm?" Rhaina asked. "Did it ever stop?"

"Stop?" Ramiro said. "Jackin' mo, we are in the wet season here. This rain stops for no man." He turned to Cailin. "For a beautiful lady, though...you never know."

"No, ma'am," Cailin said, ignoring him.

"Our visitors made it stop."

"Everywhere?" Cailin asked.

"It appeared to be a localized event," Majid said. "We arrived at the spot in which they'd been standing just moments after they left, and the jungle was nearly dry."

"It hit some invisible barrier just beneath the canopy," Rhaina continued.

"Proximity barriers," Ramiro said with a shrug. "A couple million will get you one easy at a surplus shop."

"Yeah, right," Cailin said. "The lost tribe of the Ramirons – never before seen by any scientist – does all their shopping at your local army surplus store."

"No," Rhaina said. "We crossed into it. A proximity barrier would have kept us out too."

"There was no evidence of modern technology anywhere out there," Majid said. "And the event remained for several moments after their departure. They would have had to take the proximity barrier with them to keep the rain from falling on them as they traveled."

"And they're nearly worthless in this jungle," Khonane said, sitting forward again and crossing his legs. "Too many obstructions: trees, bushes, hills. Believe me, I wanted to bring some along."

"So you're proposing...what?" Cailin asked, shaking her head. "Magic?"

"I'm proposing we keep a very good watch," Rhaina said. "This jungle got its reputation from somewhere, and I want all of us getting back out. Even you, Majid."

Majid nodded but didn't say anything.

"If there are no other questions, finish your breakfasts and let's strike camp. Cailin, destroy our trail. We'll meet you a kilotic due north, then we'll continue heading east when you catch up with us."

"Sounds like fun," Cailin said.

"You're a born tree-hopper, aren't you?" Ramiro said, grinning.

"At least I can trace my ancestors beyond the local whore-house."

"Actually, I think they were cattle rustlers."

"Go," Rhaina said. "Leave my tent. Get some work done."

The meeting broke up with everyone complaining about having to go back into the thunderstorm as they flipped their hoods back into place and trudged through the open tent flap. When she was alone again, Rhaina sent her Geminai for a quick glance around their camp perimeter but found nothing unusual. She laid back on the cot and sighed.

She was more worried about this job than she was willing to tell the others. No modern expedition had ever returned successfully from this jungle, and the few folk legends Rhaina had been able to uncover spoke of an invisible death that stole people away during the night. Whatever those creatures were that watched her camp, they were not invisible, but they could certainly hide well. An ability like that could start all kinds of rumors and legends, especially if they were as skilled at killing as they were at hiding.

14

Rhaina

It wasn't difficult duty following Khonane when he took his turn at point. Rhaina enjoyed the way his body moved, especially his legs. The rain poured off his oiled, leather hat and ran down the back of his camouflaged slicker every time he stopped to look up into the trees. The slicker really didn't do much for his physique, and it was no replacement for the old jean jacket he wore back at his ranch. That showed off his back quite well, especially when he leaned down to inspect a horse's hooves....

The click interrupted her thoughts. They all stopped, and Rhaina put her hand up to listen more carefully to the wireless speaker in her ear. The single click was to get everyone's attention. The next couple clicks confirmed it was Ramiro. They'd reached the distance Rhaina set for their lunch-hour goal.

Rhaina clicked her tongue to bring the conversation back to herself. She instructed Khonane to find cover so they could eat. He winked his reply, then turned and continued forward. The wink, of course, was to say that he knew what she'd been thinking. There were times she preferred a little privacy instead of the close association she had with Geminais. Sometimes secrets were best kept secret.

They found shelter within the hollowed-out body of a fallen cingland tree. Cailin took lookout and everyone else slipped through the tree's tall, tangled roots. They walked nearly upright through the hollowed-out trunk until they found a good place to rest. They sat in a loose circle, and everyone avoided the center of the log where a thin line of mud had formed. Cailin clicked that she was safe and in position up a tree.

"Voices low," Rhaina said, speaking barely above a whisper. The earpieces amplified her voice so everyone heard her anyway.

Nobody said much as they unpacked their rations, water flicking through the air as they shed their slickers. Rhaina sat with her legs crossed and fussed with the weapons stowed across her body before doing anything with her lunch. She flipped the hip holster out so the barrel didn't cut into her thigh, slid the boot sheath around her ankle, shifted the rifle holster to her back, and pulled the palm-sized Tricker pistol from her right boot and set it on the floor of the log beside her. When she finished, she pulled a soup cube from the food pouch and dropped it into her flexisteel cup.

"I can't believe you can eat that," Khonane said, leaning over to stare at the cube.

"Just because it's not some gourmet meal is no reason to insult my lunch."

"No, that's not what I mean. Aren't you wet enough already? You have to put more water inside you?"

"It's chicken soup. I like chicken soup. It'll warm me up." She looked at what he'd dropped on his plate, but it didn't look like any of the rations she'd seen at the store. "What is that?"

"This?" he said, staring at the cube like it had magically appeared on his plate. "Just a little something I whipped up at home before we left."

"You bought yourself a Cuber," Ramiro said with a chuckle. He set the canned flame in the center of the log and held his plate over it to melt his cube – beans from the look of it. "How much did you end up paying for that thing?"

"99,999," Khonane said. "Cred or money order."

"What were you watching?" Rhaina asked. "The Infomercial Hotline?"

"Just because you are too stuck-up to take advantage of a good deal doesn't mean that I have to be."

"Do you mind?" Cailin whispered through their earpieces. "I have chicken kiev waiting for me when I get down there, and all this food talk is making my stomach growl."

"Stop talking," Rhaina said to her. "You're on watch. And *chicken kiev*? Where did you find that?" She turned to Khonane, the answer sitting right beside her. "You packed lunches for her?"

"Sure," he said with a shrug. "She came out to the ranch for a couple weeks when I was teaching her to ride, and I guess she saw the Cuber, and she asked me to pack lunches for her. Not a big deal."

Rhaina repeated the words in her mind: "she came out to my ranch for a couple weeks." Had he shown any interest in Cailin – ever? So what was this about teaching her to ride? And staying at his ranch for a couple weeks? When did all this happen?

Majid leaned forward. "I'd like to discuss some ideas I've theorized regarding our midnight visitors."

"Shut up," Rhaina said. Then, turning to Khonane, "You could have made lunches for me too."

"You never asked." He stared back at her, his eyes wide as he feigned innocence.

"Okay, flame's open," Ramiro said, removing his plate of rehydrated beans and gravy.

Khonane leaned forward, but Rhaina caught his arm.

"Uh uh," she said, holding her cup of soup cube to the flame. "You can eat last."

"You're not seriously mad at me, are you?"

"I guess you'll find out when you see how long I put you on watch tonight." She didn't look up from the melting soup cube as she spoke. She didn't really know how she felt, and she didn't want to have to look into his eyes. On the one hand, she had no legitimate reason for being mad at him. They had a great friendship, and nothing had ever gone beyond the flirtatious banter they enjoyed so much. Part of her liked the distance. Part of her just wanted to take him home and rip all his clothes off.

It was that second part of herself that really didn't like the idea that Khonane had packed lunches for Cailin just because she "happened to notice the Cuber" while she was at his ranch for a couple weeks. There were plenty of things she could have noticed in a couple weeks with the man – his chef's training being only one of them. And when Cailin asked him to pack her lunches, was it morning, noon or night? Were they alone? Was she wearing anything?

"All right, Rhaina," Khonane said, leaning against the log. "Put me on watch all night. I've learned my lesson, and I promise to pack everyone's lunch the next time we leave home."

Never get your honey where you get your money, Rhaina thought with a sigh. She turned to him and grinned.

"That's better," she said. "If you two get to eat decent food, then the rest of us get to eat decent food."

"You little imp," Khonane said. "You weren't mad at all."

"Of course not. I just wanted to make sure we could all eat like kings next time out."

Ramiro barely contained his laughter as he scooped another spoonful of beans into his mouth. "Can I get my order in early? I'll take some pork with my beans."

"I always knew chef's school would improve my life," Khonane said.

Rhaina pulled her steaming cup of soup from the flame. "Get cooking," she said. "We have some things to discuss."

"Oh, are we ready to get back to business?" Majid asked, sitting forward again.

"Let me go relieve Cailin." Ramiro scraped his plate clean.

Cailin clicked her agreement, but that didn't stop Majid from talking.

"I believe our midnight visitors may have been some Lygme Majestic Hunters," he said.

Rhaina recalled the reference from her studies, but she failed to see the connection.

"Never heard of 'em," Ramiro said.

Thank you, Rhaina thought. *Let's see what this plastic man is willing to reveal.*

"As near as any of the research has been able to determine," Majid said, "the Majestic Hunters are reconnaissance members of Pgymy tribes. They are revered for their jungle skills even though those skills do not include actually killing anything. They will get as close as they can to their prey so the tribal hunters can take it down later – if they even do. Sometimes, as I suspect happened last night, the Majestic Hunters will just come up on a target simply for the fun of it. They're very similar to the Native North American tribes who 'counted coup,' or revered the hunter who got close enough to cut something off his opponent's garment without actually killing or injuring his opponent."

He is so full of shit, Rhaina thought. *Whatever those things were last night, they were not Majestic Hunters. They didn't even look like real Lygmies.*

"Well, I don't much like the idea of someone countin' their coo on me," Ramiro said as he threw on his slicker and headed into the rain. "Cailin, I'm coming out to relieve you. Get down from your tree."

"I thought the Majestic Hunters were only found in the Southern Hemisphere," Rhaina said. "This far north, I would never expect to see them."

"True," Majid said with a nod. "But remember, nobody's ever gone as deep into this jungle as we're going and lived to tell of it. We really have no way of knowing what we'll find. The Majestic Hunters make the most logical sense given the scant information we have."

"Hey, guys," Cailin said, shaking the water off her slicker as she sat down by the canned flame. "You know, I think the rain's actually getting heavier out there."

"We'll have to watch for flooding when we head out," Rhaina said.

"I was thinking about last night, too," Khonane said, pulling his plate of rehydrated lobster tail from the canned flame. "It seems to me those things might actually be the basis for the Lygme of Death myth. Do you know that one?"

"Yes, now that you mention it." Majid nodded.

Of course he recalls it, Rhaina thought. *He's trying to keep us from thinking about it. What's he hiding?*

"Don't you think those visitors seemed more like the Lygme of Death?" Khonane continued. "Everything from the stealthy way they moved through the jungle to the way they controlled the weather. It all seems to fit, especially when you compare it against the Majestic Hunters. And Rhaina's right; the Majestic Hunters have only ever been found in the south. The Lygme of Death actually originates from this northern continent."

"You may be right," Majid said, shrugging. "I was just proposing what seemed the most logical explanation to me. Either way, I think Rhaina was right to get us out of there as quickly as we did."

"Absolutely," Khonane said. "I don't care if I'm being watched by Majestic Hunters or stalked by some Lygme of Death, I do not want to stand around and wait for it to come back."

That was the point of this entire charade, Rhaina thought, sipping her soup. For some reason, the plastic man did not want them to make contact with whatever was out there. Why? What did he know?

"Wha–?" Ramiro's voice cut out through the earpiece.

"Report," Rhaina said, holding up a hand to silence everyone.

Ramiro didn't say anything else.

"Ramiro, go ahead," Rhaina said.

Silence.

Rhaina's Geminai raced through the log and into the tree where Ramiro had been standing. The rain poured through the upper branches, a thin pool of blood spreading along the bark.

Geminai spun around, looking for any sign of Ramiro in the trees or on the ground. She left the branch and flew in ever-widening circles around the spot where he'd been standing, but she found nothing.

"Let's go," Rhaina said, setting down her plate and stowing the Tricker pistol back in her boot. She pulled a scanner from her pack and clipped it to her belt.

Geminai hovered above the log and kept watch. She saw nothing moving in the jungle around them, not even bugs or birds. It was like something scared them all off.

Rhaina clicked through the earpieces for Majid to stay with her. A pang of jealousy tried to race through her at the thought of Khonane and Cailin working together, but she stifled it. This was business, and she wasn't about to let the plastic man out of her sight. Her jealousy would have to wait.

They stood just inside the entrance to the log, their weapons drawn, while Rhaina looked one last time through Geminai to be sure the area was clear. Except for the rain, nothing moved.

"Ramiro?" Cailin asked.

Rhaina shook her head. If her Geminai didn't see him out there, then he wasn't out there. She pointed for Cailin and Khonane to leave the log and check to the south while she and the plastic man went north. Two minutes out and two minutes back, she stressed to them, making sure they all saw the fingers she held up.

She glanced out the log, double-checking what she already knew from Geminai. She didn't see anything out there. She checked the scanner and ran it through the settings: motion, heat, sound. The scanner spotted nothing unusual, but the rain interfered with it so much Rhaina wasn't sure she could trust it. She filtered out the rain as best she could, and that extended the machine's range a few more tics.

She gestured for Majid and Cailin to lead the way. Between Cailin's tech'd eyes and whatever fancy equipment Majid had installed, they should be able to find something out there. Assuming something was still there to be found.

Rhaina followed the plastic man as he headed north and east from their log. His head jerked back and forth as he watched the ground and trees around them, and Rhaina kept checking the readings on her scanner to be sure he didn't miss anything. If something even blinked out there, they would spot it.

Majid froze.

Rhaina clicked <What?> to him.

Majid clicked a direction and distance to her, and she looked. Straight east and five tics. Nearly half a dozen trees crowded into that spot, but she didn't see anything unusual. She checked the scanner. Nothing.

"A pair of eyes," Majid subvocalized.

Rhaina looked harder. Nothing.

<How many?> she asked.

Majid held up one finger.

Rhaina looked at the spot through Geminai's eyes. Was the plastic man lying to her?

<Need help?> Khonane clicked.

<Monitor,> Rhaina said. She stepped forward, and one of the trees shimmered for a moment.

"It moved," Majid said. "It's gone."

"Where?" Rhaina asked.

"I don't know. I lost it."

<What is it?> Cailin asked.

<It's invisible,> Rhaina said. <Get over here. Now.>

<There,> Majid said, pointing through the rain.

Rhaina turned, and for a split-second she saw a pair of eyes reflecting red back at her from the bark of a tree. The eyes shut, and the thing disappeared.

<We are four tics northeast of the hollowed log,> Rhaina clicked. <Khonane and Cailin, circle to our south.>

<Acknowledged,> Khonane said.

She checked the scanner, but the thing didn't appear on it. How could it mask its heat and sound? She looked through Geminai, but the creature was invisible to her too. This was just weird, she thought. Nothing should be able to hide from them this well.

Majid walked further north, angling away from a direct path at the creature. Rhaina walked straight at the thing.

The eyes opened. The tree shimmered, and the thing was gone again.

<I saw it,> Cailin said. <It's right in front of me.>

Rhaina turned. Majid was a couple tics away and moving farther east. Khonane stepped out from behind a tree nearly ten tics away, and she couldn't even see Cailin.

<Everyone stop,> she said. She looked up into the trees above her, turned around to the hollowed-out log behind her, and studied the waist-high ferns all around.

<I've got a shot,> Cailin said.

The thing's invisible, Rhaina thought. We can't see it on scanners, and it's able to hide from my Geminai. Why would it show itself?

<Regroup,> she said.

<Can I take my shot?> Cailin asked.

"No, dammit," Rhaina said. "Everyone back here now."

The ground erupted beneath her feet. She flew backwards, crashing through the ferns and sliding across the muddy ground.

She heard somebody call her name, and then the ferns above her spread apart. A tall, slender creature reached down and scooped her from the mud. She fumbled on the ground for her gun, but she didn't find it before the thing tossed her across its shoulder.

Majid raced at the thing, a knife in his hand. He sliced across the creature's arm, but the thing flicked him away.

It lifted its arms to spread a flap of skin from its hands to its feet, and it leaped to a branch nearly twenty tics off the ground. It slammed Rhaina against the tree trunk and pinned her arms and legs with its own. The thing's fur bristled across its body, and it suddenly matched the green and brown of the tree they were standing in. It turned its long snout toward her and stared.

Rhaina listened through the earpiece. One creature was still on the ground with them. Majid seemed okay, and it sounded like he was helping Khonane. Cailin called out to Rhaina.

"Yes," Rhaina subvocalized back to her.

The creature cocked its head, its eyes going black as it studied Rhaina's throat.

"Where?" Cailin asked.

<In the trees,> she clicked back. Pistol shots echoed through the trees, and she heard Majid yell for Khonane to watch his back.

The creature pressed its snout against Rhaina's neck and sniffed. Its hot breath rushed past her throat, and the thing growled so low she felt it in her toes.

She tried to move, but the thing had her feet and hands pinned. Somewhere below, Khonane screamed. The creature clamped its mouth across Rhaina's throat.

She stiffened, waiting for the thing to bite down. The teeth pressed slowly into her skin.

"Rhaina?" Cailin asked. "Talk to me, Rhaina. I'm in the trees, but I don't see you."

The creature growled. It didn't bite down, but it gripped her right wrist with its powerful paws. It brought her hand to her ear, and it growled into her neck again.

This isn't an animal, Rhaina thought as she realized what it demanded. *It's an intelligent creature.*

"Rhaina?" Cailin said. "I need something, please. Tell me you're still there."

Rhaina stuck her finger in her ear and pulled out the ring-shaped transceiver. She flicked the tiny "Off" switch and dropped the ring into the creature's paw.

The animal released her neck and leaned back to stare at her as it let the transceiver fall to the ground.

"Okay, we're alone." Rhaina felt silly talking to this growling beast that towered over her, but the thing showed intelligence. For now, she'd give it the benefit of the doubt.

The shooting below suddenly stopped. Either Majid had killed the creature, or it had killed them. She preferred the first possibility, but she had to go on the assumption she and Cailin were now alone.

She called to her Geminai and found the spirit hovering on a nearby branch.

"I assume you want to talk?" Rhaina whispered to the animal.

The thing lifted its head and sniffed at the rain, its eyes glancing at the branches above and around them. It shivered.

Rhaina's Geminai flew closer.

"Do you have a soul?" Rhaina asked.

The animal looked down at her. Geminai slid into it from behind.

Rhaina gasped. Dozens of minds and souls inhabited the animal's body, guiding it, controlling it, forcing it to do whatever its primal instincts allowed to be controlled.

The thing swatted Rhaina aside and turned to face Geminai.

Rhaina pitched forward and fell across a tangled mass of vines and smaller branches. She gripped the rifle from its holster on her back and rolled around to get off a shot.

The animal stood on the branch above her, its fur shimmering orange as it swatted at Geminai flying around it.

Rhaina raised the rifle's sight to her eye, put the animal's spinning chest in the cross hair, and squeezed off three consecutive shots before the thing even turned back toward her.

The animal slumped to the branch, its fur fading to a dingy gray. It lifted its head toward Rhaina, reached out one bloody paw, and fell forward onto the same tangle of branches and vines that supported her.

Their weights bowed the wet branches. Several of the thinnest vines snapped loose, and the vine net slipped.

Rhaina stowed the rifle, twisted, and gripped the nearest, thickest branch she could find.

The creature's weight split the vines apart, and it tumbled through the rain and branches to crash to the ground below.

"Hold on!" Cailin called from above her.

As if I have a choice, Rhaina thought, gripping the branch. She looked up to see Cailin leap from the same branch the creature had used a moment before.

Cailin dangled above Rhaina and reached down. "Take my hand."

Rhaina gripped Cailin's wrist, and Cailin supported her as she stumbled across the wet branches to the trunk.

"Thanks," Rhaina said.

"And the others?"

Geminai flew to the ground and found Majid kneeling over Khonane's still body. The plastic man ripped off Khonane's shirt to expose deep gashes.

"Khonane looks bad."

Cailin flinched. It was subtle, but Rhaina noticed.

"And the plastic man's losing fluids out his shoulder," she finished. She brought her attention completely back inside herself. She didn't have to say another word as Cailin started climbing back down to the forest floor. Without Ramiro, they couldn't afford to let anything happen to Khonane. Rhaina did not want to be alone in the jungle with a plastic man.

15

Jake

deep in the jungle, Udo

Jake stopped as Sawn put a hand to his arm. The rain poured down his face, and he opened his mouth to take a few drops. Turning, he saw the four Lygmies and their pack frizzes had stopped further back. Sawn held a portable scope out for him to see.

"What am I looking at?" Jake said, not even bothering to glance at the thing. He was wet, his perma-skin itched like measles, and he was really sick of trudging through the jungle. If he hadn't already invested a couple years of his life into this expedition, he would have turned around long ago and gone home. There were diamonds in high-security vaults easier to get to than this thing.

"Apparently you're looking at the jungle around you," Sawn said, staring at him through those insufferable black glasses. "I, however, am looking at small weapons fire."

"Weapons?" Now Jake was interested. He turned to the scope.

"About 30 kilotics back," Sawn said, pointing to the scope. "Looks like multiple shots fired from several different pistol models. This one looks like small rifle fire."

"Where is that? What would they be shooting at?"

"That's the area our Lygmies said looked like meshet hunting grounds," Sawn said with a grin. "We avoided it."

"Someone else wasn't so lucky." Jake looked at the Lygmies shuffling beside their ugly pack frizzes. Their clothes were soaked, hair plastered to their heads – either from the rain or from some tribal gunk they put on it – and not one of them even came close to smiling. He called to the leader. *"Bek da hoo."* Come here.

The shortest male in the group handed the reins of his frizz to the Lygme beside him and ran forward. The male ducked under and around the foliage that usually towered over his head. Jake had walked through those same plants and they didn't even come up to his waist. The Lygme's black hair locks sprayed excess water as he ran to a stop.

"Cleck dae brench, eh?" the Lygme said. How may I serve you?

Jake wasn't fooled by the servile attitude from this Lygme, Ko. Behind every "Yes, ma'am" and "Yes, Sir" the Lygmies spewed was the unspoken "I hate you" or "I'll kill you." He had seen the result of a servant revolt, and it was gruesome. People strung from the rafters by their hair, others with every finger and toe cut off. No, the Lygmies were not to be trusted, especially not in great numbers. If Sawn hadn't insisted they needed all three Lygmies for this trip, Jake never would have agreed.

"Brekka dae jospeh yip, eh? Qi na yip, vras uip resgaba." Is there a good spot to camp? We'll need to set up for several nights.

Of course, the Lygme had no real concept of several nights. Jake had to put it in terms the Lygme would understand – they might need to camp for a couple rainstorms. The Lygme got it, and the Lygme didn't like it.

Ko started a long tirade in Lygmese, and Jake only caught every few words. Something about the necessity of always moving, the short time frame they were under, the dangers that might find them, and on and on. The little man barely stopped long enough to take a breath between arguments.

"Jake, what's your plan?" Sawn whispered into his ear.

Jake turned his back on the Lygme and leaned close. The thunderstorm had gotten heavier, and a private conversation had to be rather loud to be heard, but they tried.

"I'm going back," Jake said.

"That's ridiculous. That's a couple days of traveling through this jungle just to get near whoever else is out there."

"A couple days for us with these Lygmies and their smelly frizzes. What if that other group's as tech'd as you and me? We could cover 30 kilotics in hours. I do not want to race against an opponent that's as fast as me – but isn't dealing with the extra baggage we have."

"And if they're as tech'd as you and me, you'll also have trouble taking them down by yourself. I counted four weapon signatures on the scope. Four to one is not good odds."

"That's why you're staying with the Lygmies. Track me on the scope, and if I have any problems, I'll come right back. But you be ready to fight with everything you've got when I do come back." He leaned closer to Sawn's ear and spoke as softly as he could. "If all else fails, we'll ditch the Lygmies and head back for the colonies."

"That's not a smart idea."

"Then let's hope it doesn't come to that."

16

Tone

Sol-Win, Udo

Commander Tone Dalal and Avery Wilson strolled through the front door of the Ai New Skin and Retread Shop. They wound their way past the chairs crammed along the walls and down the center of the tiny outer lobby. The place reeked of burnt oils and plastics mixed with antiseptic overtones. Since the lights burned strong, Tone assumed the proprietor/doctor was not entertaining a patient.

The metal accordion-style door crashed open and a reception-roboto stepped forward. Its metal gears, wires, and joints hadn't even been covered, and the thing stared at them through bright, yellow eyes that looked more like they belonged on a corpse.

"May I help you gentlemen?" the thing said in its tinny voice.

"We'd like to see the proprietor," Tone said.

"I am sorry, sir," the roboto squeaked. "The doctor is occupied at the moment. If you would like to schedule a preliminary consultation, then I'm sure I can work you in for a half-hour tomorrow afternoon. Maybe after lunch?"

"I believe we'll see him now," Tone said, stepping forward.

"No, sir," the roboto said, raising its metal arm to block the way. "The doctor is occupied at the moment. I can take a message and have him call you, or you can make an appointment."

Avery reached forward and stabbed his index finger against the roboto's chest. He twisted his hand and a bolt of electricity raced from his finger and arced between the roboto's head and the light fixtures. Smoke spewed from every joint and exposed circuit on the roboto's body. The yellow eyes went dead and the roboto fell backwards.

"Thank you, Mr. Wilson," Tone said, stepping forward.

Avery blew the charred remains of wires from the tip of his index finger.

They followed the narrow hall to the two operating rooms and opened the doors. They found the rooms fully stocked with cans of perma-skin, sterilized saws, needles, and brushes, and even a holographic mannequin displaying fashions of skin design. They opened the last door at the end of the hallway and stepped into the drying room. A gold star had been painted in the center of the circular room, and heat lamps and drier fans were all aimed at that spot. Dried perma-skin had baked into a splattered sunburst around the star. They did not, however, find the doctor.

"Is he even here?" Tone asked.

"Shh," Avery said. He cocked his head as he turned in a slow circle, his tech'd eyes focusing on the nearly seamless walls. He stopped and pointed at a spot opposite the door. "There's an electronically shielded door. And I can hear...some voices on the other side. They're not talking though."

"Whispering?" Tone asked. It was conceivable the roboto had a built-in feature to alert the proprietor when it was shut down.

"No," Avery said. He put his ear to the wall. "It really sounds like they're...blowing bubbles."

"You're not funny," Tone said. "Pop the thing."

Avery backed away from the hidden door, picked at a hair on his arm until it came loose, and yanked out a micro-filament line from beneath his skin. He ran the line along the crack between the wall and the floor and backed away, still yanking extra line out of his arm as he went.

"Cover your eyes," he said.

Tone did. He heard a high, electric whine followed by several sparks and the soft sputter of wires fusing. The shielding dropped to reveal a door.

After retracting the filament line, Avery yanked the door open. Nearly a dozen retread tanks lined the walls and center aisle, the green foamy gurgling beneath each locked lid – except inside the last tank where the foamy sloshed over the sides in a rhythmic motion. Electricity sputtered toward the ceiling.

Tone approached, and he saw a foamy-covered butt bouncing up and down to the beat of the electric sparks. A dark green woman had her arms wrapped around the butt, and the electricity seemed to be coming from beneath her skin. Tone reached forward.

"No," Avery said, gripping his arm. "Several hundred volts running through that tank."

"Who are they?"

"I don't have the woman's face on file, but the man is 2 Glorious, the proprietor. He seems to be…uh…testing some modifications on her."

"Can you get him out of there?"

"Ground me," Avery said, pulling a couple tics of filament line from beneath his skin.

Tone took the line and tied it around the leg of a nearby retread tank. Avery extended the metallic ends of all five of his fingers and reached through the foamy to grip the man's neck. The grounded retread tank jolted from the electric surge.

Avery yanked up the proprietor, green foamy flying through the air, and dumped his naked, slimy body to the floor.

"Wha' da jackin' hell?" the man yelled, spitting a breathing tube from his mouth and wiping his goggles clean. His hands and legs slipped across the floor, and he struggled to sit up.

The green woman sat up in the tank and slicked the hair back from around her face. The gill slits beneath her jaw line spewed out excess foamy and then sealed shut as she began breathing through her mouth again. She stretched her neck and torso, the foamy sliding off her shimmering scales, and she turned her silver eyes on Tone and Avery.

"Who took away my toy?" she asked, the words nearly bubbling from her throat. She spit foamy from between her pointed teeth.

"Sorry, ma'am," Avery said, yanking 2 Glorious back to his feet.

"Da little oilies, they better be good 'n ready to do some 'splanation." 2 Glorious ripped the goggles from his face. "Eezle bin charged up for 2 Glorious for ny on two weeks!"

"But, the electricity?" the woman in the tank – Eezle? – asked.

"I've been tech'd to withstand electric shocks," Avery said with a proud grin.

"Really?" Eezle's silver eyes grew wide. She reached a scaly hand to touch Avery's arm. "How high?"

"I'm rated at nearly 5,000 volts, but that really jacks with my head."

Before any of them could say anything more, Eezle yanked Avery's shirt and pulled him into the tank with her, foamy sloshing over the sides.

"No!" 2 Glorious yelled.

Lightning burst from the retread tank as Eezle ripped off Avery's shirt and tossed it aside. The woman clamped her mouth across Avery's mouth, wrapped her scaly arms around his back, and began working his pants off with her surprisingly dexterous legs and fins.

The grounded tank bounced to the woman's gyrations, electric surges sparking across the floor.

Tone and 2 Glorious backed away.

"She's not going to hurt him, is she?" Tone asked.

2 Glorious spun around and slapped his foamy-covered hands against Tone's chest.

"She be mine, ya jackin' little oilie!" Foamy flew from his naked body as he shoved Tone away from the sparking tank. "Ya'z takin' her illeglly! I be fightin' ya honer!"

Tone pulled out his gun. Foamy fell in giant glops from his shirt and arm, and he wondered if any had gotten into the gun's chamber. It didn't matter because the moment 2 Glorious saw the thing pointing at his nose, he shut up and raised his hands over his head. He turned and stared at Avery and the eel-woman in the sparking tank.

"Once more," Tone said, more than a little frustrated. "Will she hurt him – and make it a straight answer. None of this vig-talk."

"She be hurtin' him in the most wonderest of ways," he said with a sigh.

"So she's hurting him?"

"You bein' a bark? Da man be gettin' the jackin' of a lifetime." 2 Glorious turned back to Tone. "What ya wantin'?"

"You had a patient see you a couple weeks ago, a Mr. Jake Alon."

"Dot's what dis iz 'bout? You talkin' bizness? You go out 'n you talkin' with my 'boto!"

"Your roboto is incapacitated."

Foamy erupted in a shower of sparks. 2 Glorious watched the remaining foamy steam and slosh to the couple's rhythm.

"Ya," he finally said. "Jake was here."

"Did he talk to you? Maybe say where he'd been or where he was going?"

"Ya. He bin out killin' plastique. And sum bud meet him here so they kin run off 'n find a gem in da jungle."

"He told you all this?" Jake would confide in this little skin doctor?

"No, he tellin' me 'bout the plastique. He tellin' his friend 'bout the gem."

"Did he say where the gem was hidden?"

The glow faded inside the retread tank, the foamy still steaming. Avery and the eel woman rocked gently back and forth with the dwindling current.

"Not for six more months," 2 Glorious mumbled.

Tone saw tears run down 2 Glorious's foamy-streaked face.

"Just tell me," he whispered. "And we'll leave. Did he say where the gem was hidden?"

"He tellin' his friend." 2 Glorious pointed to a desk at the other end of the room. "Take da pink datafile. It gots da pix."

Tone went to the desk and picked up the datafile. Foamy slid down 2 Glorious's naked body and formed a puddle at his feet. His shoulders slouched, but his eyes never left the tanks. Tone shoved the datafile into the computer and Jake and a large man appeared on the screen. Tone made sure the files weren't corrupted, then stowed the datafile in his pocket. By the time he returned to 2 Glorious's side, the eel-woman was helping Avery stumble from the tank.

"You okay?" he asked as he took Avery's slick arm.

The foamy ran off Avery's body in hot rivers, and the man only turned to Tone and grinned. Tiny sparks bounced over the bridge of his nose and between his eyes.

"Oh, thank you," the eel-woman said, getting out to stand beside Avery. She ran her webbed hands across the green scales of her body to slough off the remaining foamy, her wide, silver eyes blinking. She plugged her nose and blew more foamy through the gills in her throat, then turned to 2 Glorious. "Now that was a test run."

"Ya, it all works good," 2 Glorious mumbled.

"Thanks for the new look, doc," she said as she turned to strut from the room. "I'll be back in six months for my check-up."

Tone couldn't help but watch her shimmering green backside as she walked away, her hips swaying and her feet leaving wet web-prints along the floor. A spark crackled from the center of her back, split into four smaller pieces, and snaked out to her arms and legs like slow-motion lightning.

"You're good," Tone said to the proprietor.

"Ya," 2 Glorious said with a sigh. He looked at Tone and Avery, his eyes a little wider. "Ya wantin' 'lectric package like hers? I cut ya big deal. Ya, and even gots financing."

"Yes!" Avery gasped.

"No," Tone said. "We're going."

"But," Avery said. "She was.... I was...."

Tone propped Avery against a tank, untied the filament wire, and gave the hot line to Avery to hold.

"But I could...," Avery continued.

"No, you couldn't." Tone retrieved the man's foamy-soaked clothes, put an arm around him, and led him from the room.

17

Rhaina

jungle campsite, Northern Continent

"Are you trying to get yourself killed?"

Khonane barely moved on the cot, the lantern light casting blue shadows across his face and bandaged chest.

"You've been sleeping for exactly six hours," Rhaina continued. "Just like the plastic man said you would."

He blinked, but otherwise didn't react.

"I didn't know this," Rhaina said, glancing at the scanner on the floor. It still showed the area free of bad guys. "But did you know that a plastic man can have drugs pumped into his system that he can later inject into another person?"

Khonane blinked again, and this time he focused on Rhaina.

"He pumped you full of one of those drugs." She looked him in the eyes again. "Said it would make you sleep for exactly six hours while we bandaged you up, and he was right. Six hours. Almost to the minute."

"Ow," Khonane said, sliding one hand across the bandages.

"You should hurt; you were sliced up pretty good. Fortunately, that thing didn't hit any organs. Thank God for rib cages."

Khonane tried to sit up, but only got his head above the pillow before he fell back.

"Ramiro?" he gasped.

"No," Rhaina said, quieter. "The rain washed away most of the blood by the time we killed those things. Cailin climbed the trees and searched, but she never found anything. I don't know what they did with him."

"Cailin?"

His eyes were alert, and his strength had returned. Whatever drug Majid gave him, it seemed to wear off quickly. And one of the first things on his mind was Cailin. That must have been a good couple weeks at the ranch. Damn.

"She's fine," Rhaina said. She checked that his bandages were secure and that none of his stitches had popped, then clipped the scanner to her belt, threw on the slicker, and headed back into the midnight thundershower.

She stood in the rain outside Khonane's tent and let her eyes get adjusted to the darkness. They'd set up the two tents near each other, and if Cailin was awake, she probably heard most of the conversation. She shouldn't be awake, though; she should be sleeping to take watch in an hour.

"How is he?" Majid asked, stepping from the darkness.

"Awake."

"He should have been awake nine minutes ago. How is he? Does he need his bandages changed?"

"He's fine." She took a moment to look through Geminai. She didn't see anything unusual, but Geminai hadn't seen those creatures the last time they attacked. It made her nervous that her Geminai was blind to those things. She had never encountered anything that could hide so well. It made her wish she had tech'd eyes. Almost.

"There's nothing out there," Majid said.

"How do you know? You were blind to those things, too."

"Their camouflage is excellent," he said with a nod. "But I watched them change when they attacked. I'm sure I can spot them again."

Rhaina led him a few paces from the tent where they could talk in private. The rain seemed to be getting lighter, but it still poured off her hat and slicker.

"Tell me about your programming," she said.

"I prefer not to think of it as programming," the plastic man said, coming up beside her. "I like to think of it more as my natural inclinations."

"That's bullshit. You're a machine. You were programmed. Explain your programming to me."

"What do you want to know?" he sighed.

"Are you programmed to lie?"

"How would you like me to answer? Anything I say will condemn me."

"Then you have nothing to lose."

"The truth, then. Yes, I'm programmed with the ability to lie."

Rhaina stared into the thundershower, but she was pleasantly surprised at the plastic man's candor. She doubted it would last, but she was glad to see it emerge for a few moments. She glanced at the scanner on her belt. Nothing outside the camp perimeter.

"It's my turn now," Majid said. "The truth. Are you planning to kill me and leave me in this jungle?"

Where did this come from? Was Mr. Rosh stupid enough to program this plastic man with some insecurities? If so, it was a weakness she would remember if she ever needed it.

"The thought's crossed my mind," she finally said. "But I'd prefer not to do that. As long as we're being so blunt, is that part of your programming? To kill us out here and return the jewel to Mr. Rosh?"

"The truth?"

"I thought that's what we were talking about, yes."

"My programming says that I'm to do everything possible to keep you and your team alive until we find that gem."

"And after?"

"Actively working to keep you alive after we find the gem is at my discretion. But I'm inclined to do so. We stand a better chance of surviving if we're a larger group. My turn."

Rhaina nodded. She didn't like being questioned like this, but she was willing to do it if it kept the plastic man talking with such candor.

"Can your Geminai see on the spiritual level?"

"What do you mean?" And what could this possibly have to do with their mission?

"I mean...." He stared into the rain for several seconds, and when he finally spoke, it was so soft Rhaina barely heard him. "Do I have a soul?"

"It doesn't work that way." She took a moment to look at him through Geminai, but she only saw a man-shaped machine. "Have you ever heard of the Eternity of Souls?"

"No. I doubt Mr. Rosh considered it relevant to this mission."

Odd, Rhaina thought, *that a man-spirit like Mr. Rosh wouldn't program his plastic man with even a basic understanding of the spiritual Sea.*

"Think of it like another plain of existence," she said. "Or like another universe. It's the mirror image of this physical world, and the creatures that live there are the second souls to the people who live on this side. I have to travel with my Geminai into that world to see the souls you're speaking of, and then it's not always successful. If someone tried to find my second soul over there, they wouldn't find her because I've brought her over here with me."

Majid stared into the rain, apparently considering what she said.

"I'll make you a deal, though," she continued. "When we get through this, I'll look."

"Check your scanner," he said, turning to face the camp. "Quickly, though, like you did before."

She reached to her belt and tilted the scanner up, glancing at the readings. It showed something fairly large out there, not quite as big as the animals that attacked them during the day. This thing looked to be the right size for another human, but it gave off hardly any heat and it stopped moving almost as soon as Rhaina saw it. Whatever – whoever – it was, it was watching them.

"Well, I think the Banshees can go all the way this year," Majid said, his voice loud enough to carry through the rain.

Rhaina grinned. The Banshees were her favorite sandstone team.

"No guarantees," she said. She sent her Geminai to find their midnight visitor. "Their offense looks good – it has for the last couple years – but they can't get their defense into shape. You're right, though, this is the best lineup they've had in a decade."

"I gotta take a piss," Majid said with a sigh. He headed to the west of camp. "And no following me, either. This is the little boy's room."

She watched him disappear into the darkness, then studied the trees. The rain made it difficult to see, hear, and sometimes even to think, and she wished for the hundredth time that it would stop for even one hour so she could dry off. If wishes really came true, though, she'd have the gem sold and be back on Earth sipping hot chocolate by the fire and reading the latest Temple Jones romance novel. The universe didn't care what she wished.

Rhaina flipped up the scanner, but it was empty now. Whoever this mark was, he was good if he could hide himself at will from her scanner. She studied Majid's path. The plastic man was too smart to head directly at the mark, so Rhaina guessed their contact was working his way to the east of camp. She sent her Geminai in that direction. Birds sleeping in their nests, some kind of giant lizard scuttling through the branches, and dozens of nocturnal insects.

When Geminai caught up with the man in the woods, Rhaina recognized him immediately. Tech'd from head to foot, he looked more like some human/roboto cross-breed than a real man, but he was definitely Jake Alon. She'd seen his Geminai when she was still on Earth, and she'd seen the prize that brought him to Udo. It wasn't the same gem she was after, but she didn't think she'd convince him of that.

She turned to the east and stepped into the darkness. She watched the muddy ground pass beneath her feet, and her Geminai watched Jake. He paced himself with her, tracking her movements, his path leading closer to her with every step they took. The knife in his hand made it obvious he wasn't out there to say "Hello."

She stopped nearly ten tics from the camp and stared into the woods, her back to Jake's silent approach. Geminai watched him crouch behind a tree, the knife at his side. He studied the forest around them, apparently making sure they were alone, then crept from behind the tree and headed straight at her.

Rhaina spun and dropped to her knees, the waist-high ferns enveloping her.

Jake ducked behind a tree.

Geminai watched him stow the knife in a wrist sheath and bring out a pistol.

Rhaina grinned. She scuttled beneath the ferns to come up on him from the other side of the tree.

He studied the forest where she had been a moment before.

Rhaina sprang at him from behind, cupped her hand across his pistol, and slammed her body against his, trying to pin him to the tree.

He slid to the ground and gripped her around the waist.

She jumped, wrapped her legs around his neck, and dropped on his shoulders with all her weight.

He didn't even flinch as he sprang back up from the ground and shoved her off, tossing her backwards into the ferns.

Rhaina hit the ground in a ball and used the momentum to roll herself a couple tics from the point of impact. She crouched behind a tree and forced her breathing to slow.

Geminai watched Jake kneel behind a tree of his own. He fussed with a scanner at his belt, trying to detect Rhaina. It wouldn't be long before he succeeded, and she grinned at the fun she was having.

"I know you," she called into the darkness. "You're that bad shot from the Bronx."

He looked up. They'd decided on the codes years ago, and she assumed he'd remember them. If he didn't, she'd just given away her position.

He aimed the scanner at her and studied the readings.

She tensed.

"When were you last in New York?" he asked.

She smiled and stepped from behind the tree. It was the second part of the code phrase. He remembered her.

"Sorry," she said. "San Diego's my –"

Majid sprang from between a couple trees, knocking Jake to the ground and sending them both skidding through the muddy underbrush.

"No!" Rhaina yelled.

Majid shoved Jake against a tree, a knife already at the man's throat.

"Stop!" Rhaina said.

Majid stopped, the blade pressed hard against Jake's neck. He turned his glowing eyes on Rhaina.

"First rule of the mission," he said. "Protect the people escorting me."

"Shit!" Jake said. "Where did you come from?"

"Stand down," Rhaina said. She knew the plastic man's kill-switch phrase, but she didn't want to use it so soon into their mission.

"This man is a threat to our safety," Majid said.

"I know this man. He's Jake Alon. He is not a threat to our safety."

"Jake Alon?" the plastic man said, turning his glowing eyes on Jake.

Rhaina had no idea what Mr. Rosh might have programmed regarding Jake, but he obviously knew something about the man.

"I trust him," Rhaina said. "Now back away."

Majid's eyes faded until they didn't glow at all, but he still watched Jake. He slipped the knife away from Jake's neck and stepped back a couple paces.

"Rhaina?" Jake finally said as he slid the pistol back in his holster. "What the hell are you doing out here with a plastic man?"

"Good evening." She stepped forward to take his hand. "Want some coffee?"

18

Jake

Rhaina's jungle campsite

Jake wasn't happy as he sat on the cot in Rhaina's tent and sipped coffee. Pissed best described his mood. He didn't like being side-swiped, especially by yet another plastic man, and he didn't like it that Rhaina and her team were in this jungle. He knew no other reason to be out here than to be after the God's Ear gem, and that was his treasure. He didn't want to have to see Cailin and Khonane again, he didn't like making small talk with that plastic man, and he was grateful to finally be alone with Rhaina to tell her all this. But then she smiled at him and spoke first.

"I'm glad we finally met."

My god, I miss her, he thought.

"I'm glad, too." He took another sip of coffee.

"I got that little present you left at my place. Do I really need a big brother?"

"I meant it in the best Orwellian sense of the word."

"Ah, yes, of course. George and I go way back." She crossed her legs and sat further back on the cot.

Jake enjoyed watching her move, especially when that movement stretched her baggy outfit tighter around her body, around the curve of her hips and thighs.... He cleared his throat and drank more coffee.

"So what brings you out here?" he asked.

"What brings you?"

"Tourist traps. Gift shops. The usual."

She smiled.

"They're all the rage," he continued, gesturing to the jungle outside. "The natives set up these little tree houses where they hawk their hand-made jewelry and pendants and things. The only problem is that you have to buy a full-length Lygme necklace to even get the thing to fit around your ankle. Makes it hard to buy good gifts for friends."

"So you're saying you have an anklet for me?"

"Uh...."

She laughed. It was a good sound, something he hadn't heard in far too long. How could he ever be upset with her?

"I thought maybe you were getting something else for me," she said. "Like maybe...a God's Ear gem?"

Oh, yes, he thought. *I could be mad at this woman.*

"Rhaina, I don't want to compete with you."

"Good, because you won't have to."

"Good," he said. "Then you can return to the outer colony towns, my team and I will get the gem, and we'll meet for a romantic dinner in a couple weeks."

"How long's it been, Jake? Two years?"

"Since we worked together last? About that."

"I'd forgotten what an ass you can be."

"If I remember correctly, you used to like my ass."

"That was before you kept sticking it in my face."

Jake sighed as he stared at her firm eyes. Her smile had disappeared almost completely while they talked, and all hint of affection for him lost in that last comment. She would not turn back now. He knew her well enough to know that she was more resolved than ever to find the gem first.

"It's dangerous out here," he said.

"Who's on your team?"

"Sawn Walsh."

"And?"

"That's it. Me and Sawn. A few Lygme guides to carry the supplies."

"Sawn's good," she said, uncrossing her legs and sitting forward. "But what are you going to do if you run into trouble? Or if your Lygmies revolt?"

"I'm not worried about Lygmies. And you may have noticed I've installed some impressive new tech."

"I noticed when you threw me at that tree, yes."

He cringed.

"But here's what I'm suggesting."

No, he thought. *Don't make any suggestions. Just leave.*

"The God's Ear gem is not going to be out in the open for us to find. We're going to have to do some searching and digging."

"Okay." He had a strong suspicion he knew where she was going.

"I propose we combine our teams until we get there."

He was right. Why did he always have to be right?

"It'll increase our travel time, but it will also increase our chances of defending ourselves."

"Against what?" he said with a snort. "You're the one who led your team into the meshet hunting grounds. We avoided this place."

She smiled, but it wasn't pleasant anymore. He really wished they could go back to the relationship they had, where they worked together, ate together, slept together.

"We caravan together until we get to where the gem is hidden," she said. "Then we split up to search for it. If I find the God's Ear before you do, I'll cut you in for 25%. You find it before I do, and you cut me in for 25%."

"Sawn and I are 30 kilotics ahead of you, and I'm the one with the maps and guides. What have you got? Some mystical premonition that the gem is out here 'somewhere?' I think I should leave now and let you fend for yourself."

"And my plastic man could have your Lygme guides sliced in two before you got back to your camp. I know you, Jake. If you were really as confident as you say, you wouldn't be relying on Lygmies."

He sat back on the cot and stared at her. She had ten times more confidence than she ever had when they worked together last, and she seemed to have the resolve to back up what she threatened.

But she was also right. Sawn seemed to think the Lygmies were necessary to the mission, and maybe they were, but Jake still didn't like that the little beasts outnumbered him. Lygmies were too wild, too unpredictable. And just because they recognized the danger of the meshet didn't mean they would recognize whatever danger they ran into next.

The percentages Rhaina proposed bothered him, though. Only 25%? If the God's Ear was really as valuable as he believed, 25% would be quite a fortune. But why would she settle for so little? He couldn't believe she had changed so much that she'd let go of that much money.

"Okay," he said, setting the empty cup on the floor. "But if I find the gem first, I'm only cutting you in for 10%."

"Twenty," she said.

"Fifteen."

"It's a deal."

She held out her hand, and Jake knew beyond a doubt that she wasn't out there for the God's Ear. In fact, she probably never planned to look for the thing. Which meant...there was something else out here that held more attraction for her than a huge, rare gem. And the deal she struck would be a nice little bonus on top of whatever it was she was really after.

He smiled and shook her hand.

"Partner," he said.

"Traveling companion," she said, wagging a finger at him.

"Whatever." He grinned. It had been far too long since he'd played games with this woman. The expedition didn't seem quite so dreary anymore.

19

Tone

Mother Earth jungle campsite,
Northern Continent, Udo

Tone watched with fascination as the little Lygmies set up camp
for the evening. All the books he'd read and all the pictures he'd seen
hadn't prepared him for meeting a group of these creatures. The tallest
of them didn't come up past his chest, and the shortest of them could
hide in the tall ferns.

Even more fascinating, though, was the fluid way they moved, and
how they communicated through their minds. He'd never heard that
Lygmies had ESP.

And their hair! It hadn't stopped raining since they entered the jungle, and the Lygmies' bright, orange hair looked exactly as it had in the
morning, almost as if the rain bounced right off.

But he was also certain he'd seen a pair of eyes staring at him from
within the bark of a tree. The jungle played tricks with the mind. Or
maybe it was the rain playing the tricks. Either way, trees should not
have eyes.

"Keep their grubby little paws off," Silny hissed from within his cage.

A Lygme scurried away.

"I thought you liked them," Tone said.

Silny smacked his lips together, a gesture Tone had come to recognize as laughter.

"Well you certainly got on well enough with your precious Ms. Boriskov to make us all believe you liked Lygmies."

Within minutes, the Lygmies had looped vines through the corner flaps of their tents and strung them through tree branches. They tightened the vines, snapped the tent flaps taut, and secured the ends. It was some of the most expeditious work Tone had seen performed in years. He wondered if any of these industrious Lygmies would be willing to return with him to the moon and teach their recruits how to work like real men.

The tallest of the Lygmies, Jane, ran up to him. Her name wasn't really "Jane," but Tone couldn't pronounce the little woman's name so he called her Jane. The Lygme didn't seem to mind. She responded to "Jane" as quickly as she responded to her real name when the Lygmies said it.

"All is ready, good Sir," Jane said.

"Wonderful. But you should tell Colonel Walraven, not me."

"If we please you, Sir, please be it for you to tell the colonel yourself that our work for the moment is complete."

They didn't quite grasp the language, but they were certainly polite. Every one of them, however, seemed to have some innate fear of the colonel, and they avoided talking to him. Colonel Walraven seemed only too happy to be ignored by the little people, so Tone accommodated their quirky behavior.

"If it please you, good Sir, we transport the prisoner-animal to your tent for safest keeping."

Silny stood up in the cage and arched his back.

"Thank you for the offer, but we should handle him," Tone said. He opened and closed his hand in what he hoped got across the image of toothy jaws. "Very dangerous. He bites."

"Ah," Jane said, studying the animal with what appeared to be even greater fascination. "Dangerous. Yes, I observed that."

Tone called to Avery to take the cage and guard it. After a few sparks bounced between Avery's hand and the metal cage, the man carried it away. Tone headed for the colonel's tent, but Jane caught his arm.

"If it please the good Sir," Jane said. "Stop, please, for a few sentences."

"What is it?" He wanted to get inside one of the newly constructed tents. He was tired of being wet.

"The jungle, Sir, is dangerous. Why come through such danger?"

Tone smiled. Of course these little natives would be curious about the purpose of this expedition. He also knew he couldn't tell them the true purpose. If this gem was as sacred as Silny claimed, then the Lygmies wouldn't like them taking it. One thing might lead to another, shots might be fired, and Lygmies might die. Better to keep them uninformed as long as possible.

"We heard there's a treasure out here," Tone said. The best lies always contained a grain of truth. "The Fountain of Youth. It'll keep us from growing old, and we want to live for a thousand years."

Jane stared at him. Tone wondered if the little woman believed him. There was no reason for her not to. The jungle was a mysterious place, and it was just as likely that a bunch of humans would be out looking for the Fountain of Youth as they would be looking for a priceless gem.

Tone thanked God as the rain stopped beating against his head. He heard the rain hitting branches and leaves all around him, so he assumed it was a fluke that kept him momentarily dry, but he didn't care. A few dry moments were worth it.

He looked up to see if there was a break in the clouds, and that's when he saw the rain hitting some kind of invisible barrier nearly a tic above his head. It splattered against something solid and ran to the side, falling all around him like a clear umbrella.

"Do you see that?"

"Yes," Jane said, nodding. "I believe, good Sir, that the jungle is a mysterious place. Anything possible here."

She turned and walked away. The barrier disappeared, drenching Tone in a flood of pent-up rainwater. He wiped his face with his soaked jacket, smearing the water from his eyes. He turned to watch Jane trudging back to the tents, and a tingle worked its way up his spine. If the Lygmies could talk back and forth through their minds, what kept them from being able to read other people's minds? And if they could read other people's minds, wouldn't they already know the true reason for this expedition?

Tone shook his head at the thought. Jane certainly didn't know why they were here. She may not have believed Tone's answer about the Fountain of Youth, but she still had to ask to get an answer from him.

Unless the little woman had been testing him. And if that was true, Tone failed the test. Jane could have read the answer straight from his mind.

He had to talk to the colonel.

20

Rhaina

Jake's campsite, Northern Continent

Jake's camp resembled a war zone. Sawn had cut down almost every vine, leaf, and branch that hung within the camp's perimeter. The trees looked like they were scoured through to the bark. A frizz was tied to a stake near Sawn's tent, and blood was streaked across the Lygmes' tent. They found mobile motion detectors, trip-wire strung between trees, flash cubes mounted to tree trunks to light up hidden targets, and a motion-activated automatic rifle set in the center of camp and aimed straight up into the forest canopy.

Sawn strode toward them through the rain and past the frizz. Rhaina could tell from several tics away that his jaw was clenched firm and his eyes – even from behind the dark glasses – were aimed straight at Jake. He stopped in front of them, his hands clenched at his sides.

"Hello, Sawn," Rhaina said. He didn't offer to shake her hand so she didn't offer to shake his. This didn't seem the most cordial meeting.

"You okay?" Jake asked.

Sawn moved too fast for Rhaina to see more than the blur of his body. His foot punched Jake in the chest. Jake sailed backwards into a tree, his mouth open as he tried to take a breath.

Rhaina, Khonane, Majid and Cailin all had their guns out and aimed at Sawn by the time he steadied himself and turned to them. He looked from the guns to their faces and his fists opened.

"One tent," Sawn said, holding up a finger to them. "Butt it up against the north side of mine and have it done before dark. Rhaina, come with me." He turned and marched back through the rain.

"Wow," Cailin said. "Who was that?"

Khonane went to Jake and helped him stand.

"I'll...be fine," Jake said.

Rhaina could tell he'd cranked up his tech. He looked fine, no matter how bad he sounded for the others.

"What's the plan?" she asked, returning the gun to its holster.

"No problem," Jake said. He stood up straight and took a deep breath. It was all show, and Rhaina knew it. "Sawn's a little grumpy about something, probably got up on the wrong side of the tent. We'll be fine. Really."

Jake led the way into the camp, but Rhaina kept her people back.

"Don't set up the tent," she whispered. "Let's make sure we're staying."

* * *

Stacks of equipment, ammunition, and provisions cluttered nearly every corner of Sawn's tent. A blanket had been wadded up at the foot of one cot, and a second cot had been folded up and tossed into a corner to make room for more supplies.

Sawn sat on the edge of the cot and rummaged through one pile until he found a crumpled piece of paper sketched with the outline of the camp. He smoothed it out and set it on a box of pistol batteries.

"What did you do to our tent?" Jake said, his eyes wide as he surveyed the piles.

"Rhaina, have a seat," Sawn said. He patted the cot next to him.

"Are you going to kick me too?" she asked.

"Of course not." Sawn looked up, his black glasses aimed straight at her. The glasses were some kind of fancy tech hard-wired into his brain, and he could probably see better than anybody else in the camp – except the plastic man, of course – but it was still disconcerting for Rhaina to look at them.

She sat beside him on the narrow cot and looked at the map.

"We've been attacked the last three nights," Sawn said. "These things are nearly invisible, and the first night they took out two of the frizzes before I realized they were in the perimeter."

Rhaina nodded. Now his attitude made sense. It still didn't excuse what he did to Jake.

"The first two nights, they came from the West," he continued. "And then last night they dropped down on us from the canopy. That's when I lost one of the Lygmies."

"Their fur changes colors," Rhaina said. "They're not really invisible, but it's some of the best camouflage I've seen."

"They are not chameleons," Sawn said. "If all they did was change the color of their fur, I could find them; I could stop them."

"I thought the Lygmies said it was safe to set up camp here," Jake said, pushing aside a couple shovels so he could sit on the floor.

"They were wrong." Sawn made eye contact with him, then turned back to Rhaina.

"There's something spiritual going on inside them," she said. "They saw my Geminai."

"That's unique."

"For an animal, yes, and it's actually a two-edged sword. They're probably using our Geminais to find us, but I used mine to distract one. She's the reason I'm alive right now." Rhaina hesitated, unsure what else to say. She knew Jake wouldn't question what she had learned, but Sawn was always so cold, so mechanized. Kicking Jake in the chest was probably the most emotion she'd ever seen him express. And he didn't believe in Gemainais.

"What else?" Jake asked.

"They're not just animals. The one that tried to take me had dozens of minds working inside it, all of them controlling the creature in some way."

"Multiple personalities?" Sawn asked.

"Or that they're puppets?" Jake asked.

Rhaina thought about that. Her Geminai only had contact with the thing for a second, and she'd been able to see all the different minds working to control it. At the time, she'd assumed the minds were competing for control. It would mean something different, though, if the minds were working together.

"I like that," she said to Jake. "Run with it." This was what she missed, the way they worked together, the way they took an idea and played with it. She and Khonane did this sometimes, but never with the same flair she and Jake had.

"The animals can see your second soul," Jake said.

"And affect her."

"So they have some level of spirituality inside them. Which means they're not completely animals."

"Or they're animals with souls."

"Or that their ability comes from the people controlling them." Jake stood and paced the two steps from one pile to another. "We're getting distracted, though. This isn't the important part."

Realizing where Jake was going with his thought, Rhaina turned to Sawn. "Did they try to kidnap any of you?"

"No. They sneak into the camp and kill."

"They killed Ramiro, but they didn't try to kidnap anyone but me."

Jake stopped and turned to her.

"You're not here for the God's Ear," he said.

Rhaina almost laughed at him. She didn't expect him to blurt it out in front of Sawn. She thought he'd wait for some quiet moment, just the two of them, when he could try to work the information out of her.

"I'm out here for the same thing you are," she said. "The gem." It almost wasn't a lie.

Sawn turned to her. She could tell without even seeing his eyes that he was glaring. He would be doing the numbers in his head, figuring the profit that he would have gotten before, and then re-figuring that same profit after her cut. Then he would do the numbers a third time to include her entire team.

"Okay, the gem," Jake said, pacing again. "Assuming we're all out here for the gem, there's still something you know or something you possess that makes you valuable to them."

"She's female," Sawn said.

"I don't think that's the reason." Rhaina shook her head. "If they wanted women, they would have gone after Cailin too."

"And isn't one of our Lygmies female?" Jake asked.

"Yes," Sawn mumbled. "The dead one."

"They're not after women," Rhaina said.

"Your Geminai?" Jake gestured to the air around him, like he could point to her if he tried hard enough.

"Everyone has a Geminai."

"But you use yours. You believe yours can make a difference."

"I have a relationship with mine," she corrected. "But Khonane is attuned to his too."

"Then we're still missing something," Jake said. "There's something you know or something you have that makes you more valuable than the rest of us."

"Maybe they wanted to eat her while she was still alive," Sawn said. "You two might be making more of this than it deserves. We'll all be fools if we walk up to one of these things and try to talk to it – and then we discover that it prefers its meat warm."

"No," Rhaina said. "There's an intelligence there. I'm certain of it."

"Because your Geminai felt it?" Sawn asked.

"Because one of them made me remove my earpiece." He sounded like he was mocking her, and she didn't like it. "It wanted me isolated from my team. No animal would do that."

"No Earth-side animal would do that," Sawn corrected.

Rhaina had to admit that was a good point. They were dealing with an alien world, an alien jungle from which no one had ever returned. Just because it made no sense to her didn't mean the animal itself was confused.

Except there were other minds at work inside that thing. Thoughts floated around in its head – real thoughts, real voices, real instructions and conversations. How could that be ignored?

"Rhaina?" Jake said, loud enough to bring her back to the conversation.

"What?"

"I said, 'What are you thinking?'"

"I think it'll be dark soon," she said. "And we still have to set up our tent."

"Your people aren't doing that?" Sawn asked.

"No. We weren't sure we were welcome."

"Do it," Sawn said, folding up the map and shoving it in his pocket. "I'll need your people ready to fight as soon as possible, not making beds and cooking suppers."

Rhaina didn't think that comment worth acknowledging so she got up, flopped the cap back on her head, and headed out into the rain.

21

Tone

Mother Earth jungle campsite,
Northern Continent

Tone watched through the lanterns' harsh blue light as the rain drizzle outside the tent. They had put Robinson on first watch, and they had told Avery not to electrocute anyone, especially not the Lygmies. The man hadn't stopped sparking since they left that eel-woman back at the colony town. Rain popped and sizzled every time it touched his skin, and Tone was afraid the man would short-circuit.

"I'm damp," Silny said from his cage at the back of the tent.

"Shut up," Colonel Walraven said with a sigh.

Tone didn't even acknowledge the pouncer. Silny hadn't stopped irritating them since they entered the forest, and his latest set of complaints focused on his physical discomfort. He was hot, then cold, hungry, then thirsty. Apparently it was time to be "damp."

"I don't need to be here," Silny mumbled. "Told you what I knew, pointed you in the right direction. Even helped you make a map. And here I am. Wet."

"You're here because we enjoy the pleasure of your company," Tone said, not even trying to mask the sarcasm.

"I haven't been very pleasant the last few days," Silny said. "Are you sure you want me around?"

"We wouldn't have it any other way," Colonel Walraven said.

Tone chuckled and took another sip of brandy from the flexisteel cup.

"Mock me in my misery," Silny said. "How human."

Tone didn't even try to keep from laughing. He'd never been around a pouncer before, but Silny was so overly-dramatic. Tone imagined some government lab on Pluto where the caged pouncer mocked the scientist's bad toupee as the scientist stabbed a syringe into the animal's neck.

"You guys have to see this," Robinson said as he slid around the corner. He brushed the long, red bangs from his eyes and waved his rifle through the air. "There's these animals – and they're huge. They're at least as big as a bear. And they came up to the southern end of the camp, and the Lygmies walked right up to them and started petting them. It was like they were pets or something. And the claws! They're huge!" He spread his hands wide, too wide for Tone to believe.

"Where are they now?" the Colonel asked.

"They're still there, right by me and Avery's tent. Avery's out there now, too. He's petting them!"

"Stay here and guard the pouncer," Tone said as he stood and threw on his slicker. He unsnapped the clip from one of the electric lanterns, the blue light flashing chaotically. He followed Colonel Walraven around their tent, past the Lygmes' tent – a long, water-resistant cloth they'd stretched like a lean-to between three trees – and around to the southern end of the camp.

The rain had given way to this misting drizzle after sunset. The sky had lightened enough for them to know – for a brief moment – that the sun still shone before it went down for the night. Bugs and birds chirped and squawked as the last of the rainwater drained from the canopy.

Tone stopped in mid-stride behind the colonel. Dozens of eyes stared back at them from the dark. They watched him from the trees and along the ground, tracking his movements. The eyes blinked and bobbed as if they floated through the air.

"Can you believe this?" Avery said, petting the furry, orange head of the animal crouched before him.

Jane stroked the orange backside of the same animal, jamming her fingers through the matted, wet fur to massage its shoulders. She leaned close to the thing's long, pointed ears and whispered. The animal turned to Colonel Walraven, and its eyes seemed to focus on him.

"What are they?" Tone asked.

"Sir, they be meshet," Jane said. Her bright, orange hair stuck out from her head in long points that Tone found more distracting every time he tried to talk to her. "Gentle animals, good Sir. They live high in trees and come down to see things. They are curious about us, about you."

"So they're safe to touch?" the colonel asked.

Jane took the animal's paw in her hand and stroked the claws. They were more like long, curved knives than claws, and each was sharpened to a fine point that looked like it could slice open a repulsor vest. He didn't know how strong they were, but he didn't want to make any of them mad to find out.

"You must respect them, Sir," Jane said, looking back at Tone. "You treat them as friend."

"A friend," Tone said, not completely convinced. "Right."

Jane took his hand in hers, and he felt like he held the hand of a six-year-old. His first reaction was to yank this child away from the big jungle monster. Instead, she held his hand to the meshet's soft, fine fur. He buried his fingers until he felt the rough hide beneath.

The meshet turned its massive head to him, and Tone had the impression it was acknowledging his existence for the first time. It pressed its long, toothy snout against his chest and sniffed, the hot breath almost sucking him in and then shoving him over. Its ears flicked up and around as it inspected him, and its eyes shut as it breathed in the sleeve of his coat. Within moments, its long, rough tongue flicked out and around his arm, slurping something off.

"You spilled drink there," Jane said, inspecting the damp spot.

"A couple months ago," Tone admitted. "He could smell that?"

"He smell good."

"He's a magnificent animal." Tone stroked the soft fur. The meshet inspected his clothes and hair. It sniffed him several times, then ran its massive, sharp claws across his clothes and through his hair. Tone tried not to cringe.

"What's it doing?" Colonel Walraven asked.

"Good Sir, don't be angry," Jane said, putting her head down and averting her eyes. "He is knowing Commander Tone."

"Well, I think he knows him enough." The colonel took hold of Tone's arm and pulled him away. "We have things to do."

They turned to leave, and every meshet jerked forward, staring past them and through the camp. Tone put a hand on his pistol, but restrained himself from drawing the gun.

The meshet stood still, their fur changing to greens and browns to match the forest around them. Soon, all Tone could see were pairs of glowing eyes staring past him.

"Something in camp," Jane whispered. She twisted a lock of orange hair with her finger, curling the ends forward around her ear.

Avery stopped petting the animal and brought his rifle down from around his shoulder. Tone and Colonel Walraven each brought out a pistol as they scanned the camp for signs of movement. But nothing moved. No squawking birds, no chirping bugs. It was as if the jungle stood perfectly still. They stepped forward.

Tone turned, and for one second he thought he saw Jane kissing the meshet. His eyes might have been playing tricks on him, though, because it wasn't the simple kiss of a woman to a cute animal. The meshet's huge, scratchy tongue slipped out of her mouth and Jane licked her lips and smiled.

Tone pressed the palm of his hand against his eyes. He didn't really see what he thought he saw, did he? And if he did, what did that mean? The Lygmies were strange creatures, but...yuck! He shivered and opened his eyes.

The orange meshet planted its hind feet and stood up straight, raising its arms to the sky. A flap of skin stretched from the wrists of its front paws and down into the undergrowth. It crouched, then leapt into the air like a coiled spring, disappearing into the branches above. Tone heard other skin flaps snap tight as every meshet sprang away, leaping and flying through the branches until he couldn't see a single one.

"They scared," Jane said.

Tone found it hard to believe that creatures that powerful, who could fly, and who had the ability to change their colors to match their environment would be afraid of anything. But Jane knew these animals better than he did, so he didn't argue.

She wiped her mouth on the hem of her roughly woven shirt, and Tone had to look away again. That tongue...in her mouth. Yuck.

"Nothing's moving," Avery said. He held out the scanner, waving it back and forth across the camp.

"What about Robinson?" the Colonel asked.

"No, Sir." Avery adjusted the scanner's settings. "There is nothing moving."

"The other Lygmies?" Tone asked.

"They're not in their tent."

They cast the sharp beams of their lights around the camp, searching for signs of movement, any signs of whatever scared away the meshet. The light and shadows danced through the mist and around the tents and trees. There was hardly any wind, and the dense undergrowth stood motionless before them.

Colonel Walraven waved them forward.

Avery led the way, the scanner's pulsating light reflecting off his face.

Tone took position behind and to the right of Avery, his gun down and in front of him. The flaps of the Lygmies' lean-to waved gently as he walked by and peered inside. As Avery had said, nothing.

They came around the side of Avery's tent. The screen was tied back, and Tone shone his light inside. Nothing.

They continued on, Tone glancing back to be sure Jane and the colonel were still behind them. The forest around them seemed much more ominous, more threatening now. Tone remembered the eyes he'd seen in the dark. Of course that had been nothing more than the meshet, but it still made him nervous. If this forest could hide friendly animals like that, what kind of ferocious beast was he about to discover in their camp?

Avery was first around the corner of the colonel's tent. He stopped, the rifle aimed at something.

"That is jack'd," he whispered.

Tone came up beside him. The pouncer's cage stood open, and Robinson's bloodied and shredded uniform lay in pieces across the ground.

"I'm gonna kill that pouncer," Avery said.

"The pouncer didn't do that," Colonel Walraven said, joining them at the tent entrance. "They're violent little animals, but that's the problem: they're little. And look at the way Robinson's blood splatters against the tent. No, someone killed Robinson and then took away our pouncer."

Tone turned and saw the two missing Lygmies rise from the underbrush behind him. He jerked his pistol up to defend himself, but Jane stepped to block the shot.

"Friends did nothing," Jane blurted.

"How do you know?"

"Friends too afraid," Jane said as she reached to pet the nearest Lygme. "Friends outnumbered, and friends do nothing."

"Did they see who did this?" Colonel Walraven asked.

"Yes," Jane said, looking to the ground. She wiped her eyes, apparently crying. "The water-breathers. We tree-climbers, we are good. The water-breathers are the bad ones."

22

Jake

jungle campsite

Jake sat in the crackling glow of the firelight and watched Rhaina. Of course she was beautiful; he could never forget that. The memories haunted his dreams. "Firestorm" hardly came close to describing her beauty, her intensity, but Jake had called her that anyway. Years ago.

What he had almost forgotten was the sheer presence the woman had, even sitting in the middle of a jungle that wanted to rip them apart. But there she sat, calm as the last time he'd seen her, radiating beauty and power without moving so much as a finger. Her crouching stance almost screamed at the forest, "Come get me!"

He flipped on the imaging software and focused his eye's digital lens. He blinked twice, and the pic loaded into his brain.

"Don't you have enough shots of me?" Rhaina asked.

"Not with your clothes on." He grinned.

"How could I forget? The only man in the universe with flip-porn of me saved to his brain."

"It's better than any of that ancient junk they have on display at the Smithsonian."

"Same plot," Rhaina said with a sigh. "Different girls."

Jake scanned the camp. The tech analyzed the trees, the ground, and even the light levels. There was nothing out there. Maybe they would make it through the night without incident. Then they could leave this little rain-soaked hell and get their gem and get out.

"So where have you been for two years, Jake? Certainly not stomping around this jungle."

"Almost." He looked to her, but she was still studying the shadows around them. "A couple years ago, I had a scrap of information land in my lap about this rock. The fact that the thing really did exist."

"Who did you kill?"

"No one you know."

"Comforting."

"That's all I could find out, though. It was like everyone I knew suddenly realized this thing was real, but nobody knew how they knew or where they could find it."

"I remember that." Her eyes sparkled in the firelight. "The nets were filled with chats about Udoian mythology."

"And most of it was wrong."

"Wrong? Most of it was made up by prepubescent boys."

"No, that was me."

"I rest my case."

"I got on the nets and spread a lot of disinformation under a dozen aliases while I did some legitimate research into the thing. You know what I discovered? This gem is mentioned in almost –"

"Thirty unique legends and ancient myths," Rhaina finished for him. "I know. I found the same information. Did you also notice that the gem is pivotal to a battle in almost all of those legends?"

"Sure, but that didn't surprise me. It's a 'magical gem.' So what?"

"I thought it was interesting that a race of people whose mythology is so sedate developed such violent stories around this one artifact."

"That didn't bother me. We know the Lygmies are anything but se-date. Ask anyone who's tried to hire one. Hell, look at these two with us. Sawn said the first night I was gone they lit a fire and danced naked and carried on until the middle of the night, cutting themselves up."

Rhaina shrugged and went back to watching the woods. Jake's tech pulled up all the Lygme myths and ran a quick analysis. As Rhaina had said, most of them were peaceful, with the Lygmies learning and grow-ing and evolving. They taught virtues like patience and knowledge.

Not that they were all like that, of course. The longest Lygme epic was a million words and contained some of the bloodiest battles ever described. But that was the exception, not the rule. In fact, if all he'd ever learned of Lygmies was based on their mythology, he'd think they were a benevolent, peaceful people.

"Where was I?" he asked, shaking his head to get back into the con-versation.

"Researching," Rhaina said.

"Right. Well, the only place I found good, consistent information was when I hacked into the Federal databases. Unfortunately, their probes shut me down every time. Can you believe the Feds hired some firm out of Toronto to work security? If they had been using anything out of the Dells, I wouldn't have had that problem. So instead of hav-ing to find a clean port every morning, I walked into my local Federal Recruiting office and signed up in the Outland Security Agency."

"And that's the last I heard from you."

"Sorry about that. I would have left you more notes, but that first one almost blew my cover. I couldn't risk it. But you wouldn't believe the data I was getting from the inside. Did you know we've got nearly a hundred birds up there?" He pointed at the sky and looked up, but he couldn't see through the thick, dark canopy. "They're all shootin' pix and samples straight back to Earth, every day. It's a gold mine of in-formation, except that nobody has any jackin' idea what they're look-ing for. So I casually requisitioned every scrap of data that might have anything to do with this gem – along with about a hundred other non-essential files. I labeled them all 'Inconclusive,' and sent them to that great memory bank in the sky. Of course, my own digital memory kept records of everything."

"Good plan."

"Thank you. It would have been a perfect plan, too, if my Director hadn't figured out something was going on and stuck me with a plastic man with orders to kill me."

"I'm glad he failed."

"It would have ruined my day, yeah."

"I'm serious."

Jake realized she had turned to look him in the eye, and he wondered how he could have left her behind. She was a smart, sexy woman, and he left her so he could chase...what? What was so important to make him leave?

On that cue, his tech brought up a blueback before his eyes. He'd instructed his tech to bring up that image when he had doubts about this mission. Apparently his current thoughts constituted doubts.

He turned off the blueback image. Looking at Rhaina now, he didn't think it was worth it.

"What about you?" he asked. His voice felt like an intrusion on the night. He'd missed something...some moment. What should he have done? A kiss would have been good.

"After you abandoned me," Rhaina said, turning back to watch the perimeter. "I decided to strike out on my own. I put together a team, got a few good jobs, and really liked the work."

"Couldn't have been that much fun without me." Jake grinned.

"It was nice to make my own decisions. And I've made some pretty good ones."

The plastic man stepped into the light of the fire. His eyes glowed brilliant yellow, and he held a gun in each hand.

"What is it?" Rhaina whispered.

"The meshet are approaching," he said.

23

Jake

"There," Sawn said, pointing above them.

Jake looked, but he didn't see anything wrong. The leaves waved in the gentle breeze, and the firelight cast flickering shadows against the branches.

The rifle swivelled on its universal mount in the center of camp, its motion sensors tracking something above them. It spun clockwise, then jerked counter-clockwise as it focused on a new target.

Cailin assisted Khonane to the fire ring where he nearly collapsed to the ground, a pistol in his free hand.

"What about the Lygmies?" Jake asked, looking for them.

"They'll be here," Sawn said. "They know we can protect them."

"How many meshet?" Rhaina asked.

"I've counted nine," Majid replied.

Frustrated, Jake blinked and twisted his eyes to the right. The forest came to life in a brilliant, digital display, his optic sensors slamming the data into his brain. In a split-second flash, the tech analyzed the entire camp and its makeshift perimeter. It recalled from Jake's memory the location of every sensor and trip-wire they'd placed in the dwindling twilight. At the time, it seemed extravagant. Now he wished they had a dozen more.

They'd wrapped the trip-wire in a zig-zag circle from one tree to another around the camp. They'd mounted four of their pistols and two of their rifles to stationary poles and wired them to proximity sensors. Nothing was getting close without something shooting at it.

One of the mounted pistols fired into the forest, and Jake turned at a meshet's scream. The bloodied branches swung from the animal's retreating bulk.

"What are their weaknesses, Sawn?" Jake asked as he scanned the forest.

"I tried fire, noise, light, anything I could think of. They didn't care. The only thing that stopped them was to kill them, and that didn't stop the survivors from dragging away the corpses."

Three Lygmies burst from the underbrush and dove into the safety of the camp's center, their black hair bobbing before their eyes. Jake recognized the Lygme he'd named Ko, as well as the other one that never talked. The third Lygme was a new one Jake had never seen before, and he was a little taller than the other two. His face looked bruised, like he'd recently been in a fight, and Ko and the silent one supported him between them.

"Who's the new guy?" he asked Ko.

Two shots echoed from the rifle on the swivel mount behind them, drowning out most of the Lygme's response, but Jake heard the word "food."

Two meshet launched themselves from a tree and sailed straight at him. He revved to Fighting Mode, and the attack continued in slow motion. The targeting cross-hairs flashed before his eyes as the tech calculated the speed of the flying meshet, the angle of the fall, and the most probable angle for hitting them. Jake raised his arms, and the tech squeezed his finger. Two bullets, fired off in quick succession, punctured the chest of the first and then the second meshet.

Jake grinned. Two shots, two hits. Great way to start the night.

The bodies slammed into the ground at Jake's feet and slid through the mud right back out of the camp and into the dark forest. He switched down from Fighting Mode, and the world reverted to its faster, regular speed. His hearing returned to normal, and his muscles loosened as the tech released its hold.

The swivel-mounted rifle spun to a stop. The forest lay silent, nearly still except for the light breeze brushing through the trees.

"Where'd they go?" Khonane asked from his place beside the fire.

"They're still out there," Rhaina said. Her eyes glittered in the darkness, like flecks of confetti caught the light. Jake always got creeped out by how she looked when she communed with her spiritual twin. It made him think of some holo ghoul that lost its soul.

"They attack from the air first," Sawn said, checking the clip in his gun. "I suspect it's a diversion to hide the fact that the rest of them are climbing down and surrounding us."

"Sawn's right," Rhaina whispered, her vacant eyes flicking left and right as she looked at something through her Geminai. "There are dozens of them out there."

"Jake," Cailin said, sitting up from her spot beside Khonane. "Who's the dead guy with your Lygmies?"

Jake turned. The third person, the one Jake had mistaken for another Lygme, lay stretched out on the ground. He wore torn and bloodied camos, and his face had been beaten until his eyes had swollen nearly shut. Blood ran from every open crevice from his chin to his brow. His legs had been chopped off below the knees, and blood-soaked bandages around the stumps leaked red pools into the muddy ground.

"What the hell is this?" Sawn asked, stepping forward.

"The meshet will leave with food," Ko said, kneeling beside the remains of the man. "See? We offer him to the flying gods. They leave us alone. You will see. See?"

"Where did he come from?" Jake asked. "Who was he?"

"Him with the evil ones," Ko whispered. "Bad, evil pyggies who live in the sky. We take him from them. We offer him to the gods on all of our behalfs."

"Does anyone know what this jackin' Lygme is babbling about?" Jake asked, looking around the camp.

"It sounds as if we're being followed," Majid said, his glowing yellow eyes still scanning the forest.

"Yes, followed," Ko said, nodding his head.

"Weapons up!" Rhaina yelled, spinning around and pointing to the southeast.

Jake turned to fire, but the two Lygmies jumped in his way. The limp form of the man flopped behind them. He revved back into Fighting Mode and lunged to the side in time for the tech to register three meshet racing toward the camp. Their fur bristled green, then black, then brown as they darted through the dark forest.

He raised his arm as the targeting cross-hairs flashed across his vision, lining up a shot at the first meshet. Someone behind him fired first, striking the animal in the chest. He shifted his focus to the second, but a movement in the trees above distracted him.

Four meshet leapt from branches in the near darkness above.

The Lygmies lifted the battered man above their heads. More shots zipped past him as the rest of the team fired into the forest.

The meshet brushed aside the Lygmies and their human offering only to be gunned down before they got past the first tent. Their glistening fur changed to a bright orange as their bodies slid into the campsite.

"They've changed again," Sawn yelled. "They never attacked in small groups before."

It's a distraction, Jake realized. *Two attacking from the ground, four attacking from the air – and nobody's watching our backs.*

He spun around, but the tech didn't see anything. He scanned the trees, the limbs, and the darkness beyond the campfire glow. Nothing.

Looking up, the four meshet had positioned themselves above the camp again where they sat waiting.

"Jake, what is it?" Rhaina asked, following his gaze.

He turned to tell her what he saw, and that's when the tech picked up the lone meshet sprawled across the ground at her feet. Its fur bristled as it tried to blend in with the mud, the water, and the blood all at once.

"Move!" Jake yelled. The tech raised his hand and the cross-hairs flashed across the animal's head.

The forest exploded with thunderous screams. A dozen meshet revealed themselves around the camp, their camouflage fur flashing to a bright orange. They raised their arms to spread their wing flaps and crouched to the ground.

Everyone else started shooting, but Jake ducked low and tried to see what was happening to Rhaina. Meshet spread all around him, revealing themselves with flashes of orange and long, piercing screams. The creature at her feet stayed still, watching the fight break around it. What was it waiting for?

Something gripped the back of Jake's collar and lifted him off the ground.

He kicked out with tech-enhanced speed, and his foot met the solid grip of the plastic man's hand.

"Are you a coward?" Majid yelled over the battle around them. "Fight!"

The plastic man let him go, and Jake whirled around to see the meshet leap to its feet and grip Rhaina around her waist.

Jake darted to Rhaina's side in a few quick steps. She twisted in the animal's grip, and Jake grabbed her arm to pull her free.

The meshet turned its fierce, black eyes on him, and he shoved the barrel of his gun against its chest. The tech flashed before his eyes a 100% chance of hitting the target, and he squeezed the trigger three times. The shots erupted out the animal's back, sending it sprawling to the muddy ground behind her.

Rhaina yanked the meshet's severed claws from her slicker.

Jake started to ask if she was all right, but the four meshet landing around them seriously impeded the conversation.

One of the creature's scooped Rhaina up in its arms while the other three turned on Jake. His tech was kind enough to flash before his eyes a 1-in-100 chance of surviving this particular encounter. It also recommended that the most prudent course of action was to retreat. He didn't feel like being prudent when these beasts were trying to steal away the woman he loved.

Ugh, he thought. *Did I just think that?*

Ignoring his own conflicted feelings, he flicked the laser knife from its wrist sheath into his left hand while the tech guided his right hand to a perfect aim at the nearest meshet's chest. He fired three times while his left hand slashed out to defend his blind side. The first two shots hit their mark, sending the meshet sprawling to the ground, but the laser knife struck nothing but air. Worse, Jake got a set of claws raked across his arm for his troubles with the knife.

He turned to defend his left side, and the meshet on his right pounded his shoulder, knocking the gun from his hand. As he turned back, the one on his left shoved him to the ground.

"Emergency," the tech flashed before his eyes – like he couldn't figure out that on his own.

He let the tech guide his knife into the nearest meshet's chest, shoving the blade in to the hilt and twisting it around. The creature roared into his face and slashed at his arms and head, but Jake kept twisting, the knife's laser blade chipping away at some hard, skeletal frame inside. He hoped he was doing some damage.

The meshet lifted off Jake's body and rose into the air above him, its arms and legs thrashing at the hand gripping the scruff of its neck. Majid stepped forward and tossed the animal into the bushes.

The tech said he now had a 50-50 chance. He liked those odds.

He rolled away as the third meshet jumped onto Majid's back. He activated the tech's Recall, the pistol leaped back into his hand from wherever it had fallen, and he turned to aim. The cross-hairs jumped across his vision, trying to get a lock on the meshet without hurting Majid. Jake doubted the bullet would harm the plastic man, but he didn't want to explain why he didn't bother to miss.

Majid rolled forward, trying to pitch the creature off his back, and Jake took the shot.

The meshet jerked up at the noise, and the bullet punctured the creatures's lower jaw and neck. Not exactly where Jake was aiming, but he didn't complain. The animal leaped off Majid's back and thrashed across the ground, its claws raking the hole in its neck.

The plastic man flicked a laser knife from some hidden holster and punched the creature in the chest, burying the blade past the hilt and slicing the thing open from its sternum to its crotch. The meshet's muscles jerked, but it was dead.

Jake surveyed the nearly-destroyed camp. Cailin and Khonane were soaked in blood at their place by the fire, but it didn't look like much of it was their own. Sawn's arms and chest were sliced in a dozen places, and he wore a devil's grin that said the man was having the time of his life. The Lygmies cowered over their rejected human sacrifice, and the two remaining frizzes jerked at their ties.

Not one live meshet remained in the camp, but the bodies of the fallen were scattered around.

"Rhaina!" Jake yelled.

Majid gripped Jake's shoulder and pointed into the darkness above them.

He looked up to see the meshet pack leaping through the branches, the last one struggling to keep Rhaina in its arms.

24

Jake

"Rhaina!" Jake yelled, darting after the escaping meshet.

A hand gripped his shoulder and slammed him to the ground. If not for his tech, he'd have had the wind knocked out of him. Instead, he stared up into Majid's glowing eyes.

"Out of my way," Jake hissed. "I've already killed one plastic man this month."

"The plastic man's right," Sawn said.

Jake stared at the two men standing above him while Rhaina's screams grew fainter in the distance. They had to understand: this was his Rhaina! The woman he wanted at his side – if he hadn't been stupid and let her go. He would not lose her again.

Jake stood and looked at Sawn.

"Stay here with the others."

"Don't do this," Sawn said. "Those creatures will rip you to shreds."

"Plastic man, you're with me."

"But you've already killed one plastic man this month," Majid said.

Jake shoved the barrel of his gun against Majid's chest.

"I am ordering you to do this, you piece of soulless hardware," he said.

Majid grinned. He grabbed Jake into the air and threw him across his back.

"What the hell are you doing?" Jake yelled.

"Hang on," Majid said, looking up. "This will be bumpy."

Jake clung to Majid's shoulders as the plastic man sprang into the air. Majid swung onto a low-hanging branch, turned and sighted another, then jumped again, the first branch cracking under their weight. He leaped from one branch to another until they were beneath the forest's canopy, then he stopped and stared after the fleeing meshet.

"I didn't know you were programmed to leap through trees like that," Jake said.

"I'm not." Majid turned his glowing eyes back to Jake and winked. "It looked like fun when they did it."

Did the plastic man tell a joke? Could they do that?

"Hang on," Majid said, looking up.

Jake clung tighter as Majid jumped straight up and into the dense foliage of the canopy. Huge, rubbery leaves slapped back at them, splattering them with rain water. A black swarm of tiny bugs dispersed at the interruption, and some long centipede-like thing scuttled away.

Even more impressive, though, was the brown path that opened before them. Constructed of wide boards woven together with dried vines, the entire contraption looked ancient, rickety, and unstable.

Majid stepped onto it.

"What are you doing?" Jake asked.

Surprisingly, the entire suspended path didn't come crashing down from their combined weight. It did, however, creak and sway as Jake struggled off Majid's back.

"Those creatures use the trees to move quickly from one place to another," Majid said. "This path appears to be the quickest way to do that, and it's well worn. Possibly by the meshet."

Jake followed Majid's gaze to the shredded and broken leaves dangling above the center of the path. They spoke of a regular traffic flow that snapped away the low hanging foliage. One of the boards looked recently replaced, the grain still green and fresh, tight vines binding it.

In fact, Jake thought, kneeling down to inspect it more carefully. It didn't look like wood at all. The thick board was rubbery, wet. It had been sliced down the center, and the ends were curling outward as it dried. Some kind of thick resin oozed from the cut and was drying across the top and sides.

Majid knelt and placed his left hand on one board and his right on another.

"They're leaves," Jake said.

"Yes." Majid looked left. "I feel vibrations from that direction."

"Then let's go."

Majid stayed kneeling over the dried boards, his glowing eyes staring dispassionately down the path.

"They're coming toward us," he said.

"So? Get up."

"It feels like...dozens of them."

Jake stood and backed to the edge of the path. He didn't feel like taking on "dozens" of these beasts, but if that's what it took to rescue Rhaina....

"Come on, Majid," he said, gesturing for the plastic man to join him.

Majid turned and looked at him with those piercing, yellow eyes, and something about that stare put Jake on edge. Majid's face didn't give anything away – plastic men were some of the best poker players – but that dead stare made Jake think the plastic man was calculating something.

Majid gripped two boards – the ones supporting Jake – and yanked them from their woven ties.

Jake dropped his pistol as he reached out to catch anything to stop the fall. His right foot caught the edge of the path and jerked him sideways. He slammed against the path and struggled to get a grip on any of the hard, rubbery boards. His fingers looped around a couple of the vines and he held on tight, his momentum swinging him around the path where his back slammed against the underside. He bounced back and hung suspended in the trees.

"I thought you'd already killed one plastic man this month," Majid said, pointing his pistol into Jake's face. "Let's see you take out one more."

"You sorry-ass hunk of plastic!" Jake said, struggling to get back onto the path. With his body stretched like it was, his tech noticed the vibrations of heavy footsteps getting closer. It was amazing the thoughts that passed through his head as he was about to get shot. "You're going to kill me because I took out one of your brothers?"

"Plastic men don't get mad." He knelt down and shoved the barrel of the gun against Jake's neck. "Not unless we're programmed to. But either way, that's not what this is about. This is about keeping you from getting the gem before me. And if you're out of the picture, there's no one left to avenge Rhaina's death when this whole thing is over."

"You son of a bitch," Jake whispered.

"I will rescue her now," he said with a smile. "I still need her as a guide."

The tech calculated Jake's chance of survival against the gun: 0%. What did he have to lose?

"We're not through," Jake said, smiling back. He released his grip and fell away. The last thing he saw was the plastic man's frown before the canopy enveloped him and the branches slammed into his back and head. It was a fast, hard fall, and he lost consciousness long before the bone-crushing roots snapped him in half.

25

Rhaina

jungle canopy

Rhaina ran as fast as she could along the suspended path, her Geminai flying before her and telling her when the path dipped or turned. Behind her, dozens of meshet screamed at her as they leaped and flew, occasionally swatting at her arms or legs.

Part of her mind realized something quite useful about these creatures: they were not runners. If she kept going at a full-out run, they couldn't keep up with her, and in the thick foliage of the canopy they did not have the room to really spread their wings and overtake her, especially if she stayed on the suspended path.

She ducked beneath a thick, leafy branch, then heard it torn from the trunk by the animal swatting at her back. Shredded leaves and splinters of wood flew around her, and she raised her arms to protect herself from the debris.

Her Geminai noticed someone blocking her path only a few seconds before she rounded the corner and nearly ran into him. He was crouched at the path's edge, and he held two of the boards in his hands, undoubtedly to slow her escape. She leaped over him.

He pivoted beneath her, and his hand shot out, catching her foot in midair. She crashed to the ground, her elbows and knees slamming into the path's solid boards and sending shockwaves through her body.

She kicked out hard with her free foot, but the creature gripped that one too, completely immobilizing her legs. She spun around, flicked the laser knife from her wrist sheath, and sat up to cut her way free.

"Stop!" Majid said, holding up his hand.

She wanted to cry out for joy at the sight of him. If he hadn't been a plastic man, she would have kissed him.

Instead, a stampede of meshet rounded the corner behind him, their cries and flailing wings beating at the branches.

Majid leaped on top of Rhaina, wrapped his arms around her, and rolled her off the edge. He gripped a vine support, swung them around beneath the path, and hoisted her up to grip the underside of the boards. She clung to the board, only then remembering to stow the knife back in its wrist sheath – a tricky procedure when she dangled a hundred tics above the ground.

"Do you have your weapons?" Majid asked.

The path shuddered as the pursuing meshet took flight from its edges and circled around them through the air.

"They took everything but the knife," she said. The first thing they did when they brought her into the canopy was disarm her. They took her pistol so she pulled her second gun out and injured one of the creatures before they took that one from her too. After that, they patted her down and took everything else. They only missed the knife because they were in too much of a hurry.

She watched in fascination as the creatures sailed to branches all around. They gripped the damp wood, pivoted on the swaying trees, and leaped back into the air.

She hadn't noticed before, but she now saw that the meshet's hands looked like human hands. Four fingers spread from the flat palm, and an opposable thumb helped them grip and balance as much as their long claws. Their fingers were longer than those on human hands, and they were much more flexible. Rhaina saw one of the creatures bend its fingers almost completely to the back of its hand as it gripped a tree trunk and spun around to take flight again. She would have loved to stay and watch – except that the meshet wanted to take her back and eat her.

Majid let go of the underside of the path, and Rhaina gasped. He flipped around in the air and gripped the path from behind so that Rhaina stared at his back.

"Grab hold!"

She hesitated. She didn't trust the plastic man, and she didn't like the idea of relying on him to carry her back to the ground. Although...he risked his life to come up and rescue her. She looked down, then behind her, trying to see if there was any other way.

"Rhaina, I cannot defend you from them all," Majid said. "Please. I can get you back to the camp where we can make a fighting stand."

He wasn't particularly persuasive, but she had no other options. She wrapped her legs around his waist, uttered a prayer she knew only her Geminai heard, then gripped his shoulders and neck.

He let go.

The drop was almost more terrifying than anything the meshet had done with her. At least when they sailed through the air she felt they were in control, like they knew the wind and the currents and they were using them to get where they were going. Majid just fell. The wind and the trees and the flying meshet all raced past her as she clung to the plastic man's neck.

He slammed into a thick, low branch with enough force that it split from the tree. He spun with the breaking branch's momentum and kicked away, sending them falling past the web of roots to crash through the waist-high foliage covering the muddy ground.

He threw Rhaina to the ground and rolled over to stand and guard her.

She lay in the mud and stared at the underside of a hundred leaves flapping above her face. She was getting really tired of everyone carrying her around, and she didn't like the fact that no one put her down gently.

"Come," Majid said, thrusting his hand through the foliage. "We must hurry."

She heard the shrieks and flaps of the meshet racing to steal her away again, and she rolled over to stand, shoving aside the plastic man's helping hand. That's when she saw the gun.

It lay half-buried in the mud, but she would have recognized it anywhere: a Pedge .318. More importantly, it was Jake's Pedge. He carried it everywhere, and he had it so completely tied in to his tech that the thing could almost fire itself. So what was it doing out here? Unless Jake was also here.

That made much more sense. The plastic man said he was programmed to keep her alive, but she found it hard to believe he'd risk his own life climbing into the canopy to do it. But Jake.... There had been a time when they were partners that he would have done almost anything for her.

"Rhaina," Majid said, gripping her arm. "We must leave. Now!"

All around, she heard the rustling, scraping, and snorting of the meshet beasts. She gripped the gun as Majid pulled her up. Standing, she saw their situation had become worse than she imagined. The forest around them rippled with the meshet's ever-changing fur. She saw one, and a second later it camouflaged away.

The tree next to that one appeared to move, and another meshet flashed past her vision, its bright orange fur making it stand out better than any target at a firing range. She couldn't even begin to estimate how many were out there, but the forest flashed a dizzying array of patterns and colors as the meshet played their hide and seek in front of her. Above them, more of the beasts sailed along the air currents from the canopy to the ground.

"Run!" Majid yelled, yanking her along. He fired ahead of them into the forest, hitting the first few meshet who didn't flee fast enough.

Geminai screamed a warning from above, and Rhaina pointed the gun at the sky and pulled the trigger. Nothing happened.

The meshet hit the ground and rolled into the underbrush at her side. It gripped her ankle, and her hand almost wrenched away as Majid tried to hold on. She fell through the ground foliage and landed face-first in the muddy path.

The creature yanked her backwards by her ankle. She dug in with her hand and scraped through the mud as she tried to turn herself over and get a clean shot at the meshet dragging her along. Rocks and roots and vines snagged her arms and legs, slicing long gouges in her clothes and skin.

She kicked against the creature's clawed hand, and she must have hurt it because it almost let her go. She kicked again, and this time she got the creature to stop and turn on her. That was all she needed.

She shoved herself over in the thick mud, brought the gun level with the animal's chest, and squeezed the trigger. Again, nothing happened.

The meshet's claws raked across her face, sending blood flying from her cheek as her body slammed back to the ground. The animal gripped her by her foot and wrenched her along.

Her face stung as the thing dragged her through the mud. In the distance, she heard Majid yelling and shooting. She wasn't sure, but she thought he was getting closer.

She bounced across a rock and almost lost her grip on the Pedge. The gun hadn't done her any good, and she could only assume it was broken. So why didn't she drop it, let it go? It took a surprising amount of will to keep her fingers wrapped around the cold metal, and she could use that will to resist the meshet dragging her through the forest. But if she was being dragged to her death, she wanted to do it with at least one thing of Jake's.

"Rhaina!" someone yelled. But was that Majid, or was it her Geminai calling to her?

The meshet's claws dug deeper into her ankle, like the thing almost understood that someone called for her, that someone still cared she not get eaten alive.

It's Jake's gun, she thought, suddenly realizing what was wrong. *Jake has it tied to his tech. It won't fire unless Jake's the one with his finger on the trigger.*

Except that it used to work for her, back when she and Jake were partners. He had encoded the Pedge with a security code to override the tech locking mechanism so she could use it in an emergency. This certainly constituted an emergency.

She brought the gun to her face and switched on the display. Nothing happened. She gripped the pistol with her right hand, praying this would work as she flicked the Recall button in her palm. The installed tech in her hand clamped tight, and the display flickered to life as the gun finally recognized her. It registered a full charge.

She kicked the meshet's hand again, but the animal didn't seem to care. She kicked a second and third time, and the creature grunted and tightened its grip around her ankle. She slammed the heel of her boot into the meshet's wrist, and the beast finally stopped, probably to slap her again.

Rhaina twisted her hips and pivoted around to face the animal's toothy growl. It raised its left arm, claws glinting even in the dark night, and she squeezed off three shots straight into the thing's chest. The gun's discharges flashed like lightning, and the meshet slammed backwards into a tree.

She fell into the mud, panting. Her ankle throbbed, her chest and back felt like a thousand rocks were grinding beneath her skin, and her face felt slick from the blood running down her cheek. She wanted to lie there and let the universe move on without her.

"Rhaina!" It was that same voice, the one that yelled at her before.

"Geminai," she said with a smile. "You're still here."

"You have to get up," Geminai said. "Look."

She looked out from Geminai and saw the forest alive with dozens of meshet, all converging on her. Bullets flashed through the air behind them as Majid struggled to clear a path.

Rhaina wasn't sure why this plastic man was going through so much trouble to rescue her, but she didn't remember ever being so glad to have one of the machines with her.

"Behind you!" Geminai said.

Rhaina turned, allowing Geminai to guide her aim, and she pulled the trigger. A meshet spun around and fled into the darkness, holding its clawed hand against the hole Rhaina had put in it. She wouldn't survive much longer.

"Come to me," she whispered.

Her Geminai heard, and she settled inside Rhaina's skin, looked out through Rhaina's eyes and felt through Rhaina's hands and feet. They turned around, in the opposite direction from the one the meshet had been dragging them, and they saw the forest glowing with the physical and spiritual energy of the forest, the animals, and even Majid.

"You lead," Rhaina said, her head spinning too much for her to see straight. She was in no condition to get through this onslaught.

Her Geminai guided the way, and Rhaina followed her subtle leadings. They dodged to the left, pirouetted beneath a meshet's outstretched arm, rolled around a fallen log, and shot point-blank into a meshet's chest.

The animals roared their fierce anger, but Rhaina barely noticed as she allowed her Geminai to guide her through the fray. They danced past claws and teeth and flying meshet who swatted at their hair and clothes. They knew that Majid was up there somewhere, trying to reach them as desperately as they wanted to reach him, but they let the rhythm of the forest guide them, confident they would reach their goal.

A mammoth of a meshet stood before them, its camouflage fur rippling from the deepest, darkest green into the bright orange the animals favored when they wanted to be seen. It put its arms out to the side, and Rhaina feared she had been captured once again. But instead of a barrage of claws, everything became perfectly still.

Every meshet stopped in its place, and Rhaina saw them all change to bright orange and hold the color. The ones swooping through the air landed as quickly as they could and didn't move from whatever un-comfortable position they happened to be in.

Even Majid noticed the change and stopped shooting. He stood his ground only a dozen tics from Rhaina.

The meshet-mountain-of-a-creature turned toward Rhaina, and it was all she could do to stand her ground before the beast's piercing eyes. It opened its mouth.

Majid aimed his gun, but he didn't shoot.

Inspired by some instinct within her Geminai, Rhaina lifted her hand to the meshet's muzzle. She tried to put out of her mind the real-ity that this animal could bite her entire hand off in one snap of its jaws.

The beast licked her palm, and it tickled her Geminai.

The meshet narrowed its eyes and stepped aside.

"Rhaina, let's go," Majid said.

She wanted to scream at the plastic man to shut up, that this was some...moment...that he could never hope to understand. She didn't understand. This mountain of a meshet was letting her go, and for some reason that made her sad.

"Rhaina," Majid said again, taking a step forward. If she didn't leave now, he might do something truly terrible. He might start shooting again, and she didn't want this big one to get hurt.

She forced her Geminai to turn away, and she walked back to Ma-jid. Every pair of meshet eyes followed her. They watched her pick her way through the mud, lean against Majid for support, and stumble for-ward. She kept her eyes down, never looking back, never wanting to see the creatures turn on them both and tear them to shreds from be-hind.

But then it felt like they were gone, like their presence had left the area. She didn't want to believe that, but she didn't want to turn around to prove the feeling wrong.

Geminai turned, and Rhaina looked through her eyes. The meshet had all disappeared. She didn't even see the dead ones lying on the ground.

"What happened?" Majid asked.

"We got lucky," Rhaina said, wiping the blood from her cheek with her shredded shirt sleeve. "But I don't want to press that luck, so don't question it."

26

Tone

Mother Earth jungle camp

Tone set the scanner to "Power Save," and the display went dark. It would still scan their immediate vicinity, but it wouldn't light up again unless it found something – like the weapons fire twenty kilotics from their current position. He and the colonel had hovered over the display, watching the firefight move around a small position in the forest. Dozens of shots had been fired, and then it all stopped.

"We're not alone," Tone said, pushing the scanner away from him on the table. He sat back on the empty pouncer cage, playing with the shattered lock and staring at the bloody ground.

"Just say it."

Tone looked up. Colonel Walraven rubbed his hand across the stubble of his chin.

"I think we're in over our heads."

The colonel pursed his lips. Tone continued.

"We left this tent for five minutes, and we lost Robinson and our pouncer – the only guide we had to this treasure. Then we watched a firefight that could be anything – it could be other treasure hunters out there fighting over this gem right now. Hell, it might even be some bloody Lygme revolution with stolen guns and who knows what the hell else."

"You don't need to yell," the colonel said, still playing with his chin stubble.

"I think we should leave."

"And do what?" Colonel Walraven leaned back in his chair and sighed.

"Do what? We stop getting distracted by treasure hunts like this one, and we get back to the business of saving the Earth. There's a new lab out in Tokyo that's raising genetically enhanced iguanas the size of cows. That certainly sounds more worth our time than this little adventure."

"You never were much into the practical considerations, were you?" The colonel shut his eyes. "Tone, I'm going to let you in on a secret. There is nothing to go back to. By now the bank enforcers have taken our lunar home, everyone else has been incarcerated – or died defending the base – and even if that hadn't happened, the Earth is no longer on the verge of self-destruction."

Tone stared back at the man, too stunned to reply. He didn't want to believe – no, he could not believe that everything he'd heard was true. Sure, they'd been having financial problems, but they'd faced those kinds of problems before. They could see their way through it. And to say that the Earth wasn't self-destructing? That bordered on blasphemy.

"Face it," Colonel Walraven continued. "Things aren't like they were back in the 22nd. Back then we would have been getting donations and volunteers from all over the globe to help us fight our war. But eco-terrorism isn't in style anymore."

"But, Beijing...?"

"And Los Angeles, and Toronto...." Colonel Walraven sat up and looked Tone in the eye. "I know some scientists are doing stupid things back home, but most of the new research and development is so well documented that by the time they actually begin the testing there's almost nothing that deviates from the computer models. Haven't you noticed?"

The colonel stood up and paced. "When we first got together we burned that little test forest out in Oregon. Remember that?"

Tone nodded. Of course he remembered. Dr. Johnson-Sievrud had claimed to take all the computer models into account, but Tone hacked into the university's own network and found that the current crop had a five percent chance of spreading sterility into the general forest. The "respected doctor" deemed that an acceptable risk, as if he was God to let the rest of the world know that trees would fail to reproduce within the next fifty years.

"Now that was a victory," Colonel Walraven said. "When was the last time we had a real one like that? One that we could look back on and say, 'We did great?'"

"I can't believe I'm hearing this," Tone said. He sat forward on the cage, then sat back again, unsure what to do with his hands and not wanting to look the colonel in the eye. "You're abandoning everything we've worked for? After all these years?"

The colonel strode forward and gripped Tone's shoulders. "I brought you here with me. We're going to find this gem and we're going to get back to Earth and sell it to the highest bidder – maybe the president, maybe not. It doesn't matter. Don't you see? The Earth doesn't need us anymore. We can retire."

"But not Robinson."

"No, not Robinson."

"You bastard!" Tone jumped up and threw the colonel's hands off his shoulders. He didn't want to believe what he'd heard. Sure, they were sucking down funds. Donations had been falling for years, their operational success rate steadily declining, and the caliber of their recruits dropping to the point that they could probably do better by drafting kids out of mech school.

But Tone didn't want to be convinced, not now, not out here in the middle of this God-forsaken jungle, and not when the colonel was so blithely declaring that this gem – which might get them all killed – was "for both of them."

"Listen to me," the colonel said, spreading his hands. "There's no amount of money that's going to bring Robinson back –"

"This isn't about Robinson," Tone said, stepping forward. "It's about all of us – it's about you deciding that the world has healed itself. It's about you dragging us out to this jungle where we're all going to die – and for what? Not for Mother Earth. Oh no, this is for Mother Money! To get a few more bluebacks in the bank. Well, I don't want it, and Avery doesn't want it either."

He stopped and stared at the colonel, praying the man would see reason. They were in way over their heads, and the best thing was to get out now. Maybe the lunar base had been taken by the bank. They would just have to find some cheap place Earth-side. It would be a tough couple years, but they could do it.

"Let's ask." Colonel Walraven turned to the open tent flap and called for Avery.

"Yes, Sir," Avery said, jogging around the corner and almost slipping in the mud.

"Avery, I'm afraid we have to do something you may not like." Colonel Walraven stepped back, giving equal distance between himself and Tone. "You see, Tone doesn't believe we should be out here. He thinks we'd be better off if we turned around now and went back to saving the planet – without the proper funds to do that, of course."

"Avery, listen to me," Tone said, jumping in to explain himself.

"No, Avery," the colonel interrupted. "Arrest him."

Tone stopped, his arguments stuck in his throat. Arrest him? For what?

"Sorry," Avery said, stepping forward as he brought the rifle around.

"Colonel...," Tone began, watching the man leave the tent. "What...?"

"We are here," Colonel Walraven said, stopping in the harsh lantern glow beyond the tent's opening. "The gem is here. We have nothing left on the moon. We are not leaving empty-handed."

Tone turned to Avery. The man stood there with his gun trained on Tone's belly.

"You knew about this?"

He nodded.

"Who else was in on it?"

"Actually, that's about it," Walraven said with a sigh. "Me, Avery, and Robinson. The pouncer gave us a unique opportunity to leave that hell-hole, and we took it."

Which meant that everyone back at the lunar base had been abandoned, but they never knew it. They differed from Tone only in the fact that Tone was ever-so-graciously allowed to tag along on this expedition, allowed to get rich with them – and all it would cost him was his soul.

He sprang forward, focused on squeezing the life from the colonel.

Avery shouted.

Tone's hands clamped the colonel's neck and they fell into the forest outside the tent. They crashed through the ground foliage, splattered in the mud before the tent, and slid into the dark night.

Tone didn't think as he squeezed, cutting off the colonel's air. Some part of him knew that his ribs were being punched. He felt the stinging of the colonel's hits to his cheeks. But he would not stop – he could not stop. Never had he been so betrayed by anyone, and he wanted the colonel to suffer for that betrayal, to realize it had been a mistake, to know that the one thing in life worth living for was the salvation of their home planet – the same planet being genetically altered and DNA-rearranged by the scientific aristocracy–

The electric shock jolted him. He spun off the colonel, the electricity coursing through his body and sending his limbs into uncontrollable spasms. He slid face-first into the mud, his side aching and his fingers and neck twitching.

A hand gripped him by the collar and hoisted him up, and Tone stared into the blurry image of Avery's face. Tiny, blue sparks bounced between the man's teeth as he talked.

"Get up there!" Avery yelled, shoving Tone back to the tent.

Tone stumbled forward, his limbs still not moving where he wanted them to go, and he collapsed into the chair in front of the table. The lantern hanging above him buzzed with electric intensity. The room seemed to waver before his eyes, and he had to wonder just how many times the colonel hit him before Avery intervened.

And now that his thoughts were focused on Avery, he realized the man had been yelling at him since picking him out of the mud.

"...base was dead anyway," Avery said. "It wasn't like we pulled the plug on it. We got out before the whole thing blew in our faces."

"Avery, please shut up," Colonel Walraven said. He staggered into the tent, coughing and rubbing the bright red splotches across his cheek. "That was a bloody stupid thing to do, Tone." He spun around and slapped Tone's cheek with the back of his hand.

Tone's head snapped to the side, and he tasted the bitter blood oozing through his mouth.

"What the hell did you think you would accomplish?"

"Excuse, please," a tentative, female voice said from behind Tone.

"What?" the Colonel yelled.

Tone didn't have to see her to know the little Lygme, Jane, was bobbing her orange-haired head up and down in a subservient gesture to the colonel's outrage. He felt sorry for the little woman. Whatever she thought she was doing by interrupting, it was going to get her hurt.

"Pardon, please," the woman continued, a little quieter than before. "Your animal was taking you to the God's Gem, eh?"

Colonel Walraven's eyebrows shot up, and he stared at the woman. Tone had to wonder how long it would be before the colonel ordered this Lygme arrested too.

"What if we are?" the colonel muttered.

"Have you a guide?"

"Not since your 'Bad Ones' took our pouncer. Why do you even care?"

"The others in the forest, the ones shooting at everything. They want the gem, eh?"

"Probably."

"We show you," Jane said. Tone could tell without even turning that the woman had raised her head again, apparently proud that she could be of assistance.

"You'll show us what?" the colonel asked. "The gem?"

"We take you. We show you the gem."

"Why?"

"You must stop the others from reaching it," Jane whispered. "The ones ahead of you, the ones shooting at the forest. You must make them not get the gem."

The colonel's eyes narrowed, and he said, "Are you asking us to kill them? In exchange for you showing us where this gem is?"

The deal sounded too sweet, even to Tone's rattled brain. They had done many things during their time together, but Tone was proud of the fact they never killed anyone, not even by accident.

"You help, eh?" Jane asked. "You stop them?"

"I don't have a problem with that." Colonel Walraven turned to Avery. "You?"

"I don't care," Avery said, shrugging. "I've always thought our pussy-footin' around was a waste of time. It might be fun to actually go in and kill something for a change."

"You have a deal," the colonel said. He turned back to Jane and extended his hand. "Shake on it?"

"No," Jane said. "My ears do not itch."

"But we have a deal?" the colonel said with a grin. "We kill the bad people, and you show us the gem?"

"Yes, we will do this."

"Excellent. Tone, I'm afraid we're still going to keep you tied up. But think of it this way: I was going to let you fend for yourself in this jungle. With us, you'll be safe – even if you are tied up." He finally burst out laughing and strode from the tent, not even bothering to look at Avery as he said, "Tie him up. Keep him away from the guns."

Avery stood and rummaged through the supplies. It wouldn't be long before he found the binders Colonel Walraven brought along.

The colonel insisted they were necessary, even though he never said why. Now he knew.

He glanced around, searching for some way to get out of the tent without getting shot. He didn't know where he'd go once he escaped, but he would deal with that later. He had no intention of being tied up.

A hand gripped his shoulder. It squeezed, and it felt like claws digging into his skin.

Jane stood beside him, near enough that their noses almost touched. Her long, sharp fingernails dug down in his shoulder, and Tone wondered if she hadn't already drawn blood. Her orange hair hung in front of her face, tickling the sweat on Tone's forehead.

He started to turn away, but she gripped his chin in rough, calloused fingers and made him face her again.

"*Dadretska, ee tem oosha vruk,*" she said. "*Plick'a ya Inavaka. Eh?*"

Tone nodded.

She released him, turned, and left the tent, her head high.

"What was that?" Avery asked.

"I don't know," Tone croaked out. "I don't speak their bloody language."

But he did know. Somehow, the translation entered his mind a second after her words. It was like something inside of himself connected with her, and that part understood perfectly. She said the colonel was destined to die in this jungle. But to live, Tone had to stay near Jane. She would "preserve" him.

27

Geminai

jungle camp

Rhaina's Geminai raced through the forest. The dark night was quickly receding, casting the trees in dull shades of greenish-orange. The ground foliage waved in the morning breeze, spraying dew across the muddy ground and moss-covered roots. The branches and leaves flashed through Geminai as she scanned the ground, desperately searching, hoping to find any sign that Jake was alive. She had probably covered ten kilotics in the past half hour, and she would cover that same ground again if Rhaina insisted. And she knew Rhaina would insist.

The path suspended through the trees frustrated her search. Not because it got in her way, but because she couldn't find it anymore. It was like the whole thing had vanished, or that it was now invisible to her senses. She had no idea how that could happen, but without Rhaina climbing back up to the canopy, the path was effectively blocked from them.

Majid said there was no way Jake could have survived his fall when the meshet attacked them, but Rhaina had seen Jake survive other impossible situations. This seemed the most hopeless, but she wasn't willing to give up. There was always the possibility that something had cushioned his fall, that he had been able to grab hold of some branch or vine on the way down. Maybe he had even climbed back up to the suspended path, and that was why she hadn't found him.

Those were all wonderful thoughts.

Geminai circled the forest again, ready to work her way back to the center of the radius she'd been flying, but Rhaina whispered for her to stop. It was time to return to camp and get to work.

* * *

Rhaina felt the wind of her Geminai re-entering her body, and she opened her eyes with a sigh. The early morning light drifted through the open tent flap, and Rhaina smelled bacon. That would be Cailin's cooking. She ate the worst food.

She turned on the cot and stared at Khonane where he sat on the floor. He smiled, but it never reached his eyes. The night had been hard on them all, and there was little Khonane could do about any of it with his broken leg. The meshet had left the camp alone the rest of the night, and that gave them time to deal with the Lygmies' mutilated man. He'd lost so much blood from his severed limbs there was no way they could save him, and he drifted in and out of consciousness until he finally died, thankfully while he was unconscious. Sawn was burying the remains, and Majid was guarding the Lygmies so they didn't run into the forest and drag back more "sacrifices."

They'd found the man's passport and I.D. papers. He was a lunar emigrant from New Acres, a little mining settlement that hadn't survived beyond its second season. The place had been resettled by The Resurrected Mother, one of those fringe environmental groups that didn't want to come to terms with the fact that scientists really did love the Earth too. So what was some Resurrected Mother mercenary doing out here in the middle of a Udoian jungle?

"Did you find Jake?" Khonane asked.

"You already know I didn't." Their ties to Geminais made them naturally intuitive to each other's deepest emotions. She could never hide her renewed love of Jake, and Khonane would feel her sorrow as deeply as if it was his own.

"Still thought I should ask," he said.

She reached for his shoulder, and his hand met hers. She squeezed tight, glad for the companionship. Khonane was a good man, and she loved his friendship. She would never want to lose that.

But she had things to do, and the first of those was telling Sawn that Jake really was dead. It was a chore she didn't want, and she hoped Khonane would stay with her when she did it.

She started to get up but found herself staring into Khonane's eyes. He leaned forward and pressed his lips against hers. She shut her eyes. His firm, salty lips wrapped around hers, and the stubble of his chin brushed against her.

She wanted to wrap her arm around his neck and pull him towards her, to continue that kiss and never let it end. Instead, she opened her eyes and looked at him.

"I know you love Jake," Khonane whispered. "But I'm glad you're safe."

Jake. For those few seconds, she hadn't even thought of him.

"Excuse me." She slid past Khonane, then looked down at him leaning against the cot, his broken leg stretched out in front of him. Safety in duty, she thought, steeling her emotions. "We have to get moving before those things come back."

Rhaina strode past Cailin, rehydrated bacon still sizzling on a plate. She passed Majid standing guard over the three Lygmies and came up beside Sawn. He used a camp shovel to pat the muddy mound where he'd buried the remains of the Resurrected Mother man the Lygmies killed. He stood up straight as she approached and wiped his muddy hands on the ground foliage. His black tech glasses stared at her, not giving away his feelings or thoughts.

"Jake's dead?" Sawn asked before she said anything.

Rhaina nodded.

Sawn turned and stared into the forest, the muscles of his back twitching through the sweaty, muddy t-shirt. Rhaina didn't know what to say or do for the man. She knew him only from a few jobs they'd worked together years before, and she had no idea if Sawn even considered Jake a friend. She doubted she'd see much emotion from him – she'd never seen any more emotion than yesterday when he punched Jake.

"Cailin said you lost a man already," Sawn said, still facing the forest.

"They got Ramiro a few days ago." Was it only a few days? It felt like a year.

"Do you need me?"

"I could use another hand," Rhaina said. "But I'll be up-front with you. I'm sure Jake was offering you nearly half; I can't do that."

"How much?" Sawn turned around, his cold, black glasses fixed straight on her face.

"Two-thirds of the final sale price gets divided among all team members. You would get an equal share of that."

"Khonane is injured." He glanced to the tents behind Rhiana. "And he still gets a full share?"

"It's my team. My rules. But you've already come this far. Why turn back now?"

Sawn sighed. Rhaina couldn't help but notice how big the man was. His arms were folded in front of his chest, and his muscles nearly burst through his shirt. The man probably bench-pressed houses in his spare time – literally, since he was about as tech'd as Jake.

"Deal," he said, holding out his hand.

"Deal," Rhaina agreed, taking the hand and shaking it. His grip was solid, but he didn't use it to squeeze the feeling out of her. She appreciated that bit of courtesy. "I want to be out of here before those things come back."

"It's already too late for that." He pointed at the trees. "Three of the beasts watched while I buried this man. I suspect he won't stay buried once we leave."

Rhaina looked, but she didn't see anything. That meant little since the creatures could blend in so completely.

"The eyes," Sawn said, pointing to his own tech'd glasses. "They can't camouflage their eyes, and they have to open them to shift position."

"You're already earning your keep," Rhaina said. She headed back into camp.

"Have some breakfast," Cailin said, shoving a plate of greasy bacon into her hands.

"Thanks." Rhaina stared at the lukewarm, fatty slabs of rehydrated meat. She shoved a strip into her mouth and tried not to think about the fact that it used to be a cute little piglet before it was sliced and smoked and fried into this shriveled, blackened chunk. It slid down her throat, and she tried not to gag. She smiled and carried the plate with her as she spoke to the rest of the group. "Listen up. This is the most expensive job we've ever attempted, and we haven't even reached the gem yet. We lost Ramiro and Jake, and I don't want to lose anyone else. Sawn has agreed to come on board as a full partner. You better believe we'll be making use of his skills and his tech."

"Ooh," Cailin said, eyeing Sawn from head to toe. "How many skills does he have?"

Sawn snorted.

Rhaina wondered how many men it would take to satisfy Cailin, then checked her thoughts. "Strike camp. I want to be out of here within the hour."

"Rhaina," Majid said, calling her to the Lygmies.

She handed the plate back to Cailin. The Lygmies sat subdued on the roots of a giant tree with thick, rubbery leaves. It had begun to sprinkle again, but the Lygmies didn't seem to care as the water ran down their oily, black hair.

"I have seen two meshet stalking us from within the forest," Majid said.

"There were three more watching Sawn. What do you suggest?"

"It is actually Sawn's Lygmies who have the most interesting suggestion."

Rhaina turned to the three little people, but they sat with their eyes to the ground.

"They claim to have an abandoned camp near here where they can get us to the gem within only a few days."

"You told them we were after the gem?"

"They already knew." Majid turned back to the Lygmies as he continued. "Apparently, we're not the first humans to attempt this."

"Why do they want to help? What do they get in return?"

"They claim the gem belongs to a rival tribe, 'the Bad Ones,' and they would enjoy seeing it stolen from them."

"All's fair, eh?"

"Something like that." He turned back to her and guided her a couple tics from the Lygmies. "They say they have a boat that can get us all across the river, including the remaining frizz."

"What river?"

"Apparently there's a river. They talked like we should already know this."

"No, there was never a river in any of my visions. And Jake never said anything about crossing a river."

Majid shrugged. "I have no reason to doubt their words."

Rhaina stared at the three Lygmies seated on the roots, apparently moping. At least that's what it looked like to Rhaina. The Lygmies were such weird little creatures she had no way of knowing if normal, human emotions even applied. For all she knew, they were moping because Sawn buried their captured human, and that thought sent shivers down her spine.

"Can you keep them under control if they turn on us?"

"Absolutely," Majid said. Rhaina thought she saw a smile flick at the corners of his mouth. Was he actually looking forward to hurting the little demons?

"Fine," she said, wiping away the first drops of morning rain. "You control them. I want to be at their camp as soon as possible, by tonight if we can."

28

Tone

jungle trail

"Nothing," Avery said, stowing the motion detector back in the pouch. "Whoever was here, they're long gone."

Tone didn't even give him the courtesy of a smile as Avery turned around. They'd marched hard the entire day to reach this site, and since Tone was now officially their prisoner, they had decreed only half rations for him. They hadn't made him march in shackles, but they tied him to a tree every time they stopped. They wouldn't even let him pee in private.

Tone wondered what had become of the people he used to know, the ones he used to call his friends, the ones who used to go on raiding missions with him one night and to the bars with the next. And most importantly, what happened to the colonel he used to know?

"Move," Colonel Walraven said, shoving the butt of his rifle into Tone's shoulder.

They slogged their way through the pouring rain and mud to enter the deserted camp. The ground foliage was mashed into the ground where three tents had stood. A fourth area had been trampled, possibly by supplies, or maybe where a lean-to had been set up. Almost every tree in the clearing had been stripped of its leaves and branches, and several trunks bore the scars of gunfire. Rainwater pooled in the small fire pit and ran into the muddy tracks.

"Who were they fighting?" Avery asked as he stared at the ravaged clearing.

Jane gasped, and Tone turned to see her staring at the blood-covered stump of a fallen tree. She pressed her palm to a tuft of fur, closed her eyes, and started humming. Tone stepped closer, and she jerked her head around to stare wide-eyed at him.

"Were they fighting the meshet?" he asked.

"We should leave," Jane said, her eyes flicking to different spots across the camp.

"Why?" Tone looked around, but he didn't see anything except Avery watching him from a couple tics away. He turned back. "What is it?"

"Please, we must leave. A partome may be near."

"A what?"

"They swim the oceans of the earth. We must leave."

A shrill whistle broke into the conversation. Tone looked back to see Colonel Walraven beckoning them over, and Avery gestured for Tone to lead the way. He glanced once more at Jane, and her eyes were wide as she scanned the ground and the pools all around them.

Tone led Avery through the camp, his own gaze now focused on the ground. What was Jane looking for? What was a "partome," and how would he know when he saw one? For all he knew, they might be poisonous water slugs, or maybe piranhas with attitudes.

They met the colonel standing over a freshly dug hole, and all thoughts of partomes vanished from his mind. Within and all around the hole lay Robinson's muddied, mutilated form. The stump of his body had been propped up in the mud like a trophy, his blood and organs dumped into the hole to be pounded into soup by the rain. His severed head had been shoved onto the end of a branch, the hair yanked out and twigs poking through his eye sockets.

Tone stared, his mind not really comprehending what he saw. Avery spun around and threw up in a mud puddle.

"The partomes," Jane whispered.

"Who are the partomes?" Colonel Walraven said. Tone could hear the anger in his voice, the need for vengeance.

"Please," Jane said. "We must leave. We are not safe in this place. The partomes hunt in this place."

Tone turned around and saw that the other two Lygmies were standing near trees on the opposite side of the clearing. They were watching Jane, and they shifted back and forth.

"Colonel, maybe we should take her advice," he said.

"I want to know where I can find these partomes," Colonel Walraven said through clenched teeth. His head shook as he continued to speak. "After we know where to find the partomes, we will tear them limb from limb and shove their heads onto trees and –"

"Colonel!" Tone said, gripping the man's arm.

Colonel Walraven turned toward him, but his eyes were huge. His gaze flicked from Tone to the ground to Jane and back to Tone again, never focusing on anything long enough to really see it.

"No," the colonel said. "No. No, no, no." His eyes stayed with Tone for a few seconds. "No, I – I brought him out here. It's right that I should be the one to...well, to...." He looked at Jane. "Don't you see? The partomes, they're – they're helping those bastards out there. They're helping them to find food and shelter and – and the gem."

Jane backed away.

"They want our gem." He gripped Tone's shoulders and yelled into his face. "Don't you see? They are trying to steal our gem!"

Avery had finally recovered, and stood at Tone's side. His eyes had the same wild gleam, and his grin was so wide it looked like it sliced his face in half.

"Oh, yeah," Avery said, nodding at the colonel. "Oh, yeah. Yeah, we can kill them all. We will make them pay for what they did to Robinson."

Tone tried to back away, but the colonel wouldn't let him go. Neither of these two men had ever been blood-thirsty and greedy before. They cared about helping people, about preserving the environment so that people a thousand years from now would still have an Earth. That was a noble vision. Not this revenge and lust for wealth. Unless everything before had been an act, and this true nature had been sitting under the surface, waiting for the opportunity to show itself? But for more than 15 years? That seemed to incredible to believe.

"We cannot let them live," Colonel Walraven said, releasing Tone and turning to Avery. "They must be made to account for this."

No sooner had the colonel let him go than Jane grabbed hold of him and tugged him away. He nearly slipped in the mud as she yanked him along, trying to drag him across the camp to where the other two Lygmies anxiously waited.

"What are you doing?" he said as he jerked his arm away.

"We must leave," Jane said, grabbing his hand again. "Come."

"Yeah, you've made it very clear. The partomes." Avery and the colonel suddenly yelled, and Tone turned to see them waving their guns through the air, obviously enjoying their new-found love of violence. He looked back at Jane. "Why should we be worried about these partomes? We haven't seen any. Have we?"

"Come!" She started to pull him forward again, then she slid to a halt and stared at the edge of the clearing.

Tone followed her gaze. The rain pounded the ground, and one of the Lygmies spun around and shimmied up the nearest tree.

"P'rook!" Jane yelled.

The second Lygme turned to follow the first. He gripped the tree's trunk, lifted himself off the ground, and started climbing.

The ground beneath him seemed to explode and an arm of mud snaked up from between the roots.

The Lygme screamed as it was yanked down the tree, its fingers digging bloody streaks into the bark.

Tone reached for his gun, then remembered he didn't have one anymore. He cursed the colonel's stupidity. He rushed back to retrieve anything he could use to defend himself, but Avery and the colonel had their rifles aimed straight at him. He fell to the ground, dragging Jane down with him.

The Lygme's screams were pierced by the eruption of gun fire.

Tone lifted his head and saw the two men laughing hysterically as they pounded shot after shot through the air above his head.

Jane started howling, and Tone turned to see her staring behind them. A Lygme was pinned to the tree by the hail of gunfire. His body jerked and shuddered and gyrated with each life-wrenching shot.

Tone couldn't let this go on. He rolled away, dragging Jane with him as he tried to get out of the line of fire. They slid and crawled across the muddy ground.

And then, the gunfire stopped.

Tone had to listen around the ringing in his ears for several seconds before he actually believed it, and he lifted his head to view the desolation. The tree had been shredded, and the Lygme's body was a mass of red pulp at its base.

Jane turned to see for herself, and her incessant howling became more frantic as her eyes grew wide.

"Would you shut that jackin' Lygme up!" Avery yelled as he scrunched his eyes shut and shook his head.

Tone saw no reason to get Jane quiet. Let her grieve, he thought, as he pushed himself up from the ground.

That's when he noticed the ground shift beneath him. He stopped and stared into the mud, rain pouring down his head and slicker and pooling beneath him. The mud seemed to wash around him in miniature waves, and the pile he watched rolled over and around itself before settling into a ridged pattern that could almost have been mistaken for a face.

Muddy lids flicked open revealing the brightest pair of black eyes Tone had ever seen. He sprang backwards, and the creature lunged at him, mud flying all around as it wrapped huge arms around him. Mud spewed from its sharp-toothed mouth, and the thing fell on Tone, arched its back, flipped forward to tear out his throat – and then it was tackled by an orange blur.

Tone didn't wait to see if the meshet was stronger than the partome thing that had just tried to eat him. He jumped to his feet, nearly slid into the fire pit, and raced for the edge of camp where Jane beckoned.

Gunfire erupted from the other side of camp as Avery and Colonel Walraven screamed in delight. Bullets pounded the ground and trees again, and Tone tried to duck low to keep from getting hit.

A pillar of mud sprang up before him, and he slammed into the solid body of another partome. The creature spun around to him, its long, black hair spraying water and mud across his face, and its skinny arms clawing wildly at his face.

Several bullets punctured the creature's chest, and the thing lost all interest in Tone as it seemed to melt back into the mud before him. It dove forward and slid along the surface of the earth before submerging completely, its long-finned feet leaving a muddy wake to mark its trail.

Tone leaped back to his own feet and nearly tripped over Jane as he rushed from the clearing. She hoisted him up, and he gripped the slick bark of the nearest tree, only to slide back down.

She shoved her hands into his backside and tried to keep him from slipping, but she was too small, and he didn't have a good enough grip.

"Climb!" she yelled.

The thick, rubbery leaves exploded all around him as Avery and the colonel swept their aim from one end of the clearing to the other.

"I can't!" he yelled at Jane. "I don't have claws on the ends of my fingers like you!"

A huge, powerful hand wrapped around his wrist, and Tone looked up to see a wet, orange meshet gripping the trunk. It hoisted him up in one powerful motion and threw him across its back. Then it leaped from the tree, spread its arms and legs wide, and sailed toward the canopy, high above the destruction of the clearing.

Tone spared a quick glance as the ground fell away, and he saw Avery and Colonel Walraven get scooped up by two other flying meshet. The muddy camp churned like an angry ocean as the partomes swam through the earth.

Tone had to struggle to hold onto the meshet's powerful form as it jumped and sailed through the trees, almost tossing him over its head one second and then popping the joints in his shoulders the next as it gripped branches and sprang higher.

It landed on all fours on a wide path suspended in the canopy, and Tone rolled off the creature's back to land on the solid boards. He couldn't remember ever being so thankful to be alive. He'd never ridden a wild animal before, and he saw no reason to do it again after this experience.

Avery and the colonel were dumped unceremoniously next to him on the path by two other meshet.

Tone's meshet reached toward Avery and the colonel, yanked the rifles from their hands, and threw them down the rubbery path.

"What the bloody hell are you doing?" Avery said, jumping to unsteady feet.

The meshet spun around and screamed in his face, a deafening noise that almost made Tone want to jump off the path.

Avery stumbled back, but he was smart enough not to say anything else as the meshet kicked the weapons to Tone's feet.

"What's the meaning of this?" Colonel Walraven said as he gripped the rope vines of the path and steadied himself. "Tone, what are you doing?"

Jane strode down the path, and she didn't even flinch as she watched the colonel rise. She walked up to him and shoved a finger into his chest.

"*Brakopreha uingh jajantepla freshjaha!*" she said.

"What?" Colonel Walraven said.

Tone wasn't sure how he knew, but he knew the duty of translation fell to him for this little exchange. He didn't like it much, but Jane had no intention of speaking to him in anything other than her own tongue. But how did he even know that?

"She says that you're not...fit to command," Tone said.

Colonel Walraven laughed.

"Keedli'pa gnok ha porokfor miin bruknimah."

"She says you both kill indiscriminately, and she can't have you harming her meshet." But what made the creatures her own, Tone wondered. Except, that wasn't exactly what she'd said. She said she couldn't have them harming "any and my one" meshet. He didn't know how to translate "any and my one," though, when he had no idea what the phrase meant. He didn't even know how he knew the words he was translating.

"We didn't do anything but defend ourselves against those jungle beasts," the colonel said.

Jane's eyes slid to narrow slits, and her jaw clenched tight. She snapped her fingers, never taking her eyes off the colonel.

The branches all around them shuddered, and more than a dozen meshet flashed from their green and brown camouflage to bright orange. Two of the meshet jumped from a branch behind Tone and strode toward Jane. The path creaked under their combined weight, and Tone felt the boards shudder as they squeezed past him. He couldn't see Jane at all with the meshet standing before him, but he had no trouble hearing her.

"Kiploo," she said.

The meshet spread their arms, revealing bloody holes in the thick flaps of skin that attached at their wrists and ankles. He had to believe the injuries hurt, but the meshet didn't even shudder as they stretched the wounds wide enough that Tone could see through them.

"Tone will lead," Jane said, enunciating every syllable with exquisite care.

The meshet backed to the edges of the path, and Jane strode between them and helped Tone to his feet. She retrieved the weapons and thrust them into his hands.

"Lead," she said, pointing down the path.

"Jane," Tone said, glancing back at Avery and the colonel. "I think we need to talk. I don't...want to be out here anymore. I'm ready to go home."

She turned to him and sighed, then yanked on his shirt for him to kneel. He did. She took his face in her hands and leaned him near to herself, near enough that Tone could again smell that musky, sweaty odor that seemed to permeate not only Jane but everything she wore and used.

"Tone," she whispered with a smile. "Lead. Or return to the forest floor with the partomes."

The meshet behind her closed the gap between them, cutting off any chance that either Avery or the colonel could help him – assuming, of course, that they would. The threat was real. He either led this party "voluntarily," or he wouldn't be leading anything ever again. And he had no desire to take his chances with those mud-swimming partomes down below.

"Will this path take us all the way to the gem?" Tone asked, pointing down the suspended path.

"Almost." She patted his head and grinned like a girl who'd had a good temper-tantrum.

29

Computer Circuit Board

location unknown

>Rerouting Power +
>Systems Analysis -
>Tech Network Operational +
>Field Coils Operational +
>Main Power Supply Damaged +
>Bones Damaged +
>Muscles Damaged +
>Joints Damaged +
> Internal Organs -
> 29% Damaged +
>Brain Functioning Below Optimal Levels -
>Rerouting Power +
>Body Subroutines Initiated -
>Heart Restarted +
> Operating Below Nominal -
>Lungs Restarted +

>Danger: Interior Blockage -
>Rerouting Power +
>Respiratory Clearance Subroutines Initiated -
>Cough -
>Check -
>Blocked +
>Cough -
>Check -
>Blocked +
>Cough -
>Check -
>48% Clearance \ Adequate +
>Rerouting Power +
>Body Subroutines Initiated -
>Heart Restarted -
> Operating Within Nominal Parameters
>Lungs Restarted +
>Rerouting Power +
>Brain Functioning Below Optimal Levels -
>Rerouting Brain Functions to Tech Network +
>Awaiting Authorization -

Damn, Jake thought. *I died again.*

30

Rhaina

river trail

Rhaina sat on the bench at the edge of the boat and watched the rain pound the river as they passed through the night. The Lygmies insisted on calling it a river, but to all the humans on board it felt like a lake. Or maybe even a bayou. But if it was a river, it was certainly the largest, slowest river any of them had ever been on.

They had reached the shores of the river-lake-bayou by late afternoon, and the Lygmies said they all had to get in the boat and leave immediately. So they stowed their bags, and the Lygmies shoved off.

The boat itself was spacious, and the first thing they did was make a quick dinner. After that, Rhaina sent the rest of her team to bed – except Majid, who didn't need to rest – and took the first watch. She sat on the main deck just above water level with the remaining frizz stamping its feet in the stall behind her. Two of the Lygmies poled the water to her right, shoving the boat along and pushing away from the thriving trees with their elaborate root systems that wound and spread into towering support rods for the trunks and branches that stretched into the air, blocking all light from the sun, moon, and stars. Rhaina felt like she drifted through a king's banquet hall that had been overrun by the surrounding forest.

The boat's second level housed quarters that were probably quite comfortable for all the Lygmies on board, but were slightly less spacious than a child's bunk bed for the humans. Even Cailin, as short as she was, couldn't stretch out.

Rhaina jerked back from the edge as a long, bulky form drifted beside the boat. It rolled its head to the side and blinked up at her, the water rolling down its long, black snout and beading on its fur. The animal swam with surprising speed and agility for something so large.

She turned to ask what it was, and she saw two more of the animals trailing through the water. That was concerning. One was a novelty, but three had the potential to cause some damage. She couldn't see anything more than the very tops of the creatures, but it wasn't hard to imagine something with the size and ferocity of an alligator, or maybe even a hippopotamus, drifting beneath the surface.

She was about to call out to the Lygmies when they pulled up their poles and rushed to the rear of the boat. They leaned far over and stroked a couple of the creatures on their snouts, calling out to them in their gibberish language. The creatures responded by swimming nearer, nuzzling the Lygmies' hands, and bumping the boat with their heads. The wood creaked and the boat shuddered with each passing animal.

"Ever heard of a partome?" Khonane asked, hobbling over to join Rhaina at the side of the boat.

"Never," she said. "And you're supposed to be resting."

"Who can sleep through all that Lygme chatter? Listen."

The Lygmies talked to each other, and the one word she heard repeated most often sounded like "partome." She turned back to watch the animals swimming through the water. One of them strained its neck to turn to her, exposing a row of sharp teeth that glinted in the dim lantern light.

"I wonder what they eat?" she said.

Khonane chuckled as he leaned in. She didn't know whether she liked the closeness. What would Cailin think? Did she really care what Cailin thought? Actually, she did. She needed her team working as a team, not infighting about relationship issues.

"Shouldn't you be sleeping?" She turned to face him.

"Probably. But you'd have trouble sleeping too if you knew a plastic man stood a few tics away from your head."

"What's he doing?" She looked to the front of the boat, but she couldn't see Majid beyond the housing.

"I don't know," Khonane said. "He was talking to himself, something about rosh."

"Mr. Rosh?"

"He never said 'mister,' but sure. Maybe. Who's Mr. Rosh?"

"He's the man funding our trip." But why would the plastic man be talking about Mr. Rosh? The man was nothing more than a wisp of a ghost anymore, and he couldn't have any affect on the plastic man – unless Rosh programmed the plastic man to talk about him? But with who? And why?

Or was he talking to Rosh? There wasn't a transmitter in the galaxy that could beam a signal that far and allow conversation. A recording then? To be retransmitted later? But from where? And by whom? It wasn't like there was any technology in this jungle to allow him to report in.

"You're sure he was alone?" Rhaina asked. "Our third Lygme wasn't up there with him?"

"No," Khonane said, shaking his head. "That third Lygme was laying in the bunk above me and talking in his sleep. You do not want to know what he was saying."

Rhaina lifted an eyebrow, expecting him to continue.

"I'm not repeating it."

"That bad?"

He rolled his eyes and turned to stare into the night.

Rhaina watched him, his face silhouetted against the blue lantern light and his profile showing off the straight, hard line of his nose and jaw. The brim of his cowboy hat extended far enough beyond his brow to keep the light from hitting any of his face except his chin, where she noticed several days' worth of scruff.

Khonane cleared his throat, glanced at her, and said, "How's your Geminai?"

Rhaina met his gaze and smiled. It was an odd question. He usually avoided talk of their Geminais, and he had never asked like hers was a separate person. Was he finally starting to acknowledge his own second soul?

"She's good," Rhaina said. She pointed to a spot above the second deck. "She's right there, in fact, watching that one Lygme who's still petting the partomes off the end of the boat."

"Oh, sure," Khonane said. He turned to look first at the Lygmies, then to the spot above the housing where her Geminai hovered. "Right there. Good."

Rhaina smiled. He was so obviously uncomfortable that it charmed her, and she reached forward to kiss him on the cheek. She knew it wasn't the smartest thing to do, but she didn't care. Besides, they were good friends. Nothing wrong with one good friend giving the other friend a peck on the cheek.

But Khonane turned his head at the last second, and her kiss landed on his lips. Her eyes widened.

"I'm sorry," she said, backing away. She looked out over the river. "Sorry. I didn't mean to...you know. I didn't mean to do that."

"Are you actually at a loss for words?"

"Yes," she said with a laugh.

She turned to see his expression, to laugh along with him and to let the moment slide away forgotten – hopefully with nothing more said about it ever. But when her eyes met his, they were so close to her that she could see nothing else. He kissed her again, and this time she didn't back away. She hadn't really wanted the first kiss to end, and she wasn't about to stop this one.

His hand stretched around behind her neck, and she leaned in closer to him, watching his eyes as he watched her. She liked that, the intimacy of watching each other as they kissed. Jake had never done that, not for a kiss and certainly not a one-night stand.

Hmm, she wondered. What would a night be like with Khonane? Would she get to watch those wonderful, inviting brown eyes all night long? Does he close them?

It was a delicious thought, and she was willing to let it continue, until she saw something moving in the darkness beyond the frizz's little enclosure. Her eyes drifted from Khonane, and his brows furrowed at the distraction.

The frizz stamped its feet and swayed its head as the little shadow darted between its legs. The shape was too small to be a Lygme. A rat maybe? Did rats even live in this jungle? Or on this planet?

Khonane turned to say something, but Rhaina held him tight and pressed her lips to his ear.

"Behind you," she whispered. She ran her hand across his back to maintain the illusion of their intimacy. "One mark in the shadows."

She felt his arms tense as he nuzzled her neck, his hat slipping backwards. He slipped his hand to her waist and pulled the pistol from its holster as she sent her Geminai to investigate the shadows.

She flinched as Khonane's whiskers scraped her jaw. He would definitely need to shave if kissing became a habit.

Her Geminai drifted above the frizz and scanned the dark corners of the housing.

"I see him," Rhaina whispered as she pulled Khonane's gun from his holster. "One cat."

"Cat?" Khonane asked, nibbling her ear lobe. "Out here?"

"Directly behind you," Rhaina said, using her Geminai to sight her shot through the darkness. "It's sniffing around Sawn's pack."

"Count of three." Khonane shifted his weight, grimacing at the pain in his leg.

"One," Rhaina said. The cat stood on its back legs and sniffed the knot at the top of Sawn's bag. "Two." She considered that the animal might not be anything more than a common house cat, and they were about to scare the thing half to death. If so, she'd have to apologize. But they couldn't take that chance. If it was a pouncer.... "Three."

Rhaina and Khonane released each other, and Rhaina flung herself left. Khonane lunged forward, and the animal shrieked as the man tried to grasp it.

"It got away!" he yelled.

She watched through her Geminai as the cat darted through the housing to the front of the boat.

"I see it!" she yelled back, leaping away as the frizz kicked at the noises. Rhaina sprinted through the housing and burst into the rain.

Majid's glowing eyes met her in the darkness, and she could see him studying the furry, thrashing cat he held by the scruff of its neck. The animal wrapped itself around his arm and sank its teeth in deep. It would have been enough to get free of any of the humans on board.

"Do you know how little pressure it takes to snap a pouncer's spine?" Majid said.

The animal released its grip on his hand and growled, its ears pressed flat against its head.

"Lose something?" Majid said, turning to Rhaina.

Khonane limped up to the door of the housing, the lantern in his hand to illuminate the front of the boat. The blue glow made the rain sparkle like tinsel, and Majid's face shone like the dead. All three Lygmies rushed past Khonane, nearly knocking him over as they surrounded Majid and pleaded for the pouncer's release. They petted it and kissed it and supported its legs to ease the strain of Majid's grip.

"Please," Ko said, turning to face Rhaina. "Do not harm our Sigpa. He is good. He not harm any things."

Rhaina stepped closer. The animal watched her the entire time. Oh, yeah, Rhaina thought. There's a mind behind that glare, a consciousness you don't find in normal cats. She shoved Khonane's gun into the animal's ear.

"No!" all three Lygmies screamed at once.

"Shut up," Majid said.

They did, turning to Rhaina and pleading for the animal's life with their big eyes.

"Talk," Rhaina said to the pouncer.

"Bite me, bitch," the pouncer growled.

"No no," Ko said. "He not mean what he says. Please –"

Majid gripped Ko's neck. The Lygme stopped talking.

"'Sigpa,' is it?" Rhaina said.

"The name's Silny."

"Silny? Okay. What are you doing out here, Silny?"

"Seeing the sights." If pouncers grinned, this one was certainly doing it. His whole attitude screamed superiority.

Rhaina grinned back and pulled the gun away from his face. "Dunk him," she said.

Majid swung around, shoved both the pouncer and Ko into the river, then hoisted them back up. He slammed Ko onto the deck of the boat and held the soaking, coughing pouncer in the air in front of Rhaina. Ko slipped off his feet, and Majid hoisted him back up. The other two Lygmies backed away.

"Just the pouncer next time," Rhaina said.

"Yes, ma'am." Majid's yellow eyes betrayed nothing. Did he not know which "him" Rhaina wanted dunked? Plastic men were anything but stupid, so he had to know what he was doing.

The pouncer lashed out, swatting at Rhaina and twisting its body to wrap around Majid's hand again. It spit river water at them and shook its head, more water flying from its ears. When it couldn't get loose, it stopped struggling and growled at them, its flat eyes glowing red.

"Once more," Rhaina said as she wiped a smudge from the gun's polished black handle. "Why are you here?"

"You think I want to be here?" Silny said. "You think I like being all wet and muddy?"

"You wouldn't be out here if you didn't gain something from it. Talk." She stopped cleaning the pistol and waved it beneath the pouncer's nose.

"Oh sure, blame it all on the pouncer. You wouldn't be having any problems if the pouncer wasn't here. One great mind in an ocean of critters, and you have to try to squelch it."

"What are you babbling about?" Rhaina asked. She swiped at the rain in her eyes. "Dunk him again."

"Wait!" Silny said as Majid lifted him high in the air. "I can help you! I can give you information!"

Majid lowered his arm until Silny was eye level with Rhaina again.

"The information I want to know is why you're out here," Rhaina said.

"I can do that. I can give you that, plus more." At this, his eyes narrowed and his claws extended. "But I'll only help you if you put me down and stop dunking me in the river."

"Give me some reason to trust you," Rhaina said, "and not to drop you overboard for the partomes to eat."

"You're not the only humans in this jungle."

Rhaina stared at the pouncer's soaking face. Black eyes met her gaze without flinching, and whiskers twitched at the strain of the grip on its neck. She really had been ready to toss the little animal overboard. The last thing she needed was a petty, vindictive pouncer slowing them all down.

This information was interesting. She already knew they weren't alone – the Lygmies had proven that when they brought back that mutilated soldier from Resurrected Mother. But if this pouncer actually knew who they were, where they came from, how many were out there.... She had to decide if she could trust the word of a pouncer.

"You've earned a temporary reprieve," she said. "Majid, let's bring him inside."

"I don't get to drown him?" Majid said.

"Not today. And let the Lygme go, too."

The plastic man sighed, but did as he was told. Rhaina turned to lead them back into the dry housing, and that's when she realized everyone on the boat was awake and watching. Sawn stood in the rain, Khonane behind him and leaning against the rickety door frame. But more importantly, Cailin leaned against Khonane's chest. She seemed perfectly at ease within his personal space, as if it was the most natural place in the world for her to be. Apparently, it was.

"Show's over," Rhaina said, waving them all back inside. "Back to bed. Cailin, you have watch in an hour."

"Yes, ma'am."

They filed back through the tiny door, and Rhaina avoided Khonane's gaze. Then she realized she was doing exactly what she didn't want her team to do, allow her personal feelings to get in the way of her job. She was the leader. She could look at whoever she pleased, whenever she pleased, and in whatever way she pleased.

She looked up in time to see Khonane disappear through the door as he followed Cailin inside.

Stay out of it, she thought with a sigh. Leave them alone. You're here to get the gem and get the hell out. So do your job and quit jackin' around with the team members.

"Can somebody towel-dry me?" Silny said.

Rhaina smiled as she led the plastic man and the pouncer back into the covered housing.

"Get a leash on him," she said to Majid. "He answers questions, and then he can dry himself off."

31

Tone

tree canopy trail

Tone marched silently behind Jane's tiny body. Except she didn't look all that tiny anymore. Had she actually grown, or did she just seem taller because he didn't want to be hostage to a munchkin and her ferocious pets?

"We need to rest," Colonel Walraven said from behind him.

"We rest later." Jane didn't even slow her pace.

They walked along the suspended path, the wood creaking and the whole path swaying in the light, midnight breeze. Tone heard the rain falling all around them, but it had been at least a couple hours since any drops hit him. Not that he was anywhere near being dry. His hair and pants were still soaked, and the cool air sent shivers down his back.

"Hey," Colonel Walraven whispered, shoving Tone's shoulder. "You're supposed to be the bloody leader now. Let's stop and rest."

"Um, Jane?" Tone said.

"Yes, my dear?" She glanced back at him, and he nearly stumbled as he saw her brilliant, orange eyes glowing through the darkness ahead of him.

"The, um, the men are tired." He had to look away, just for a second, to compose himself again. When did her eyes start glowing? Did all Lygmies' eyes glow in the dark? She looked like a little demon. "We've been walking most of the night, and, to be honest, I'm tired too."

"Oh, I'm sorry." She stopped and snapped her fingers. The two meshet that had been lumbering behind them came rushing forward, pounding the rickety planks and shoving Avery and the colonel out of the way.

Jane spoke to them in Lygmese, and they turned, grabbed Tone, and lifted him up onto their shoulders. They started marching forward again, and Tone had to work to balance himself. Their shifting weight and uneven strides made him feel like he would topple head-first at any minute. A group of low-hanging branches snapped into his face, scratching his arms and neck.

"Wait!" he yelled, slapping away leaves and sticks. The meshet stopped, and he struggled from their grip and fell back to the path. The colonel stood over him and laughed, the first real laugh Tone remembered from him in months.

"Oh, my pet!" Jane said, rushing to his side. She stroked his hair and nuzzled his cheek with her nose as she helped him sit up. "Are you all right?"

"Jane," he said as he leaned against the path's securing ropes. "We need to rest. That means we need to stop. All of us."

She turned and looked at the colonel who had finally stopped laughing, then she turned to the meshet and spoke to them in her language. They jumped into the trees above and disappeared from view, but Tone heard them rustling around. Leaves rained onto the path, and there was a scraping sound from above, thudding and stomping as if the meshet walked on another platform right above them.

"It's okay, my pet," Jane said, her orange eyes glowing brilliantly before him. "If you want to rest, we will rest."

The meshet returned moments later, long, wooden boards secured beneath their arms.

"Tell your friends to behave themselves, though," Jane whispered.

Tone looked, and Colonel Walraven and Avery were backing away, tensing as if to make a break for it.

"Don't," Tone mouthed to them, pleading with his eyes for them not to leave him alone with these animals. He couldn't look at Jane without her licking her lips at him – was that supposed to be seductive? – and he couldn't take a deep breath anymore without that musky scent of hers filling his nostrils.

Colonel Walraven winked at him, then turned and ran.

The air shimmered around them, and half a dozen meshet rippled into view as their fur changed to bright orange. They seemed to light up the darkness as they blocked Avery's and the colonel's escape.

"This is torture!" Avery yelled, spinning around and advancing on Tone and Jane. He shook his hands free of the gloves and let the lightning spark between his fingers.

Jane bared her teeth in a savage snarl, her orange hair seeming to stand on end.

Two of the surrounding meshet launched themselves at Avery. He turned on them, spinning his hands to form a tiny lightning ball that lit the path and surrounding trees in a brilliant, white glow. He never got a chance to throw the lightning as the animals jumped on top of him and crushed him against the path with their weight. At least one bone snapped.

The meshet stood up and leapt back into the trees above, leaving Avery to writhe on the path by himself, hollow gasps the only thing escaping from his mouth.

"You animals!" Colonel Walraven yelled. He started to run to Avery, but the meshet on either side of him gripped his shoulders.

Jane turned to Tone, her orange eyes and hair like tiny flames against her pale skin. She closed her mouth, a growl still emanating from somewhere deep within her throat, and she leaned forward.

"Is he your friend?" she asked, pointing at Avery.

"Yes," Tone said. He gripped the edge of the path so fiercely he thought he might snap the boards. Actually, he wished he could snap the boards so he could fall to his death and never see these nightmare creatures again.

"Then we will not let him die," she said. She leaned forward, her eyes flickering at him in the harsh lantern light. She extended her tongue and licked him from his stubbly chin, past his lips, to the point of his nose, and up to his forehead. She sat back and giggled.

32

Jake

location unknown

Jake tasted the sweet, clean water falling into his mouth and knew his body had finally healed itself enough for him to slip back into consciousness. He hated this part. He'd only used his Resurrection Tech once before, during a particularly tough job with Rhaina years ago. Like now, the two of them had managed to get separated, and he ended up walking in front of a bullet. The thing hurt going in, and it hurt even more coming back out. And that brief moment, slipping back into reality, hurt like hell.

The computer flashed the final warning at him:

>Physical Repairs complete -

>30 seconds to Forced Consciousness +

>29 -

>28 -

>27 -

Oh, no.

>24 -

>23 -

Wasn't there anything else to heal? Anywhere in his body?

>19 -

>18 -

It would hurt more if he let the countdown reach zero.

>13 -

>12 -

Okay. Let's do this.

>8 -

>7 -

His mind sent the activation code to stop the countdown. He forced himself to look outside the computerized images floating around him, to think beyond them, to acknowledge more of the real world.

Where was that water he'd tasted earlier? The sensation flooded back over his body, drops pounding against his skin, water filling his mouth and nose.

He began to choke, and his body flung itself forward. He felt the cool, soft earth ooze between his fingers as he spewed the rain water from his mouth.

He dragged the air back inside himself with a long, low wheeze.

All around, he heard the rain hammering against the leaves, the branches, the ground. Everything was so loud!

His eyes flew open. What was he looking at? White and green-streaked froth mixed with the rain and ran across the muddy ground. He must have thrown up, but he couldn't imagine anything like that coming out of his own stomach. Either way, it was not the first thing he wanted to see when he regained consciousness.

Shutting his eyes again, he pushed himself away and leaned backwards. His foot slipped in the mud, and he landed hard on his butt. The jolt reverberated all the way up his spine, making every joint in his back tingle.

He twisted his eyes to the right, and the tech flashed status reports before his closed lids. First up was the damage report. He scanned through it. It probably would have been easier to count the number of bones that hadn't broken instead of the ones that had.

He checked his internal clock and saw that he'd been out for just over three days. He checked his position against the maps, charts, and photographs stored in his tech and found that he hadn't even reached the halfway point. He could turn back now. He probably should turn back, get himself fixed at 2 Glorious' shop, and then head home. Except that he never was a quitter.

The tech flashed the power indicator before his eyes, and he saw that he still had over 50% of his batteries left. That was one of the best features of his Resurrection Tech, its own power source. It used some of his main supply, but not much.

So, he thought, sitting in the mud and feeling his bones, joints, and muscles scream at him. Forward or backward? Backward or forward? He was alone in this jungle, completely defenseless against those vicious meshet. Or was he?

He activated the return switch in his palm, but his gun did not come back. The tech flashed a warning at him that the gun was out of range. Probably taken by that murdering plastic man.

Ah, the plastic man, he thought. Where did Rhaina say she got him? From her employer? And, like all plastic men, he was a trained killer. And now he was alone with Rhaina.

Two years. That was a long time to go without seeing someone, and she was as extraordinary now as the day he left to join the Feds. And he was just as much of an idiot for leaving.

He opened his eyes again, slowly, and looked around the tiny clearing. The rain fell in large drops from the canopy far above, the canopy from where he'd fallen several days ago. That canopy hid a suspended path he assumed was used by the Lygmies, and he could make better time up there than across the forest floor. He'd have warning about the meshet from vibrations; no need to skulk around trees and wonder if the meshet were camouflaged right in front of him.

Standing, he noticed that the leaves on the ground all around him.

Ugh, he thought. The Resurrection Tech was supposed to use the nearest nutritional source to give his body the energy it needed to heal, but...no wonder he was puking green.

33

Tone

jungle canopy trail

Tone lay on the narrow board, too scared to move, almost too scared to breathe. Jane said Lygmies slept in the trees all the time, lying on boards to either side of the suspended path. Nobody ever fell. Children liked to jump around and play on them. Don't give in to your fear, she said.

After she said all that, she climbed onto Tone's board with him, curled up, and fell asleep in his arms. He had no idea where this sudden affection came from, but he didn't want it. She'd been acting weird for days. She smelled so strongly of musk he could barely breathe, and she was freaky with her glowing eyes and orange hair sticking off the top of her head. He'd never spent much time around a Lygme before, and this one made him never want to see one again.

She shifted in his arms, her fingernails digging like daggers through his shirt and across his chest. He gritted his teeth and tried not to move.

Her eyes flashed open, and Tone gripped the edges of the board.

She slid across his chest and muttered some Lygmese at him as she ran her fingers across the buttons of his wet camo shirt. Grinning, she started grinding her hips across his crotch, licking her pointed teeth and letting the disheveled strands of her orange hair fall across her face.

Tone shut his eyes, but that made things worse. He had to watch her, had to remind his body that this wasn't some beautiful woman on top of him. This was a sick Lygme – a freak of nature. An abomination.

She threw herself forward, barely reaching the top of his chest, bit one of the buttons of his shirt, and tugged. Her eyes flashed bright orange at him, and her pupils contracted to narrow, black slits. She looked demonic in the crackling glow of the lanterns.

She grasped the sides of his body and growled at him, her teeth still wrapped around the button. He tried to look away, but she gripped his face. Her breathing grew deeper, gasping as her body undulated to whatever rhythm bounced inside her head.

Tone felt his body giving in to the desire, and he tried to think of anything else but the Lygme's tiny, sweaty body. Engine schematics, a mission back on Earth, his last vacation to the beaches of Italy.... He looked at the suspended path. A meshet shimmered into existence, its eyes glowing in the dim light as it stared at them.

"Oh, shit!" Tone tried to push the Lygme away, but she dug her fingernails in deeper, scraping through the shirt and drawing a thin line of blood.

"No," he said, trying to turn her head. "Look. Behind us." He had no trouble keeping his mind off her sweaty, musky body now as the meshet watched them and growled.

The animal leaned forward, across the length of the sleeping board, and braced its hands on the wooden edges. The board creaked under the combined weight, and Tone watched the horizon tilt at a disturbing angle. He tried to hook his boot to the edge of the path, but he couldn't get a grip. He felt himself sliding backwards.

The meshet grabbed the back of Jane's ragged shirt and lifted her off Tone. Her eyes flitted around, and she gasped in ragged, short bursts. The meshet leaned back to the path and turned Jane around.

She shrieked, but Tone couldn't tell if she was surprised or relieved. Either way, she flung herself at the creature, wrapped her arms and legs around the beast, and buried her face in the fur of its neck. Her fingers clung to the beast's head, and she started licking its muzzle and stroking its fur.

The meshet laid her down in the center of the path and straddled her hips. It stretched its skin flaps tight, blocking her from view as it settled down on top of her.

Tone squeezed his eyes shut, turned to the side of his sleeping board, and curled into a fetal position. He still heard every snap and growl, every gasp and wheeze. The path rocked and the sleeping board swayed. If he concentrated really hard, he could imagine that he was back on a beach in Italy. If he concentrated even harder, he could almost imagine that he really had met some beautiful woman and that he was there with her now, and they were the ones who made the bed shake and the world spin....

* * *

Jake circled behind the tree trunk and stared down the dark, suspended path. His optical sensors lit up the path for him, and the digitized data told him about his surroundings, from the wind speed to the air temperature. What the sensors didn't tell him was who those humans and Lygmies were on the other side of the tree, or why they were so friendly with the meshet.

He'd watched them for nearly fifteen minutes, and they were dressed like that human the Lygmies brought back to the camp, the one they had torn the legs off. It was more obvious now that they were eco-terrorists since Jake had a chance to see them close – and alive.

Everything about them, from their outfits to the fact that none of them carried any weapons, screamed amateurism.

And what was that guy doing with that Lygme? Jake shuddered at the thought of even touching a Lygme for that long, and he certainly wouldn't want one pawing him up like that. Maybe these eco-terrorists had gone native.

Of course, they could also be out here searching for the God's Ear gem. A rock worth as much as this one was bound to attract attention sooner or later. But why couldn't it have been much later? Like after he already had it in hand?

Which left the question of what to do. A straight-forward assault would be stupid. Eco-terrorists, meshet, and Lygmies against one, lone Jake were not good odds, even if he'd had his guns. And sneaking past them without trying to slow them down? Probably the safest course of action, but Jake didn't like to play it safe. What to do, what to do, he wondered.

He slipped his hand up his right sleeve and felt the wrist holster. The laser knife sat securely in its sheath. He grinned.

34

Tone

"Are you okay?" Tone whispered, leaning forward on the wobbly sleeping board.

Jane sat cross-legged in the middle of the path, her eyes half closed and her body swaying. Dried, bloody streaks wound their way across her face and criss-crossed her mouth. Her clothes hung on her like tattered, bloodied rags, and her arms and neck bore ragged slashes that looked distinctly like teeth marks.

"I should go home," Jane said, swaying. "But I can't. And so...I grow weary." She held her hand up to her face and seemed to inspect the teeth marks along each finger. "The responsibility is mine, the burden is mine, and I'm afraid that I do not have the strength of will to succeed."

"Barlow," Tone said, recognizing the quote he'd been thinking.

"Yes," Jane said. "Phinneas Barlow, *The Works of the Common Mind.* His essays apply well to our situation."

"But, how do you know...?"

"We are not a stupid people," Jane said. "But we are smart enough to act it."

"And now you're dropping the act?"

Jane stopped swaying and toppled onto Tone's feet. He jerked back, scared of what the Lygme would do to him now. But instead of pouncing on him or licking his boots or anything freaky like that, she rolled onto her side and stared at him from the foot of the board.

"Your friends," she said. "They do not care for your cause – but you do? It means little to them, especially to your colonel. He is a fractured man, a dangerous man whose spirits fly in opposite directions and feed on power."

"Colonel Walraven is a great man," Tone said. "He has led our organization for nearly twenty years. You wouldn't know the first thing about what he's done to improve Earth."

Jane smiled at him, then said, "Are you rested enough to travel?"

"Sure. But I need you to tell me why you attacked me last night."

"Oh." She rolled her head to the side and stared out at the trees. Her orange hair flopped in front of her eyes, and she swished a bug away from her face. "Tone, you are a good man, but I will not tell you everything."

It wasn't much of an answer, but it was the last thing she said before she went to wake her Lygme friends. He crawled on his hands and knees back onto the path, checking the branches above for signs of the meshet. He saw none.

Avery and the colonel were already awake and whispering when Tone reached them several tics down the path. They stopped talking as soon as he approached, and they acknowledged with curt nods his call to get ready. He saw them leaning together and whispering again as soon as he walked away. Probably planning their escape, he thought.

Jane had called the colonel a fractured man. What did she mean by that? Certainly nothing physical; the colonel was as healthy now as the day they left. Was she talking about his lust for the gem? That had made him more volatile, but Tone found it hard to believe he was as dangerous as the Lygme said.

Then again, he couldn't remember the colonel ever pulling a gun on him. Was the man acting so irrationally because of these Lygmies and whatever game they were playing? Or maybe losing Robinson affected him more deeply than any of them had thought.

And what did a Lygme know about true peace, compassion, or mercy? Those were human qualities, not something Lygmies could understand. The colonel wasn't exactly himself, sure. That didn't change who he was at the core, and Tone had seen the man's core over the years: a true believer in their mission to help restore Earth.

With barely a rustle of leaves or branches, Jane dropped from the trees. Two unknown Lygmies landed at her side. Jane's eyes flashed bright orange, obscurring the black of her pupils. Her lips were set tight before her clenched jaw. She yanked a hand through her ratted hair, then shoved Tone's hip to spin him around.

"We're leaving," she said, marching him forward.

"But what about my stuff?" He tried to turn around. "And the sleeping board."

"Leave it." She shoved him again. "We have supplies, and the meshet will clean up after us."

Jane ducked ahead of Tone and kicked Avery's sleeping board.

"Hey!" he said, gripping the edges of the bouncing board.

Avery and the colonel looked at Jane's flaring eyes and didn't say another word. They crawled to the path, stepped in front of her, and starting walking without another look back.

The early morning humidity seemed to have seeped into Tone's clothes, and while he wasn't getting rained on, it sounded like the drops struck right above his head. His boots squeaked against the wet boards and his fingers slid along the rubbery vine supports.

"When do we get our weapons back?" Colonel Walraven said. He had stopped in the middle of the path, blocking the way, and Avery stood behind him, electric sparks rolling in the palms of his hands. The new Lygmies gripped Tone's arms and yanked him back as Jane took a step toward the colonel.

"Move," she said.

"I don't think I've made my request clear," Colonel Walraven said.

Avery thrust his arm out and sent a bolt of electricity arching down the path and into Tone's chest.

Tone flew backward, electricity dancing across his body. His heart stopped, his breathing stopped, it even felt like his life stopped. He hit the boards and skidded to a halt, his entire body tingling. He lay there several seconds, letting the feeling seep back into his limbs.

"That is some jackin' shit, ain't it?" Avery yelled. "Whew, that eel woman was hot, and she charged me good!"

Tone sat up and leaned against the vine railings. The two Lygmies were lying at his feet, shaking their heads and trying to stand. Their clawed paws were scorched black where they'd been holding him.

Tone looked at the rage building in Jane's eyes. She clenched her fists at her sides and spun back to them, her orange hair whipping around her neck.

"Turn around," she growled to the colonel. "Start walking."

"You're out of line, little Lygme," the colonel said with a smile. "We hired you to take us to this sacred temple out here."

"And we're going."

"Right, right." He knelt down in front of Jane and straightened the rags of her shirt.

Tone pulled himself up and leaned against the railing. He didn't know the plan, but he suspected he wasn't part of it anyway.

"The problem I'm having with the arrangement now," Colonel Walraven said, "is that we humans aren't in charge. We hired you. Remember?"

"I have a clear memory," Jane said.

"Good. Then you can remember where you put our weapons."

"You will get your weapons back when we reach this temple and you kill the others."

"That just doesn't work," the colonel said, shaking his head. "We need them back now. We need to be able to defend ourselves from all the wild animals out here. You know, like you."

"This is our jungle. You will do as we say."

Rolling another electric ball, Avery said, "You don't get it, little piggy. We're here now. Humans. We can handle this jungle of yours and anything it has to throw at us."

"Give us our weapons, and we'll be on our way," the colonel said with a smile. "We'll kill those people out there, and then we'll leave. You'll never see us again."

Jane unclenched her fists, and Tone saw that her nails had grown out to form small, pointed daggers at the ends of her fingers. How did she do that?

"Colonel, be careful –"

"Shut up, Tone," the colonel said, barely glancing at him. "I don't need to hear a traitor's opinion."

"Let me hit him again," Avery said as he waved the electric sparks through the air.

"Wait," Tone said. "You don't think that I'm working with these...things, do you?"

"Woo!" Avery said, rolling his eyes. "We heard you and this little glikdo last night. Hell, I think you woke the whole jungle. Sounded like bloody animals in heat."

Tone stood there, too stunned to even move. They really thought he'd turned against them? They really thought he'd had sex with this little beast? And that he'd made those god-awful noises while doing it?

"Our weapons," Colonel Walraven said.

Jane launched herself onto his neck, spun him around and onto his knees, and stabbed her dagger-nails through his shirt. Blood oozed out of his side. If Tone had blinked, he would have missed the whole maneuver.

Jane turned to Avery, all of her body hidden behind the colonel except her forehead and eyes.

"Go ahead," she taunted him. "Shoot your lightning at me! Do you think you're such a good shot you can hit me before he's dead?"

"Colonel?" Avery said, the electricity sparking off the ends of his fingers. He shifted back and forth on the balls of his feet, backing away and glancing at the trees and the other two Lygmies who had finally stood up in front of Tone.

The colonel grunted as he tried to grip Jane's hand.

"You would abandon your colonel to the enemy?" Jane said.

"I'm going to kill you!" Avery screamed. He shot a bolt of lightning down the path, completely missing Jane, but sheering off a low-hanging branch beside Tone.

"Avery, don't!" the colonel said. Then, to Jane he whispered, "I can order him to do it and he'll electrocute us both. You don't stand a chance if I tell him to. You have to let me go, and you have to give us our weapons."

"You really think a little lightning can kill me, Colonel?" Jane bit his ear and wouldn't let go.

The colonel grunted as blood dripped down his neck.

"Let go of him!" Avery said, stepping forward again and wadding another electric bolt in his hands.

The trees above him shook with life as three meshet shimmered bright orange. Avery looked up in time to see them land around him.

The path trembled beneath Tone's feet. The vine he held with his right hand snapped and flew back toward his face. As he dodged out of the way, he felt the vine slice across his mouth and cheek. The wooden planks collapsed, the path unraveled, and as Tone fell forward he saw the world tilt and the ground rush up at him.

Water slapped against his face, and he frantically reached out for anything to catch his fall. The vines tangled around him, the planks battered his head and chest, and he gripped something slick and hard. The path slid from the forest canopy, and Tone gripped the sliced branch, riding with the vines through the rain.

The tree flashed into view for only a second before he slammed into the trunk. He lost his grip on the branch, spun upside-down, and slammed his back into the tree. He dangled there several moments, trying to take a breath, trying to see through the pounding rain, trying to figure out why he hadn't fallen to his death. He looked down and saw water everywhere, like a giant lake, except there were trees growing in it.

Something tightened its grip on his ankle, and Tone lifted his head. A bright, orange meshet clung to the trunk above him, one powerful hand gripping his left ankle. It jerked its legs and hoisted him a little ways up the tree, his back and head cracking against the tree and fallen path. It repeated the motion, and this time Tone braced himself so he wouldn't get a concussion.

The rainwater poured down Tone's body, soaking his legs, pooling in the crotch of his pants, and streaming across his chest and face. The meshet pulled him back up the tree one yank at a time until they reached the remainder of the shattered path.

The animal tossed him back against the loose, vine railing, then knelt down on all fours and shook the water from its fur. The fluffy fur rippled as the creature turned green and leaped back into the branches above.

"Kriptu j'ois 'u fen!" Jane yelled as she pulled herself up the tree behind Tone.

He ignored her and stretched his back, the cuts and bruises screaming at him to sit still. He decided they were right, and he touched his stinging face where the vine had sliced him. When he brought his hand away, his fingers were smeared with blood.

"Poojda na ma tr'lena ka ysriptava," Jane said, striding past him. She sounded pissed, but she was ignoring Tone. He decided to sit still until her tirade ended. Besides, he could almost ignore the pain if he didn't move.

A meshet landed with a thud beside Tone, dumped Avery's still body at his feet, then launched itself in the opposite direction, apparently retrieving someone else.

"Baku da gr'oopdhu!" Jane said, waving a finger at Avery.

Two more meshet flew onto the remains of the path and dropped two Lygmies. The first Lygme sat up, shaking its head, but the second lay still where the animal dumped it. Jane waved the meshet off, then knelt beside the still body.

"Nemashtyka," she whispered, pushing aside the Lygme's orange bangs. *"Dup plinta."* She wrapped her arms around the Lygme's neck, hoisted the body up, and started rocking the Lygme.

It was tough to tell through the rain pounding across them, but Tone thought Jane was crying as she hugged the lifeless body to herself.

"Nemashtyka," she said with a sniffle. *"Nemashtyka, plinta."*

The other Lygme shuffled to Jane's side and wrapped her arms around Jane and the dead Lygme. They sat like that for several minutes, rocking and crying, their eyes clenched shut while Tone tried to look anywhere else. He felt like an intruder staring at them, but he didn't know what else to do.

He could see their pain, and he understood their loss, but he had trouble feeling any sorrow. It was a death, sure, but it was only a Lygme death, and moments before, Jane had been threatening to kill the colonel. As far as he was concerned, she got what she deserved. It wasn't a pretty thought, but it was how he felt.

Another meshet landed on the edge of the path and deposited Colonel Walraven's body on the planks. The colonel sat up and crawled to the supporting vines at the side, propping himself up as the meshet jumped into the branches above.

Moments later, another meshet crawled over the broken edge of the path and approached the three Lygmies, a torn vine in one of its paws. It got down on all fours, set its head on Jane's shoulder, and let out a sigh that blew more rainwater into Tone's face. It set the vine beside Jane.

"What a tender moment," Colonel Walraven said. He inspected his shirt where Jane had sliced him with her dagger-nails. "One less Lygme in the galaxy. Oh well."

Jane's eyes slid open and she turned toward the colonel. Tone saw enough of her face to know that she absolutely hated the colonel at that moment. The meshet on her shoulder leaned toward her face and growled at her.

She responded to the meshet with more of her language and then sat back from the dead Lygme. The meshet scooped the Lygme under one arm, gripped the nearest tree, and climbed into the branches above.

Jane turned to Tone.

"He lives," she said, pointing at Avery's body.

Tone didn't know what to say so he just nodded.

"I think we've seen how good your protection is," Walraven said as he struggled to stand. "I believe you were about to give us our weapons and send us on our way."

Jane retrieved the vine snippet the meshet had left at her feet. She shoved it against her nose and inhaled, nearly sucking up the entire thing in one breath, then she turned back to Tone.

"The mechanical human was here," she said.

Jake Alon, that fellow the robots had recorded, was the only "mechanical human" Tone could think of. Was that who she wanted them to kill?

Jane inhaled again, then continued. "He used something to...burn the vines, to make them weak."

A laser knife would do the trick, Tone thought.

"You will kill this mechanical human," Jane said, her eyes clenched shut as she held the vine to her face.

"We'll do no such thing," Colonel Walraven said. "We've been your prisoners and your pawns long enough. Now give us our weapons and let us go."

Jane's orange eyes flashed open. She thrust her hand to her side and spun around, her tiny body seeming to grow with her anger.

"Wait," Tone said, reaching forward to grip her shoulder.

Jane spun on him, her jaw muscles bulging as she ground her teeth. Tone wondered for a moment if he was doing the right thing. He had an idea, but now, staring back at Jane's fiery orange eyes, he wondered if he should have kept his mouth shut. What other choice did they have, though? The colonel wasn't getting anywhere by arguing.

"We'll do it," Tone said, glancing from Jane's hate-filled gaze to Colonel Walraven's hate-filled gaze. "We'll kill the mechanical human."

"Oh, thank you." Jane's clenched jaw transformed into a smile that nearly split her face. She leapt forward, wrapped her tiny arms around Tone's waist, and buried her head in his shirt.

Colonel Walraven glowered and turned away.

35

Rhaina

river trail

Rhaina stepped from the boat, her boots squishing into the muddy beach and the rain pounding against her poncho. She shielded her eyes and stared. The lake water lapped across the beach, spreading through the mud and washing across the carved step leading to the overgrown path and further on to the stone temple hidden beneath the forest canopy.

The temple's three tiers ascended to the canopy's lowest branches, and the temple's mammoth rock structure spread across the clearing as far as Rhaina could see from the right to the left. Slits were cut into each of the levels, apparently for windows. Long, stone walkways extended around the perimeter of each roof. Defense? Sight-seeing? Wide gutters had been carved along the edges of each level, either by the pounding rain or by the Lygme occupants years ago, and the rain ran like waterfalls off every corner and into an overflowing pool that encircled the building.

Deep green moss hung like a ragged, tattered quilt across the temple, accenting the sharp, black and white lines of the immense stone walls. She had known that something like this existed, but none of her research had prepared her for the grand scale on which it had been built.

Sawn coughed behind her.

"Are we going?" he said, his sunglassed eyes staring at her. "Or are we going to admire the architecture all day?"

She looked from him to Cailin. Khonane stood behind her, finally well enough to walk without assistance. Majid stared at her from his place at the boat's railing, and the three Lygmies held the pouncer, Silny.

"Cailin," she said, stepping aside, "you and Sawn grab earpieces and scout the perimeter. Make sure we're alone, and see if you can find an underground passage into this thing."

"We can't walk straight in?" Cailin asked.

"When has anything ever been that easy?" She turned to Khonane. "Feeling good enough to load up that frizz?"

"I think so."

"Good. Do it." The Lygmies started to edge past her and she put a hand on Ko's shoulder. "Tell your little friends to tie that pouncer to a tree, then help me get our supplies."

Silny squirmed from his place in the Lygme's arms. "I'll get wet," he said.

"Yeah, we all have problems."

Within a half hour, Cailin and Sawn returned from finding an underground entrance, the frizz was loaded down with their camp supplies, and they secured the boat to the same tree the Lygmies used for Silny. They marched up the slick, stone steps through the rain, the frizz bellowing its complaints at every step.

Rhaina remembered back to all the times she'd seen this gem in the Eternity of Souls. There was the jungle, which they'd already walked through, the barrier, which she could only assume was the lake/river they'd crossed, and then there was some kind of stasis field, something that protected this gem from the outside world. She'd always assumed the field would be obvious, maybe even running when they arrived, something they would have to break through to get in, or maybe something that hid the entire area from view. But she saw nothing like that now. In fact, nothing but the surrounding jungle kept this temple from view. She sent her Geminai to scout the area. She'd already seen so many things go wrong on this trip that she wasn't going to take any chances now.

Geminai soared ahead of everyone else, scanning the ground and air, sailing around trees and rocks and over the expansive moat surrounding the temple. The place was deserted. There were hardly any animals except insects and birds. The trees and vines, however, seemed to have grown into and out of the temple walls until they were as much a part of the building as the stones and mortar.

Two more passes around the temple, and Geminai returned to Rhaina's body with nothing new to report.

"Everything okay?" Khonane asked, hanging back from the rest of the group.

"I don't know." She shielded her face with her hand as she walked, trying to make out anything dangerous within or around the mammoth structure. "Are you getting any vibes? Anything wrong, or anything bad?" She meant his Geminai, of course.

"No. You?"

"No. And that's what worries me. This...." She gestured at the temple, the path, the confident stride of the Lygmies leading them along. "It's too easy."

"Maybe the Lygmies are lying to us. Maybe they took us to a different temple."

"This is the right place," she said, recalling Geminai's visions. "But something's not right. Keep an eye out."

They caught up with everyone else at the mouth to the underground entrance. Sawn and Majid looked at Rhaina through their cold, tech'd eyes, while Cailin and the Lygmies hovered under the stone archway to keep out of the rain.

Rhaina looked past them all, through the opening, and down the stone steps, shining a light into the darkness below. The rain ran down the steps and pooled at the bottom. She couldn't tell how deep. The walls were coated with moist, brown algae. The tunnel went on farther than her light could reach.

"As if we weren't wet enough already," Cailin said from beside her.

"I am not going down there," Silny said.

"Majid," Rhaina said, turning to the plastic man. "You and Khonane stay up here with the Lygmies. Sawn and Cailin, you're with me."

"That is unacceptable," Majid said, stepping forward. "Mr. Rosh has instructed that I stay with you until you find the gem."

"And I'm instructing you to stay up here with the Lygmies. Believe me, finding this gem will not be simple. I'm going down there, take a look around, and then I'll be right back. Fifteen minutes at the most."

"If you are gone longer, I'll come after you."

"You leave these Lygmies alone with our supplies, and I'll deactivate you."

"You do not know how."

Rhaina smirked, then turned and led the way down the steps, Cailin and Sawn behind her. *This is the home stretch,* she thought. *Riches beyond my imagination, and then I can retire from hellholes like this.* She reached to steady herself against the wall, and her fingers sank into the cold, brown moss.

"Yuck," she said, flicking the sticky strands into the water below.

36

Jake

jungle canopy trail

End of the line, Jake thought as he came to a halt. The suspended path stopped, open air and a few hanging vines the only thing beyond the last board. He dropped to his knees and pushed aside the branches, expecting to see the expanse of lake water still beneath him. Instead, he saw the open roof of a pinnacle, the stones and mortar crumbled away beneath the weight of vines and branches stretching down from the canopy.

He checked his implants, found his place on all the charts, maps, and schematics he'd stored, and determined that he was at the hidden temple. He grinned. His work for the past couple years was finally paying off. All that sucking up to jackin' federal bosses, all the manipulation of data, all the secret rendezvous – another few steps, and it would all be worth it. He'd be wealthier than he ever imagined possible.

He gripped a vine, checked that it was secure, and slid down from the canopy. The clearing stretched out beneath him, all mud and vegetation and flowing water. The temple seemed to ripple from the water flowing in streams down every side of it, like he was looking down on a reflection in a pool. He almost believed the image, except for the solid peak directly beneath him, the beams and stones sticking out at life-threatening angles to him as he worked his way down.

The vine ended several tics off the floor of the pinnacle's open platform. Jake spotted what looked like the sturdiest part and let go. He landed with a thudding splash in the pooled water and slipped to his knees. He sat up and rubbed at the pain in his legs as he studied the small room. The long, narrow windows were set high in the stone walls and were nearly overgrown with moss and tiny bushes that grew from the cracks in the mortar. There was no door to the room, and Jake wasn't sure how he was supposed to get out except to scale the walls.

He stood and started searching through the water on the floor, looking for any kind of hole or door. Nothing.

Walking to the center of the room again, he stared at the vine dangling above his head. He could get to it easily, but any un-tech'd human would find it nearly impossible. A Lygme would never stand a chance.

He realized then what he had to do, that he had to think like a Lygme. It made sense they would design some way to get out of this little room. They were short, they were fast, and they were tough. So what would they do to get in and out of here?

Jake walked the perimeter of the room and inspected the corners. They were solid, stone against stone in the walls, and the wooden floor beams were installed tight. So where did the water go when it drained out?

He pounded his left foot against the floor, splashing his boot through the water, and watched the little bubbles drift away from him until they popped. He stepped forward and repeated the process several times until he found the narrow drain slit in the floor by one wall. He knelt down and felt around until his hand hit on a lever installed within the drain.

"Clever little Lygmies," he muttered, flicking the switch.

The floor dropped away beneath him, dumping him in a current of water down a blackened chute. He struggled to grab hold of anything, but the sides were slick from years of polishing by the rushing rainwater. A twist, a turn, and Jake flipped onto his back, then back onto his stomach. He blinked, twisted his eyes to the right, and the implants kicked on. The visual amplifiers brought the tunnel to life in blurring greens and blacks, and the tech estimated he'd dropped nearly thirty tics already.

The tunnel twisted to the right and suddenly ended, shooting Jake across a pool of water on his belly. He struggled against the momentum as a wall rushed at him. The water filled his mouth and nose, and he came to a coughing, sputtering halt, his arms in front of him and the wall half a tic from his head.

He put his feet down and rammed his knee into the floor. Cussing at the pain, he splashed around until he finally stood up in the knee-deep water and looked around through the darkness. He was in a long, narrow hallway, the water leisurely drifting past him on its way to wherever it went next.

"Great," he muttered, looking back and forth down the tunnel. "I travel halfway across the galaxy to fall into the alien sewer system." The tech didn't find anything unique about either the left or the right passages, so on a whim he turned left. As he did, he saw a large head disappear back into the wall and a rock get replaced.

All the stories of giant sewer rats and alligators came to his mind. It was an irrational fear, and he knew that, but he still decided that the right-hand tunnel was the better way to go.

37

Rhaina

jungle temple

Rhaina led the way through nearly waist-deep water, Majid at her side. Sawn walked behind her, then Khonane, and Cailin watched the rear. She focused on the task at hand, looking for a place to begin their search for the God's Eye gem.

The Lygmies waded along behind her, their necks strained to keep their heads above water. Ko had tried to hold the pouncer in front of him and above the water, but the little animal struggled for several minutes, hissed for several more, and finally climbed to the top of his head and arched its back. The Lygme didn't seem to mind, not even when Silny's claws cut through his thick, black hair and into his scalp.

The pouncer was an unknown factor in this whole trek. He claimed that the Resurrected Mother soldiers brought him along, but he couldn't give a good reason why. He said he knew why the Resurrected Mothers were in the jungle, but he claimed that reason was sight-seeing. He said he'd been separated from the group accidentally, but he didn't want anyone to take him back – not that Rhaina had been serious when she offered. Simply put, the little animal was lying, and he was terrible at it.

But that left Rhaina with a whole different set of problems. What did the pouncer really know, especially about their gem? Had he been the Resurrected Mothers' prisoner? If so, what made him so valuable? If not, why didn't he want to go back? Above all, why did the pouncer want to be with the Lygmies all the time? It almost seemed like he knew them, and that thought bothered her more than all the others.

"You said there was a place to store our supplies," Majid said. "When do we get to it?"

"Stop questioning me," she said with a sigh. The plastic man had repeatedly asked her about the temple. How far had they gone? What was down there? And in several different ways, had they found any evidence of the gem? If she hadn't known he was a plastic man, she would have thought he was excited.

They turned down a corridor to their right, climbed a short flight of stairs out of the water, and entered a long, narrow room. The tattered, moldy remains of a thin curtain hung from the ceiling at the far end and probably divided the room years before being abandoned to the elements.

"Finally," Silny said. He jumped off Ko's head, ran to a corner, and started bathing himself.

"Khonane, see if you can make those work," Rhaina said, gesturing to the lamps set in small alcoves along the walls. She turned to Cailin. "You and Sawn unload the supplies and set up camp."

"This will never work," Majid said as he surveyed the dark room. "There's no ventilation, and there's no way of escape if those Resurrected Mothers corner us in here."

"Are you joking?" Rhaina asked, staring at the plastic man. She pointed at the wall above the stairs and shone her light through a narrow slit. "Ventilation," she said. She turned around and aimed the beam at the wall behind the dais. "And there's a hidden door in those rocks. It's a little short, probably Lygme-size, but we can fit." She looked back at the plastic man standing with his hands on his hips. He seemed to be studying the wall behind the dais, almost as if he was having trouble seeing it in the dark.

"Wow," Cailin said with a chuckle. "I can't believe you missed that. I always thought plastic men were perfect."

"I hadn't yet turned around to see the ventilation," he said with a sigh. "Now I'm going to scout the hallway below, make sure we're really alone." He spun around and stomped back down the stone steps, the water splashing around him.

Sawn stepped forward and leaned to Rhaina's ear.

"I've never seen a plastic man act that way."

"It did seem odd," she whispered back.

"Did you get a kill switch for him?"

"Of course."

"I suggest you keep it nearby."

A light flared through the room, bathing them all in its warm, orange glow. The walls seemed to flicker, reflecting the single point of light back and around them. Khonane replaced a small, lit lamp into its alcove, the room dimming only slightly, and turned back to Rhaina.

"Still had fuel," he said with a shrug.

"Good work." Rhaina turned her attention back to the stairwell and wondered what the plastic man was doing down there. He didn't need to go down there to see if someone was coming; he could use his plastic-man-augmented-ears to hear anyone walking through all that water.

She sent her Geminai down the stairs and looked at the temple through her eyes. The walls glowed shimmering blue, and the water seemed like silver glass. Geminai floated above the surface of the silver water and scanned the hallways left and right. Ripples drifted back from the right, deeper into the temple than any of them had gone.

He's searching for the gem, Rhaina thought. She brought herself back with such a gasp that everyone in the room turned to her.

"Sawn, you're with me," Rhaina said, grabbing her flashlight. She unclipped the pistol from her belt and headed down the stairs, not even turning to see if Sawn followed her. "Cailin, Khonane, keep an eye on the Lygmies."

She crept down the stairs and back into the cold water, disturbing the ripples as little as possible. Sawn walked behind her, his gun out and at his side. She signaled for him to stay quiet, then glanced through Geminai to get directions. Geminai had moved down the hall to the right about twenty tics, and she was waiting at the next bend where the walkway angled higher and the water ran at knee height.

Rhaina put her hand to the shirt pocket that held the plastic man's kill switch, then moved slowly forward. She kept the light dimmed and pointed at the water, bright enough that she wouldn't walk into anything. She tried not to touch the wall as she came upon Geminai.

The plastic man stood around the corner and down the hall, about fifteen tics away. Rhaina could hear the machine splashing through the water with each step it took, and it seemed to be talking to itself. Or was it talking to someone else? She strained to hear, but she couldn't make out the words.

Geminai glanced around the corner, but what she saw confused both her and Rhaina. The plastic man stood in the center of the hallway with his back to them, and he spoke into the darkness ahead. But another image, a second presence, hovered within the plastic man's shell, making his mechanical body glow a brilliant black. It looked like a double-exposure.

Majid stepped to the right with a violent splash, and the second image followed a split-second later. The machine kept up the babbling, and the double-exposure seemed to babble right along with him, but neither Rhaina nor Geminai could catch the words.

She stepped around the corner, catching Geminai within herself as she did. She started to say something to Majid when the double-exposed image turned around. A head, and then an entire body leaped out of Majid's mechanical skin. The eyes opened wide, and the second person gaped at her for almost a second. The image rounded back on the plastic man and vanished with a muffled pop.

Majid turned around.

"What's going on?" Rhaina asked, shining the light into the plastic man's face. Geminai raced ahead and scanned the water, the walls, and further down the hall for any sign of the second image – a free-floating spirit – but she couldn't find that it had even been there.

"I saw something," Majid said, pointing further down the hall. He seemed calm now, more like the machine she'd met back on Earth than the erratic one she'd seen since reaching the temple. Could the temple itself be affecting him?

"Well I heard something." Rhaina watched the machine carefully. She really didn't think it would flinch at her comment, but she had to try.

"I doubt you heard anything," Majid said, turning around to face the darkness again. "It's not making any noise."

"So what's there?" she asked, stepping forward.

"I don't know. Watch the water."

She watched. Small waves lapped at the walls, and ripples washed past them. Tiny bubbles bounced along the water's surface where Rhaina's light struck them.

"It's us," Rhaina said.

The plastic man lifted his foot and stomped down with enough force to splash Rhaina's shirt. She jumped back. Water sprayed around them, and Majid pointed down the hall.

"That is us," he said, indicating the new, larger ripples.

"Why don't you just yell that we're here," Rhaina said, wading back to his side.

Sawn gripped her shoulder and tugged her back. "They already know," he said.

"You see them too?" Majid asked.

"Tell me what's there," Rhaina said. She struggled to see anything through the darkness, then urged her Geminai forward to see through her eyes. The shimmering blue walls grew damp and dingy as slivers of brown oozed from between the cracks, poured down the walls, and streamed into the water. They pooled into globs that floated on the silvery surface. The globs drifted into the center of the stream and fused into larger masses, spreading from one side of the hall to the other.

"It's like a dance of light," Sawn whispered.

Rhaina stared at him. Were they even looking at the same thing?

"Light?" Majid said. "It's more like a hole that's swallowing all the light into itself."

"Let's go," Rhaina said, stepping back.

"Why?" Majid asked. "What do you see?"

"Something different. Now let's move." She led the way back to the corner, turned left and tried to rush through the deepening water.

"We should investigate that hallway," Majid said as he splashed along behind her.

"We should get back to the rest of our team."

"Then I'll go back alone."

"You will stay with us." She turned to make sure he was following, and that's when she saw the face behind Sawn's left shoulder. It was a woman's face, dark brown with streaks of silver running from the line of her soaking wet hair, down her forehead and past her eyes, across her cheeks and down her neck. Dark green eyes glittered through the darkness, and the woman grinned.

Rhaina started to yell a warning when the woman gripped Sawn's shoulders and yanked him into the air. Bright, silver wings fanned out behind her, and the woman lifted Sawn to the ceiling. Her wings beat the air around her and tipped into the river, spraying water.

Sawn struggled in her grip, beating at her hands and arms to break free, but the woman turned to fly away with him.

Majid lunged forward and gripped Sawn's boot, pulling both him and the woman into the water. He struggled against her arms and wings, finally dragging Sawn out from beneath her and staggering back to Rhaina.

The woman's wings unfurled from the water and spread to touch both sides of the hall. She lifted her head from the water and turned to glare at them, her eyes wide. Her wings locked against the walls and lifted her silver body from the water.

Rhaina sited her gun at the woman and pulled the trigger. The shot struck. Liquid gushed from the wound in the woman's belly, and she started to collapse back into the river. Her wings shrunk and she lost her grip on the walls. Her hair dissolved down her face. Her arms shriveled into mere sticks of their powerful form. The woman slipped beneath the surface of the water, her body dissolving away.

Majid leaned a hand down where the woman had disappeared, then looked at Rhaina.

"Nothing," he said.

"Like hell that was nothing," Sawn said as he stood back up. "That jackin' beast was trying to kidnap me."

"Come on," Rhaina said, waving them with her. "Let's go ask our Lygmies some questions."

38

Rhaina

"Guardians," Ko whispered, nodding at his Lygme companions.

"Yes," the other two said. "Guardians."

"What the hell is a guardian?" Sawn said from where he sat across the dimly lit room. He wiped the last of the mossy grime from his hair, then threw his towel into a wadded ball in the corner.

"A creature of *bwyuchi kai gure*," Ko said. *"Kluirehu bin jhazhre sling. Kendium pindulumsyn hre nab gastlisnk-"*

"Hey!" Rhaina said. "Enough with the Lygmese."

"They said the guardians are a creature of the king of the water wall," Majid said.

"I understood them," Rhaina said. "And the word wasn't 'water wall,' it was 'stormfall.'"

"In the vernacular, certainly," Majid said, nodding. "But predicated by the formal '*kai*' title, the word takes on the less ambiguous translation of 'water wall.'"

"Forget the grammar lessons," Sawn said. "Ko, how many of these guardians are down here?"

"They are creatures of the water," Ko said, shrugging.

"Meaning you won't tell us?"

"He is telling us," Rhaina said with a sigh. "He's telling us he doesn't know."

"No," Ko said, standing up and glaring at Rhaina. "They are here, everywhere. They are creatures of the water."

"You already said that." Rhaina glanced from Ko to the other Lygmies, and she saw the fear in their wide eyes. Something about these guardians had to be really nasty if they could make the Lygmies so scared.

"Bu dishka di," Ko muttered. He stepped forward and gripped Rhaina's hand in his own tiny, calloused fingers. He continued, speaking each word slowly and precisely. "Guardians - are - water."

"Shit," Sawn said.

"Oh, we are so jacked," Cailin whispered.

"Ko," Rhaina said, kneeling down to look him in the eye. "Let's make sure we're saying the same thing. Are you telling me those creatures don't live in the water, but that they are water?"

"Yes."

"Through and through?"

"Yes."

Silny started snuffling from his place in the corner.

Sawn whipped his gun around and aimed at the pouncer. "Shut up," he said.

Silny licked his lips, then lowered his head to his paws with a sigh. He shut his eyes, but kept his ears cocked to the conversation.

"Tell us how to kill them," Rhaina said.

"You cannot," Ko said. "They are water."

Rhaina stared into the Lygme's golden eyes and tried to decide how much to trust his explanation. He sounded sincere, and he certainly looked scared. Living water creatures was something she'd never heard before, not in any of her research. If the Lygmies knew so much about them, why didn't they mention the things before now? Was this some tricky Lygme ploy?

"Rhaina," Khonane said from his place standing guard. "I think we have visitors." He backed away from the stairs and into the room, his gun drawn and aimed at the water below.

Majid rushed to his side.

"What's down there?" Rhaina asked, standing up and gripping the pistol at her belt.

"More guardians," Majid said.

39

Jake

jungle temple

Jake splashed through ankle-deep water, his implants feeding the digitized data into his brain that allowed him to navigate the black tunnel. The creature he'd first seen had followed him all afternoon. He could hear the thing walking, but every time he turned to see it, the noises stopped, and the tunnel looked empty.

He knew it wasn't his imagination. The thing had a rhythm to the way it followed him, to the way it moved and breathed. Its steps sounded heavy in the darkness, like it was bulky or sluggish. But if the thing was that cumbersome, it shouldn't have been able to hide so well.

He rounded a corner and almost ran head-first into a set of metal bars blocking his way. His implants analyzed them in a flash: old and slightly oxidized, they looked like they had been pounded into the stone ceiling and floor centuries earlier. Pale vines twined around the bars, and their leaves felt sticky and alive. A quick jerk at the bars proved they were still solid.

Jake pushed aside the tangle of vines and peered out from between the bars to the hallway beyond. Another barred door stood directly opposite him. His tech spotted a pile of bones in the corner that were about the size of a Lygme adult. Half a dozen gated doors lined the hallway to the right. The wall to the left had been chiseled in a jumble of Lygmese that warned everyone that death waited for them inside this cell – the cell Jake was now standing in.

Not only the sewer system, he thought, but also the death chamber. This just got better and better.

The lumbering, shuffling steps advanced, and Jake peered back the way he'd come. The hallway was empty, but this time the steps didn't stop. For the first time, his tech was able to capture the sounds clearly enough to analyze them and make some estimates about their nature. Assuming the thing weighed two hundred kels – which was probably a good estimate considering how much noise it made – then the tech calculated the creature to be at least four tics high.

That thought sent a shiver down Jake's sweaty back. He scanned the walls, the floor, the ceiling, anything he could see for a way to get out. Everything looked solid.

The steps splashed closer, and Jake glimpsed a pair of eyes on the end of short stalks poking up from the shallow water. His tech recalculated the creature's mass based on those eyes and told him the thing was probably four to five tics long instead of only four tics tall. *As if I couldn't have figured that out on my own,* he thought.

He turned back to the metal bars and tried to pry them loose. They didn't budge. He felt along the edges for weaknesses. The bars and gate were strong enough they could have been installed yesterday.

Water sloshed behind him, and the tech estimated the creature to be twenty tics away. He did not feel like fighting something that large, no matter how slow it moved through the water. He shoved one foot through a tangle of vines, gripped the bars, and hoisted himself up. His boots slid along the flaking rust, and he struggled to stay up. Yanking himself higher, his foot snapped a thin vine. His hand caught the cell's upper ledge, and he swung himself up.

The ledge ran along the cell's wall, beneath the ceiling, and Jake swung around and onto it. Loose gravel scraped against his arms and legs as he shoved himself deeper. This wouldn't do at all when the creature attacked, he thought, but at least he had a different perspective on the long hallway and its water-logged drainage system.

The creature snorted and snuffled beneath him as if it knew he was there. It sprayed water against the wall, and Jake thought he heard claws scraping the stones. He would have to move soon, and he still didn't have a plan that didn't involve fighting – or lots and lots of running.

A woman's face suddenly appeared before him, her features dark brown with silver highlights running down her forehead, past her eyes and cheeks, and down her long neck. Her eyes flashed silver as she gripped Jake's shirt and yanked him from the protective alcove.

He fell to the ground, water splashing all around and his knees and hands scraping the hard floor. He scrabbled up to find the woman who attacked him. Instead, the water creature sprang up on its hind legs, reared back, and took a swipe at his head.

Jake revved to Fighting Mode and let his tech take over. The creature seemed to slow to a crawl as the tech sped up Jake's thought and motor processes. He ducked and rolled through the water and to the side of the creature. As his tech had calculated, the thing stood nearly five tics high. Its arms and legs were thick with rolling fat, and its hide blood-streaked where patches of fur were torn away.

The thing let out a bellow as it twisted its stubby snout around to find Jake again. Its eye stalks swivelled and bent around to search him out in the darkness.

Jake turned to sprint back down the hallway when something gripped him by his belt and yanked him backwards. He twisted around and grabbed the slick, wet arm of the silver-eyed woman still holding his belt. She grinned.

Jake slapped her hand from his belt.

Her other hand came around so fast that Jake's tech barely caught the movement. She gripped his jacket.

The bug-eyed creature snarled, and they turned to see it charging at them.

As the woman released Jake, he sprang to the wall behind him.

A pair of silver wings fanned out to the woman's sides, and she lifted off the ground and out of the water.

Jake's tech calculated his odds and found them pretty low. He could probably handle the slow, bug-eyed creature, or he could take on the lightning-fast winged woman, but even in Fighting Mode, he would have a hard time fighting them both at once. As much as he hated to do it, he turned and ran.

He splashed down the long, black tunnel, his tech mapping the return route. He heard the bug-eyed creature howl as it lumbered along, and he heard the powerful woosh of the woman's wings behind him.

He dropped to the ground, and the woman flew past him. She circled in the narrow tunnel and hovered a dozen tics away. Jake could still hear the bug-eyed creature approaching from behind, and he didn't like being caught between these two.

The woman cocked her head at Jake as she ran her hands down the front of her body to smooth out her shimmering robe. The silver streaks down her dark face seemed to shine more brilliantly as she spread her lips to display a pair of fangs.

Still in Fighting Mode, Jake bolted forward and took a swing at the woman's head. She blocked his fist, then aimed a punch at his kidneys.

He side-stepped her, threw an upper-cut to her jaw.

She backed out of reach, her wings beating rapidly, and aimed a kick at his groin.

He caught her foot and shoved her away.

They kicked and punched and slashed at each other as Jake desperately tried to outpace her. She matched him at every turn, no matter what offense his tech tried to throw. She was amazing, and he made sure that his implants recorded her every move so he could review them later.

The bug-eyed creature roared, and Jake took a little of his attention away from the fight. His defense slowed, and the winged-woman landed a punch to his stomach.

He stumbled back, and the woman laughed as he fell on his behind in the middle of the water-logged hall.

The bug-eyed creature thundered behind him, and Jake turned to see the thing lunging at his head.

He struggled to stand and defend himself.

The winged woman flew at him, landed on top of him, and wrapped her arms and legs around his body. She forced him under the water, then shoved him along beneath her as she flew toward the bug-eyed thing.

His tech sealed up his nose and mouth. He felt a bone-wrenching jolt as they struck the bug-eyed creature and knocked it off its feet. The woman continued down the hallway, dragging Jake beneath the water.

As they reached the end of the hall, the woman arced toward the ceiling. She shoved aside a hinged stone, flew through the opening, then slammed the stone back into place and dropped Jake onto it.

He stepped back as far as he could, which wasn't far in the claustrophobia-inducing pit. Except it wasn't really a pit, Jake thought as he glanced at the trap door at his feet. He hoped those hinges were strong enough to hold both him and this winged woman because it was at least a six tic drop back to the water-logged tunnel.

He looked back at the woman, but her wings had disappeared. She stared at him with intense, bright silver eyes, but she didn't make any move to hurt him. He smiled at her.

She smiled back.

"You're...uh...a really good fighter," he said.

She raised her hand, and Jake tensed. Instead of taking another swing at him, though, she brushed one dark finger against his lips.

"Bootah," she said. It was Lygmese, and it meant "fighter." It was more than that, though. She was calling him a great fighter, an expert warrior, one who had vanquished a great evil.

"No," he said, shaking his head. "I didn't kill that...whatever it was. You did."

"Likde bur," she said, but he didn't know what that meant. It almost sounded like a name, or maybe a title. Was she calling him that, or was she referring to the creature in the hallway below? Of course, he could have been way off and she was telling him what she ate for dinner.

He took her hand away from his mouth and held it lightly. Her skin felt slick, almost oily, and he noticed for the first time that she smelled a little salty, almost like she'd spent too long playing in the ocean.

"What are you?" he whispered.

She withdrew her hand from his and pointed up the long tunnel above. Jake followed her gaze and saw a series of rungs pounded into the stones.

"Up," she said.

"You know my language?"

"Up."

"Okay, I'll climb up. Great. But first, you have to tell me what you are. Please."

The silver streaks down her dark face started to glow more brilliantly again, and she smiled at him. Then her form collapsed in a gush of water that sprayed across Jake's body. The water splashed against the walls, pooled at his feet, and started draining through the cracks in the stone door beneath him.

Jake wiped the water from his face and eyes. His tech had been recording when the woman disappeared so he instructed it to replay the last few seconds. The recording played in slow-motion within his mind, and he watched as the woman's "skin" melted away. Her face, her body, her clothes...everything vanished, leaving a body of water standing before him with nothing holding it together. Then it collapsed at his feet.

Jake told his implants to file those last few seconds of images in a secure place in his head where he could look at it again later. That woman was worth much more study, he thought. He put his hands to the cold, wet rungs and started climbing.

40

Tone

jungle canopy trail

"Yes," Jane hissed.

Tone stood far back from the abrupt end of the suspended bridge. Jane, however, clung to a vine and hung beyond the bridge, her bare feet clinging to the edge of the last rubbery board as she studied something beneath them. Tone stared at her bright orange toenails and filthy, blackened feet and wondered when she'd removed her shoes. Did she paint those nails that god-awful color, or did they just grow that way naturally?

"Yes," Jane said as she swung herself back onto the end of the bridge and stared at Tone. "Yes."

Tone shuffled his feet and tried to look at anything but her. She had that same hungry glaze to her eyes that she'd had last night when she attacked him. It was getting toward evening again, and Tone did not want a repeat of that sexual display. He glanced at Colonel Walraven and found him peering over the vine railing too. What did they find so interesting down there?

"Tone," Jane said, tugging on his shirt.

He tried not to twitch away as he looked down.

"You're coming with me," she said.

"No," Tone said, almost in a panic.

Avery and the colonel turned to watch.

"Yes," Jane said, tugging him down to kneel before her. "Tone, I need you."

He started to look around, tried to find somewhere to run, some way to get away from this crazy Lygme and her perverted ideas. He glanced back at her dilated eyes, and he had to wonder if this would be the end of him.

"Good," she said, nodding. She turned to the other two Lygmies, snapped her fingers at them, and pointed at Colonel Walraven and Avery.

"Now just one damn minute!" the colonel said, taking a quick step back. "We are not your little sex toys, no matter what you do with Tone."

It wasn't exactly the support Tone hoped for, but he was glad to hear the colonel was at least arguing.

"Sex toys?" Jane said, turning to the colonel and grinning. Tone couldn't tell if she was honestly amused or savoring his discomfort. "That is what you believe?"

"Give us a reason not to," Avery said. He cracked his knuckles and tiny sparks bounced between his fingers.

Jane burst out laughing. Cackling at the men, she bent over and clutched her belly. She snorted the air back through her nose and almost fell over as she was caught up in a bout of laughter.

Tone backed away. He couldn't go far with the other two Lygmies watching so closely, but he put another tic between himself and Jane.

She stopped laughing as suddenly as she'd begun, and she stood up straight and looked at Colonel Walraven. Her face had grown hard and her jaw shook as she spoke.

"It is no concern of yours what I do to keep off the *midpa'ah*." She turned to Tone, but she didn't touch him this time. "Come. You are still safe with me."

Before he had a chance to argue, a large paw settled on his shoulder, and he turned to see a meshet towering behind him. He started to back away, but the animal scooped him up in its arms and threw him over its shoulder. Jane climbed the meshet's back and clung to its furry hide as it shuffled to the edge of the bridge.

Tone had enough time to see the colonel and Avery, under great protest, get thrown across the other meshet with the remaining two Lygmies, and then they all took flight. The creature spread its skin flap and dropped away from the bridge. Tone tried to see where they were going, but the meshet fell on a large branch, pivoted forward until Tone saw the world upside-down, then snapped back with enough force to make him dizzy.

Jane grinned up at him from her place on the animal's back.

The meshet spun around and dropped away again. This time the rain pelted Tone's back and washed down his head. He watched the tree they were on disappear in a blur of movement, and then the meshet landed on something distinctly solid. It pivoted forward and released its grip on Tone.

He panicked as he thought of falling a hundred tics to his death. Instead, he landed with a crack to his head on a hard, wet stone.

The meshet stood over him, studying his face as Jane climbed off its back. Apparently satisfied it hadn't killed him, the meshet stood up straight and launched itself back into the trees and rain. Tone watched it fly until its orange fur rippled green and it blended back into the forest. The other two meshet swooped down and deposited Avery and Colonel Walraven.

Wiping the rainwater from his eyes, Tone turned around on the long, rough stone. They had landed on a narrow roof, and the surrounding forest looked like something out of a holoshow. Pillars and other rooftops surrounded them. Water pooled in the corners and poured in great falls into a large moat overflowing the expanse of buildings. Green, white, and red vines clung to the walls like multi-hued carpets encircling them.

Jane walked to the center of the rooftop, swept her hand along the stones, and gripped a metal ring. Her eyes flashed orange and her arm muscles bulged as she hefted open a black, stone trap door.

"Follow me," she said, and she dropped down the hole.

Tone went to the hole and looked. The room beneath was dim, the light shining through the hole illuminating enough for Tone to know he wouldn't hurt himself getting down.

He knelt, swung his legs into the hole, and jumped. He landed with a splash in the center of the room, then turned back up to the hole above him. The rainwater wasn't falling on him anymore, and it looked like it struck an invisible barrier where the stone used to be. Had the Lygmies developed some sort of matter displacing technology? If so, he was impressed. That was something the Earth scientists were still trying to do.

Tone turned to stare at Jane. Did that explain why they hadn't gotten wet the entire time they'd walked along that bridge? He'd heard rain falling all around him, but he hadn't gotten wet until the meshet rushed them down to this building. The Lygmies could have turned off their machines for the flight down, then turned them back on once they safely landed. And since the only one down here was Jane, then she must be the one carrying the tech. But where?

That thought made him hesitate. Jane was the most unstable Lygme he'd ever seen. He'd heard stories about them going crazy, about them wiping out whole groups of people, but he'd never seen one actually spiraling into that madness. Matter displacement technology would be an incredible thing to bring back to Earth, assuming he didn't get himself killed trying to get it from her.

He heard raised voices above him and turned to look back through the hole. The Lygmies were babbling so fast in their own language that Tone couldn't understand a word they said, and Colonel Walraven and Avery were shouting back obscenities.

Tone looked at Jane, but she didn't seem to care. She had her hands pressed against the rocks. Her eyes were closed, and she hummed some tune as she swayed back and forth against the wall.

A bolt of lightning lanced through the hole, nearly striking Tone's arm, and he ducked to a side wall. Jane still didn't move.

Avery slid through the hole and fell to the floor on his back in a wash of water and gravel. Something cracked, and he screamed, rolling to his side and clutching his right arm.

Tone started to go to him, but one of the Lygmies jumped down the hole and landed at Avery's side. The Lygme's eyes were huge, and he thrust the point of a knife under Avery's throat. The Lygme's shirt was in tatters, and his shoulder and arm were scorched black.

Jane snapped her fingers, and the Lygme turned to her.

"Let the human go," she whispered. She kept her eyes closed and her hands pressed against the stone wall.

The Lygme snarled something in his language, then slipped the knife in a sheath and stepped away.

"Tone," Jane said. "Care for your companion."

Before Tone could move, Colonel Walraven jumped down the hole. Blood ran from his nose, and his left eye looked red and swollen. The third Lygme jumped down after him, and the colonel backed away from him.

Tone went to Avery and started examining the arm.

The two Lygmies mimicked Jane's actions on two other walls, placing their hands against the stones and humming as they swayed.

Tone was far from medically trained, but he couldn't feel any breaks in Avery's arm. The man could have fractured something during the fall, especially since he winced every time Tone got near his wrist. Tone ripped a few strips of cloth from the end of his shirt and wrapped Avery's arm from the wrist to the elbow.

By the time he'd finished, the Lygmies had turned around and faced the center of the small room. Their mouths moved, but nothing came out. Their eyes glazed, cloudy as they stared straight ahead.

The room started to shake as a low rumble echoed through the windows. Tone stood and looked outside and saw the moat water churning as if it boiled. Steam began to rise from the surface, punctuated by the falling rain.

Colonel Walraven joined Tone at the window.

"What's happening?" Avery asked from the middle of the room.

Creatures rose from the churning water. The long hair hung before their eyes, their speckled hides looked knobby, and their long snouts extended far beyond their short necks. Tone saw a row of teeth flash as one of the creatures opened its mouth and bellowed into the rain. The rest of the creatures in the water reared back on their hind legs and responded to the cry with their own howls. They all stood up on their short legs and started to move out of the moat, joining their leader on the muddy ground. Tone remembered the Lygmies called them "partomes."

"Avery," Jane said. "Strike your lightning at the bubbling water."

Avery went to the window and looked at the creatures below.

"Are those the things that attacked us?" he asked.

"They are," Jane said.

"Just shoot the bastards," Colonel Walraven said, turning from the window.

Avery held his left hand out the window and threw a bolt of electricity down at the moat. It struck the water and flared through the moat, along the banks, and across several tics of the muddy ground. The partomes screamed as the electricity coursed through their bodies. They fell to the ground, writhing in pain as Avery kept the power discharging from his hand.

The Lygmies started to hum again, more loudly this time, and with more of a sense of direction to their music. One of them stomped his boot in rhythm against the stone floor.

Tone caught words and phrases that he knew, things he'd heard before. The song sounded like a prayer, like the Lygmies were imploring some hero figure, maybe even a divine figure, for help in what they were doing. He didn't realize the little beasts had any sense of spirituality. He'd never seen it in their dealings with humans.

The water bubbled higher and started to look more like a wall of water than any kind of pool or moat. Avery's electrical charges flashed and rippled through the rising water, sparking to the ground like lightning from a violent storm.

"I think that's enough," Tone said, watching the lightning flash to the ground.

"I stopped a long time ago," Avery whispered.

The electric wall of water arced higher, angling toward the top of the buildings. Tone saw other fingers of water coming from behind their tower, and from both sides of it. Straining out the window, he saw they were surrounded by the electrified wall of water. It rose into the air above them and splashed to a point in the center of the sky, blocking out the last of the late afternoon light and rain. Lightning flashed inside the wall, sometimes escaping to the ground.

Tone looked down and saw several shapes moving through the darkness below. White teeth and long, oily hair reflected the bursts of lightning. Avery hadn't killed them all.

"Come," Jane said.

Tone and Avery turned from the window. Colonel Walraven sat against one wall, fussing with the cut on his cheek. Jane held another trap door open in the floor and gestured for them to go down.

"What the jackin' hell are you going to do with us now?" the colonel asked.

"You go find the other humans and kill them."

"Why did you trap us with that water wall?" Tone asked. "Is this to be our prison now?"

"Your prison?" Jane said with a chuckle. "No. It is our grave."

41

Rhaina

jungle temple

Rhaina stumbled back through the waist-deep water as the guardian's talons grasped at the air above her head. She brought her pistol around and took aim at the man's liquid chest, but he slid away before she got off a shot.

The second guardian, the winged woman, sprang forward and knocked Rhaina off balance into the water, then swung a killing blow. Sawn sliced the woman's legs in half with the barrel of his rifle, then yanked Rhaina back.

The woman's legs fell into the water and vanished. She spread her wings as the water poured from the holes at her knees. Her body shrank until she slipped beneath the churning surface. Then the bubbles started again, the water swirled, and the woman's head rose from the same spot she'd fallen. Her eyes flashed bright silver, her wet hair hung in long curls before her face, and her wings splashed up to lift her back into the air.

"We can't win this!" Sawn yelled.

They'd already retreated from the narrow room they'd chosen as their camp. The guardians forced them down the stairs and back into the hallway, and they were pushing the team to the open ground surrounding the temple. Rhaina had no idea what would happen once they got there, but she hoped the shallow water and mud would restrict the guardians' movements.

Khonane and Cailin skirted along the side walls, taking aim at the guardians and helping the Lygmies retreat with the pouncer. Sawn and Majid stayed up front where they could get in close and use their tech to fight.

Rhaina watched the winged woman hover before them, and she knew Sawn was right. They could slow these creatures, but they couldn't beat them. She turned and gripped Khonane's arm.

"Go," she said. "Get everyone out."

"No!" he said.

Rhaina ducked as the winged man flew over their heads and circled behind them. The woman kept her place several tics in front of them while the man tried to scoop one of the Lygmies from the water. Majid fired twice and struck the male guardian in the chest. The Lygme slipped from his grip as water gushed from the holes.

Rhaina grabbed Khonane's shirt and almost threw him past the deflating guardian. "No heroics!" she said.

"No!" Khonane spun around to her. "We can't go outside. Can't you feel it?"

Rhaina touched her Geminai by reflex. She was hovering at Rhaina's side, watching the guardians and whispering warnings and advice to help Rhaina fight. But even more unusual, Khonane's Geminai was nearby, circling the group in wide arcs that took it outside the temple for several moments, then back in and near the team. Khonane's uneasy feelings would be coming from his Geminai. Rhaina wondered what was outside that made his spirit so nervous, but they didn't have any choice. They could not beat these reincarnating guardians.

"It doesn't matter," Rhaina said, slipping back inside herself. "Go!"

Khonane didn't argue. He turned, shoved the Lygmies after Cailin, and they ran as fast as they could through the water and toward the temple entrance, Majid following to guard their retreat.

As Rhaina slipped past the rising guardian, Sawn pounded the butt of his rifle through the creature's water skull. The guardian collapsed again, and Rhaina and Sawn took aim at the woman still hovering down the hall. One shot struck, and the woman staggered back as water poured from her abdomen.

Rhaina grabbed Sawn's arm and pulled him after her as she turned to run. She let her Geminai guide the way as they turned left, right, left again through the dark, narrow passageways. They turned a corner, and Rhaina saw the stairwell leading back out. Lightning flashed from above, and the rainwater rolled down the stairs in pounding waves.

Geminai looked back to see the male guardian flying up behind them. Pushing Sawn ahead, Rhaina turned and took aim. Her shot struck the right wing, and the creature tumbled head first into Rhaina, knocking her beneath the water and pinning her under the guardian's disintegrating bulk.

Rhaina closed her mouth tight as she struggled to push off the guardian. Geminai touched Sawn's mind to bring the man back for her.

Silver beams flashed through the black water, and Rhaina looked up and into the guardian's eyes as he stared down at her. He gripped her arms with his fierce strength and wrapped himself around her, his glowing eyes studying her face as they sank to the temple's floor. Rhaina felt the creature's form shriveling away as he leaned his head next to hers. She felt his watery breath blow past her ear, felt the beating of the creature's liquid heart against her chest.

He pressed his mouth against her ear. His breath warmed the water swirling around her neck, and his voice seemed to echo across the short distance between them.

"Come with me," he said.

The muscles in his arms collapsed and his body fell across her like dead weight.

"I will show you," he continued.

Show what? Rhaina wondered.

"His eye," the creature said.

Sawn gripped Rhaina's shoulder and tugged her from beneath the guardian's body to haul her out of the water.

Rhaina stumbled against Sawn and coughed the water from her mouth and nose. She shoved the soaking pistol into her holster and pulled the rifle from around her back.

"Let's go!" Sawn yelled.

Rhaina's Geminai touched her mind and told her the female guardian was swimming toward them, twenty tics away.

She flipped the rifle on its side and fumbled at the keypad.

"Rhaina!"

She pressed the code for the rifle's self-cleaning mode. Water spurted from every crack, out from the pins and screws, and drained from the rifle's barrel.

Geminai whispered a direction. Rhaina raised the rifle and used the laser sight to aim at the spot in the black water. She fired, and the hallway erupted as the female guardian flew into the air. Water spewed from her back, and her wings thrashed as she struggled to stay airborne.

Rhaina didn't stay to watch. She followed Sawn up the slick steps and onto the muddy ground surrounding the temple. They both stopped to stare.

The sky strobed with bursts of refracted lightning darting within a dome of water that stretched high into the air above them. The roiling, energized wall of water rose from what used to be the temple's moat. Lightning bursts struck the ground, scattering mud and water and electric sparks high into the air.

Six slick, mud-covered partomes strode forward through the chaos, Majid at their side. The Lygmies followed close behind, Ko shielding the flat-eared pouncer beneath his ragged shirt. Cailin and Khonane walked nearby, the rain pouring down their hats and slickers.

"What happened?" Rhaina asked, pointing into the sky. She swiped her soaking bangs from her eyes and leaned close to Cailin and Khonane.

"According to our Lygmies," Cailin said, "this mess was caused by that other tribe of Lygmies, the ones who worship those meshet animals."

The partomes growled and shook their long, stringy manes. One partome flexed its scaly hand, its claws shining in the flashing light. Rhaina shifted so she could see all of the creatures.

"If those other Lygmies can do this," she said, "there's no telling what else they'll do to try to stop us. And if those Resurrected Mother soldiers are really as desperate as Silny says they are, then this is just the beginning."

"Please, ma'am," Ko said, tugging on the end of Rhaina's shirt. "Let us help." He gestured to the two partomes squatting behind him.

"Can you do magic like this too?" Rhaina asked.

"That?" Ko asked, pointing at the domed sky. "That will disappear when those evil Lygmies are dead."

"You're volunteering to stop them?"

"Yes, ma'am."

"And what about those guardians?"

"We have our partomes to keep us safe."

Rhaina considered. She didn't want to let the Lygmies out of her sight, but she didn't want to waste the time avoiding the Resurrected Mother soldiers. On the other hand, it might be handy to have the Lygmies far from her when she started stealing sacred relics from their temple. And the Lygmies were natural killers anyway. Why not let them do her dirty work for her?

"You can do that, but you're taking one of my people with you," she said, pointing at Sawn.

"That is acceptable," Ko said. He turned and led the partomes back to the temple entrance.

"Don't let your guard down," Rhaina said, pulling Sawn close to her.

"Never," Sawn said.

"And keep radio contact."

"Of course."

She turned to see the Lygmies and partomes waiting at the top of the stairs – both sets of aliens with slick, black hair glistening in the flashing light. For the first time, she was struck by the resemblance the Lygmies had to their partome pets. The same oily, black hair, and they had similar stocky builds. Was there some common ancestor between them, like humans and monkeys?

"Anything else?" Sawn asked, leaning toward Rhaina.

"No," she said, putting aside her train of thought. "Just remember that those Lygmies and their partomes can be as much of an enemy as any Resurrected Mother soldier."

"Yes, ma'am." With that, he trotted off through the storm to start the hunt.

"What about us?" Khonane asked, shielding his eyes from the rain. "We can't stay out here all night."

"We're going back in," Rhaina said. "But this time we're going to find that gem and get the hell out." She turned to Majid. "Can you handle both of those guardians when they attack again?"

"If you insist," he said.

"Good," Rhaina said with a grin. "Then let's get out of the rain."

42

Jake

jungle temple

One more, Jake thought, stepping up the ladder's metal rungs. And another one. And another one after that. He stopped climbing, looked up the long, black well to the stone door still twenty tics away, and sighed. He could think of several things he'd rather be doing than this, things like seeing that new Dane Stone action flick, or sitting on the beach in Sidney. At this point, he'd even take a West Texas dust storm over this tediousness.

He gripped the next rung and started humming to himself. Ninety-nine steps of steel in the wall...ninety-nine steps of steel...climb one more, and where do you go...ninety-eight steps of jackin' steel in the wall....

He stopped. Was it his imagination, or did he feel a tremor? He cranked up his audio amplifiers. He definitely heard something, but it didn't sound like an earthquake. It was more like the dull roar of falling water. A thunderstorm? It would have to be one powerful thunderstorm for him to hear it inside this stone well.

That thought made him quicken his pace. If he could hear this thunderstorm from inside the well, then it must be one gigantic thunderstorm. He powered his implants and raced up the remaining steps, his boots pounding on the metal rungs and sending loose pebbles raining down.

He reached the stone door at the top and pressed his shoulder into it. Nothing.

He listened again with his implants, and he definitely heard rushing water. He wondered if he'd been tricked by that guardian. Did she stuff him inside this well to let him drown? He'd seen her liquid body drain through the cracks at the bottom of the well so he knew the rocks weren't sealed tight, but it didn't take much water to drown a person.

Sending more power to his tech, Jake pressed his shoulder against the stone. He heard a seal crack, and he shoved at the stone again until it broke away. He slid his fingers around the stone's edge and pushed it aside, then poked his head above the lip of the well.

Dim light streamed through an open window to his right, and he heard the rushing water echoing from outside. Occasional bursts of lightning flashed through the window, lighting the room in stark white and forcing the tech to constrict his pupils. The room itself was empty except for vines and moss that had grown in through the window and taken over the walls and the floor. He shoved himself up and out of the well and went to the open window.

A wall of water rippled from the ground and passed very near the room's outer wall and window. Lightning coursed through the waves crashing up the wall and into the sky. Jake was sure he could reach out and touch the electrified water, but he didn't feel like becoming a piece of charcoal.

He turned to examine the rest of the room, and he startled backward. Two people stood there. By reflex, he revved to Fighting Mode. Time slowed, the bursts of lightning became lengthy explosions of white light, and the muscles in his body tensed as the tech took over.

The two people watched him. His implants scanned them, and he realized he knew the woman, the winged woman he'd fought in the tunnels below. The man standing beside her was also made of water, and he was dressed in the same kinds of liquid robes that fit so nicely on her body. It just didn't look as good on the guy, he thought.

He powered down his tech and took a step back from the liquid pair. They didn't move.

"Hi," Jake said, raising his hand to give them a small wave.

"Hi," they echoed back, raising their hands in imitation of him.

Jake grinned.

"You, uh...you really took me by surprise."

The pair looked at each other but didn't say anything this time.

"I don't remember if I said before," Jake said to the woman. "But I do want to thank you for saving me from that animal down there."

"You'll have his ear," the woman said.

"What?" Jake turned from her to the man, but neither seemed inclined to explain.

"Go that way." The woman pointed at the wall behind her.

Jake's tech analyzed the dark wall. A door-shaped seam was cut into the stones. It was a little small, about Lygme-sized, but he could fit.

"Why?" he asked.

"To be his ear," the woman said, cocking her head to the side.

Jake repeated the words to himself. Whose ear? Were they really telling him about the God's Ear gem?

"Do you know why I'm here?"

"Yes," the man said.

"You wish to be his ears," the woman said.

"You mean the God's Ear?"

"Yes," the man said.

"And you're okay with that?"

"It is your destiny." The woman turned, ran her hand along the hidden seam in the wall, and opened the narrow, stone door with hardly any effort.

"My destiny," Jake muttered. Something wasn't right. These creatures were too accommodating, and he had the feeling he was being manipulated somehow. What did they really want from him? And what kind of "destiny" would they be talking about that would bring him halfway across the galaxy to steal their sacred stone?

As he approached, both creatures touched his shoulders.

"Until the other side," they said in unison.

Jake stepped through the door and walked down a steep staircase. The stairs glowed beneath his feet, lighting with each step he took, showing him where he was and where he would go for the next couple steps. The creatures shut the stone door behind him, blocking the last of the lightning flashes and plunging the stairwell into ringing silence.

Jake sighed as he stopped to look back. He could go back up there, use his tech to shove open that door, and then what? His only options would still be death by lightning water or death by mauling from that slug in the dungeon. If he followed the stairs, at least he'd have a new option for death.

And who knew? Maybe those water creatures really were letting him walk in and take their sacred gem. Yeah, and maybe he could take a swim in the Rocky Mountain Acid Wells and live through it. He knew he was being set up, but he'd have to play this through to see where and how.

43

Tone

jungle temple

"Come," Jane said, beckoning them to the center of the room.

Tone didn't move from his spot by the window. If this bloody temple was to be his grave, then he would stay where he was and make death come to him.

"Tone?" Jane said, cocking her head. She brushed the wet, orange bangs from her eyes, then looked to Colonel Walraven and Avery.

The three stayed in their places by the wall, staring back at her.

Jane sighed and looked at the floor. The other two Lygmies backed away. Jane ran her fingers through the dirt on the floor, tracing odd patterns with her orange nails. She chanted a soft, mourning tune as she stirred the dirt into the air.

Tone coughed as the dust spread. It swirled around their heads, but it never settled back to the floor. Within moments, the air had grown brown. The lightning flashes lit the open windows and shone like harsh beams through the fog of dirt.

Through it all, Jane chanted from her spot at the center of the room. Tone pressed his hands into the floor beneath him, comforted by the thought that something was still there. The clouds of dust made him feel like he floated, like the room stood still and he sailed in circles, that Jane was his anchor and he would fly into oblivion if he didn't have her grounding him to his place.

The dusty air fluttered, and a different world opened around them. Tone sat in water up to his neck in a dark, narrow hallway. The air smelled damp, musty. The water rippled around him, and Tone heard footsteps splashing closer.

He rose from his spot, but instead of water falling off him, the air shimmered with clouds of dust until they coalesced back into the mirage of the darkened hallway.

"Colonel Walraven," Jane said through the fog. "You will find and kill these people."

As Jane spoke, a group of three Lygmies and a large man with sunglasses stepped around the corner of the hallway. The Lygmies looked to be in even worse shape than Jane and her companions. Their black hair hung in long, wet curls down their heads and in front of their faces, their clothes were soaked in mud, and their eyes were sunken and bloodshot.

The human, however, looked tech'd for battle. His eyes were covered by a wrap-around sight visor, his shirt bulged from all the implants he had installed in his arms and chest, and he walked through the water with a machine's precision. Tone knew this man would not die easily.

"I'm through with this," the colonel said. "If you want them dead, Lygme, then you kill them."

"Kill them," Jane said, "and I will take you to the gem you seek."

Colonel Walraven stepped to Tone's side, scattering the mirage for several seconds until the dust settled into its windy pattern again.

"Show us the gem now," the colonel said. "And then we'll kill these people."

Jane appeared through the dust. Her eyes glowed bright orange, and her arm circled as if she still stirred the dirt from the ground.

"Kill them now, or you get nothing."

"This is an old argument, bitch," the colonel said. "We hired you to take us to the gem. You think you've kidnapped us. We won't do anything more for you until we get our gem."

Jane put her hand behind her back, then brought it forward again. She held the colonel's rifle out to him.

The colonel shied away from the weapon and glanced to his left and right through the mirage. Then he turned back to Jane, studied her glowing face for several moments, and whipped the gun from her hand. He spun it around and shoved the barrel toward her. She didn't even flinch. She stood her ground and watched him, her one hand still spinning the dust through the air.

"You don't really want to see your gem, do you?" she said.

"You said we'd all die in this temple. Who cares about a bloody rock."

Jane's arm came forward again, and she offered another rifle to the colonel. This one belonged to Avery.

"What's your game?" Colonel Walraven asked as he studied the newly offered weapon.

"Take it and see."

Avery stepped forward, disturbing more of the dusty mirage. He cradled his bandaged left arm and looked from the rifle to the colonel.

"I don't need it, sir," he said. "I've got my electrical charge."

"Which hasn't been very effective yet against these beasts," the colonel muttered. He lowered his own rifle and backed away. "Take it," he said.

Avery took the rifle.

"Very good," Jane said. Her eyes dimmed and she stopped moving her hand. She sank back down from the mirage as the dust settled.

The hallway with its knee-deep water drifted to the floor. The tower room returned to normal, the lightning flashes cutting through the darkened interior to reveal that Tone and Jane were now alone.

Tone spun around, but Avery, the colonel, and the other two Lyg-mies had all vanished. Jane lay sprawled across the center of the floor, her eyes shut and her breathing harsh and uneven.

"What did you do with them?" he asked.

"For those who know how," Jane gasped, "the temple's passageways can be bridged."

"Oh, I...see." Tone didn't think it was much of an answer, but it was probably the only one he'd get. He glanced to the walls and windows, trying to see any way he could escape the dark, tight room. This Lygme had been acting erratically for days, and now he was alone with her.

What if she tried to jump on him again? She didn't look to have the energy for anything, but Tone had learned not to be surprised. And if she could make two-thirds of their party disappear through some "bridge," then he had no way of knowing what else she could do.

"Do not fear, Tone," she said.

"Oh, I'm not afraid," Tone lied.

Jane pushed herself onto her elbows.

"You must come with me."

"Where?"

"I will take you to the gem you seek."

He just stared at her.

"Your colonel should not have it." She struggled to stand up. "He is a broken man whose spirits fly in opposite directions. He would only corrupt it."

As the lightning flashed outside the windows, Jane's silhouette im-printed in Tone's mind. He would have bet his life that she had grown fur and a set of skin-flap wings like those meshet beasts that flew through the trees. Then another flash, and he saw that it was only her, standing in the center of the room with her hand outstretched to him. He rubbed his eyes to clear away the image.

"Come," she said. "I will show you the gem, and then you will be free to do as you please."

"You mean you'll let me go?"

"I will free you to the gem." With that she reached out, took his hand, and led him through the open window outside the temple walls.

44

Tone

The view would have been breathtaking if Tone hadn't been worried that everything would kill him. The temple walls were slick and coated with layers of moss and vines, the lightning arced through the watery dome above him, and the loose rocks on the narrow ledge threatened to spill him over.

Jane had no problems as she strode to the corner and turned back to him. He shuffled along with his back to the wall, not sure whether to be thankful the narrow ledge was there or to curse the fact that Jane was making him walk it.

"Come," Jane said, taking his hand. She pulled him to her side and crouched down. She kept her eyes forward, and Tone saw she was eyeing another ledge several tics away.

His foot slipped beneath him, he landed on a loose vine, and his momentum sent him over the side. He scrabbled for anything to stop himself and caught hold of another vine. It unraveled from the side of the wall and threw him around the edge of the building where he hung like a swinging pendulum above the muddy ground.

He clenched his eyes shut and tried to slow his breathing as the vine rocked him back and forth.

"Tone," Jane called from above. "Tone, are you hurt?"

He clung to the vine, not daring to breathe.

"Tone, speak." She jiggled the vine.

"Stop," he whispered.

She did. "Give me your hand."

Tone opened his eyes a crack. The lightning still flashed, and the water-covered sky had darkened with the onset of evening. The temple wall brushed past him, wet and matted in green and red moss, vines, and thick, leafy plants. But wrapped around the swinging vine, he felt safer, more secure. He did not want to move.

"Tone."

He opened his eyes a little further and tilted his head. Jane leaned over the edge, her head not even a tic above him. She smelled musky, and the beaded sweat dripped off her dark forehead. She held one hand out to him, her orange nails filed to fine points and looking like tiny claws. Tone scrunched his eyes.

"No," he said. "I'm fine."

"Tone, you are in danger. That vine will not hold you."

"I know."

"Then give me your hand."

Tone thought about moving his right hand up the vine. He even flexed his shaking fingers, but he could not will himself to move.

Yesterday I would have thrown myself off that sleeping board, he thought. *And today I can't let go long enough to climb back up.*

That thought stopped him. What was it that made him want to end it all yesterday? What was it that made him so afraid to even move today? Was it the Lygmies themselves? Colonel Walraven? This mission?

Tone opened his eyes as he discovered what he didn't like about this mission: it was to be his final mission with the colonel. No matter how this turned out, there was no way he could return to the life they'd had on the moon, all the good they were doing back on Earth. And what did he have left in "retirement?"

Ah, but with the gem in his own possession, he thought, he might still be able to affect some good, even without everyone else – without the colonel. Politicians could always be bought. After all, President Tudor had seemed more than willing to grant any concession to know this gem existed. Think of the good that could be done in the world with that kind of money....

Jane's gritty, firm hand wrapped around his wrist, and Tone looked up at her. Her orange eyes glowed, and the muscles in her tiny arm and shoulder bulged as she hoisted him up. The vine went slack in Tone's grip. Jane shuffled back on the narrow ledge, and Tone reached up and grabbed the slick stone.

He climbed over the edge, crawled to Jane's side, and sat beside her. She wasn't even breathing hard.

Tone stared out across the temple grounds and watched the lightning flash for several moments. Jane seemed content to let the silence go on. Finally, he turned to her.

"What is it you don't like about the colonel?" he asked.

"I told you," she said. "His spirits fly in separate directions. It makes him dangerous, unpredictable. Uncontrollable."

"And what about me? Am I 'controllable?'"

Jane smiled, and the glow in her orange eyes seemed somehow brighter.

"You have changed," she said.

"No." Tone looked back at the night. "I don't think I ever wanted the colonel to get this gem."

"That is wise."

"I want to use it for good, to do something that will make an impact for humanity."

"I knew you were the only one of your party who would say that."

"And that's why you want me to have it?"

"Yes."

Tone turned back to her and grinned.

"Can you get me back out of this jungle without any problems from Colonel Walraven?"

"Yes."

"Then let's do it."

He stood up, keeping his back pressed against the temple wall, and reached down to offer Jane his hand.

"You are kind," she said, eyeing his hand. "I will miss you."

"You know, I think I'll miss you too."

45

Tone

Tone followed Jane for almost a half-hour, around and through towers, from one roof to another, down long, narrow passages that smelled musty, like no one had walked those passages in hundreds of years. They brachiated along suspended vines, climbed down the slick walls to drop to lower levels, and finally entered the window of a lone spire in the center of the temple. The spire stretched above them nearly to the height of the watery dome, and they climbed up the inside stairs, circling around the interior walls until they reached a small antechamber at the spire's peak.

Jane stood before a small, wooden door with silver bands across the top and bottom. There was no doorknob that Tone could see, but only a ring set in the center of the wooden beams.

The lightning flashed violently behind them, and Tone could make out the image of a Lygme face carved into the wood, the metal ring hinged through the face's nose.

"How do we get in?" Tone asked.

"You must open the door."

"Why me?"

"I cannot. It must be you."

Tone gasped at the thin air and set his hand against the door. The wood was smooth and hard, polished to a shine as if it had been placed in this tower only yesterday. He shoved his shoulder against the wood, but the door didn't budge. He searched the frame for any kind of trip lever or hidden handle, but he didn't see anything that looked like it would open the door.

"How do I open it?" he asked.

Jane had shut her eyes and leaned against the wall, lightning flashing against her orange hair. She didn't say anything.

Tone turned back to the door and gripped the metal ring. He pulled it, but nothing happened. He turned it around on its hinge. He finally pounded it against the wood, hoping there might be someone on the other side to open it.

The eyes of the carving flipped open, and the Lygme face stared at him.

Tone stumbled backwards as the lightning flashed across the animated carving. The nose ring clanged against the door as the face followed Tone's movements.

"What the hell is that thing?" Tone asked, grabbing Jane and yanking her away from the wall.

"The Guardian," Jane whispered, staring wide-eyed at the thing.

"Tone Dalal," the door said, its voice echoing down the stairwell. "You may enter."

The carving opened its mouth, the jaw stretching wide until its bottom lip was on the floor and its upper lip nearly to the ceiling. Its eyes were shoved to the sides of its nose, the metal ring dangling between them as it watched Tone.

The room beyond was lit with a subtle blue light that seemed to emanate from something Tone couldn't see. The walls were barren of any markings, decorations, or even windows.

"The gem is in there?" he asked Jane.

"Yes."

Not even an hour ago, Tone thought, he would have turned around and run as fast as he could from this evil looking door. But now, fully resolved to do the right thing back on Earth, he felt it was his moral duty to walk through that door, retrieve the gem, and go back home to make Earth a better place.

Without waiting for Jane, he stepped through the gaping door. The room curved to his left, and Tone got his first look at the gem.

Glowing brilliant blue as if from a fire within, the gem sat mounted in the ceiling above Tone's head. Its light shone into every part of the room, even around the corner of the wall where he had first peered through. It looked to be the size of his fist, and its corners were cut with a sharp precision. The blue light swirled through the gem like gasses in a crystal ball.

Tone stepped forward, in awe of the gem's beauty. He had no idea where he'd find a buyer for it back home, but he was certain it would bring a fortune for him.

He stood beneath its glow and stared. That's when he saw the intricate carvings in the stones around the ceiling. Wide, looping circles extended out from the gem toward the center of the room, and two longer ovals pointed toward the back wall. Two of the front-facing ovals joined together at the gem, making a total of nine loops. The carvings extended to the back wall where they made four parallel lines down into the floor and disappeared. It looked like a pair of legs carved upside-down, the feet and toes huge above his head.

"Of course," Tone said, grinning as the thought occurred to him. "The God's Foot gem, like that pouncer said."

He reached up to feel the sides of it, and the gem came loose in his hands. He fumbled with it, almost dropping it to the floor before he got a good grip on its edges. The gem was surprisingly light. It glowed in his hands, the blue light almost seeping through his fingers.

Tone grinned. He had been dragged to this god-forsaken planet against his better judgement, kidnapped, nearly raped, and almost fallen to his death more times than he cared to remember, but it suddenly all seemed worth it as he stared into the mesmerizing glow.

Dust spilled across his hands.

Tone looked up.

The carvings had changed. The "feet" had moved, no longer intersecting at the spot where the stone had been placed. Instead, the carvings showed the feet spread wide and the toes split apart, like someone stretching after a long sleep.

There was a crack, and Tone turned to see one of the carved toes flex down and away from the stone. More dust sprinkled across his shoulder.

"Jane?" Tone said, glancing back out.

She wasn't there.

He started to move but couldn't. He looked down and saw that his feet had sunk into the stone beneath him.

"Jane!" he said.

More dust fell across him, and he looked up to see the carved feet meet above his head. The stone splintered out in a dozen directions, and the feet slammed across Tone's shoulders, crushing him down through the liquified stone.

46

Rhaina

jungle temple

Cailin removed the ascent rifle from her back and unwound a few tics of micro cable from the pouch at her belt. She tied the cable to a bolt, loaded the bolt into the rifle, and fired at the ceiling. A quick, high-pitched chink told them the bolt had lodged into place. Cailin tested the line, then braced herself against the wall and climbed to the ceiling.

"I don't see anything," she said when she reached the top.

Rhaina sent her Geminai into the wall. The second-soul flew through the stonework and mortar and into the narrow passageway that had been cut through it. She traced her way back to the wall and found the way blocked by a hinged stone that had been swung across the entrance.

"Look at the stones up there," Rhaina said. "One of them is hinged on the inside, and you should be able to pull it out. I didn't see any locking mechanisms."

"Okay," Cailin said, sounding unconvinced. She shone her lamp along the wall and felt the cracks between the stones.

Rhaina glanced up and down the flooded hallway, expecting the guardians to attack them at any moment. Water dripped off a stone behind them, plinking with each drop. Lightning flashed through the open stairwell at the far end of the hall, but the rain had finally stopped.

"Got it." Cailin swung a long, narrow stone away from the wall.

Light spilled out from the passageway, and Cailin had to turn her head to block the glare. She swung to the side of the entrance and waited.

"There's no way we missed that," Rhaina said.

"There was no light before," Majid said.

"Hey," Cailin called down. "It's jackin' bright up here. What's the move?"

"What do you see?" Rhaina asked.

Cailin squinted around the corner. "A tunnel. Takes a turn to the left about three or four tics in."

"And the light?"

"Can't tell," she said with a shrug. "I don't see anything in there that would make that much light." She adjusted the cable, balanced on the edge of the passageway, and squinted forward. "In fact, I don't see what's making that light at all. It's almost like the light comes from somewhere farther down the tunnel."

"All right," Rhaina said with a sigh. "Go in. What's around that corner."

Cailin swung off the cable and into the tunnel. She pulled out her pistol and stepped forward, her shadow flickering across the walls as she walked out of view.

Rhaina looked around, then spared a glance through Geminai. Neither of them saw any Guardians, and that worried Rhaina. Those creatures had followed and attacked them most of the day, and now that her team was standing in one place, they weren't anywhere to be found.

Geminai rushed down the hall to view Sawn's fight, but it was already over. Two of those partome creatures walked along behind Sawn and the Lygmies. They were inspecting the body of a slain meshet. The Resurrected Mother soldiers had apparently fled since their bodies weren't anywhere to be seen.

"Thoughts?" Khonane said, stepping to her side.

Rhaina smiled. "How's the leg?" she asked.

"A little sore." He massaged the muscles in his thigh as he continued. "Overall, I'd say I recovered pretty quick, probably because of all the drugs Cailin kept pumping into my system."

"I'm sure." Rhaina pointed to the cable hanging from the ceiling. "Would you have any problems with that rope and tunnel?"

" I hate climbing," Khonane said, "but I shouldn't have any problems. It's only a few tics up."

Cailin appeared at the crawlspace entrance again and leaned over the edge. She blinked and rubbed her eyes.

"Rhaina?" she said, looking around and squinting.

"We're here."

"Tunnel's clear." Cailin pointed back. "It curves around on itself and climbs up a couple flights."

"And the light?"

"Couldn't tell," she said with a shrug. "It got really bright two turns in, and then it started getting dim again. You'll think I'm crazy, but it almost seemed like the light was coming up through one of the stones in the floor."

Rhaina looked down the water-logged tunnel behind her and thought. The main tunnel was now clear of the fighting, at least for now. There was no reason for them to bother with this passageway, but she would keep it in mind for later, in case they wanted to go up another couple levels. But the Sea of Souls had been very clear when Geminai looked: this gem was beneath the temple. If anything, they had to go down, not up.

"Okay," Rhaina said, turning back around. "Cailin, get down here. We'll explore that area later, if we need to."

"Cailin, move!" Khonane yelled. "Now!"

Rhaina looked up in time to see one of the water guardians in the passageway wrap his huge, wet arms around Cailin and throw her over his shoulder. He turned and disappeared into the light.

"No!" Khonane yelled, jumping on the cable.

"Wait!" Rhaina said. She gripped his leg, but he was up and over the edge of the tunnel before she could pull him back.

"Do you want me to bring them back?" Majid asked.

"Wait." Rhaina flew with her Geminai into the wall, down the tunnel, and after Cailin and the guardian. The creature ducked around a corner and jumped down a hole in the floor, then he pulled a hinged stone, shutting the hole. Khonane ran around the corner, past the hole, and down the next hall, not even noticing the displaced seam in the floor.

Go get him, Rhaina said to her Geminai. *Bring him back to the trap door.* She pulled herself back into her own body.

"Oh, let's," Rhaina said with a sigh. She gripped the thin cable and pulled herself up, bracing her feet against the wall.

Majid leaped through the air and landed in the tunnel above her. He gripped her hand and pulled her up beside him.

"Where?" he asked.

"Three turns in."

They ran down the tunnel, light bleeding from the rocks around them. Three turns to the right and they nearly ran over Khonane standing in the middle of the hall and rubbing his right ear.

"Are you hurt?" Majid asked.

"Yes," Khonane said, turning to Rhaina. "Someone screamed in my ear that I had to come back."

"I'm sure my Geminai only did what she had to." Rhaina knelt to the floor and felt along the seam for any handle. She didn't find anything, and the light shining through the floor was making blue spots bounce before her eyes.

"Another stone door?" Majid asked, kneeling beside her.

Rhaina nodded.

Majid punched his hands into the narrow seam, sending shards of stone flying up at them. He gripped the edges, yanked the stone off its hinge, and pulled it out of the floor.

Intense, white light flashed through the hole. Rhaina and Khonane covered their faces while Majid stared straight into the blinding glare. The light shone through Rhaina's hand, making her bones stand in dark contrast to her red fingers. She moved until Majid's body blocked the direct light.

"It's a circular stairwell," Majid said. "Do we follow?"

Rhaina reached out to her Geminai and found the second soul trailing close behind Cailin and the guardian down these stairs.

She shut her eyes, the blinding light almost piercing her eyelids, and she considered the options. That same male guardian had offered to show Rhaina the God's Eye gem, and now he kidnapped Cailin. Was he taking her to the gem instead of Rhaina?

"Jackin' hell," she muttered. "Yes, we're going in. Majid, you first. I'll take the rear, make sure that other guardian bitch doesn't come up on us."

Majid led the way down the circular, stone stairwell, Khonane following close behind. The light grew stronger, more piercing, with each step they took. Rhaina grabbed hold of Khonane's shoulder, shut her eyes, then covered her eyes with her hand. The light still shone through.

Rhaina's Geminai didn't even notice the light through her spiritual eyes. She floated down the stairs and watched for any signs of danger. There were none, which actually had Rhaina more concerned than if a hundred men had laser launchers chasing them. That guardian had to know he was being followed. So why was he allowing it?

He's not allowing it, Rhaina thought, nearly coming to a stop on the stairwell. *He's encouraging it.*

She thought back to the Sea of Souls and the snake-thing she'd seen guarding the knowledge. She'd always believed those Guardians of Knowledge to be mythological creatures until her Geminai found two of them. What if these temple guardians were nothing more than the physical equivalent? And what if these physical guardians were leading her around like that spiritual one had, allowing her to see and do only what they wanted her to see and do?

But then why attack her? Why not lead her straight to the gem?

Because now it's my idea, she thought. *I'm not being led around by some mystical Guardian; I'm trying to rescue my friend from an enemy, and if I happen to find the God's Eye gem while I'm doing it...well, I'm lucky.*

"Stop," Majid said.

They stopped. Rhaina considered opening her eyes, but the light still penetrated her hand and eyelids, so she relied on her Geminai to see.

Majid stood before an archway that had been carved into a face with a gaping mouth. An eye close set to each side of the nose at the ceiling, and a metal ring dangled between the nostrils. Through the mouth, though, Geminai saw images flitting through the air, scenes of the jungle outside, other hallways throughout the temple, the narrow room they'd tried to use as their camp. The scenes floated through the air, their images waving as if from a breeze Rhaina didn't feel.

"Cailin must be on the other side of this carved mouth," Majid said. "I did not see any other passageways as we descended."

"Go," Rhaina said. "We're getting Cailin and getting the hell out of here."

Majid stepped through the mouth-shaped door and beyond the swirling images. Khonane and Rhaina followed.

The light faded as soon as they crossed the threshold.

"Rhaina," Cailin called.

Rhaina opened her eyes and saw Cailin standing a few tics away, apparently unharmed as she grinned back at them.

"Isn't it incredible?" she said.

Rhaina looked at the walls, the ceiling, and even the floor as clouds of images floated all around the room. The few she'd seen through the door were only a small fraction of the scenes the room contained. She saw villages of partomes, Lygmies running through the jungle, meshet flying above the forest canopy, and even a human city built in a clear-cut portion of the forest. She gasped as she recognized it: the colony city Sol-Win.

"It's...weird," Khonane said.

"Not those," Cailin said. She pointed at the ceiling. "That!"

A tall, skinny column of rock shot up from the center of the room nearly to the ceiling. Atop that column sat a glowing, green rock. Refracted beams of light shot from it in all directions, piercing the rocks above and making them glow from the inside out. Even the pillar emanated light.

Rhaina clenched her fists as she stared up at it.

Khonane turned. "Is that ...?"

"The God's Eye gem," Majid said, a huge grin spreading across his plastic face.

"Isn't it great?" Cailin said. "That Guardian brought me right to it."

47

Rhaina

"Let's get out of here," Rhaina said.

"I am not leaving without that gem," Majid said, pointing to the top of the pillar.

"We've been set up! Get that through your plastic head. That creature wasn't keeping us from it. Cailin said it herself: he led us right to it."

"Then we take advantage of its stupidity. This is what Mr. Rosh created me to do, and this is what I will do."

"You will leave with us," Rhaina said, raising her pistol. "Or you won't leave at all."

Khonane and Cailin pointed their guns at the plastic man too.

"Treachery?" Majid said. "Mr. Rosh programmed me to trust you. Why would you betray our trust like this?"

"Cut the act," Rhaina said. "Now let's go."

The room brightened as the swirling images changed to show another room, this one glowing blue. The randomness of the scenes quickly returned, but Rhaina could have sworn she saw a man in military fatigues holding a blue gem. *Damn,* Rhaina thought. *This temple has more looters than the pyramids.*

"Was he a friend of yours?" Majid asked.

"You saw him too?"

"Hard to miss." Majid started pacing, turning from one to another of them as he walked in circles. "So was this the plan? Split up the group, have Sawn meet your friend somewhere else, and then kill the plastic man? Did you anticipate me finding this room with its second gem, or was this a bonus discovery?"

He stopped with his back to Rhaina, and he stared up the pillar to the green gem. Rhaina slid her hand into her shirt pocket and removed the kill switch. She cupped it in her palm.

"You know, Rhaina," Majid said. "You can't stop me." He crouched down, then leaped halfway up the stone pillar and started climbing.

Khonane and Cailin spun to shoot, but Rhaina raised her hand to stop them. She punched the code into the kill switch and hit the "Send" button.

The plastic man stopped. His body twitched as he tried to climb higher, then he lost his grip and fell to the ground. His plastic body cracked and popped, but he did not shatter. The yellow glow faded from his bio-mechanical eyes, and he stayed as still as the rocks around him.

"Let's go," Rhaina said, stowing the kill switch in her pocket again. She turned and led them across the room to what she believed to be the door. The images spinning around them made it hard to know what direction to go, but her Geminai assured her she was right.

"You of all people," said Majid, "underestimate me."

Rhaina turned and saw the plastic man standing at the base of the pillar and staring at them. His eyes were dark, though, as if the power hadn't returned to the machine.

"I never underestimate a plastic man," Rhaina said.

She signaled Cailin, and Cailin unsnapped a grenade from her belt. She flicked a dial on the grenade's base and threw it at Majid. The bomb exploded in mid-air with a thundering pop, showering the plastic man in electronic debris that sparked and crackled as it struck him.

"A pulse grenade?" Majid said, watching the electro-magnetic shards rain down. "Ms. Bruci, I am quite impressed."

Ms. Bruci? Where did that come from?

She glanced through her Geminai and saw a shadowy figure hiding within the plastic man's dead shell. Its black shape flitted around inside Majid's body, moving the face, the arms, and the legs to make it look like the plastic man was still alive. The kill switch had done its job, but something else had taken Majid's plastic body, something else that could only be....

"Mr. Rosh," Rhaina said. "How did you do it?"

"I discovered there is something I love more than that prison of a tower I built." Majid's mouth opened and closed as Mr. Rosh spoke, but the movements were more like a puppet than a real person. "I love my life. And once my building was destroyed, it didn't hold onto my spirit nearly as much as it had for all those years."

As if on cue, the images dancing on the dust changed to Mr. Rosh's office tower exploding from the inside out. Strobing flashes lit the building's interior from top to bottom. The windows shattered, the walls dislodged, fires erupted, and the entire 200-story complex imploded to the ground.

"Magnificent, isn't it?"

"You really are a monster," Rhaina said.

"What?" The floating scenes flitted to their randomness again as Mr. Rosh turned to her. "Oh, no, you misunderstand. The destruction of my building was tragic, of course. I made sure to do it at night so that I wouldn't kill that many people. They were mostly custodians and such, the cheap labor."

Rhaina shook her head. Was she actually working for this beast? A beast with money. That's what got her into this in the first place.

"Now then," Mr. Rosh said, gazing at the gem far above. "I believe we were about to claim our prize."

"No, we are leaving." Rhaina sited her pistol on Mr. Rosh's back.

"Rhaina," he said, spreading his arms wide. "May I call you Rhaina? Anyway, Rhaina, I heard all of your arguments to Majid a few minutes ago. Remember, I was here. You believe this is a trap, and that we'll all get killed, etc. Think, woman." He spun around. "How long have we been in this room? And nothing's happened?"

"If we shoot him," Cailin asked, "will he shut up?"

"Go ahead and shoot. I have a plastic man's body now, and I'm sure I can take more punishment than you." He looked back at Rhaina. "But this is a breach of contract for you, Ms. Rhaina Bruci, and I'll make sure everyone Earth-side knows about it. It will ruin you. You'll never work that side of the galaxy again."

With that, he turned and started climbing the rock pillar.

Rhaina aimed for the plastic man's shoulder and pulled the trigger. The shot struck, but it didn't even slow him down.

Cailin and Khonane fired several shots, but he kept climbing.

Rhaina tried the kill switch once more, but nothing happened.

"Come on," she finally said, grabbing Cailin and Khonane. "Let's get out of here while we still can."

They turned and sprinted for the door, Rhaina relying on her Geminai to guide her through the floating pictures. They entered the blinding light and Rhaina slapped one hand across her eyes. She tugged Khonane after her as she ran through the gaping mouth and back up the stairs.

The ground started shaking. The walls rumbled, and bits of dust and stones rained down on them. Rhaina held Khonane's hand as they wound their way around the center stone column. The light dimmed with each revolution. A loud, rushing sound started far below them, as if from a torrential wind. According to Geminai, they were very near the top.

Rhaina slammed into something solid. She would have fallen backwards except Khonane and Cailin ran into her from behind. She opened her eyes and saw one of the Guardians – the female this time – standing before them.

In one, swift movement, the Guardian had Rhaina, Khonane, and Cailin pinned together in her outstretched wings. She flew back down the stairs with them.

Rhaina struggled against the Guardian's slick body, but she couldn't work her way free. She tried to get to the pistol at her belt, but the Guardian had her arms pinned tight. She tried to kick her way free, but the Guardian seemed impervious to pain.

After only a few seconds, the Guardian stopped, spread her wings, and shoved them back through the mouth carving.

They skidded across the dirt flood and came to a halt in the center of the rotating collage of pictures.

Rhaina spun around and looked up the stone pillar. Dust swirled on the air near the ceiling, and refracted beams of green light shone out from the God's Eye gem. Mr. Rosh gripped the pillar, and his hand reached for the glowing stone.

"No!" Rhaina yelled.

He took it, and he grinned.

The air grew suddenly still. The floating pictures stopped their rotation and started blending into one another, wrapping the images across each other. The scenes washed into a collage of translucent greens and whites swirling across the ceiling and walls. The room seemed to be spinning around them, and Rhaina had to look down to keep from getting sick.

Mr. Rosh landed on the ground in front of them, the glowing, green gem in his hand.

"This is what you were afraid of?" he asked, looking around at the spinning pictures.

"You bastard!" Rhaina yelled. She ran and hit Mr. Rosh in the stomach, sending his plastic body to the ground, then pounded his head with her fists.

His free hand shot up and gripped her neck.

Cailin sliced through his arm with her laser knife, and Khonane yanked Rhaina back off him. They jumped away, Mr. Rosh's plastic arm dangling from Rhaina's neck and leaking yellow plasti-fluid across the ground.

The green and white swirls stopped rotating around the room and froze into a marble-like pattern across the walls and ceiling. The color seeped out of the ground beneath them, leaving the rocks a streaky, white collage.

Rhaina grabbed the leaking arm from her throat and tossed it to the ground.

"I think it's time I let the professional handle you three," Mr. Rosh said. He slipped the gem into his pocket, and stood. More plasti-fluid drained from his elbow, staining the bleached ground a splattered gray. "Ms. Bruci, good-bye."

The plastic man's body drooped for a second, and then his eyes lit bright yellow and he stood straight again. He raised the stub of his arm and looked at the damage from the laser knife, then he turned to Rhaina.

"I'm deactivated for only a few minutes, and this is what you do to me?"

The ground started shaking, and the green and white swirls lifted off the ground to their left, rotating across the dome of the room to reveal images of the surrounding jungle. The swirls continued to recede, revealing the forest canopy, thunderstorm clouds, and even the deep blue sky far above their heads. It rotated behind them with more thunderclouds and trees until it looked like they were standing in the middle of the jungle again.

"You didn't do that, did you?" Majid asked, pointing at the surrounding trees. Then his head jerked still and his eyes went dark. "Kill them," he muttered – but it was Mr. Rosh's voice that emerged. His head snapped straight, and his eyes lit yellow again. "Mr. Rosh, that is not a rational course of action. We're in an unfamiliar, potentially dangerous situation, and these people may be able to help keep me alive."

"A split-personality plastic man," Cailin muttered. "Just what we need."

Majid continued arguing with Mr. Rosh's spirit as the jungle around them suddenly erupted in moving bodies. Dozens of partomes burst from the muddy ground to meet even more meshet rippling from their camouflage. They met in fierce battle, blood flying through the air. Meshet dropped from the sky to strike at the partomes, while the partomes jumped up to yank the meshet to the ground in mid-flight. Blood and fur flew through the air. A meshet impaled a partome on a branch high above their heads. A partome gripped a flying meshet and shoved him into the ground, pounding his orange body beneath the mud.

Rhaina looked for the door back out of the room, but the jungle images obscured everything except the floor. She looked at Majid who had stopped arguing with himself and seemed to be engrossed in watching the battle around them.

A black oval began rising from the floor to their left. It expanded and contracted as it rose higher along the wall. It blotted out the fighting animals, then moved higher to block a line of trees, and finally centered in the sky like a black slit above them. Rhaina couldn't help but think it looked like the pupil of an animal's eye staring down on them.

Of course, she thought. *The God's eye, and we awakened him.*

The pupil contracted, and Rhaina felt like she was being watched. It flicked back and forth, seeming to focus on one person and then another.

"Everybody stand perfectly still," Majid said, staring into the eye.

"Oh, now you're being cautious," Cailin said.

The jungle scene melted away from the walls and drifted to the floor, only to be replaced by repeated images of Rhaina and her party. The mirror-like images surrounded them along the walls, then repeated up to the ceiling until thousands of Rhainas, Cailins, Khonanes, and Majids stacked to the ceiling.

"I think it's seen us," Cailin whispered.

A dark shroud, like the lid of the god's eye, lifted off the floor in front of them, circled across the ceiling, and slammed into the floor behind them, covering the entire room in darkness. Rhaina looked through her Geminai, but the room seemed perfectly still. The pictures were gone, the pupil was gone. She even had an unobstructed view of the door for the first time.

She allowed herself a small sigh, hoping this was the worst that would happen.

Before her next breath, the floor melted away beneath them.

48

Jake

jungle temple

Jake sat on the stone floor with his eyes shut and listened to the conversations around him. He heard Lygmies and humans throughout the temple, snatches of dialogue that told him there were at least another dozen people roaming the halls. He heard Sawn and his Lygme buddies fighting four others, a couple humans and two Lygmies who spoke with a weird dialect. He heard that jackin' plastic man bragging about how he might allow Rhaina to live.

He focused in on Rhaina and let the sound of her voice wash across him. She was mad. She fought with the plastic man, and Jake nearly jumped from his spot when he heard her choking, but then Rhaina's friends pulled her back, and somehow they hurt the plastic man.

Good, Jake thought. *Makes him easier for me to kill.*

The sounds of gunfire intruded on his thoughts. With a sigh, he turned his attention away from Rhaina and opened his eyes, trying to ignore the sounds of Sawn's fighting.

The brown gem sat on its shelf in the wall, lighting the room with its dim glow and seeming to mock him. *This is the God's Ear gem,* Jake thought. Those guardian spirits pointed him in the right direction, practically opened all the doors for him, and now he sat before his precious prize. But he wouldn't touch the thing.

The stairs had led him to a door carved like the face of an ugly Lygme, and all sounds disappeared, like he'd walked into some vacuum. When he yanked on the carved face's nose ring, the mouth opened to reveal a room where voices echoed from within the stone walls. Things had been too weird, though, too magical for Jake's liking. His world did not revolve around spirit guardians and yawning doors and talking walls, as interesting as they might be.

He flipped on his optic receptors and scanned the gem. The analysis came back in seconds: a large calamite stone, chipped into its lumpy shape, and encasing a mass of crystalized sien that made it glow from the inside out. There was nothing mystical, or even highly unusual, about this gem except that it was huge. He could have the thing cut into hundreds of pieces and make a fortune. He could probably buy a moon with the money he'd make off that thing.

His mind knew all those facts, but that didn't make his gut reaction any less real. He should find Rhaina, and they should get as far away as they could. He knew of a great hotel on Pluto where they could go, a little five-star place with a honeymoon suite overlooking the Crystal Caves.

Sawn yelled.

Jake turned and stared at the wall to his left, the wall that still echoed Sawn's voice. The wall shook. Jumping up, he scanned the stones, and his tech told him they had been cracked, apparently by something large and heavy.

He ducked back through the open door, and the sounds in the other room vanished. The oppressive silence felt like a weight shoved against his ears. He ignored the enforced silence as he crouched behind the corner of the stairs and watched through the mouth-door.

Stones and mortar exploded soundlessly from the room's left wall, spraying dusty debris across the floor, and a meshet burst through the hole, flying through the air on top of a really ugly beast with filthy, black hair. The first critter looked like it could have passed for any modern trumpeter with the tangled hair, the scarred face, and the massively powerful arms. But then the thing clambered out from beneath the meshet and Jake saw its dorsal fin and gills.

The animals tumbled across the floor, biting and kicking and clawing each other until the water thing finally bit down on the meshet's neck and tore it open. The beast flicked its head back, spraying the room with the animal's blood. It opened its stained mouth, arched its back and roared in victory.

Jake scratched at his ears. He had no idea how loud the beast was yelling, but it was weird and frustrating not to hear.

A lightning bolt shot through the air and struck the thing in the back. The animal shook several seconds as the electricity coursed through its body, then collapsed to the floor, showing a black scorch mark in its back and sparks flickering off its blackened fingers.

Two black-haired Lygmies ran into the room. One of the Lygmies ducked into the corner, picked up a large rock, and looked like he was about to strike anything that came near him. The other Lygme threw himself on top of the fallen beast with gills and started petting the thing vigorously. He even knelt down and licked the animal's face.

Gunfire erupted across the floor. One shot struck the kneeling Lygme in the head, and he fell across his pet.

Sawn ran into the room and crouched behind what was left of the broken wall. Blood ran from several cuts across his chest, and his arms and face were bruised and bleeding. He exchanged tense words with the Lygme in the corner as he swapped out the power conversion cartridge in his gun.

Another meshet entered the room and headed straight for the cowering Lygme. Sawn turned to shoot, but a bolt of lightning struck his gun. He scrambled to retrieve it, but two men in fatigues walked into the room. Two meshet trailed behind them.

One of the men waved his hands in the air until a ball of electricity formed between them. He held it out, and Sawn stood where he was.

The first meshet went to the cowering Lygme with the black hair, gripped him by the shirt, and lifted him into the air. He slammed the Lygme's head against the wall, cracking his skull and splattering the stones with thick blood, then he tossed the Lygme's loose body back into the corner. Everyone turned to Sawn.

Jake shifted as he thought through his options. The big guy in the middle, apparently the boss, held a gun that Jake hadn't seen him use. The little guy was obviously a crack shot with those lightning bolts.

And whose brilliant idea was it to install lightning bolts on that idiot? As soon as he thought it, though, his mind flashed on 2 Glorious. That little plankton would do anything for the right price.

Jake flipped on his optical receptors and scanned the meshet. His tech estimated that in Fighting Mode he could take down one. He even stood a decent chance fighting two, but then his chances dropped against three or more. Mr. Shocker and his boss made the odds even worse, even factoring in Sawn's help. Jake looked around for anything he could use as a weapon, but the hallway offered only stones and sand. Not really effective against the powerful meshet.

Mr. Shocker darted toward the wall where the God's Ear gem sat. The boss gripped his shoulder and held him back, then moved forward to inspect the gem himself.

This is bad, Jake thought, shuffling in his spot. He pried one of the smaller stones loose from the wall and aimed it at the nearest meshet.

The boss reached for the gem.

Jake braced himself against the corner and yelled, but nothing came out. No one in the room even flinched at the noise he tried to make.

The boss plucked the gem from its alcove.

"No!" Jake tried to scream through the silence. He jumped up and ran for the door.

The boss turned and saw Jake running toward them. He opened his mouth and spoke, and the others in the room all turned.

Jake revved to Fighting Mode and saw several things at once: Sawn gripped a meshet and flung him against a wall; Mr. Shocker spun around and threw the ball of energy he'd been playing with at the door; the boss shoved the God's Ear gem into his pocket; and the carved door slammed its mouth shut.

Jake flung the rock forward, and the Lygme mouth-door caught the stone between its carved teeth. Jake skidded to the floor and peered between the open lines of the door's mouth.

Sawn had cracked the skull of the meshet, but the other two had thrown him to the floor for his efforts. Shocker wove another ball of energy between his hands, and the boss headed back out through the hole in the wall.

Jake screamed at them, tried to warn them to put the gem back, but they couldn't hear him. Mr. Shocker laughed at Jake as he followed the boss across the room.

Damn! All he needed was a pistol.

The boss stopped and looked down at his pocket. The gem glowed dull brown through the green and white fabric. He and Shocker grinned about it, then they cupped their hands over their ears and winced. The meshet shook their orange mains and scratched at their ears. They opened their mouths and seemed to howl.

A hole opened in the center of the floor, and wind whipped everyone's hair. Shocker and his boss dropped to their knees and held themselves against the wind. One of the meshet, the one closest to the hole, was pulled down by the force of the wind and sucked through the floor.

The second meshet released its grip on Sawn and let him be dragged down the hole.

"No!" Jake said, pounding his fists against the stone face.

In quick succession, the second meshet, then Shocker, and finally the boss himself were flung through the hole.

Jake stared through the gap in the carved face. The wind died down the moment the boss and the gem disappeared.

"I knew something like this would happen," Jake muttered. "I mean, I didn't know this-this would happen, but I knew it would be something like this. Something really bad. Why do I always have to be right?"

49

Jake

Jake looked around for anything to pry open the carved mouth. He saw rocks and sand and more rocks. Deciding a rock was his best option, he picked one up and started pounding it against the carved nose. It chinked against the door, and chips of rock flew back at him.

Wait, Jake thought, holding the stone in mid-strike. He'd heard the door. He snapped his fingers, and he heard the snap. He tapped the stone against the door, and he heard the tap.

"This can't be good," he heard himself say. Recalling that bad things always came in three's, he looked around to see what else had changed, and that's when he saw the lamp in the wall light by itself. One second it was dark, and the next second – poof! – bright, shiny, oil-lamp light.

"Oh, I hate weird, magical things," he said. He turned his attention back to the door. With all the other things he'd seen, he half expected the door to come to life while his back was turned. Thankfully, it didn't.

He boosted the power to his arms and smashed the rock against the door's mouth. A stone tooth chipped out of the door and flew into the room beyond. Encouraged, he struck the tooth next to it and knocked that one out too. He continued across the door until he'd knocked out enough teeth that he could fit. He wriggled his way through, chuckling at the thought of his rear end sticking out the mouth of a carved door. Then the thought of the door biting him in half made him hurry.

The room had lost its magical ability to let him hear things throughout the temple. He could only assume that ability came from the gem itself.

Ah, the gem. He'd known there were other people looking for this gem, but he had no idea who those people were or where they'd found their furry, orange meshet.

He knelt to the floor and peered down the hole in the center of the room. He boosted the power to his ears, but he didn't hear anything beneath him. He used his optical receptors to scan the walls of the hole, and he saw that the stone floor had crumbled down into it and scattered bits of rock across the damp walls. The hole itself was carved almost perfectly into a circle. It went down nearly twenty tics and then angled away from him, toward what was probably the center of the temple.

He started to bring up the maps with his tech when his audio amplifiers picked up the sound of shuffling feet in the hallway. He jumped back from the hole and crouched against the wall.

He didn't see anyone, but the hallway was lit with those same oil lamps recessed into the walls. It had probably made quite a show when all those lamps magically lit. He turned up his audio amplifiers and caught snatches of Lygmese.

He heard a lone, female voice that sounded like she was talking to herself. She said she regretted what she'd done, she'd really liked that human, she wondered if she had done the right thing, and on and on.

A grunt echoed down the hallway, and Jake slapped his hands across his ears at the noise. He cranked down the power to his audio amplifiers. Along with shuffling steps, he now heard heavy breathing, grunting, and a babbling of whispered Lygmese.

The babbling still came from the female Lygme who was gushing about somebody now. She told this guy how wonderful he was, how grateful she was that he was around, how she couldn't have done this without his help. The only response Jake heard was the shuffling and grunting.

He edged away from the hole as a meshet stepped into view. The creature cooed and grunted with each step, looking back and forth over its right shoulder and then its left at the Lygme woman gripping the orange fur around its neck.

"*Kepta suwee da,*" the woman said. Take me home, my love.

Jake thought he must have heard wrong. Lygmies were weird creatures, but he'd never heard of any of them playing house with the meshet.

"*Pootah ah indmee Urkay, eh?*" Did we capture Urkay?

The meshet nodded its head and grunted. Jake nearly fell over from the shock.

They're sentient! He leaned forward to get a better view of the animal as it walked away.

"*Beeta pluh. Kepta de padakaso, suwee.*" I'm very tired. Take me to our home, my love.

The meshet nodded and kept walking.

She's not crazy, Jake thought, staring at the floor and listening to the meshet's footsteps. *She's carrying on an intelligent conversation with a jungle animal that can think and respond to her.* And she seemed to know something more about what was going on than any of the other Lygmies Jake had met.

He made the decision about what to do next, and he acted before his brain could stop him. He stepped into the hallway and cleared his throat.

The Lygme leapt off the meshet's back before the animal could even spin around. She ran at Jake, her orange nails pointed at his face and her hair flying wildly behind her.

Jake revved to Fighting Mode and sidestepped her attack, backing against the wall and raising his hands above his head.

"Wait!" he said. "I want to talk."

The meshet had spun around by this time and launched past Jake's face to land on the Lygme. It held her to the ground with one powerful hand while she thrashed and screamed beneath its grip.

"I have no weapon," Jake said, powering down his implants. He wasn't sure how smart it was to leave himself vulnerable to attack, but he wanted information, not a fight.

The meshet turned to him and snarled, but it kept its hand on the Lygme woman's back. She screamed and clawed at the stone floor with those wicked, orange nails of hers until the fight seemed to leave her, and she threw her arms to the side and lay still and quiet.

The meshet looked down at her, and Jake wondered if she was unconscious or dead. She drew in a sharp, ragged breath that answered that question for him, and the meshet lifted its clawed hand from her back.

"Speak fast, human," she said, her voice ragged and harsh against the stone floor. "Next time, he may not be able to stop me."

"You can talk to him, can't you?" Jake said.

She pulled her arms back to her side and forced herself to sit up. The meshet supported her as it glared at Jake. The Lygme woman looked terrible, even by normal Lygme standards. Her eyes were bloodshot red and orange, her fingers were bloodied where the floor had broken off her nails, her head lolled back and forth like she couldn't support the weight, and her breaths came in short, uneven gasps.

"Are you okay?" Jake asked.

Her eyes focused on him for a few seconds, and she squinted like she was having trouble seeing him.

"Jake Alon?" she said.

He tensed. It was always bad when the other person knew your name.

"You sought the God's Ear," the Lygme woman said, her head falling forward again. "Did you not find it?"

"What do you know about that?"

"Did you find it?" the woman screamed.

The meshet gripped her shirt and kept her from lunging at Jake again. Her eyes bulged wide and orange at him, though, and Jake felt like backing a little further from this dangerous little Lygme.

"Yeah, I found it," he said.

"Then, where is it?" she said, looking back and forth across the hallway. *"Pukalah breek, eh? Nimblah lo fwe, eh?"* Why are you here? Where did you hide it?

Jake squatted so he could look the Lygme in the eyes those few times she actually looked up from the floor.

"You knew that gem was dangerous, didn't you?"

The meshet growled low, its eyes narrowing on him.

"Bokah lim sa milnatha, eh?" Who has the stone?

"What do you know about that gem?"

"Bokah lim sa milnatha, eh?" the Lygme screamed again.

Jake waited for something more, anything she would say that would make more sense.

"Voshta uim sa milnatha." Tell me about the stone.

Jake grinned. He glanced from the wild-eyed Lygme to her furry friend, then back to her again. His tech estimated he could easily fight or run from these two, and they could do little to hurt him. He had the upper hand, and he wasn't going to let it go.

"No," he said.

The Lygme lunged forward, her bloody fingers waving in the air.

Jake jumped back, ready to go into Fighting Mode, but the meshet had hold of the Lygme's shirt and shoulders. Her bare feet scraped against the floor, but the meshet didn't let her get any closer.

"Thanks," Jake said to the meshet.

The creature growled at him, then pulled the Lygme toward itself and wrapped her up in its furry arms. She calmed almost immediately, her head falling forward again as the animal petted her ragged, orange hair.

"Please," she whispered.

"An even exchange then," Jake said. "Question for question, and total honesty." He wasn't sure she would be honest with him, but he didn't have any information that would help her anyway. What did he have to lose?

"Agreed," she said. Her voice was muffled by the meshet's furry arm, but Jake heard her anyway.

"How did you know I came looking for the God's Ear gem?"

"We directed it to you." She lifted her head and really looked at him as she continued. "Now: who has the stone?"

Jake considered her answer before saying anything. She said they had directed the stone to him. What did she mean by that? Was she saying they planted the information for him to find? Did that mean the Lygme on the cruise ship wasn't really a renegade selling "secret information?" Or was it some trick of the translation that let her reverse her words? There were so many ways he could interpret her.

"Say that once more," Jake said, "but in your own language."

The Lygme sighed. *"Plitta vree, 'Sreh nemer kliptaling ee' tipaey, rek.'"*

Sreh nemer kliptaling, Jake thought. "We pointed to you...." *Ee' tipaey,* "God's Ear."

"You told the God's Ear where to find me?" Jake said.

"Bokah lim sa milnatha, eh?" Who has the stone?

"Right, our deal," Jake said. "The stone was taken by a guy in green and white...damn. Do you know the word 'fatigues,' or maybe 'camos?'"

"Yes," the Lygme said, clenching her eyes shut.

"Good. He was in green and white fatigues. He had a bunch of meshet with him, and his buddy was shooting lightning bolts everywhere."

The Lygme dropped her head against the meshet's arm. Her body jerked as a coughing fit hit her, and Jake saw tears pooling in the corners of her eyes.

"Okay, I get the feeling that's bad," Jake said.

"Why didn't you take the God's Ear?" the Lygme cried.

"No, this is my question." Jake thought through everything this little Lygme had told him: he had been set up from the start, the guy who had the gem now was a bad guy, and for some reason it would have been a much better thing if Jake had taken the gem like he was supposed to. But then he would have been sucked down that hole in the floor, and now he would be...where? "What does that gem do?" he asked.

"Lum de blankdeso Urkay, remda fin pilna sa."

"One-third of Urkay?" Jake said. "The part that lets him hear?"

"Why didn't you take the gem?"

"You're joking, right?"

The meshet growled.

"You told me that this whole thing was a trap, and you want to know why I wouldn't fall into it?"

"But your souls are in balance. We could have reached you. We could have worked with you." She opened her eyes and stared at him, and he noticed again the dark rings that encircled her bloodshot eyes. "Colonel Walraven, though.... We will not be able to stop him. He will kill us all, and then he will feed off our souls."

"Right," Jake said. Maybe the woman really was delusional. "One more question. My buddy, Sawn, he was with this Colonel when they were all sucked down a hole in the floor. I need to know where that hole goes so I can help him."

"Jake, you do not understand." The meshet hefted the Lygme's limp body into its arms. The tiny woman looked like she was about to collapse. "Your friend, and all the other humans we brought to this temple, they are all food for Urkay."

"You mean...this Urkay, he's going to eat them all?"

"First their bodies, and then their souls."

He'll eat them all. Jake turned and looked back into the small room where the God's Ear gem had been. He'd listened to conversations throughout the temple. He'd listened to Rhaina find another gem, the God's Eye gem that he didn't even know existed. They had been arguing about that gem, and their plastic man was determined to take it no matter what. But if he took the gem, and if Rhaina was still in that same room when it happened, then she probably got sucked down as food –

He turned to the Lygme again.

"Where are they?" he asked.

"Leave with us," the Lygme mumbled.

"Where is Rhaina?" Jake yelled.

The Lygme opened her orange eyes again and stared at Jake for several seconds, her breathing coming in shallow gasps.

"I told you," she said. "Food for Urkay."

50

Rhaina

Urkay pit

Rhaina shot from the tunnel and skidded on her back across the surface of the water, her arms flailing through the darkness. Her head hit something firm, and she tried to put her feet down in the water. A cold, plastic hand gripped her neck.

"Don't struggle," Majid whispered. "Tell me where we are."

"How do I know?" she choked out.

"You knew we would come here when we took the gem."

"I knew something bad would happen, but I didn't know what. Now let go."

Surprisingly, he did. Rhaina sat up in the shallow water, the ripples soaking her pants. She was tired of being wet no matter where she went in this awful jungle.

She called her Geminai and looked out through the spirit's eyes. They had fallen into a long, wide hallway interspersed with large holes along the bottom of the wall. Geminai flashed through all the holes and discovered that most were too steep to climb, and all were too slippery from years of algae growth.

With a pair of long screams, Cailin and Khonane shot from the same tunnel behind her and skidded across the shallow water. Rhaina jumped out of the way and grabbed at them as they raced past her. She caught hold and swung them to a halt beside her.

Khonane grunted as Cailin disentangled herself from him.

"You okay?" Cailin whispered.

He gave another grunting reply, and Rhaina's Geminai leapt into his body. She traveled from his head, down his spine, along his rib cage, past his hips, and stopped at the fracture in his leg. It had happened in the same spot already weakened from the crack several days earlier. She had no doubt he was in a lot of pain.

"It's a clean break," she said, jumping back into her own body again.

Majid gripped her shoulder, and she fought the urge to slap his hand away.

"Someone's coming," he whispered.

She looked past him and saw a dim glow approaching from far down the hallway. That could be a person, she thought, or it could be one more mystical surprise in this temple of traps. She thought it best not to take any chances, especially with Khonane hurt again.

"It's a man," Majid said. "He's alone."

"He's one of those Resurrected Mother people," Rhaina said as she looked through Geminai. "And he's carrying another gem like ours."

"Ah, your partner," Majid said.

"You're an idiot, even by plastic-man standards."

"Hello?" the man called, faint but clear. "Is...Is someone there?"

"What's the move?" Cailin whispered. She had her gun out and by her side. She'd also given Khonane a strip of cloth to bite down on.

"For now," Rhaina said, "I'll play friend. But you watch my back." She stood up, Majid at her side, and walked toward the stranger.

"Hello?" the man said.

"We're here," Majid yelled back.

"Oh, thank God," the man said. The light bounced as he started running down the hall.

"So who is he?" Majid whispered.

"I told you. I don't know."

"That's right. I'm supposed to believe you."

"The only reason we're down here is because Mr. Rosh is a stupid, greedy fool who didn't trust me enough to let me do my job."

"You were going to leave that gem. He did not want that, and I could not allow that."

"So here we are."

"I don't think I've ever been so glad to see someone before," the stranger said between quick breaths. He shone the light into Majid's face, then Rhaina's as he approached.

Rhaina blocked the light with her hand to try to see the stranger's face. According to Geminai, the man had a gun in the holster at his belt, but he made no move toward it. He was either trusting or stupid.

"Who are you people?" the man asked. "Have you found a way out of here?"

"Who are you?" Majid said.

"Sorry." The man stowed the light beneath his arm and extended his hand to the plastic man, apparently not even noticing that Majid's arm had been torn off at the elbow. Majid turned to hide the missing arm and clumsily shook the stranger's hand.

"Tone Dalal," the man said as he turned to Rhaina.

"What's with the outfit?" she asked, pointing to the man's camouflage shirt and pants.

He looked down like it was the first time he'd seen what he was wearing, then looked back at Rhaina and grinned. "Hey," he said, "it's a jungle out there."

He spun around and shone his light down the dark tunnel behind him. He flicked the beam back and forth, then turned to Rhaina and Majid and pretended to be calm again.

"Can we go now?" he asked.

Rhaina sent her Geminai down the hallway, but she didn't find anything unusual, certainly nothing that should make this man, this Tone Dalal, so agitated.

"What's down there?" Majid said, looking past Tone.

"I don't know," he said with a shrug. "Some animal; a big animal."

"Sure you're not just worried about that gem in your pocket?" Rhaina asked.

Tone's hand dropped to the pistol, but Majid's gun was shoved against his cheek before Tone could even react. He stared down the long, black barrel at Majid and held his breath.

Rhaina put her hand over Majid's and lowered the plastic man's gun.

"Don't worry," she said to Tone. "We're not going to take your gem. We have one of our own."

"You're a plastic man, aren't you?" Tone asked, his eyes wide at Majid.

Majid nodded.

"Then I'll stay with you, if you don't mind." He turned to Rhaina. "Unless...are you plastic, too?"

"Tone Dalal," Majid said. "What exactly are you running from?"

"I told you," he said with a twitch of his hand over the gun. "Some animal. Can we go before it comes back?"

Rhaina glanced down and saw a green circle glowing through Tone's shirt pocket. That's where he'd stowed the gem, but why was it glowing? She looked at Majid, and she saw the God's Eye gem glowing blue through his shirt.

That can't be good, she thought.

A barking roar caught their attention, and they all turned to one of the large holes along the wall. Tone shone his light, and a snarling meshet came shooting out. The bright orange animal twisted itself upright and dug its claws through the shallow water and into the floor. It came to a stop in the middle of the hall and twisted its head to look at them.

Rhaina tensed, ready for another fight, but Tone approached the thing.

"Jane?" he said. "Did you bring Jane?"

Sawn skidded out of the tunnel, followed closely by another meshet and two humans that Rhaina could only assume were the Resurrected Mother nuts. The first meshet reached out to stop the humans from sliding across the surface of the water while the new meshet stopped itself.

Before they could stand back up, Sawn grabbed the rifles from the Resurrected Mother soldiers. He tossed one to Rhaina and leveled the second on the two new men.

"Jackin' hell, that was fast!" the shorter man said.

"Shut up," Sawn said to him. "And do not spin another lightning bolt, or I'll shoot you between the eyes."

The two meshet stood up tall and sniffed the air.

"Tell them to settle down," Sawn said, gesturing to the animals.

"Tell them yourself," the second, taller man said. He turned around and saw Tone. "And look who we found in the sewers. Of course."

Tone didn't reply. He shuffled nervously from one foot to another.

Rhaina sent her Geminai to search these two new men while they postured. She found a couple knives stowed on each, a small pistol strapped above the big man's ankle, and a glowing, brown stone in the big man's pant pocket.

"Which gem did you find?" she asked, interrupting whatever blather they were spouting.

They all turned to her, and the big guy got a narrow-eyed grin on his face.

"I don't believe I've had the pleasure," he said, stepping forward and extending his hand.

"Do not go near her," Sawn said.

"You already have my gun," the stranger said with a drawn out sigh. He gave Rhaina what was probably his best, most charming smile. "What could I do to her?"

"I don't know," Rhaina said, returning his fakey grin. "Maybe something with that blade strapped to your arm?"

The man stopped grinning, sighed, and raised his hands. Sawn stepped forward and searched the man's left sleeve, pulling out a short-handled Borchard knife.

"And his right leg," Rhaina said.

"So the Amazon woman's in charge?" the man said as Sawn yanked the small gun from the ankle holster. "I'm Colonel Walraven, in case you were wondering."

A snappy retort sprang into Rhaina's mind, but before she could say anything her Geminai yelled for her. Rhaina turned her attention spiritual, and she saw the walls around them quivering, waving like flags in a breeze.

Rhaina jumped back into her body and grabbed the light from Tone's hand. She aimed it at the walls, but physically they looked normal.

With a series of pops, lights ensconced near the ceiling burst into flame. Flickering lamplight flooded the hallway, casting everything in a warm, orange glow. Half-circle beams of light bounced off the rough ceiling. Shadows played within the large sewer holes. Cailin stood up from her spot in the shadows, protectively hovering near the injured Khonane.

"This can't be good," the shorter man said.

"Rhaina," Majid said, staring into the distance. "I think we should leave."

Everyone turned to look.

"I don't see anything," Rhaina said, glancing back and forth.

"It's not what I see," Majid said, "but what I hear. Something very large is coming."

51

Jake

jungle temple

"Wait," Jake said. He ran after the meshet as it shuffled down the hall with the Lygme woman in its arms. "You can't leave. You're responsible for this mess!"

The meshet turned and nipped at him, then continued on. The Lygme barely moved.

"You said it yourself," Jake continued, hoping the woman could at least hear him. "If this thing gets loose again, it'll kill us all. No one would be safe, you said. Not me, not you, not your tribe."

The meshet stopped, and Jake had to jump aside to keep from running into it. The woman touched the animal's face and whispered to it in Lygmese. The meshet turned and glared at Jake, and then the thing knelt and laid the woman on the floor. She looked so small and weak; her arms lay sprawled at her sides and her mouth was open to let in quick, shallow breaths.

"She's dying, isn't she?" Jake asked.

The meshet barked at him and shoved him to the ground beside her. Jake almost revved to Fighting Mode, but the Lygme flopped her hand onto his leg, and he calmed himself. She opened her eyes, and they were almost pure orange staring up at him. Her hand shook, and she smelled so strongly of musk that he wished he had tech in his nose that he could turn off and not smell her.

"I must leave," she said. "I should have gone home long ago, but I had to complete this. And now...I failed."

"It doesn't have to be a failure," Jake said. He had no idea what the little Lygme was babbling about, and he really didn't care. Rhaina was in danger, and this dying Lygme would not help. "Tell me how to save my friends."

The meshet behind him placed its large, hairy paw on his back, and Jake tensed.

"Do not move," the Lygme whispered.

"You're asking for a lot of trust." His tech figured the odds and told him he wouldn't even have a chance to defend himself if the meshet decided to rip open his back.

"Turn off your machines," the Lygme said.

"No."

"Do so, and I will tell you what you want to know."

"Maybe you should tell me what I want to know before I speed you to your death."

The meshet's claws extended and touched Jake's spine.

"He will not let you hurt me," the Lygme said, "and I will not hurt you. Turn off your machines."

Against all rational judgement, he powered down the implants, shutting off the tech in his arms, legs, and body.

"All of it," the Lygme said.

Jake sighed. He had no idea how this little Lygme knew that he'd left power to the implants in his brain, but it was more than a little scary that she did. What other abilities did the Lygmies hide?

He shut his eyes, powered down the tech in his brain, and the world around him went silent. He couldn't remember the last time he'd turned off his entire body; he didn't like the sensation of being alone with his own thoughts. His first reaction was to check his implants to be sure he was still alive, but the in-and-out of his own breaths assured him that he was.

A low ringing echoed through his ears, and he tried to adjust to the idea that he couldn't hear the Lygme breathing or the rustle of the meshet's fur or any other of a hundred little sounds he'd grown accustomed to his tech picking up and sorting for him automatically.

The Lygme put her hands to the sides of his head, and Jake opened his eyes as she pulled him towards her. They touched foreheads, and the world exploded.

A rolling sea of images flooded into Jake. In a second, he traversed the entire planet of Udo, scurrying back out of this jungle nightmare, flying low over rolling oceans to land on the shores of the Eastern Continent where the tall-grass prairies stretched wide across the horizon, then further north, along the foothills of the sub-arctic plains and high on top of the tallest mountains ringing the northern ice shelf. The frigid ice dropped away beneath Jake's feet, and he flew through the clouds, out of the planet's atmosphere, and into the empty, silent blackness of the space above. He floated there, watching the planet shrink into the distance, moving at incredible speed for it to disappear that quickly, yet somehow believing he was sitting perfectly still on the dirty floor of the Lygme temple hidden deep in the forest of the Northern Continent.

Jake shut his eyes to the slow, rhythmic turning of the stars around him. It wasn't real, and he refused to be sucked into a hallucination brought on by the musky scent of the Lygme woman who held his head.

A pair of eyes opened before him and stared back through his closed lids, the bright, orange flecks of the irises spinning away from tiny, black pupils. The Lygme eyes narrowed on him, and Jake knew the pupils focused tightly on his mind. He felt the Lygme's presence as it rummaged through his thoughts, pulling at memories Jake barely recalled having: personal experiences from his childhood, the happy times with his mother and father, his own escapades running errands for little money and high risk just so he could have adventures to share with his friends.

He started to close down his thoughts to this invasive mind when a second pair of eyes appeared before him, another Lygme who pulled at different memories: the times he was hurt as a child by the neighborhood bully, the dozens of evenings he stared longingly through the telescope in his back yard and wished for something more, a place he could go and people who would accept him for who he was.

A third, and then a fourth pair of eyes appeared. More minds tapped into his subconscious, pulling at memories long forgotten and parading them for Jake and everyone else to see and experience as if they were their very own. Jake grabbed at the flashes of thought, tried to pull down the screens of drama playing before the eager audience of minds, screamed at the cheering crowds of eyes who seemed determined to make him replay his entire life for no other reason than their simple viewing pleasure.

Then they were gone.

Jake spun around in the darkness of his own private thoughts again, searching for any sign of the intrusive minds. There seemed to be only one left, and he knew that one was the mind of the little Lygme kneeling before him on the dusty, stone floor.

She stood beside him, took his hand, and turned him away from his thoughts until he focused on her.

He tried to ask several questions at once: who were those other minds? Where had they come from, and where had they gone? Why were they so interested in his past?

But nothing came out, no matter how hard he tried to open his mouth and speak.

The Lygme woman, Thilemon, or "Jane" as she had been called by the Resurrected Mother soldiers, turned Jake's attention to the past. Not her past, though, but the far, ancient past, before she was born, before her tiny band of Lygmies came together to form their own family groups, before this jungle was even a jungle. They stood together on the muddy fields of an even more ancient feud that had grown to swallow up the young Lygme men in violent battles.

Thousands of Lygmies rushed onto the field of battle, surrounding Jake and Thilemon with screams, swinging swords, the clash of armor, and the overwhelming scent of bloody carnage. Lygmies fought. Lygmies died. Then, they were gone.

Seasons passed in an instant, a year, or maybe two – Jake wasn't certain – and the battle repeated itself with fresh armies. Lygme men clashed, fell, died, and dispersed as before. The seasons came and went again, the armies returned and fought again, and the seasons passed – again. The cycle continued, over and over for what seemed like hundreds, maybe thousands of years. The feud, whatever had touched it off at the start, continued throughout the generations as children, grandchildren, and the grandchildren of the grandchildren fought, died, and returned the following year to do it all over again.

And then one year, one tribe of warriors entered the field of battle with a giant in their lead, a champion to defend them. This new Lygme, if it even was a Lygme, towered over Jake as it approached. The opposing Lygmies rushed to the fight, but the champion struck down the first wave of fighters with one swift pass of its giant sword. Lygme heads, bodies, and limbs flew through the air, and the champion roared triumphant.

For the first time since Jake and Thilemon watched the battles, the fighting moved from this blood-stained field. The champion put the opposing army in retreat, and the victorious fighters pursued them relentlessly. They slaughtered Lygme warriors in their sleep, routed entire armies without a single loss, leveled towns and villages that dared to stand against them, and lined up captives for slaughter.

And the champion yawned.

Jake watched the champion's face as, battle after battle, he continued looking bored. He swung his sword, he slaughtered warriors and innocents by the hundreds, but he seemed to want something more. He grew restless at nights, walking the hillsides by himself and slaying dozens of nighttime predators just for the pure enjoyment of the fights.

He became more ruthless in the battles, no longer satisfying himself with the simple kills. He toyed with his opponents, hurt them a little at a time until they cried in anguish for death to take them. He strung pymgy warriors from the rafters of their own ransacked homes to watch them writhe in the wind. He tied children to the tails of wild beasts and laughed as the animals made sport of them. He no longer killed the captive women, but stripped them naked, tied them together, and forced them to serve his every desire. When they refused him, he sliced off an arm or a leg. If they continued to oppose him, he ran them through with his sword and forced the survivors to tow the body parts behind them.

The Champion's army – for it had become the Champion's army, not the Lygme warriors' army – found less resistance with each battle until finally they entered every town and rural village to find them deserted, abandoned. In the face of overwhelming opposition, their Lygme enemies had chosen to flee with their few remaining families rather than become an extinct tribe.

The Champion railed against his cowering, warrior subordinates. He accused them of treachery, claiming a bargain of life-long warring and bloodshed that they had broken with their first campaign. They tried to console him, to make promises of other campaigns, other enemies in faraway lands that they always wanted to destroy but never had resources to meet in battle. And then one warrior, the most scarred and beaten of the Champion's select men, came to the Champion while he was sleeping and ran him through with a two-handed sword, pinning the Champion's struggling body to the ground.

But their Champion did not die. Instead, he became like a raging animal. He yanked the sword from his body and struck down the warrior who'd tried to slay him. His rampage turned on the rest of the army, and he pursued them into the night, killing them with that same two-handed sword and hacking their bodies into small parts that lay strewn across the hills and valleys.

When all his warriors were slain, the Champion turned his attention back on the warriors' homes. He traveled far to reach villages defended by only the smallest of ineffectual forces. He slaughtered them all, stringing up the bodies as a message that he would be avenged for the treachery of his comrades.

He traveled back along the prairies, through the hill country, and onto the desolate plain where he first laid the opposing army to ruin, and he was met with a combined force the likes of which the Lygme world had never before seen. Urnto and Prakto tribes, the Illnetah and Laan families with their combined seventeen generations, and, for the first time ever, the wild meshet and partome – enemies one and all, from the smallest Lygme child to the mightiest partome beast – were brought onto the battlefield.

The Lygmies streamed forward, rushing to their deaths at the Champion's sword. Blood sprayed the field. Lygmy bodies littered the ground at the Champion's feet. And the partome and meshet locked scaly fin with furry wing to encircle the field of battle.

The animals chanted in their own barks and howls as the battle raged within their circle. Power rose from the song they chanted, and the Lygme warriors all fell dead. Their spirits fled their bodies, only to be barred from entering the afterlife by the ring of power the animals had formed.

The Champion advanced on the nearest meshet, ready to slice his way free, but the Lygme spirits tore into the Champion's physical body. They tormented him, cut into his skin, flesh, and bones with their nails of finely honed spirit.

Weakened by the onslaught of the Lygmies' spiritual attack, the Champion collapsed to the ground, and that is when the partome and meshet chanted a different melody, this one of barks, growls, yips, and mourning howls.

The dead Lygmies used their spiritual energies to slice off the Champion's ears, gouge out his eyes, and hack off his feet. The three parts of the Champion's body crystalized into gems, precious stones that would be shattered and their tiny pieces cast into oceans far removed from each other.

But instead of destroying the stones, Lygmies flocked to the site of this, the most horrific battle ever waged, and they began piling stones one on top of another to encompass the still-chanting partome and meshet. They built walls, constructed multiple floors and encased the three gems within rooms where they could paint intricate scenes detailing the horrors they had wrought upon each other.

The spirits of the slain Lygmies were trapped inside this physical shell, haunting the walls and hallways and harassing the pymgy pilgrims who came to view this shrine of destruction.

As the chanting partomes and meshet died away, the remains of the Champion's body struggled back to life. Without eyes, ears, or feet upon which to stand, the Champion crawled blindly through the dead muck encased within the ground floor walls, slaying any who dared to approach it and eating their raw remains.

Seasons passed, the temple grew more elaborate. Landscaped sections were built to beautify and reverence this Shrine of Destruction. And then the rains began to fall. Centuries came and went. Forests encroached on the temple's grounds until they overran it.

The Lygmies stopped coming. The Shrine of Destruction faded into legend, then myth, then some ancient story that was told to frighten children of old – for if they did not behave, the Champion Urkay would come and steal them away to his dungeon to eat them.

The chanting meshet and partome had known the hearts of their Lygme kinsmen, though, and they had seen the greed in the Lygme eyes as the Champion's bodily gems were placed reverently within sealed vaults as the Shrine of Destruction was built around them. And the animals' chant had changed. It was a subtle change, a bark instead of a yip, a growl in place of a purr. Just enough to alter the spell that kept the Champion bound, enough to ensure that no Lygme could ever again bring the Champion Urkay back to life.

But then, millennia later, the humans came. Lygmies died defending their homes. Humans died defending their machines. Fear, and then hatred, swelled within each group until a tribe of young Lygmies ventured into the forgotten forests to resurrect the Champion Urkay who would drive away the human invaders and restore the stolen Lygme land, restore the memory of the tortured and slain Lygme warriors. But the ways to the gems had been blocked, and no pymgy hand could reopen them. No Lygme hand could ever again hold them.

Rumors of the gems were spread. Information – maps, inflated values, tales of danger and riches – was spread throughout the human colonies and distilled into the conversations of humans returning to Earth until the young Lygmies finally attracted enough attention to coax three groups of humans into the forest to lay their alien hands on the magical stones and restore the Champion Urkay–

Jake fell back with a gasp. He shook his head. He blinked at the blinding torch-light all around. He tried to see clearly through the tears that had welled up in his eyes. The tale of centuries of destruction still swam before his eyes.

The Lygme woman lay dying at his feet, her arms limp at her side and her dry mouth gaping open. The meshet knelt to the floor and scooped her body in its arms.

"Wait," Jake said, grabbing the meshet's arm.

The meshet snarled, but Jake did not let go.

"How do we stop it?" he asked.

The meshet snorted and shook its head. Then it stood up and carried off the dying Lygme, not even glancing back.

52

Jake

Jake blinked and twisted his eyes to the right. Every piece of tech burst to life, and he processed the vision that Thilemon had given him. He downloaded as much as he could recall: the fierce fighting, the Champion, the meshet force, the building of the temple, and...the jackin' way he and Rhaina had been used by these hateful little Lygmies.

He muttered a curse at them and their civil war.

No, he thought. Not a civil war. A generational family feud. The Lygmies thousands of years ago had decided the fighting would stop, and now these Lygmies today decided they wanted to fight again. They probably kept the hatred alive for all those years, fed their children a steady diet of familial bloodshed and revenge.... Hell, they even trained their pets to fight each other – if those meshet and partome monsters could be called pets.

He brought his attention back to the data his tech was analyzing. The most immediately useful piece of information seemed to be the map piecing together from the temple construction part of his vision. He zoomed in and out of the three-dimensional map, first locating himself, then finding the dungeon where he'd seen the "Champion Urkay," that slug-thing that tried to eat him.

He imagined Rhaina being eaten by that slug, and he took off at a run. He overlaid the temple map across his sight, the digital schematic twisting and rotating as he ran. He turned left, then right down a flight of stairs, another right, a left down a second flight of stairs and into a flooded hallway. He slogged his way through waist-deep water, following the winding passageways back and forth through the maze-like temple. The lower he went, the more confusing the construction became, like those first builders were inept at building anything on this grand a scale.

According to the map, he had to go down one more flight of stairs, but he didn't like the idea of swimming through the stagnant water. Worse yet, the female spirit creature rose in front of him. She put out her hand to block the way, her hair waving behind her in a non-existent breeze.

"Hi," Jake said, sloshing forward. "You've been a great help. I found the gem and everything, but now I have to get down those stairs."

"No," she said.

"No. Right...well...." He stepped to the left and she glided in front of him. He stepped to the right and she followed him again. Jake looked past her and into the dark water. He couldn't see it, but the map clearly showed the stairs to the dungeon on the other side of this spirit woman. "Look, miss, you've been a great help, but I really have to get by you."

"No."

He was about to start yelling when he heard another voice behind him speaking Lygmese. He turned and saw a second creature hovering in the air behind him. The two spirits glared at each other as the one behind Jake kept talking.

His tech tried to translate for him, but most of the words didn't have an equivalent, like she spoke some Lygmese variation he'd never before heard. Instead, he had to piece together their conversation from the fragments that came through. The two creatures threatened each other – that was obvious even without the translation. Then they traded insults – quite well, judging from the twisted looks they gave each other.

And then dozens more of the creatures rose up from the water, some standing with the second creature, but most hovering around the first and blocking the way to the stairs. They looked identical, the men like all the other men and the women like the other women.

Jake stepped back as slowly as he could in the waist-high water, trying not to draw attention to himself. The creatures were all yelling, pointing, and glaring at each other. This was obviously a longstanding argument, and Jake wanted no part of it.

A frozen shiver passed through him, sending icy pinpricks down his back, neck, and arms. He took another step and came out the back side of one of the male spirits. The creature didn't seem to care as it drifted forward, adding its own raised voice to the argument echoing off the walls.

The hallway was now filled with dozens of spirits, all threatening each other and all drifting further from the underwater stairwell. Jake edged toward the wall as he watched the spirit creatures. None of them noticed him. He took a deep breath, flipped on the breathing regulator in his lungs and slipped beneath the water's surface.

He heard the argument still raging as he drifted quietly through the murky water. He had no idea how many diseases he was exposing his eyes to, but he kept them open anyway. It would be far worse to blindly bump into one of those spirit creatures.

He gently swam toward the submerged stairwell, careful to keep his strokes slow and smooth. As he got closer, though, something didn't seem quite right. Two steps down, the water looked like it wavered, like Jake was looking through a clear wall at – of all crazy things – more flaming sconces. His tech analyzed the silvery refractions – the water stopped at the second step.

He drifted to the stairs and tentatively reached his hand toward the shimmering wall. He stuck one finger through. Then a second finger. His whole hand. He flexed his fingers and twisted his hand, watching the silvery, distorted reflection. He didn't feel any water resistance on the other side. It really was a wall to hold back the water.

The argument above him stopped. Jake turned and saw the creatures drop back into the water and rush at him.

He shoved against the first stair and fell backwards through the water. He sailed through the shimmering wall and collapsed to the stairwell, cracking his head against the dark stones. Spots bounced before his eyes, and the breathing regulator shut down at the first gasp of breath.

Something gripped his ankles and yanked him back up. He smacked the back of his head against the next couple steps, then gripped the stairs with his hands and looked up through the choppy wall of water. Dozens of spirit creatures struggled against each other on the other side for a grip on his legs. He felt his ankles pop as they twisted his legs to get a better hold. Then one group took his left leg and pulled while the other group took his right leg and pulled him the other way. His groin muscles screamed as the creatures tried to tear him apart like a wishbone.

He revved to Fighting Mode and felt the muscles in his body tighten. He clamped his legs together and knocked several of the creatures into each other – not that he felt any sympathy. Bracing against the stones, he shoved away and down the stairwell. The spirits tore at his leg, dragging their claws through his pants and clouding the water with his blood.

Jerking back, his legs came free, and he tumbled down the stairs, bumping and scraping across the rough stones. He stopped beneath a flaming sconce and looked back to see one of the spirits diving through the water wall and down the stairs after him.

Jake's body responded before his mind told it to, and he jumped to his feet, ready to fight. The creature – one of the men this time – stumbled on the second step and collapsed to his hands and knees. He crawled another couple steps closer to Jake, then he seemed to lose the strength in his arms and fell face-first against the stone.

Jake's tech did a quick scan of the creature, but the results were worthless. The things were as much spirit as water, neither of which told him if this one was still alive. He looked up to the water wall at the top of the stairs, but none of the other creatures was there anymore.

"Don't...."

Jake looked down. The man's liquid body was melting on the stairs, and he had turned his head enough to look up at Jake.

"Don't what?" Jake asked, powering down his implants.

"Don't kill." His legs dissolved, the water pooling across the steps. His head started swelling, and he had to open his mouth wider for the words to come out clearly. His head burst, spraying water down the steps as the rest of his body collapsed into a muddy pool.

53

Jake

Jake bounded down the hall. The flickering lamplights shone bright before him, a long, narrow passageway with metal-barred doors down each side. He counted a dozen prison cells, a few of them standing open, but all of them in perfect, shining condition.

"Jackin' mystical shit," Jake muttered as he took a cautious step forward. He didn't see any of the overgrown moss or rusted-out bars or dilapidated stones he'd seen when he was trapped in this dungeon only a few hours earlier. He had his tech cranked up high, his ears catching every creak and groan of the temple structure, his eyes seeing through the darkest shadows cast by the cell walls, and his skin sensing every breath of wind around him –

Which made him wonder why he was feeling any wind at all.

He caught the distant sound of Rhaina's voice, and his heart beat a little faster. He had to restrain himself from running down the hall and bursting in to rescue her. He trusted his instincts enough to know when they were telling him to be cautious, and right now they were screaming at him to take it slow.

From behind, he heard a footstep on the stone floor.

In front, though, several soft footsteps came at him, and a cat's nose and whiskers poked around the corner of an open cell door.

"Jake," the cat hissed, his eyes flashing gold at him.

Jake stopped. The footsteps behind him stopped, too, but he heard at least two distinct sets of breathing. He was being set up for an ambush.

"Well, if it ain't the little nipster addict," he said.

The cat's ears cocked sideways. "I told you," he said. "I am not some junked up alley-cat."

"Oh, right," Jake said, listening to the steps behind him. "Being a junked up Pouncer-cat is much more prestigious."

"I should tear out your throat for that insolence."

"Go ahead and try," Jake said, circling around to stand directly in front of the Pouncer. His right ear still picked up the two sets of breathing, but now his left ear heard another three sets from further down the hall in the other direction. Were they with the Pouncer, or were they both being set up?

"Lick me," the Pouncer said. He sat and started washing his face with his paw, and that pretty much answered Jake's question about who was being set up by whom.

"Well, if you're going to be a jackin' wimp about it...." Jake revved to Fighting Mode, spun to his left, and took off down the hall at the fastest run his tech'd legs would give him.

Three slow-motion forms sprang at him from within the prison cells. Jake twisted and ducked and left their muddy arms and long claws slashing the air behind him. He continued down the hall, the doors sliding past his left and right side at deceptively slow crawls. As he neared the "T" junction at the end of the hall, his tech told him to take a left, and he turned in time to see a muddy, black creature with long, stringy hair and gill slits in its neck stand up and block his way.

Jake tried to stop, but his feet skidded across the floor's loose dirt. His legs twisted out from under him, and his tech tried to compensate, tried to keep him upright and steady.

The creature's hand came up, its fingers wide open to grab hold. It locked on tight to Jake's neck and threw him backwards to the ground. He felt the back of his head pound against the stone floor, and he knew the creature had cracked his skull. His tech immediately responded with a flood of nanobots to repair the damage.

Jake pounded his right fist into the creature's cheek, sending a spray of blood from his own knuckles as much from the thing's mouth. The creature spun back with a clawed slash across his face.

His Fighting Mode took control, and Jake struck back with a left, then a right, and another left to the creature's head and neck. He felt the bones crunch with each blow, and the creature finally stopped fighting back. He started to throw the thing's bloody body off himself when two more of them reached his side, gripped his arms, and sat on them.

Jake struggled against their weight, thrashing around and kicking out with his legs. Somehow, the things were able to avoid him and stay across his arms. Another of the creatures leapt from the shadows and landed on top of Jake and the already dead thing. He felt the breath knocked out of him, and blood splattered his face from the dead animal's broken mouth.

Within moments, he was immobolized by their combined weights, and his tech was kind enough to flash before his eyes his dwindling odds of escape.

The black and white pouncer trotted down the hallway toward them, licking back his whiskers and watching Jake's struggle through gleaming, golden eyes.

"You are an impressive human specimen," the pouncer purred.

The four muddy, gill-slitted creatures holding down Jake's arms all turned and watched the pouncer approach. Meanwhile, Jake's tech offered such useful suggestions as: "Kick one opponent in the crotch" and "Free your left leg." Of course, his tech failed to tell him why his left leg would work any better than his right.

"All out of escape ideas?" the pouncer asked as he sat a few tics away.

"Just lying here," Jake said, "and giving you a false sense of security."

"Jake, does your tech provide you with those pithy comments, or do they come natural to you?"

"It's a human trait. Pity you're not one of us."

The pouncer gave one of his laugh-approximating sniffles and started washing his face again.

"In a moment," he said, "you won't be 'one of us' either."

The four creatures turned and snarled at Jake.

"Wait," Jake said. "You haven't told me your role in all this yet."

"Oh," the pouncer said, standing and stretching out his long back. "You mean you want me to explain to you my evil plot to destroy all the humans on this planet and to set my fellow captives free?"

"Yes, please. In detail."

"No." The pouncer looked at the four creatures. "Kill him."

54

Rhaina

Urkay prison

Rhaina sited the gun at the slug's ample torso. She fired three shots dead into what she assumed was its belly. The thing didn't even slow down – and it was fast! It spun and knocked her to the flooded floor, sending her skidding across the hall.

Move! her Geminai yelled. She rolled away through the lapping water, and the slug rammed into the wall beside her, sending chunks of rock flying.

She heard people yelling for her to get out of the way, and she stumbled backwards as a barrage of gunfire struck the creature and the wall around it. The thing shrugged off the shots, splashed back around, and stampeded after the others again. Rhaina stood and watched the thing for a few moments as the eco-military man launched several dozen lightning bolts into its hide.

We won't win this with brute force, she thought, *and certainly not as disorganized as we are now. We need a way out of here,* and her Geminai flew away to find it.

Rhaina ran across the hall to help Khonane stand. He wrapped his arm across her shoulder and staggered up beside her, and the two of them stumbled through the splashing water. Rhaina caught Sawn's attention where he was shooting at the slug from across the hall. He grabbed Cailin's arm and they followed.

"Do you know where we're going?" Khonane asked.

"Yes," Rhaina said, pointing her gun down the hall in front of them. "That way."

The gun suddenly jerked her arm forward, and Rhaina staggered face first into the water, dragging Khonane down with her. She heard Khonane's pain-filled yell a moment before the water covered her ears, and then she lost her grip on him. The gun tugged her through the water, and it was all she could do to keep her grip on the thing as she tried to get her feet back under her again.

Someone grabbed her left arm and pulled her up.

"What happened?" Sawn yelled.

The gun strained against Rhaina's grip, and Sawn's eyes went to her outstretched arm.

"Whose weapon is that?"

"It's Jake's," Rhaina whispered. She released her grip, and the gun flew from her hand. It skipped across the surface of the water as it continued down the hall away from them. "Come on," she yelled.

They splashed after the gun, the sounds of fighting growing dim behind them. She hadn't even allowed herself the time to mourn Jake, not with this god-forsaken job threatening to kill her around every corner. A niggle of doubt played at the back of her mind: What if he wasn't really alive? What if the gun had malfunctioned and taken off on its own? Or what if the gun didn't get to him quickly enough to save him from whatever was threatening his life?

She shoved those thoughts aside.

"Wait for me!" someone yelled.

She skidded to a stop. That eco-terrorist with the funny name – Tone? – ran toward them, and he held his blue gem in his hand. The slug followed close behind, water flying to the walls as it barreled along, and Majid led the remaining eco-terrorists as they chased after the thing.

"Out of the way!" Rhaina said. She grabbed Cailin and Khonane and shoved them toward the wall.

Sawn stood his ground in the center of the hallway. He raised his pistol and sited the slug coming at him.

"Sawn," Rhaina yelled. "Get out of there!"

The slug jumped into the air and flew at Tone's back.

Sawn let loose a barrage of gunfire at the creature's head.

The creature struck Tone square in the back, pounding his body to the flooded floor and sending waves lapping down the hall. The impact sent the gem flying from Tone's hand. It arced away from him as he disappeared beneath the slug's body.

Sawn snatched the stone from the air.

The slug leapt forward again.

"No!" Rhaina yelled, reaching for the gun – that was no longer at her hip.

Sawn spun away, but the creature clipped his shoulder, yanked him beneath the water, and flopped on top of him.

Cailin and Khonane started shooting. Majid stood in the center of the hall and shot. The eco-terrorist launched lightning bolts into the thing's slimy hide, leaving scorch marks and filling the air with the stench of burnt flesh.

Geminai! Rhaina thought, and her second soul flew back to her side. The spirit circled the slug from all angles, trying to see any way to get at Sawn, but the thing had him enveloped. Its brown skin pulsed, and a blue glow emanated from the thickest part of the creature's bulk.

Geminai attacked the thing spiritually, slashing its sides and trying to penetrate it anywhere she could. She followed several of the lightning bolts into its body, digging spiritual claws ahead of the bolts to try to get them further into the thing and do more damage. The skin closed in behind her as quickly as the lightning traveled through, and Geminai had to shove her way back out. A brown muck began coating her spiritual body, and she itched all over.

The slug sprang up, Sawn's glowing, blue body suctioned to its underbelly. The rags of his clothes fell off his body in strips.

Cailin stumbled back into Rhaina. "What do we do?" she yelled.

Rhaina stared as the slug stretched to the ceiling, lifting Sawn's naked body with it. It pulled his arms and legs to their extremes and then beyond, popping his joints and stretching his muscles until Rhaina didn't have to imagine their tearing sound.

Majid, Tone, and Khonane sloshed through the standing water to Rhaina's side. The two eco-terrorists backed further down the hall.

Rhaina shut her eyes and saw through her Geminai. The spirit flitted around the stretching slug, trying to get a clear look through Sawn's body. The slug had gripped him with some sticky residue along its underbelly, and it seemed to be absorbing his body into its own. Glowing, blue slime slid across his face, down his neck, and along his shoulders and chest. Muscles twitched throughout his body as he tried to pull himself loose.

Geminai pounded her spiritual fists into the slug's underbelly. Her hands came away sticky and dripping with blue slime, but the slug actually flinched at the hits. She continued the onslaught as Sawn's body slipped inside the thing. The creature let out a deafening roar that made Geminai flinch and forced Rhaina back into her body long enough to cover her ears, and then the thing dropped to the ground.

Geminai darted out of the way as the creature crashed to the floor, water flying against the walls and soaking everyone. It sprang forward on rear-jointed legs, pouncing on the sloshing water like an animal going for the kill. It lifted its head and studied the long hallway, then bounded forward with the grace of a leopard. In a moment, it was gone, its thunderous leaps echoing back down the hall.

"What was that?" Cailin blurted.

"I think we would do well to find a way out of here," Majid said.

"Understatement of the year, Tin Man," the eco-terrorist Colonel said. He and his buddy helped Tone stumble out from beneath the water. Tone coughed, and his face and arms were bruised, but he was still alive.

"Give me the gem," Rhaina said, turning to Khonane.

"No," Khonane said. "Weren't you watching? That thing went straight for whoever was holding that stone."

"Exactly. This stone is my responsibility, not yours."

"No. We're a team, and the stone is the team's responsibility."

Rhaina pulled her rifle out of its case behind her back and pointed it to the floor. "Give me the stone," she said.

Khonane glared at her, but he pulled the glowing, green rock from his pocket and handed it over. "You know," he said, "I don't think you've ever threatened me before."

"I'm not threatening you," she said. "I'm keeping you alive."

"Wait," Majid said. He turned and listened down the long hall. "The creature is returning."

55

Jake

Urkay prison

The gun flew into Jake's hand, and his Tech sprang into action. He twisted his hand back and fired at the muddy creature sitting on his arm. The thing yelped and leapt away. The Tech calculated the next shot, zeroed in on the second creature, and Jake's fingers pulled the trigger. This shot went straight though the thing's belly, and the animal fell off.

With that off his chest, Jake sat up and took aim at the third animal. That one slashed Jake's face in one quick flick of its arm.

"Jackin' hell," he muttered. "That hurt."

As the thing reared back for another strike, Jake sited it with his tech and fired. The creature fell, and the fourth one turned and high-tailed it out of there, up the stairs and through the water wall.

Jake's tech searched the long hallway for that damn pouncer, but in the excitement of being beat up, he hadn't seen the thing run off. Pouncers still had enough real cat in them that Jake couldn't believe this one would willingly take the swimming route like its muddy thug, and that meant that the little critter was still somewhere inside the dungeon.

His amplified ears picked up the sounds of people fighting and some large animal splashing through water, but that was all coming from behind him. He couldn't hear the pouncer. The little thing had to be pulling some alley-cat hiding trick on him, and he didn't have time to play games with it.

"So long, little pouncer," Jake yelled. "Hope you can swim."

He turned back to the "T" in the hallway and headed for the cell door at the end of the left turn. Just like before, it was covered in stringy moss, and the bars were as solid from the outside as they were from within the cell. He pushed aside the moss and peered inside. The long dungeon was lit with wall sconce torch lamps as far back as he could see. The walls gleamed new, and the shallow water rippled toward the cell door.

Jake started tugging the mossy vines aside, revealing more of the cell door and the fist-wide bolts that held it in place. He uncovered three hinges on the left side, backed away, and shot them off. He yanked hard and the door fell forward until the tangled vines caught it tight. He stepped around the tilting door, through the damp vines, and back into the sprawling dungeon he'd escaped only a few hours before.

"Honey, I'm home," he whispered, looking around the dungeon. After all he'd been through, he was almost disappointed when the psycho spirit woman didn't spring out and attack him. Almost.

His tech amplified the sounds of fighting further down the hall: shouting, splashing, gunfire. He took off at a run, his tech re-analyzing the dungeon hallway now that all the torches lit it from one end to the other. Drain spouts emptied into the dungeon every ten tics, their gaping holes large enough for two people to crouch side by side. Water trickled out of them and dripped to the floor, but not nearly as much as had been gushing out when he fell through that first drain.

The hall curved as he ran. The shouting became louder, and he picked out Rhaina's voice as she yelled for her people to follow her.

Then the creature came into view, and Jake had to slow down and stare at the thing. No longer the blind, stupid slug that had tried to barrel him over, the thing had developed a rather man-like form as it stood about twice as high as Jake, its arms extended to the ceiling. Its body pulsated, and its limbs began to define themselves as real arms and legs. Fingers grew out of its stumpy arms, and it gripped the ceiling, tearing out chunks of rock and raining down pebbles onto itself.

Two ears opened up on the side of the creature's head, and the thing spun around toward Jake. Its chest and arms were dripping red, and it had a man stuck to its body like it had fallen on him. Jake didn't know the man's name, but he recognized the face as that eco-terrorist leader. The creature's body convulsed, and the eco-terrorist was swallowed up within the thing.

Jake stopped in the middle of the hall. The creature bent down and started running at him, its thick, stump-wide legs pelting water everywhere. Jake raised his gun. The tech scanned the creature's advancing form and lined up a shot.

The creature's gaping mouth and empty eye sockets looked straight at Jake, and then the thing's head sort of shifted. The slug-like features became more defined, and for a half second Jake thought he saw that eco-terrorist's face grin back at him.

The tech recalculated the shot as the creature bounded forward. Twenty tics away. Jake put a little more pressure on the trigger. Eighteen tics. The crosshair tracked the creature's bulky form, assuming the spot of greatest vulnerability. Seventeen tics.

The face changed again, and this time the shape became immediately familiar.

Sawn? He hesitated.

The creature made a sudden leap, covering the distance between them in a fraction of a second. It struck Jake's shoulder and sent him flying against the wall, then it let out a roaring laugh as Jake's body crumpled against the solid stone. He fell into the lapping water, and his tech was kind enough to inform him that he was seriously hurt.

56

Rhaina

Urkay prison

"Jake!" Rhaina watched helplessly as his body flew through the air. He struck the wall, and his neck snapped back before he fell into the water.

"Don't!" Majid said, gripping her shoulder.

"I'm not stupid," Rhaina snapped. What did he think, that she was going to rush in and get herself killed?

She turned back to her team, but everything within her ached to run to Jake and pull him from the water. She had to be smart about this if they were going to keep anyone else from getting killed.

She looked at Cailin and Khonane, and she knew she couldn't ask either of them to face this creature. They would both do it, but Khonane's leg was injured, and Cailin was his best way out of this dungeon. Sawn was dead. Those three eco-terrorists had been killed: Tone drowned, Shocker was thrown against a wall like Jake, and that pompous Colonel of theirs had been sucked inside the creature, just like Sawn. That left her alone with the plastic man, Majid.

"Cailin, get him out of here," Rhaina said, pointing to Khonane. She turned to the plastic man. "And you, Majid or Rosh or whoever is looking at me now."

"I am Majid," the plastic man said. "Mr. Rosh only inhabits this shell. I control it."

"Right. You're with me."

"I am crippled." He twisted his body, showing the empty hole where his right arm used to be. He'd tied off the exposed tubing, but the wires and circuits still sat exposed under the ragged fringes of his ripped shirt.

"You're a tough man to kill," she said. "And you're not getting out that easy."

"Wait," Khonane said. He pulled her toward him, and he wrapped his arms around her.

It was a completely unromantic moment with the slug bearing down on them, and she couldn't believe he would choose this moment to express feelings for her. On the other hand, it felt really good to have him hold her close, put his arms down her back, slip his hands inside....

"Let it go," she said, backing away. She pried the God's Eye gem from his hand.

"Rhaina, it will come after you."

"Leave." She turned to Cailin. "Both of you."

"Yes, ma'am." She braced Khonane against her shoulder and led him off. Rhaina watched them go, arm in arm. She remembered Khonane's conversation with her on the boat, his touch, his kiss. She never got to ask him where his affections truly were, with her or with Cailin, and it really didn't matter anymore. Cailin would get him out of here. She would take him from this jungle and keep him safe.

She turned away.

"You don't expect to live, do you?" Majid asked.

"No. Let's go."

"Rhaina, wait."

She watched the slug thrashing through the water at the hallway's curve. It seemed to be having fun by itself, playing in the water and flicking its head – what the hell was it doing? – but she knew it was only a matter of time before it came for her again.

"Give me the gem."

"What?" Rhaina asked, turning to the plastic man.

"This will save your life, and Mr. Rosh and I will take the gem back to Earth."

"If I lived to be a thousand, I would never see one blueback from that idea."

"And if you keep the gem, you will not live to see tomorrow."

"That slug will kill you before you get out of this temple."

"I'm a plastic man. It takes a lot to kill me."

"You're a cocky son of a jackal, that's what you are." She took a couple steps away from him. "I'm not giving you this gem."

"That's your choice." Majid looked down the hall. "But you may regret that decision."

Rhaina turned to see the slug-creature ambling toward them. She took a deep breath and wished she could actually give the gem to someone else. But it wouldn't be right. She was responsible for her team, and she would do everything she could to get them out. And Majid was a bastard of a plastic man for thinking she wouldn't see through his self-serving offer.

The slug passed by Cailin and Khonane without even a flinch, its steady advance aimed straight for Rhaina and Majid. It moved on all fours again, its legs rising from the water and dropping back in with barely a slosh with each determined step.

Its features shifted as it stalked forward, its face morphing from Sawn to the Colonel and back into the slug again. She ached at the sight of Sawn's face on that beast, but she knew it was nothing more than a trick, an evil way for this creature to get her to lose her nerve. But she wouldn't back down, and she and Majid would beat this thing – or at least keep it from hurting anymore of her people.

She turned to Majid, but he wasn't beside her. She looked around and saw him standing inside one of the sewer tunnels further down the hall.

"What are you doing?" she yelled.

"I'm a real son of a jackal, aren't I?" Majid yelled back.

The slug-creature let out an ear-splitting roar. Its face morphed into that of the colonel, and the thing galloped straight toward her.

57

Rhaina

Rhaina took a deep breath. She let her spirit connect with her second soul. They became one in the cavern, each touching the other's reality, each sensing the Urkay in both worlds, the physical and the spiritual.

Rhaina jumped aside as the Urkay trampled through the water where she'd been standing. It snorted, spun around, and lunged at her from behind. She ducked to the ground, and the thing sailed over her. It hit the floor hard, spraying water into the air, and a dull thud vibrated through the floor and walls.

Geminai sensed Cailin and Khonane close behind.

"Get out of here," Rhaina yelled, glancing at them.

Cailin had hold of Jake's arm, and she pulled his limp body from the sloshing water. Rhaina turned back to the Urkay pursuing them. She couldn't spare a moment wondering if Jake was alive. Either he was or he wasn't, but the best thing for him was to keep the Urkay from hurting him again.

The creature stalked around her, its face showing Colonel Walraven's features. Other than stretching him a little thin over the bulk of its head, the creature had duplicated Walraven's face perfectly, from the stubble across his cheeks to that damned cocky smile that spread all the way to the corners of his eyes. The fact that the Urkay had no eyes in its sockets made the cockiness seem even more sinister.

Her Geminai felt the movement a moment before it happened, and Rhaina jumped aside as the creature slashed at her with dagger claws. This couldn't go on forever, she thought, slipping her knife from the sheath at her hip. The creature was big enough it didn't have to catch her, just tire her out and then pounce.

* * *

Jake felt the arm around his shoulder. A thin arm, but strong enough to hold him up. A woman's arm.

"Rhaina," he said.

"What did you say?" the woman asked. Jake recognized her: Cailin.

Jake's side ached as Cailin lugged him around. He checked the status reports on his Tech and saw it had healed several fractured ribs and a punctured liver. That would account for the pain in his side. The Tech had sent nanobots to clean up the area around his liver, but it was slow going. Other than that, the Tech gave him a clean bill of health.

"Damn, I hurt," Jake said.

"What?" Cailin asked.

He stopped and opened his eyes.

"I can't hear you, but let's keep moving," Cailin said, tugging him forward.

"I'm fine." Jake shrugged her arm off his shoulder and turned. Khonane stood behind him, one hand supporting against the wall. "You really should get Tech'd," Jake said to him.

"Thanks, but no," Khonane said.

Jake looked past him to the fight further down the hall. Rhaina stood before the Urkay, a knife in her hand and a bloody streak down her face.

"What the hell is she doing?"

"Distracting it so we can get away." Cailin grabbed Jake's shoulder. "Now hurry."

The rage swelled within him, and Jake spun around. He gripped Cailin's arm and shoved her against the wall.

"And you're letting her?" he yelled.

"Stop!" Khonane said.

"No, we're not letting her." Cailin squirmed under Jake's grip. "But if you don't let me go, we may not have the time we need to help her."

* * *

Rhaina's muscles ached. The creature had been relentless. Rhaina suspected the only reason she was still alive was that the thing had no eyes to see her, even though its hearing seemed incredibly precise.

She spared a glance down the hall as she saw Cailin leading Jake and Khonane away, and several emotions went through her. She wanted Jake and Khonane out of this mess, safely living their lives far away from this beast. But she also wanted to be rescued, and that wasn't going to happen once they were safely away.

"Come on!" she yelled at the creature as the thing blocked her view. "Either do something or get out of my way."

The beast lunged again, and Rhaina dodged back, slashing the knife along the thing's arm. It howled as a line of blood trickled down its arm, then leapt.

Geminai saw the blow coming, but Rhaina didn't. All Rhaina saw were teeth and claws coming at her, and she couldn't get out of the way quickly enough. She felt the stinging, burning slash of a claw across her leg. Then a tooth raked her back.

She fell into the water and struggled to get out of the creature's path. Geminai guided her: turn left, turn right, duck down! But the creature pounded the floor all around her, splashing water high into the air and knocking her this way and that with the force of the waves. She struggled to get her footing again and get out of the onslaught, but the creature would not give her a second even to breathe.

A hand gripped her arm, and Rhaina almost yelled for joy. Visions of Jake and Khonane rushing in to save her at the last minute flitted through her mind.

She was yanked through the water and up into a sewer culvert before she recognized that Majid held her arm. He braced his legs wide against the walls of the stone drain, and he dangled her by the wrist in the air before him.

Rhaina coughed up a mouth full of water. She struggled with her free hand to reach out to Majid or to the walls or to anything she could to get out of the plastic man's biting grip.

"You're going to hurt yourself more," he said.

"You bastard!"

"Oh, we covered that already."

The Urkay slammed into the culvert beneath them, shaking the walls and loosing a rain of pebbles and dirt on top of them. The creature snarled, then backed out of the drain again.

"Magnificent, isn't it?" Majid said.

Rhaina struggled to get into her shirt pocket, but Majid shook her until she stopped trying. He yanked her forward, flipped his arm around the small of her back, and held her tight against himself.

She squirmed, knowing it was almost useless trying to get free of his grip.

"This is much better, isn't it?" he said. "More intimate. Rather like those special moments on the boat with Khonane."

"Go to Hell."

The creature clawed at the drain beneath them, tearing long gouges into the rock floor and growling its displeasure up at them.

Majid reached around to the front of Rhaina's shirt, slipped his hand into the pocket, and pulled out the kill switch.

"Oh," he exclaimed. "A treasure."

Rhaina grabbed for the switch, but Majid flicked it into the air. It clattered against the wall, then tumbled to the floor beneath them.

The Urkay slammed forward again, crushing the kill switch beneath its mighty legs. It bellowed its frustration at them.

"Oh, Rhaina, I'm so sorry," Majid said, looking down. "Were you trying to get that little box?" He reached into her pants pocket, and Rhaina struggled to get him out. She kicked and thrashed and clawed at his arm, but he dug deeper until his fingers wrapped around the God's Eye gem.

"You'll never make it out alive," she gasped.

Majid yanked the gem from her pants and held it tight in his hand.

"That creature will tear you apart – you and that ghost you're carrying inside."

As if on cue, the Urkay slammed into the wall beneath them. It snarled and clawed at the stone walls, and it tried to pull its body up the drain, but it couldn't squeeze through.

"You forget," Majid said. "I'm a plastic man. And a plastic man is very hard to kill. But there is one question that remains." He looked down the dark hole at the creature growling beneath them. "Do I drop you straight into its mouth, or not?"

58

Jake

Urkay prison

"Okay, it's in," Jake said. He pounded the spike once more for luck, then he followed the thin strand of sheerwire to where Cailin knotted it around the second explosive-tipped spike. She secured it in the barrel of the blow gun and sited the Urkay's exposed rear end sticking out of the drain culvert.

"Nice of the thing to give us such a big target," Jake said.

Cailin pulled the trigger.

The spike shot, trailing the sheerwire fast behind it. It struck the Urkay in the rump, the tips exploded out and secured the spike in place, and the Urkay jerked its head from the culvert with a mighty roar that shook the entire dungeon. It spun around and, for something that had only empty eye sockets, it looked straight at Jake and Cailin.

"Oh darn," Cailin said, lowering the rifle.

The Urkay launched itself across the shallow water at a full run.

Jake revved to Fighting Mode, ignoring the low-power warnings flashing before his eyes, gripped Cailin's arm, and started running.

Khonane waited for them near the end of the hall where the sheerwire would keep the Urkay from getting at them – theoretically, at least.

* * *

Rhaina's ears still rang from the creature's final roar. She didn't know what startled the thing, but she suspected her team had something to do with it. She squirmed in the plastic man's grip. He stared down, shaking his head.

"Well, there went my fun." He cocked his head, his yellow eyes sparkling at her through the darkness. "To live...and to let live. Is that the essence of humanity, Rhaina?"

"Go to Hell."

"Brilliant retort, but you used it once already." He swung her against the wall to his right. "Put your feet on the ledge."

She did. Although it was more of a crack in the rock than a ledge.

"Now when I let go, you can either fall head-first, or you can keep your hands out and catch yourself against the opposite wall. It's your choice."

Rhaina couldn't believe the plastic was going to let her go. Why did he change his mind? Or was he taunting her now?

"One last thing," he said. He spun around on the ledge, pressing his body firmly against hers and holding her wrists high above her head to keep her in place. "If we ever meet again, I hope you'll remember what we shared in Paris."

"Oh, quote it right," she muttered.

He pressed his cold lips to her mouth in an approximation of a kiss.

Rhaina tried to twist her head to the side, but Majid pressed against her, making struggle excruciating. She felt his cold, mechanized breath, and the stiff plastic lips crinkling into the corners of her mouth. His mechanized, yellow eyes glowed down at her, and Rhaina saw the smile showing through them.

Then he backed off.

"Hm," he said, frowning at her. "I'm not sure what he sees in you. That certainly didn't do anything for me."

He let go of her wrists and dropped, splashing into the water below and ducking from view.

With nothing supporting her anymore, Rhaina fell forward. She cracked her fingers against the opposite wall and hung suspended like that for several seconds. Her legs shook as she thought of the plastic man trying to feed her to that creature. Her mouth ached where he'd tried to kiss her, and her hands tingled as the blood tried to get back into her cold, stiff fingers.

She stared into the dim, golden light streaming from below, and the rage built within her. She hadn't wanted a plastic man on her team at all. The only reason she'd agreed was to.... Why did she agree? Because Mr. Rosh insisted, and because she wanted this mission. She wanted this gem. She wanted to find something so rare, so valuable, so beautiful that she could retire. That would catch Jake's attention.

That was more introspection than she cared for. She pushed those thoughts aside and focused on the most immediate thought: A plastic man had assaulted her with a kiss.

"Yuck," she said. She licked her lips, then spit into the water below. She still had that dry, plastic taste in her mouth.

Her Geminai flitted nearby, and Rhaina spared a glance through those spiritual eyes. Her team – against all orders, bless them – had leashed the creature by his butt to a wall. They were out of danger for the moment. The plastic man, however, was trying to sneak by them all, around the creature and past her team while everyone was busy looking for her.

Rhaina dropped back into her body. She leaned forward as far as she could, then pushed away from the wall. She angled back up and slipped out of the crack in the wall to slide down into the water below. She didn't care about the slug-creature anymore. She wanted her gem back. And she wanted to terminate that bastard of a plastic man.

59

Rhaina

Urkay prison

Rhaina knelt in the shallow water and felt around for the kill switch, her leg and back aching where the creature had cut her. Her fingers brushed pieces of metal and plastic, and she pulled them from the water. As she expected, the kill switch was a dozen pieces. She tossed them aside and felt through the water again. She passed by rocks and chunks of mortar in the murky, frigid water.

Something sharp pierced the tip of her finger, and she jerked back. She wiped the drop of blood on her shirt, a part of her mind wondering how many microfauna she'd just ingested, then she felt more carefully along the ground. She found the sharp point again, followed the metal blade to the leather-strapped handle and pulled the knife from the water. Brown slime dribbled off the blade, and she wiped it across her already filthy pants.

She crouched there a few moments and took in the scene down the flickering hallway. The monster thrashed against the spike protruding from its bloody hind end as it stretched the cord tight, trying to reach

Jake and Cailin and Khonane. The plastic man crept low against the wall opposite the monster, escaping unseen.

Rhaina stood and stretched her arms out before her. Her back still hurt, but her injured leg felt like it would hold her up. That was all she needed.

She edged against the wall and started after Majid.

Geminai poked the Urkay's spiritual shell, aggravating the beast and getting it to make even more noise. The beast's roars thundered around them.

Majid crouched lower to the water and slowed down.

Rhaina snuck up behind him, the creature's thrashings masking her approach. She knew Jake would never approve of what she was about to do. Khonane would try to stop her. Cailin...well, Cailin would probably shoot a spike through the bastard's butt.

To hell with sense, she thought.

She jumped on Majid's back, wrapped one arm around his neck, and punched the knife into his chest. Milky, orange fluid burst out of the hole and washed across her hand.

Majid jumped up and slammed backwards into the wall, knocking the air from Rhaina's lungs.

She didn't try to get her breath back. She yanked hard on the knife, slicing up through the plastic man's chest and neck, then pulled the knife out of his plastic body in a spray of orange fluid.

Majid staggered forward.

The monster rushed at them.

Rhaina leapt from Majid's back and tumbled through the water.

The monster clipped Majid's right arm and sent him spinning away, his orange fluids mixing in the swirling, muddy waters as he collapsed.

He's not so tough, Rhaina thought with a smile. She steadied herself again, her back throbbing from the bruises Majid had put on top of the monster's cut.

Majid jumped out of the water in front of her and gripped her throat.

Rhaina slashed at the plastic man's arm, but he only laughed at her.

"And to think I was going to let you live," he said, his voice coming out in garbled, plastic tones.

Rhaina gasped.

"What did you say?" Majid asked with a grin. "You wish now you'd left well enough alone? Too late for sentiment."

Geminai's scream nearly deafened Rhaina. She saw the monster through Geminai's eyes. She saw the sheerwire cord trailing from the thing's butt. And she saw just how smart this beast really was.

Rhaina grabbed Majid's shoulders and leveraged off his choking grip. She repelled against his chest and swung onto the top of his head.

"What...?" Majid said, staring up at her.

The monster rushed past his left side and cut sharp in front of him. The sheerwire cord snapped taut around his waist.

Majid snapped his head back in a barking, plastic laugh.

The cord sliced his body in half, spinning his legs away beneath them and sending Rhaina tumbling into the water, orange fluid spilling across her, and Majid's glowing, yellow eyes following her all the way down.

She struggled in the water against Majid's tightening grip. His eyes glowed at her through the murky water, and she could see the outline of his grin. His mouth moved, but she didn't hear any words, only the dull splashing of water.

And then someone gripped the collar of her shirt and dragged her backward. She stumbled several steps before she got her feet under her, and she turned to see Jake hauling her out of the water. Majid's hand clung to her neck, and his squirming, plastic body flopped against her chest.

"Get around its back!" Cailin yelled.

Khonane yanked hard on the plastic man's torso, but it refused to let go.

"You bastard!" Jake said, gripping Majid's arm.

Rhaina saw the intensity in Jake's eyes, and she knew he'd slipped into Fighting Mode. He twisted Majid's arm, and she heard the motors and power lines snapping inside his plastic shell.

Rhaina gasped, finally able to breathe again, and shoved her hand inside the plastic man's sliced body.

Khonane struggled to twist the thing's head off its hinges, and the motors ground.

Rhaina saw the Urkay swinging around for another pass, a sharp-toothed grin spread wide across its face.

"Ready!" Cailin yelled.

Khonane grabbed Rhaina's arm and dove aside.

Jake swung the struggling, plastic torso around and impaled it on the spike protruding from Cailin's blow-gun.

Cailin pulled the trigger, and the spike blew out through Majid's back. It shot through the air, trailing a second line of sheerwire behind it. The Urkay ducked aside, and the spike missed the thing's head to lodge deep in its shoulder. The tips exploded out, setting the spike into position and latching the Urkay to a second wall.

Majid's flailing torso bounced along the sheerwire cord as the Urkay thrashed at the restraints.

"Let's move," Jake said. He yanked up Rhaina from the ground.

She got her footing after the first couple steps, then ran along beside Jake, part thrilled that her team came back and part disappointed that Jake had to rescue her. Just once, she wanted to be the one to get him out of the fire.

Her Geminai screamed danger, and Rhaina nearly stumbled from the force of the warning. Jake was at her side. Cailin ran right behind. And Khonane –

"No," Rhaina said, yanking her arm from Jake's grip.

She spun, almost knocking over Cailin.

Khonane had shoved the plastic man's body along the sheerwire cord to the far wall. He pulled the God's Eye gem from Majid's shirt pocket.

"Khonane, no!"

The Urkay lunged forward, the first spike flying loose from its rear end in a shower of blood.

Geminai pounded against the creature's spiritual body, trying to slow it down.

The Urkay sprang forward, its mouth open wide, and slammed into the wall head-first.

Rhaina felt the blow to her Geminai and staggered back. Her head throbbed, and the tears started pouring down her cheeks as Geminai fought to free herself. Her vision blurred.

"Rhaina, I'm sorry," Jake said from somewhere, but Rhaina couldn't see him.

Thunder pounded through her head. She felt the grinding of teeth across her spiritual body, the wash of saliva drenching her spiritual self from head to toes, and the darkness of a tormented eternity swallowing her Geminai whole.

"Rhaina!" Jake said. He shook her.

Part of her heard the Urkay screaming in ecstasy from across the hall. Part of her felt that scream rattling through her bones and past her skull and down through her hips.... The darkness enveloped her. She felt the spiritual ties shriveling, and she clutched at her chest to keep them whole.

"Rhaina, what is it?" Jake said. He pushed her hands aside and felt along her stomach and chest. "Are you hurt? Talk to me!"

The cord vanished. The physical world flooded back in on her, and Rhaina shot up with a gasp. The flickering fire lamps made the walls seem to move. The pounding water jostled her back and forth where she tried to sit beside Jake. His voice sounded like lightning beside her.

"Rhaina, talk to me," he said. "What's wrong?"

"Geminai," she croaked. Rhaina felt inside herself. She searched deep for her second soul, checking dark corners of her spiritual self, but she found nothing except a searing emptiness.

"She's...gone," Rhaina said with a shiver. "Dead...." The darkness closed around her.

60

Jake

Urkay prison

No, Jake thought, hugging Rhaina tight. He pressed his face against hers, trying to feel her breathe. *Do not die.*

"Jake, let's go," Cailin said, her eyes on the Urkay.

Jake sat up and set the palm of his hand on Rhaina's forehead. His tech blinked before his eyes, and he called up the medical program. The scanners flashed through Rhaina's skull in a second, and the readout showed her temperature one degree above normal.

He moved his hand to her chest and scanned her heart.

"Jake, we need to get moving," Cailin said, kneeling beside him in the water. "We can help Rhaina later, after we're out of here." She turned, raised her rifle, and sited down the hall.

The readouts flashed before Jake: heart rate low; breathing shallow.

He requested treatment recommendations. The program suggested "Lower patient's body temperature" and "Attempt to revive patient."

"Dammit," Jake muttered to his tech. "What's wrong with her?"

His tech flashed: "Indeterminate." *Need to buy an upgrade,* he thought.

The Urkay laughed.

Jake looked up and saw Colonel Walraven's face staring back at him from the Urkay's tremendous bulk.

"Let's go," Jake said, scooping Rhaina into his arms.

"That's what I said," Cailin yelled. "Do you know the way?"

Jake didn't answer. He headed back the way he'd come. He brought up his temple maps again and laid them over his vision as he walked, while Cailin kept pace behind him. The map shifted and rotated as Jake scanned the large sewer drains to his left and right. The ground shook as the Urkay pounded the walls, nearby and obviously pursuing them.

This wasn't right, Jake thought as he ran. Where were those guardians who fought him before? Why weren't they around to keep him from escaping? They tried to feed him to this creature, they rescued him from it when it was about to eat him, and then they fought each other when he wanted to come down to stop it. But they had not left him alone since they first saw him. Why the contradictory behavior?

"Jake," the Urkay rumbled from far behind. "Do not leave. I'm almost ready for you."

They reached the end of the hall, turned left, and ducked through the broken gate out of the dungeon. The lamps flickered in the hall. The gravel skidded beneath Jake's muddy boots. They raced past the dead partomes in the hall, reached the crossway, and spun right, past the dozen empty cells with their gates standing open and to the stairwell at the end of the hall.

Jake started to run toward the stairs when Cailin grabbed his shoulder to stop him.

"What's that?" she said, pointing to the wall of water at the top of the stairs.

"It's...." Jake began. He frowned at the water suspended before them like a wavering wall. How could he quickly explain it? "Never mind," he finally said. "It's just water."

The Urkay bellowed a scream from the dungeon far behind them. The temple shook.

The water wall in front of them rippled.

"Jake?" Cailin said, taking a step back.

A thunderous explosion echoed through the corridors. The lamps in the walls fizzled out, and the water at the head of the stairs burst from its protective shell.

The water struck Jake full-on, sending him flying back into Cailin. He struggled to keep Rhaina in his arms as the water pummeled them down the hall. He tripped on a loose stone, the water washed his legs out from under him, and he fell flat. His tech kicked in automatically.

Jake heard the rushing water pouring past him in slow motion, felt the waves buffeting him along, and, from somewhere very close, heard Cailin thrashing.

His eyes augmented the blackness until he made out shapes. The water shoved him back down the hall, past the open cell doors, through the dredged up muck of thousands of years of accumulated dirt and decay. His back slammed into something solid, and he felt Cailin struggling behind him.

The tech in his body groaned as he tried to push away from Cailin and still keep hold of Rhaina's limp body. The water poured down the black hallway at them. The ceiling shook. The walls of the cells collapsed around them, sending chunks of stone and mortar through the water like floating missiles.

"Jake!" Cailin sputtered.

"I'm here," he yelled back. At least it felt like he yelled. Even with the tech, he had trouble hearing over the rising water.

He let go of Rhaina, and the water pressed her to his chest. He reached back, gripped Cailin's hand, and spun around so he was facing her with Rhaina propped between them and the water pounding against his back.

"I can barely move," Cailin said.

Jake reached for the sheerwire pouch at Cailin's side and unwound several tics of the cord. He bound Rhaina's hands together, wrapped the other end around her body a couple times, then passed the cord to Cailin.

"Around your waist," Jake said, slapping the cord into her hand.

She fumbled with it while Jake watched the water rise around them. It had climbed past his knees and was fast approaching his waist. His legs tingled from the cold – alarming since his tech was supposed to compensate for temperature extremes. And in the distance, above the pounding of the water, he heard footsteps. Loud footsteps, getting closer.

"We have to go," Jake said.

"This won't tie!"

He reached past Rhaina and grabbed the sheerwire from Cailin's shaking hands. The water surged around them as he twisted the cord tight around her waist, and he slapped the ends back into her hands. They felt like ice.

The footsteps thundered closer.

"Can you hold your weapon?" Jake asked.

She only nodded, but he could see through the darkened hall that she held her hands like loose clubs around the gun. Why couldn't people just admit that the human body functioned better with Tech?

He spun around and plowed through the surging water, clinging tight to Rhaina's limp body. His Tech's status bars flashed up to show the strain on the gears and motors in his legs. The water hit him with as much force as high-level rapids. It swirled behind him and shoved Cailin around on the other end of the sheerwire cord. She slipped and coughed and staggered behind him, but the cord kept them together.

"Jake!" the Urkay yelled above the pounding waves.

He reached the bottom of the stairs again and struggled forward. He gripped the wall and pulled them all up one step at a time.

"Jake, do not leave." The creature pounded through the waves behind them. "You are the only one left worth a good fight."

He felt the stone step slide out from beneath him. The water washed his left leg out. He fell forward, and the water shoved him back to the bottom.

A clawed hand gripped his arm and yanked him back upright. The sheerwire cord snapped tight and Cailin staggered up behind him.

An orange meshet stood before him, clinging to the ceiling by three clawed legs and lifting him up with the fourth.

"Do not interfere, young one," the Urkay growled.

The meshet snarled back, then did a backflip off the ceiling and yanked Jake, Rhaina, and Cailin the rest of the way up the stairs. They fell into the knee-deep water of the blackened hallway, surrounded by bright, orange meshet staring at them.

"Jake," Cailin said. "I can't see anything. How close are we?"

The meshet that hauled them up the stairs stepped forward and reached for Rhaina.

"Back off," Jake said, standing between the creature and Rhaina.

"Jake, what's going on?" Cailin asked as she raised her gun.

The other meshet stepped forward, and the first one gripped Rhaina by her shirt and yanked her away.

Jake's tech took over. He spun around, grabbed the gun from Cailin's hand, and turned back to aim at the meshet.

The animal dropped beneath the water's surface. A second meshet came at Jake's right side and slashed at the sheerwire cord between him and Rhaina. He staggered forward at the blow, and a second meshet slashed the cord in half. It scooped Rhaina into its arms and leaped away as Jake raised the gun again.

Two more slashes from behind, and the meshet separated him from Cailin. One of them scooped her up and followed the others.

Jake spun around in the empty hallway, searching for any remaining meshet to shoot. They'd all fled.

The Urkay trudged up the steps, Colonel Walraven's face plastered across its distorted features. It looked back and forth in the empty hallway, then turned to Jake and smiled.

"Alone at last," it said with a grin.

The water erupted beside Jake as another meshet burst through. He turned to defend himself, but the thing ducked behind him. It gripped him around the waist, flung him across its back, and launched them down the hall and away from the screaming Urkay.

Jake clung to the bright orange fur as the meshet dipped and leapt and flung them through the black, crumbling temple. He considered kissing the thing for rescuing him. Then he thought about breaking the thing's neck before it kidnapped him to someplace he couldn't escape. He finally settled into riding to its destination. If he was lucky, it would take him to the same place it took Rhaina, and then maybe he could help her.

His tech's internal map tracked their progress through the temple as they reached one of the spires in the far corner away from the Urkay. The meshet jumped onto the window ledge and balanced over the dizzying drop. The wall of water still surrounded the temple, but the forest floor had turned to a floodtide of mud. Dozens of creatures swam through the muck, speeding away from the temple and back into the forest, looking like rats deserting a sinking ship.

Jake looked up through the driving wind and rain and saw the other two meshet disappear into the tumbling water above him. He had enough time to take a quick breath before the meshet launched itself from the temple spire and fell away into the wind.

61

Tone

Urkay armory

The sticky, puckering lips slid away from Tone's mouth, and he started to gag. He jerked away, leaned over the wet stairs, and coughed dry, racking heaves. His stomach cramped, and he collapsed into a puddle of water, his head hanging over the top step. Dim light fell around the small area where Tone lay, and he heard water running somewhere in the distance.

He wiped his mouth with a shaking, frigid hand and came away with strings of tiny, black pebbles from his face and neck.

The ground beneath him shook as something pounded a nearby wall.

He struggled to sit up without falling down the stairs. He slid back from the top step, shoved away with shaking arms, and sat shivering in the water. His gut ached. His legs wouldn't listen to anything he wanted them to do. His head felt like it was spinning away from his neck.

Metal clanked, and Tone turned to see a huge person standing before a hole in the middle of the wall. The man had to be at least four or five tics tall as he flipped a sheet of metal armor across his wide back like it was nothing more than a coat. He fastened the armor across his chest and abdomen, then reached back into the hole. He pulled out another piece almost as large as the one on his back, slapped it against his chest, and started latching it at his shoulders and sides.

Tone shut his eyes. He was in Hell, he thought. That had to be the answer. Except he'd always imagined Hell a lot hotter, drier, more full of fire and pitchforks.

The man stomped across the hall, his armor clinking with each step. Tone opened his eyes again –

He recognized the man's huge, wide face. "Colonel?"

"Colonel," the man repeated. He stopped. He looked at the floor, then the walls around them, the ceiling. He seemed to be looking for something, but he brought his attention back and smiled. "Yes, you can call me Colonel. I like that." His deep voice echoed off the stone walls.

The colonel went to another wall beside the stairs, leaned back, and punched his fist forward. The stones shattered with another rumbling explosion, and dust and rocks pelted Tone. The colonel reached into the hole he'd made and withdrew a rusty sword that had to be as long as Tone was tall.

"Nothing lasts," the colonel said, eyeing the sword.

Tone shivered and looked away. His mind wasn't working well enough to process what he was seeing. If this was Hell, then all he had to do was wait for that thing to chop his head off with that sword. If this wasn't Hell, then...he had no idea what to expect.

"You thank me now," the colonel rumbled, stepping up to Tone.

Tone craned his neck. The colonel leaned over him, that rusty sword waving a breeze above Tone's head.

"Thank you," Tone whispered.

The colonel burst out laughing, then sat down with an echoing thud.

"You have no idea why?" he asked.

Tone shook his head.

"You were dead." The colonel grinned. "I had to suck so much water out of your stomach. Took me most of the night!" He threw his huge head back and laughed even harder.

Tone's hand slipped, and he collapsed into the running water. He tried to cover his ears with shaking hands.

"Hungry?" the colonel asked, tossing a long, meaty bone across the water.

Tone eyed the offering suspiciously. It was nearly a tic long, and the meat was thin and ragged. Huge chunks had been torn away from the bone, telling Tone that something else had been gnawing on this piece. He looked up –

Some other face stared back at him from the armored man.

"Where am I?" the new face asked. The man scanned the long hallway back and forth, but Tone didn't recognize this face. The eyes were wide, the brow wrinkled, and the cheeks puffed out like he was having trouble breathing.

The new man inside that huge body jumped to his feet with a thundering splash. He spotted Tone, reached forward and yanked him into the air until they were eye-level, Tone's feet dangling far above the floor.

"Where?" he yelled at Tone.

"I – I don't know." Tone looked around. The hallway didn't look like anyplace he'd been, but the stone and masonry were unmistakable. "I think...the Lygme temple."

"The temple?" The man looked around like this was a brand new thought to him. "She left the temple? How dare she! She did this to me. I'll ruin her."

The man's grip suddenly loosed, and Tone fell to the floor. The shock ripped its way through his bones and muscles, and Tone collapsed into a heap. He gripped his throbbing ankle, but kept himself from crying out.

The new man staggered backward, his hands before his face. He bumped against the far wall, lowered his arms, and turned to Tone – with a different, third face.

This face was at least familiar to Tone. He looked like one of the men who had been with that woman, Rhaina.

"Run," this third man said as he looked at Tone.

Tone just stared.

"Run! I don't control him."

Before Tone had a chance to do anything, the lines around the third man's face blurred. They blended together. The mouth twisted, the eyes changed shape, the cheeks filled out again, and the colonel stared out of that massive head once more.

"Don't move," the colonel said, panting. "I'm in control again."

"Am I dead?" Tone whispered.

"Dead?" The colonel thundered forward and sat in the water with a dull thud and a quick point at the ground. "Like Avery there?"

Tone glanced at the long bone of meat lying beside him on the floor. He felt like retching, and he turned away and shut his eyes.

"Not yet," the colonel said. "But you lead me to the flying Lygmies, or you wish I let you die." He grinned.

62

Jake

jungle canopy

It seemed like the meshet had jumped and bounced and sailed for days, but Jake's tech told him it had only been seventeen minutes. The furry, orange creature had run out of the temple and climbed halfway up the side of the building in the rain, then jumped through the wall of water surrounding the temple. Jake felt the surge of electricity course through his body, and his tech flickered at the surge but didn't die. His fingers, joints, and muscles tingled, and he had struggled to hold on to the flying meshet.

The animal gripped a branch and swung forward until Jake started, then it whipped upright, and Jake smacked his nose into the back of its orange head. The meshet growled at him, then turned its attention back to the canopy far above. Jake looked up and squinted through the pelting rain. He had enough time for a sense of dread before the meshet leapt high.

They continued up through the high branches and through the canopy until only the rain-filled sky stretched above them. The meshet surveyed the trees in every direction, then bounded across the branches, its momentum kicking sprays of water that mixed with the steady rain from above. The dark clouds rolled past them, lightning spears arcing overhead and thunder rumbling low.

The meshet suddenly ducked and landed with a splashing thud in the middle of the elevated walkway. It jerked its shoulders and sent Jake flying to the ground, then it leaned forward on all fours and shook itself from head to stubby tail.

Jake raised his arm to block the water from splashing his face, and that's when he realized that the rain had stopped. Looking up he saw water striking a solid barrier and running in wide, long streaks past him and off the sides of the walkway.

The meshet turned, gripped Jake by his arm and hoisted him up. He shoved Jake forward, and they walked like that for several minutes. Jake used the time to let his tech compute how far they'd travelled. Estimating the meshet's flight speed and discounting the time they spent dangling from precarious branches, they'd only gone three kilotics – four at the absolute most.

The walkway turned and opened onto a wide, flat platform with shorn trees sticking up between the boards and intermittent railings. Dozens of Lygmies and meshet sat and stared at Jake as he entered the clearing. Their eyes tracked him up and down, and their silent stares told him they weren't impressed. Half a dozen white sacks hung limp from bare branches spread throughout the clearing. Two bright orange meshet hung by their front legs from a branch at the other end of the clearing, thick, white strands spraying out of their bellies and forming another sack between them.

Cailin sat toward the center of the clearing, beside Rhaina's still body. She looked at Jake and started to put her finger to her lips.

"What –" Jake said.

The meshet's paw clamped across his mouth, and Jake saw every Lygme within a dozen tics sneer in disgust at him. The meshet behind him growled into his ear, then came around and released his mouth.

"*Bek'a du,*" the meshet snarled.

Jake stared wide-eyed. Rusty as his Lygmese was, this animal had unmistakably told him to shut up.

"*Bisch ka du,*" the meshet said, pointing to where Cailin sat.

Jake didn't argue. He went to Cailin and sat down. He ran a hand across Rhaina's frigid wrist. Her pulse was there, but it was weak. He had to do something, or she might not make it.

Cailin touched his arm, shaking her head.

"I need to help her," he whispered.

A dozen meshet growled and started toward them across the platform.

Cailin shook her head and put her hand across Jake's mouth.

"No," she mouthed, still shaking her head.

The meshet surrounded them, and the nearest swatted at the back of Jake's head.

Jake rubbed the knot that quickly formed there. The meshet stood around him, their hands clenching and their padded paws rippling with contained strength. He didn't need his tech to tell him he was so incredibly outmatched he should shut up and be thankful he was still alive. And if Rhaina wasn't lying beside him, obviously injured, he might have been content to do that.

The meshet turned and lumbered back to their spots along the edges of the platform, and they all turned back to the two hanging from their branch and weaving that white sack between them. The Lygmies seemed as content to watch this display as the meshet, and Jake wondered if it was some seldom-witnessed ritual they were watching.

He scanned the crowd. The silence seemed almost reverential, and the wide-eyed looks and grinning smiles displayed the ecstasy the Lygmies and meshet all seemed to feel. Then Jake stopped and stared at one face in the crowd, one bearded, human face in the midst of the jungle riffraff.

The man sat there perfectly still with his eyes shut and his face slightly tilted up. Jake's tech scanned the features and started comparing this man against the databanks of people he'd met or seen throughout the years. The answer came back almost immediately: Ramiro

Rodriguez, Rhaina's hired muscle. More brawn than ingenuity, the man could shoot and fly almost anything. From what Jake recalled, Ramiro devoured any history book he could get his hands on, and Rhaina seldom went anywhere without him.

So what was he doing in the trees with these primitives?

A loud thud and a shaking through the platform told Jake the two meshet had finished with their sack-growing and dropped from their branches. A sudden burst of activity filled the air as the Lygmies and meshet all stood up. Three of the larger meshet lumbered up to Jake and Cailin and stood menacingly over them, obviously on guard duty.

Ramiro drifted through the crowd to them. Dingy strips of cloth draped precariously down his shoulders, criss-crossed his chest where they were tied with ropes, and hung loose around his bare legs. Jake couldn't shake the image of a religious leader striding serenely toward them. He almost expected Ramiro to open his mouth and say, "Peace be upon you" or some such drivel.

"Arise," Ramiro said, gesturing with his palms turned upward.

Jake and Cailin stood, and Cailin's eyes widened.

"You...were dead," she said.

Ramiro squinted at her then turned to Jake and cocked his head.

"Jake Alon," Ramiro said. He wasn't asking a question.

Jake nodded.

Ramiro turned to Rhaina still lying on the ground at Jake's feet.

"That's so sad," Ramiro said, kneeling down to touch Rhaina's cheek.

"Yeah, it is," Jake said. He grabbed Ramiro and hauled him up. "She needs medical attention! I don't know what's wrong with her, but she's been getting weaker. Is there anything in this God-forsaken jungle that will keep her alive until we can get her back to civilization?"

"Yes," Ramiro said. He cocked his head again and seemed to be listening. With the babble of Lygmese floating around them, he could have been listening to any snippet of conversation, but nothing Jake caught sounded concerned with Rhaina's life.

"Ramiro," Cailin asked, "what happened to you?"

Jake wanted to ask that same question, following it up with a good slap.

Ramiro leaned forward, touched the sides of Cailin's head, and bumped his forward against hers. She gasped, and her eyes went huge. She stared forward, the whites of her eyes slowly filling with veins of red until it looked like she would start weeping blood. Ramiro released his grip.

Cailin took a step back, staring at Ramiro. Her eyes faded slowly back to white, and a tear – water, not blood – rolled down her cheek.

"Amazing," she whispered.

"You must see, too," Ramiro said, turning toward Jake.

"Absolutely not!" he said, backing away.

"You must understand."

"I understand perfectly fine, thank you." The conversations around them quieted down, and Jake turned to see several Lygmies and meshet staring at him. He looked back at Ramiro. "I will not have you brainwash me like –"

"He didn't brainwash me," Cailin said. "He...told me a story."

"I've already had one story told to me that way. That was enough." He reached down and started to scoop Rhaina into his arms.

"No," Ramiro said, placing a hand on Jake's shoulder.

"Don't even try anything," Jake said over his shoulder as he lifted Rhaina.

"You cannot take her," Ramiro said.

Jake turned to face the man and realized that every Lygme and meshet had stopped talking. The Lygmies glared, and the meshet snarled, their toothy fangs telling Jake their opinions better than any words. Without asking it to, his tech calculated the odds of fending them all off in a fight. The results were not encouraging.

"She stays," Ramiro said. He came forward and put his arms beneath Rhaina's still body.

Jake stared. He might lose the fight against everyone else, but he could take out Ramiro with the first punch.

"Ramiro," Cailin interrupted, "Rhaina needs our help. We have to get her back to civilization."

"She's already there." Ramiro reached for Rhaina.

Jake tightened his grip and spun away, knocking Ramiro off balance.

The meshet growled, and the whole platform rumbled their menace.

"I'm taking her," he said, backing away and watching the meshet encircle him.

Cailin pulled out her gun and followed him across the platform, alternately aiming at the meshet and then Ramiro.

"We can care for her," Ramiro said, advancing through the orange, furry crowd.

"I'm not leaving her with a pack of animals," Jake said.

Cailin fired at the ground, a hole splintering through the rough boards in front of Ramiro.

The meshet flinched, some of them rippling away in camouflage, others lowering their heads and growling.

"Jake," she said. "Go. Run!"

Jake revved to Fighting Mode. He turned and saw the world spin in slow motion. A meshet slashed at him, and he kicked the paw aside. Another swung from a branch above, and he ducked out of reach. He slid between a pair of Lygmies, leapt above a meshet slashing at his ankles, and jumped out of reach of one snapping at his arm.

He heard Cailin behind him, her gun firing and her steps stumbling to keep up. Then, with a short cry, he didn't hear her any more.

Jake's tech flashed an electronic map before him, showing him the best outline of the places he'd been in the trees – and it wasn't much. Another few seconds, and he would be running blind along the path. The tech outlined its best guess of the forest beneath him based on the trees. Another twenty tics before him was a stand of trees growing close enough together that he could climb down with Rhaina over one shoulder. His tech would keep him balanced in the trees, and the odds were in his favor that he could do it.

He pushed his tech, straining the gears in his back and legs to reach the stand of trees.

A meshet sprang at him from above, and he ducked past.

Too late, he spotted two others reaching at him from the sides. They tripped him. He lost his grip on Rhaina and sent her flying across the walkway and into the waiting arms of a fourth meshet that swung up from the branches beneath the path.

Jake punched the nearest meshet in the snout, sending a spurt of blood across its orange face. It gripped his arm as it fell backwards and yanked him off the pathway.

Jake landed on the falling meshet, and they crashed through the trees. Branches snapped. Giant leaves slapped them in the face and arms. Birds squawked and took flight, barely flapping away before Jake and the meshet crashed past.

And then the world opened up beneath them, and Jake saw an algae-covered swamp rushing at them. They hit the water, everything going black and silent as the swamp swallowed them up. Jake struggled through the murky waters to reach the surface again. His tech outlined animals – fish, he assumed – that flashed and darted.

He broke the surface with the angry meshet. The animal swung at Jake, barely clipping his shoulder. Jake struggled backward as the meshet continued its onslaught. Its claws slashed. Its teeth snapped.

Something yanked the meshet backward. Its face changed from rage to outright panic. It splashed and struggled through the water to get away from whatever grabbed it.

Two black, muddy creatures sprang out of the water. They slashed through the meshet's orange neck, blood pouring into the swamp, and they bit down hard on the thing's chest and arms. Within seconds, they disappeared beneath the water again, dragging the struggling meshet down with them.

Jake treaded water in the suddenly silent swamp. Bright red bursts clouded the water around him and *things* drifted to the surface. He had no doubt that whatever those creatures were, they could probably do to him what they'd done to the meshet. He looked around for the nearest tree – nearly a dozen tics away – and started for it.

The swamp was silent except for his own swimming. The meshet on the walkway above apparently had no interest in rescuing him – or their fallen comrade.

He reached for the roots of the tree, gripped the soggy bark, and started pulling himself out of the water.

Something gripped his ankle.

He spun around in time to see one of the black creatures, its long, stringy hair waving in the water behind it and its face covered in blood.

It yanked him off the tree and beneath the water in one swift motion.

63

Geminai

location unknown

Geminai cowered in the inky black, her sobs stifled by the deafening pressure on her from every side, the weight of her own blindness restraining her more harshly than the thickest chains ever could. She felt herself drifting, but she knew not where. She clutched the severed cord in her hands, wishing, pleading, begging the universe to make her whole again, to reconnect her with her person, with her Rhaina.

Brilliant, blinding flashes sparked in the distance again. She'd seen them before, of course, and she ran again as she'd run then. The Eaters must not find her. They must not catch her, or they would devour her – a soul left unbound outside the Sea. She knew they were only doing what came natural to them, what their own spirits urged them to do. But she wanted to live! She wasn't ready to give up, to let herself drift into their oblivion.

But she also didn't know where she could go. Without her Rhaina guiding her, thinking with her, helping her to see the physical world in all its splendor....

Never in her short existence had she seen a place like this darkness, a place that was without form, a void. She'd never heard tales, she'd never even imagined a place like this could exist. Her Rhaina had always scoffed at the idea of a Limbo or a Purgatory, a Waiting Room at the End of the World, but those seemed the best explanations Geminai had for where she now found herself.

The air around her rumbled, and the blackness receded for an instant. She gaped at the world around her – the physical world just beyond this shell. She stood in a long hallway of the temple, water rushing past her feet. An open hole in the stone wall before her held a trove of armor and weaponry, and she somehow knew it was all for her. The Resurrected Mother runt, Tone, sat cowering along the opposite wall, and a part of Geminai knew this to be right. He should cower at her greatness.

The blackness enveloped her, and Geminai screamed her frustration at having the reality taken away again. She pounded the air around her. She kicked at the darkness. She beat and stomped and punched – and the world flashed before her once more.

She stared into Tone's tear-filled eyes as she held him high, threatening to hurt him, to drop him to the floor and show him what pain really meant.

And just as quickly, the scene vanished.

Geminai drifted in the darkness, too stunned to do anything else. She'd wanted to hurt that man. She'd felt the murderous thoughts coursing through her spiritual body, and they'd felt...good. She shuddered. Was this what she was without Rhaina? When her physical self was stripped away, was she nothing more than a collection of animal instincts to do harm to those around her?

The touch at her shoulder made her cry out. She jerked around, ready to strike down the Eater that had come to cannibalize her soul – and stopped when she recognized Khonane.

She threw her arms around him and hugged him close. She felt the comfortable, wispy bonds of his spiritual body enfolding her, and for the first time since being cut off from Rhaina's physical self, she finally felt secure.

"Rhaina," he said.

"Shh."

She squeezed her eyes shut and just felt him. The strong arms. The keen mind. The attributes of his soul that drew her to him. The things that made him perfect for her.

She leaned around and kissed him.

He responded in kind for several moments, then withdrew.

"Rhaina," he said again.

"Why must we speak?" she said, shutting her eyes.

"I felt your pain from across the void."

"And you've come to take it away."

"I've come to ask your help."

Geminai opened her eyes and stared through the darkness into the soul of this man before her. This man who had always been there for her, who had always encouraged her, aided her, been her rock when the world seemed to slip away around her.

"How long have you loved Cailin?" she asked.

He stared, his eyes wide.

"Is that why you've been so distant?" he said.

She answered with a nod.

"Cailin's heart shifts daily," he said. "Her attention focused on me for a brief time, but I've always stayed true to you."

Geminai squeezed her eyes shut and felt the tears drifting down her cheeks. Why did she have to wait until now to say this to him? Why couldn't she have confronted him weeks ago – months ago! They could have been together in the physical world, together in spirit and in body.

"Rhaina," Khonane said, more seriously this time. "We must work together to break free of the darkness."

She put one hand across his mouth and wrapped the other in the spiritual threads of his hair.

"The Urkay has stolen our bodies," he continued.

Geminai pressed her lips to his cheek.

"But our souls are free to roam within him," Khonane continued with a little less urgency.

Geminai brushed her hands through his body, tugging through his spiritual self and letting the wisps of his spirit float back to his form.

Khonane turned away, his mouth open and his eyes unfocused. He pressed his hands to Geminai's sides and ran his fingers along her shimmering form. They kissed, arms entwined.

"We must...," he breathed, his eyes closed as their bodies blended together. "...get...free...."

Geminai's body tingled as she felt Khonane's spirit slide into hers. They wrapped themselves around and through each other, their spirits intertwining, and their passions carrying them through the darkness. Geminai barely saw the tongues of flames sliding from between them before she shut her eyes, her breath catching at the pure heat they poured into each other.

64

Tone

jungle temple

The vine rope tightened around Tone's neck as he slipped on the muddy steps leading up from the temple undergrounds. He coughed into the mud, then stumbled back up, the rain pelting him from every side. He wiped the water and mud from around his eyes and stared at the dome of water soaring into the sky above him and around the temple.

"Do not stop," Colonel Urkay said as he climbed the steps behind Tone.

"Look." Tone pointed at the water. It frothed and swirled around the temple, like a stormy sea that had been draped over them, forming a wall of water. Which was perfectly fine by Tone. At this point, drowning seemed a far better option than being marched through this jungle on a leash like some pet.

Colonel Urkay stepped forward and yanked Tone along. "They madden me," he bellowed, sliding out his rusty sword and waving it in the air above him. He ran forward and Tone staggered along behind.

He crashed into the wall of water, lightning arching against the ground and waves spraying around them.

Tone stumbled at the Urkay's jerking pressure on the vine. He lost his footing and fell face-forward into the water wall. He slipped through the water, reached the end of the leash, and collapsed between the barrier's edges. The water shoved his face into the ground, pounding against his head and shoving its way into his ears. Tone felt his eyes swimming against the pressure.

The vine yanked him back with a quick choke. His head slipped from beneath the barrier, and Colonel Urkay dragged him sputtering to his feet.

The Urkay punched him in the stomach, and Tone spewed water across them both.

"Stop that," Colonel Urkay said with a slap across Tone's cheek.

Tone slipped to the ground and coughed up more water.

"How you get through?" Colonel Urkay asked.

Tone stared at him, wondering what answer he could give that wouldn't get him hurt.

"Tell me," Colonel Urkay said with a quick kick to Tone's leg.

"I don't know," Tone said. "I fell."

"Get up."

Tone struggled back up, shaking the water from his ears and rubbing the muddy hair away from his eyes.

"Put hand through."

Tone shoved his hand through the water barrier. The pressure against his arm nearly knocked him over, but he finally pierced through to the other side.

Colonel Urkay tugged him back with the vine. "Glad you with me," he said with a grin. He gripped Tone and threw him across the armor on his back.

"What are you doing?" Tone asked, clenching the wide shoulders.

Colonel Urkay didn't reply. He stepped forward and shoved Tone's head into the water wall. The pressure pounded against Tone, threatening to crush him to the Urkay's back. They took a second step, and Tone's world exploded. The pressure tripled. Lightning coursed through the water around them. His ears started ringing from the pounding waves.

Another step. More lightning. Greater pressure.

Tone tried to scream, but the water forced its way down his throat.

A third step. The water felt like it solidified across Tone's back.

Step. Tone felt like he was being shoved through a brick wall. His arms went numb. His head felt like it would split open.

Step. Step. Step.

Tone slipped to the muddy ground as a wave washed across him. He shook his head and struggled to overcome the sudden change in pressure. Falling rain mixed with the mud around him, and Tone looked up to see the water wall collapsing back down like a tidal wave. The forest opened back up around him.

Colonel Urkay stood in the midst of the rushing water, arms held high and a piercing scream echoing from his throat. He beat against his chest plate, a pulsing drumbeat keeping time with a choir of voices from behind them.

Tone turned back to face the temple. Hundreds – thousands! – of ghostly forms poured from the walls and windows, most of them soaring up until they disappeared into the rain-filled sky. Others flying low to the ground and rushing past Tone and the Urkay, pounding the air around them and whispering words of warning into Tone's mind.

"He is evil!"

"Run while you can."

"Do not believe him."

"He will hurt you."

"If you –"

"Enough!" Colonel Urkay roared, and the spirits scattered into the wind.

Tone stood on the muddy ground and suddenly felt very alone with this creature. Jane had delivered him to this thing's temple – she'd practically fed him to it. That woman, Rhaina, and her team of mercenaries had left him behind in the temple, apparently escaping on their own. And now Lygme ghosts were telling him he would die.

Colonel Urkay yanked the vine leash, and Tone staggered to the ground.

"The orange-haired ones," the Urkay said as he pointed to the forest. "Lead to them."

Tone tried to loosen the noose around his neck. Maybe death was the only option left, he thought. And if that was true, then he'd bring the Urkay with him.

He turned and studied the temple, trying to orient himself with the forest. Everything looked so different from a couple dozen tics up, but he thought he remembered the way Jane had led him.

"That way," Tone said, pointing in the opposite direction.

"Good," the Urkay said, unsheathing his sword. "Lead."

Tone staggered to his feet. He started walking across the muddy ground, visions of his own death flitting before his mind. Then he smiled as he thought about the Urkay dying with him. Falling over a cliff. Drowning. Slipping beneath mud. So many possibilities in this new, random direction.

65

Jake

The black-haired swamp creature tossed Jake to the cave's damp ground and stomped off, its fur-drida swishing across its back with each step. A dull, blue glow waivered from the cave ceiling, and Jake looked up to see a net hanging above him and hundreds of little bugs crawling inside it. The blue light emanated from their bellies.

Jake stood up as much as he could and tried to shake off the water. He let his tech scan all around as he did so, and the results weren't good. Eight tunnels branched away from this one. Jake knew the one behind him led back up to the swampy area where the creature had caught him – but that was also a good thirty tics up, and that thing could swim better than a fish. He could hear water rushing through two other tunnels, but the last five carried the distinct babble of Lygmies. He was not in a good position.

"Poor little mouse," a voice whispered.

Jake knew that voice, even without his tech analyzing it. He turned around slowly, scanning the caves once more.

"My friend the pouncer," Jake said.

"My name is Silny."

"Of course. Silly Silny."

The Pouncer hissed at that, and Jake's tech locked on to the sound. The animal was down the tunnel to Jake's immediate left, probably no more than five or six tics away. He turned his back on it and pretended to look down the other tunnels.

"So, Silny, are you here to escort me to my death?"

"You're playing games." Jake heard the Pouncer pad forward a couple steps. "You know exactly where I am; I heard it in your breathing."

His tech had steadied his breathing so he knew the Pouncer was lying. He played along anyway, though, and turned around to face the tunnel where the Pouncer was now sitting and watching him.

"No more games?" Jake asked.

"I'm through with games."

Jake smiled.

"You will finish what you've come here to do," Silny said.

"Steal the jewel, get the girl, go home a rich, satisfied man?"

The Pouncer sniffled at him. Dozens of eyes appeared in the dark tunnels all around. Lygme eyes and beasty eyes. Jake estimated there had to be at least sixty creatures of one sort or another suddenly standing or sitting on the edges of this small cave.

"Do you know what Pouncers and Lygmies have in common," Silny asked.

"It's gotta be your sense of humor."

"It's the humans standing over us and making our lives miserable."

"You can't be serious," Jake said, suddenly putting some pieces together. "You lured us all out here to get back at the human race? What, are we dinner for that critter back there at the temple?"

"That's a good idea," Silny said as he started washing his face with one paw. "But we have much bigger plans than that."

"The colonies," Jake whispered, taking his thoughts to their next logical extreme.

The Pouncer started purring so loudly that Jake could hear it without his tech.

"Are you familiar with the legend of the Urkay?" Silny asked.

"Heard of it, yeah."

"Then you know he is an unstoppable creature."

Jake didn't bother to reply. He scanned the tunnels, but his tech registered another couple dozen Lygmies and swamp monsters waiting down each one. Apparently, he was the main attraction.

"And once this unstoppable creature has rid the planet of its human infestation, there will finally exist a place in the universe where Lygmies and pouncers can live side by side."

"Your own cat-topia. Nice."

"And we have you to thank." Silny stood up and stretched his back, extending his claws and scraping them across the dim floor.

"You made sure the location of those gems got out to everyone, didn't you?"

"It took us almost five years to attract the attention of someone like you, someone who could actually survive this jungle. I'm glad I'm not a betting cat, though, because I was ready to put some bluebacks on the Urkay swallowing you whole. But the good colonel was fun enough to watch."

With a sigh, Jake sat on the floor and stared at the pouncer.

"Well, let's see," he said. "You've captured me and explained the intricacies of your evil plan. So let's get on with it. I have someplace to be."

66

Rhaina

location unknown

Rhaina felt herself floating through the night, the sensation filling her with a longing for her second soul. She remembered the Sea of Souls where she and Geminai used to float above the galaxy, watching people drift in and out lives, watching them interact with each other, watching from afar as dreams were made, lives were changed, hopes were dashed. The infinite orchestra of life. The touch of eternity. The mask of godhood she wore so proudly...before it was stripped away.

She squirmed from that last thought, one she didn't think came from within herself.

"Life exists beyond the human boundaries."

Rhaina knew those words came from someone else. She turned in the drifting darkness and tried to see who had invaded her serenity.

"You must go outside of yourself."

Serenity of the soul, Rhaina thought. *Peace by example. Utopia of the never-ceasing limbo existence.* It wasn't for her, and she didn't appreciate some spirit whispering the words into her one remaining soul.

"Open your eyes and hear."

Rhaina opened her eyes. The voices flooded through her in the darkness. They overwhelmed her soul. They seeped into her consciousness. They rushed out through her ears and nose, and they jumped in through her stomach and legs to fly full-circle through her self.

"Get away!" Rhaina yelled.

The voices drifted away, and a face peered through the darkness.

"You're a Lygme," Rhaina whispered.

"I am of the Ones," she said. "I have been. I was thought into this world. And I shall forever be. Along with my brothers, sisters, my mothers and fathers."

More faces turned in the darkness, the eyes shining back green through the reflected night.

"Jane," Rhaina said.

The Lygme tilted her head and smiled. "And so it begins."

"You're going to change me, aren't you?"

"No more than you already have been. Together, we shall be restored."

"Into the likeness of you?"

"Into the likeness of your god."

"I have no god." Rhaina turned to the laughing faces around her. "I am the maker of my own self."

"Of course you are, my dear," Jane said. "Which is why you have turned out so horribly inadequate."

"You can't make me do anything."

Jane smiled, then stepped forward through the darkness. Her body burned bright orange, and her eyes blazed with intense flames that licked out from her skull.

"We have never met one like you among humans."

Rhaina backed away cautiously.

"You have come so close to touching your true self."

Rhaina looked around. The other Lygme faces might still be out there in the darkness, but she couldn't see them anymore with Jane's intense light so close.

"You are lost without her, aren't you?"

Geminai flashed at the edge of Rhaina's self, and she gasped. The longing overwhelmed her, and Rhaina lunged at the flitting existence of her second soul. But it had already vanished.

"No!" Rhaina yelled. She spun on the burning Lygme and beat the air between them with her fists. "Bring her back to me! Bring her back."

"Let me show you the nature of true life," Jane said.

Rhaina swiped at the tears streaming down her face.

Jane held out a hand, and Rhaina stared at it. Tears streaming down her face, she saw that her own hand blazed as well.

"What's happening to me?" Rhaina asked. "To you and me both?"

"We are starting down the path together."

"To where?"

"I don't know," Jane said, taking Rhaina's hand. "This is my first time to grow up as well."

They turned and looked out upon the faces in the darkness. Another Lygme stepped forward, but this one seemed old as the wind. He looked upon Rhaina and Jane with a burning intensity that seared their spirits. Then, he spoke:

"In the beginning," he said, "there was nothing. And then the Voice of the Creator spoke, and Udo was fashioned from the chaos...."

67

Tone

jungle floor

Tone staggered into the mud as Colonel Urkay yanked again on the vine leash around his neck.

"Where are they, Tone?" the Urkay bellowed. "You promised Lygmies. You said they were this direction. 'Trust me, Colonel,' is you said. Where – are – they."

He yanked Tone back up from the mud and propped him against a tree. Tone fought against the vine around his neck as he gasped in another breath. The rain burned his face and made his clothes cling to his wounded body. The Urkay's clammy hand clung to Tone's shirt.

"They're out here," Tone said with a gasp.

"I think you lie," Colonel Urkay said, his face pressed within inches of Tone's. "I think you deserve punishment."

"No, please believe me. This really is the direction."

"You may not need every limb."

"I promise. It's a little further." Tone shoved his fingers between the knot, loosening the vine until he had enough room for his entire hand between the cord and his neck.

Colonel Urkay slid his rusty sword from its sheath and stared at the glittering, wet blade. "My sword. Over five thousand of my enemies it struck dead. One more little Lygme human nothing to it."

Tone yanked the vine over his head, slipped into the mud and out of the Urkay's grip, and stumbled back up in a run through the wet forest.

"You run?" the Urkay laughed.

Tone ran. With every last bit of strength, he ran. Through the waist-high bushes and ferns, tripping past tree roots and knobby out-croppings of rocks. Anywhere, as long as it took him far from this murderous creature.

"Wait for me!" Colonel Urkay said. Tone heard the thing stomping after him, pummeling into the ground the same plants and roots that slowed Tone. The sword clanged through the air, and Tone turned to see the Urkay threshing the foliage into heaps all around him.

Tone grabbed a vine and spun around a tree.

His feet flew out from under him. His arm yanked back, and his shoulder seared with pain as it was wrenched in its socket.

He slammed back against the tree, his hand still gripping the vine and the Urkay making a steady advance. Tone looked back at the vine and saw it was covered in a gelatinous, milky slime that had oozed be-tween his fingers and around his palm. It fastened his hand firmly to itself.

Tone looked up. High above, the vine met a web of other vines, all intricately woven between the trees to snag whatever unlucky creature might be flying up there. At the web's edge, a giant, black dot with legs curled under stared down at the forest floor – stared at Tone.

"Giant, alien spider," Tone said with a gasp. He yanked on his hand. He braced himself against the tree and tried to shove away. He strained against the slime, but it refused to release his hand.

"Keep pulling," Colonel Urkay said, looking up. "Agitate it more."

Tone looked. The spider-thing had uncurled its six legs and stood at the edge of the canopy webbing. Its one, giant eye focused on him, and its pincers opened and shut beneath its mouth.

"Help me!" Tone pleaded, reaching for Colonel Urkay.

"You ran," the Urkay whispered. "Do not run."

"No. Never again. I swear it!"

The line holding Tone's hand jerked back, smashing his hand against the tree bark. He yelped, then clamped his free hand over his mouth as he stared at the web far above him – the now-empty web.

"Oh, no," he said, scanning the trees. "Where'd it go?"

"Wasn't watching." Colonel Urkay glanced around, shrugging his heavy armor with a thunderous clank.

Tone leaned back, putting all his weight into freeing his hand from the sticky web. The slime oozing around his palm and between his fingers seemed to stretch a fraction away, but it stubbornly refused to release him. Tone wiped the sweat and rain from his forehead as he searched for the giant spider.

"Lead me to the Lygmies," Colonel Urkay said as he stepped forward, "and I release you."

"Absolutely," Tone said. "I'll take you straight to them."

"That way?" the Urkay asked, pointing behind him, back the way they had been going.

"No," Tone said, shaking his head. "No, it's more...that way –"

The spider leapt from the tree above Tone. It arced through the air, its six legs spread out before it, and it landed on Colonel Urkay, pounding him into the mud. It sank its pincers into his throat, then reared back.

The Urkay pounded his fist into the spider's head. With a squeal, the thing rolled into a tree, then flipped back onto its legs and scuttled into the branches.

"No!" the Urkay bellowed. He swung his sword around and sliced the trunks of half a dozen skinny trees around him. Wood groaned. Branches snapped. Pent-up rain poured down on top of them as the trees swayed and tumbled into each other far above. With a pounding roar, the trees fell against each other, knocked loose thousands of branches and leaves, and came crashing to the forest floor, splattering mud and debris high into the air.

Tone cowered where he stood wrapped around his own tree, his free hand over one ear as he watched the enraged Urkay.

The spider had fallen to the mud at Colonel Urkay's feet. He hefted his sword and swung back around before the spider could get itself upright again. Four severed legs spun into the air in a rain of blood as the spider squealed in agony. It shoved itself across the ground with its remaining two legs, trying to distance itself from the Urkay. The gushing blood mixed with the rain in the mud at the Urkay's feet as he grinned triumphantly at the fallen creature.

The spider shoved again with its two legs. Its eye swivelled in its socket, straining to watch both the Urkay and where it was sliding along the ground at the same time. Its squeals gurgled through the pooling water.

Colonel Urkay turned back to Tone. His eyes were wide, and the two bite marks on his neck had already formed a black circle wider than Tone's hand. His face was red, and his breathing came in rasping gasps that made his armor lift away from his shoulders in rhythmic clanks.

In one swift motion, the Urkay launched himself through the rain and slammed the point of his blade against Tone's tree.

Tone gasped. His eyes saw his arm, but his mind refused to acknowledge what had just happened. Something was missing. Shouldn't he feel it, though, if he'd really lost it? Blood ran out of the wrist, but Tone could only stare.

The Urkay grabbed his freed arm. He shoved his palm into the open wound, and a puff of smoke escaped at the touch. The Urkay shoved him away and grinned.

Tone tried to move his fingers...but his hand wasn't there.

He twisted his arm around and stared at the still-smoking, cauterized stump.

He slipped in the mud at his feet and collapsed against the tree, still gaping at the remains of his arm.

"Hurt?" Colonel Urkay asked, his breathing escaping in shallow gasps through the wide, thin grin.

Tone shook his head. He looked up. His bleeding hand hung limp from the sticky vine above him.

"Next time," the Urkay said, "I'll make it hurt."

The spider gave a pained wheeze behind him as if reinforcing the point. The Urkay chuckled, but didn't turn.

"Lygmies," he said, pointing the blade of his sword at Tone's chest. "You lead."

68

Rhaina

location unknown

Rhaina drifted beside Jane in the swirling darkness. Her head ached, but her mind craved more of the knowledge that had been poured into it. Histories, philosophies, theories, and truths all bounced around inside of her until Rhaina felt she must burst. But then something else, something better, found its way inside, and Rhaina felt enlivened again. It was huge, organic, and jumbled with a myriad of thoughts and expressions, personalities and individuals. She hungered for more, and she reached out into the dark.

"No," Jane whispered.

"I must," Rhaina said. "It's there, waiting for me."

"Your time is through," Jane said. Her face filtered through the darkness. The bright orange hair draped low over Jane's eyes. Her shoulders slumped, and her nose had grown flat, rough, and black.

Rhaina stared at Jane who looked as though she could barely keep her eyes open.

"You're not coming with me, are you?" Rhaina asked.

"No."

"You're...dying?"

"I'm alive," she said with a tired grin. Her head slumped forward, her features dissolved one by one, and then she faded away.

Rhaina looked around, suddenly aware of how alone she really was. She drifted, unsure where she should go or how she should get there. Together, she had let Jane take the lead. They'd traveled the universe of space and time, visiting humans and Lygmies of the past, present, and – how Rhaina knew this she had no idea – the future. She had witnessed her own birth, flown through the treetops with a group of meshet, delved into the icy chasms of Udo's arctic oceans, and chased comets through the empty expanse of the galaxy between Udo and Earth. And now she was lost.

"Hello?" she called. She didn't know what response she wanted, but nothing came back to her from the dark.

She turned left, then right, backward and forward, up and down. The same, impenetrable black surrounded her. With no sense of direction, she had no way of knowing which way was right and which was wrong. She knew, though, that if she didn't go somewhere, she wouldn't get anywhere. She took a step forward.

A blinding pinpoint of light opened in the distance. Rhaina hesitated only a moment, then continued on. She reached out for the light and saw it open wider before her. An orange eye crossed in front of the tear, obscuring the light.

Again, Rhaina hesitated, but then a voice touched her mind. She wasn't alone. The eye watched her with concern. There was nothing threatening from the giant eye.

She could think of no reason to believe the eye was benevolent, except that she knew it to be true. She continued on as the eye drifted away.

Giant hands reached around the light. They gripped the edges and tore through the darkness, ripping it away in giant sheets until Rhaina thought the light would blind her. She squeezed her eyes shut, felt herself slipping through the darkness, and put her hands out to break her fall to the ground – to real, physical ground.

Rhaina looked. The dried, black-green boards of the forest canopy sat before her nose. Rubber-wood, she thought. Of course, that wasn't the real name, but that was the closest her mind could translate the real word from Lygmese. Broken from the rubber-wood forests of the southern mainland during the second Great Harvest. Placed in the canopy for the ease and protection of The Ones, and under the direction of Elder Slungran of Mon.

"Help her," someone said.

"Leave her!" said another.

"She lived?" asked a third.

"We knew she had the power," said the first.

"But without her essence?"

Rhaina pushed up from the ground and looked sideways at the crowd of meshet standing around her. Kas and Om and Tlee and.... She knew them all.

"Rhaina?" the meshet named Om said, stepping forward.

Rhaina stood up and looked him in the eye – that same orange eye that had pierced the darkness for her. She pressed her palm against his furry chest. His heart beat hard and fast.

"Not even Ramiro...," Kas mumbled.

Rhaina turned, keeping her hand on Om's chest. Kas stood behind her, a puzzled, clinical expression to her sniffing, black snout.

"Ramiro never claimed his essence," Om said.

As if he'd heard, Ramiro walked through the crowd of meshet and placed his hand on Rhaina's shoulder.

"I prayed you would live through it," he said. But his mouth didn't move.

"I always knew she would," Om said.

Rhaina turned. Om had not moved his mouth either. But, there was something else, something about the words he'd said.

"You lied," Rhaina said.

Om beamed, then turned to Tlee, the one who yelled at them to leave Rhaina alone.

"Yes, she's magnificent," Tlee said, though Rhaina could hear the distaste with each word. "Fit to be a sister of The Ones."

Children chattered in the distance behind The Ones gathering around Rhaina. She pressed through the crowd until she could see them all playing further away. Delightful, dirty little urchins with leaves and mud in their orange hair, their ears, and across their thin warmers.

Rhaina turned back to the crowd behind her. They watched her expectantly. Pride. Amusement. Joy. Condescension. She felt it all emanating from The Ones.

"You touched my soul," she said, reaching once again toward Om.

"Your mind heard us all," he said, gesturing to the other meshet – the other Ones standing with him.

"They wanted to take you," Ramiro said, stepping forward again. "But they were afraid of you."

Rhaina laughed. These creatures were ancient in their power and experience. She was nothing more than a babe next to the youngest of them. Unless, she thought as she glanced behind her to the children again, she stood next to the smallest of the young. But the smallest one wasn't there anymore.

She turned back and walked to the shimmering cocoon suspended between two branches. It had been torn apart, and she could see the outline of her own body within its confined space. The word entered her mind in two languages at once: cocoon. They had placed her inside that cocoon, and she had been transformed, had become something new. Something not entirely human, but not entirely native either. What was she?

"Sister...," another voice whispered.

The Ones grew silent. Even the children ceased their playing.

Rhaina turned and put a hand to the second cocoon. Still whole. Still glowing with the breath of transforming life within.

"Jane," Rhaina said with recognition, caressing the silver pod. She smiled, then leaned her head against the cocoon. "I'll see you on the other side," she whispered.

69

Jake

jungle floor

"Impotent human."

"Ass-licker," Jake replied

The Pouncer glared at him but kept silent. Since announcing Jake's execution, Silny had done nothing but hurl insults at him. The partome led up a steep, winding tunnel to the surface, apparently so the Pouncer wouldn't get his little feet all wet. After a few more mutual jabs, Jake pointed out this fact to Silny, and that's when the little monster's insults turned ugly.

The rain pounded Jake's face. The dim light filtering through the canopy told him it was getting toward evening, and he'd have to turn on his tech whether he wanted to or not just to see where he was going. He'd received a low battery warning while using the tech earlier and shut it down, saving the juice until he really needed it.

"It'll be fun to watch you die," Silny said.

Jake counted the partome around them: seventeen. They'd lost one somewhere along the way.

"Did you see the Urkay stomp your musclely friend?"

He must mean Sawn, Jake thought, avoiding the pouncer's gaze.

"Squashed him like a bloated mouse."

"Hey," Jake said, punching the nearest partome in the arm.

The animal turned and snapped at Jake, the thing's teeth barely missing his hand.

Jake stopped, his feet sinking into the mud. The partome stopped and turned, a couple of them growling at him.

"Clarenden bu miksha ding, eh?" Jake said. You like a good fight, don't you?

More growls, but a couple partomes narrowed their gaze on him. He'd struck a chord with these beasts.

"Keep moving," Silny hissed, his tail swishing through the rain.

"Den 'a slitta fing, den 'a krit du brish." Maybe a little fight now, maybe a little wager on the side?

Fewer growls this time, and Jake even noticed a couple toothy grins. They liked the idea of fighting him. But Jake had a better idea.

"Bren ken Silny."

"What are you telling them, human?" the pouncer said, his eyes black and his ears flat.

The partome let out a barking laugh, throwing their heads back and whipping their fur-drida in tight arcs through the air.

"Bisch du krendal sa'an," the nearest partome barked, his smile spread wide. *"Ben slahvapa su."* I'll fight you, tall one. The tiny animal is irrelevant.

That partome took a step forward, and Jake backed off. The other partome laughed even louder.

"You're only delaying your death," Silny hissed.

"Sark barukarndlehern," Jake said, pointing at the pouncer. *"Nlaha ty uiahkreen, eh? Pilnda bisch or tren ik weq."* You hear him taunt me. Are you afraid to let him near me? I'll fight him, and I'll make it a good show for you.

Silny's eyes flashed from Jake to the grinning partome. He put his tail up and started purring as he faced the partome.

"Whatever he's saying, remember who your friend is," he said.

"I couldn't agree more," Jake said with a grin. "And what better way to show your friendship than to let him fight his own battles?" He patted the nearest partome and got a narrow-eyed growl for his effort.

Silny's tail poofed. "What did you tell them?"

The big partome, the one who wanted to fight Jake on his own, shoved Jake forward with a laugh.

"Ben du bisch," he said.

The other partome formed a loose circle in the muddy clearing and started growling, flexing their claws and swinging their fur-drida over their heads, spraying even more rain water across everyone.

"You're a fool," Silny said, turning to Jake.

"What's the matter?" Jake asked. He blinked and twisted his eyes to the right. The tech powered up throughout his body, revving his fighting systems and tensing his muscles. "Afraid of a fair fight?"

The pouncer sprang from the ground, his teeth and claws aimed at Jake's neck.

Jake stepped aside and Silny flew past. The pouncer hit the mud and spun around, his ears flat and his eyes solid black.

The partome growled in glee.

"Wow," Jake said with a yawn. "That move almost surprised me."

"It wasn't meant to surprise you," Silny hissed. "I was merely testing you."

"Oh, of course. I don't know why I didn't notice that."

The pouncer hissed.

Jake circled, letting his tech map the forest around them. No obviously simple paths of escape, but he was confident his tech would find something for him. It always did.

"You wanted this fight," Silny said. "Let's fight."

"Mm, can't be too hasty." Jake pointed at the growling partome. "I promised them a good show of it."

Silny lunged, and Jake stepped aside again. But the pouncer kinked his back in midair to come flying at Jake's face. He swung an arm around the pouncer's back, gripped him by the scruff of his neck, and flicked him back into the mud.

With a snuffling laugh, Silny got back up and licked blood from around his mouth and nose.

Jake raised his hand to see the teeth and claw marks washing bright red in the rain.

The partome cheered all around him, and Jake returned his attention to the circling pouncer. It was unnerving how well the little critter could imitate a certain smug smile.

"So much for implants," Silny said.

"Yeah, I guess I'll have to ask for a refund."

Jake's tech flashed a red path through the bushes, up a tree, and into the canopy where he could gain some protection from a series of branches while he defended himself in hand-to-hand combat against the partome. And the best part was he had a one-in-twenty chance of making it all the way up there without getting his body broken and mangled by them.

He grinned. He'd take odds like that any day.

He feinted to his left, then jumped to his right, racing past the stunned pouncer. His tech caught the sounds of the partome scrambling to stop him. They yelped and howled and crashed through the brush behind him as he let his tech take him as fast as it would go.

The implants caught the movement a moment too late to move out of the way as a heavy branch swung through the air and pounded Jake in the chest.

The air punched from his lungs, and ribs cracked. The world spun.

He skidded through the mud, his head, shoulders, back and legs crashing against rocks and tree roots until he finally came to a halt.

His tech flashed dozens of warnings before his eyes. The list of broken bones scrolled before his left eye; the damaged and bleeding internal organs before his left.

"Look at the piggies!" a large voice bellowed from somewhere above.

Jake rolled over in the mud, coughing a mouthful of blood and curling around at the pain wracking his body.

Red, flashing warnings popped up in his eyes. What wasn't broken was bleeding, and if it wasn't bleeding, it was bruised – 28% of his body needed immediate work. The nanobots were racing around to begin repairs. The medications were pumping through his bloodstream, numbing his immediate pain so he could at least think straight.

A thunderous crash resounded from somewhere nearby. The ground shook as mud, leaves, and bark splattered across Jake from the fallen tree.

He shut his eyes and replayed the recording of the last moment before this hell swept his body. A tree branch swung at him from his right side. He stopped the replay. Zoomed in on the end of the branch. Saw the filthy, blood-stained hand at least as large as Jake's entire chest gripping the end of the branch.

"What's this?" the Urkay's voice roared.

Jake opened his eyes in time to see the giant standing over him. He rolled over in the mud and gripped a rock, but the Urkay yanked him back with a twist that dislocated his left leg.

The Urkay wrenched him up from the ground and lifted him upside-down in the air until they were eye-to-eye. His hands wrapped around Jake's torso and started to squeeze.

His tech reinforced the bones around his rib cage, and Jake watched the pressure gauge rise. The Urkay laughed, and Jake recognized the thing's face as one of those eco-terrorists that had been bumbling through the jungle.

"You're hard to pop!" the Urkay said, giving Jake a violent shake.

More warnings flashed. Jake felt a moment of panic as the low-battery warning blinked alongside all the others.

"You might be more fun than Lygmies," the Urkay said. "Let's find out."

The Urkay let go of Jake with one hand, but tightened his grip with the other. He turned around and swung Jake through the air.

Jake saw the tree flying at him in Fighting-Mode slow motion. He clawed at the Urkay's hand, struggling to break the grip. Wind and rain whipped past him. Branches scraped by.

"Emergency Safeties!" he yelled to his tech.

The Urkay slammed him face-first into the tree's trunk.

70

Rhaina

jungle canopy

Rhaina collapsed to the hard, rubbery floor, the meshet around her suddenly buzzing with worry. Something...no, someone...had cried out in pain. Someone close to her. Someone...missing. The meshet sent thoughts of safety and comfort and consolation into her mind, and Rhaina had to shove them back out to think clearly.

She sat up and stared across the sea of bright, orange meshet, not really seeing any of them. Something had struck her emotions with enough force to bring her to her knees.

She scanned the silent crowd.

"Where's Jake?" she said.

Silence from the meshet. Ramiro and Cailin stared at the floor.

Rhaina looked around the groups of meshet. One female and her naked cubs were mourning their loss. Her spouse had fallen to his death in the swamps below, and he'd taken Jake down with him.

"Jake's not dead," Rhaina said. She jumped to her feet.

The meshet tried to invade her emotions, tried to shove soothing thoughts into her mind, but she wouldn't let them. Her mind swept through the jungle, past thousands of insects and animals, through the swamp water to the network of caves hundreds of tics deep, back up to the muddy land where a party of partomes had led Jake to his death at the hands of the resurrected Urkay.

Except Jake wasn't dead.

* * *

The nanobots flooded through Jake's body, working frantically to repair the most needed bones, tissues, and mechanics for him to get back up and defend himself.

"This is fun!" the Urkay yelled, hoisting Jake back into the air by his left leg. He flopped in the Urkay's grip. "Like a little macquet that won't break."

The jungle flew past Jake's field of vision. He caught flashes of trees, the rain, partome scattering back into the jungle, and even that scheming little pouncer before the Urkay tossed him into the mud.

Jake struggled to push himself up, his tech reporting what wasn't repaired. There were too many to easily count.

The Urkay roared with laughter as Jake slipped back into the mud. The warnings flashed before his eyes: he was running low on nanobots to repair everything breaking in his body, physical or tech; his odds of living through this fight were falling faster than he cared to watch; and his batteries were telling him he was down to fifteen-percent – not nearly enough to bring him back if he died again. He had to get away, fast.

The Urkay gripped a fistful of hair and hoisted him back up. Jake saw the massive fist coming straight at his face, and he twisted himself in the creature's grip, leaving behind several tufts of hair.

As Jake slipped to the ground, he heard the thundering clap of the Urkay's fist slapping the palm. Jake scuttled through the mud before the opportunity to escape left him. The low-battery warnings flashed redder and redder.

* * *

Tone shivered in the rain. He cupped the stump of his left arm and rocked on the tangle of tree roots where the Urkay had told him to sit and wait. He could hear the sounds of fighting nearby, but he didn't care. The Urkay was hurting some other defenseless animal, and that meant it wasn't hurting him for these few moments.

The Urkay barked out a laugh, and the sound echoed through the forest. A convulsive shiver ran up his spine, and he slipped from his spot to splash into the mud. He wrapped his right arm around the root and stared at what remained of his left arm. The new, red flesh itched. He reached to scratch it, but realized it wasn't the wrist at all. It was the palm of his left hand that itched, the hand that had been chopped off, like the five-fingered ghost was mocking him. Like he hadn't been reduced enough, left to pant after some maniacal jungle monster that treated him like a golden retriever: Find the Lygmies! Heel! Stay! Move, and I'll punish you even more!

Something splashed through the mud. A man cussed, then spit.

Tone gripped his left arm, willing the non-existent hand to stop itching, and scrambled over the roots until he was as far from the noise as possible.

Something hissed, very close to where Tone had been sitting. He ducked down. He had no idea what new creature was out to get him, but he didn't want to be an easy target.

"Hello?" a voice said.

Tone recognized the voice. It wasn't a friendly voice, though.

"I see you, human. Stand up."

Tone almost obeyed, then realized it wasn't the Urkay speaking so he had no reason to.

Soft steps padded across the roots. Tone curled in on himself, willing this person, whoever he was, to go away and leave him to misery.

"Commander Tone Dalal," the voice said. It was above his head.

Tone looked up. The pouncer, Silny, stood above him on the roots, staring down and licking his chops.

"How did your species ever evolve?" the pouncer said with a sniff. He turned and disappeared from sight.

How did we evolve? Tone wondered. He was better than this, and he knew it. Better than groveling along in the mud. He'd saved forests like this one. He'd rescued animals, innocent animals who deserved to live. He was a Resurrected Mother Commander, and he'd done his bit for life and ecology and the sanctity of all that was noble in the human spirit.

So how did he evolve to this?

"A pouncer somehow ended up our lunar base," Tone said. "He promised riches that would keep us solvent for centuries...and power."

Tone shoved himself up and looked across the rain-soaked forest. The little black-and-white pouncer trotted away, mud clinging to his legs, and the rain soaking his fur.

"Pathetic," Tone said, gripping the root. "Liar." He pushed himself up and crawled across the tangle of vines and roots at the tree's base. "That...thing! Deceived me?" He shook with rage at the injustice of it all. He stumbled and slipped through the mud as the pouncer disappeared through the underbrush. "No," he said, crashing after the thing. "You won't get away!"

* * *

Rhaina strode across the labyrinth of catwalks in the forest canopy, ignoring the stream of pleas and questions coming from the meshet behind her:

Was he worth it all?

She wasn't ready to confront the Urkay.

They couldn't bring back the dead.

Didn't she want to learn the subtleties of her newfound powers?

And that was the one that kept eating at Rhaina, that these jungle creatures really believed she was something special. That one meshet, Jane, had taken Rhaina through the beginnings of their metamorphosis. She had touched Rhaina's souls, connected Rhaina with the tribe, and tried to form Rhaina into something more than she'd ever dreamed possible. But without Rhaina's consent – or even her knowledge.

Who was she kidding, though? She could feel the change within her already. The meshet saw her as more than human, more than the vast Sea of Souls they roamed in their own spiritual journeys. They saw her as more than Lygme, more than the skinny, hairless little imps that roamed freely in human society, more than the majestic, orange beasts that lumbered after her, and certainly more than the mud-grubbing monsters that swam the swamps below. They'd touched her souls when she first entered the forest, and they recognized her power, and they'd tried to kidnap her like they did Ramiro, tried to convert her to their religion of tree-dwelling superiority.

"Rhaina," one lone woman's voice echoed above the crowd.

She stopped, and the crowd chasing after her stumbled over each other to keep from bumping her.

"Yes, Mother," Rhaina said, turning back to the crowd of meshet. She cringed as soon as she'd said it. Jane wasn't her mother, and it was one more insult for these meshet to plant that emotion in her mind.

"Do not run, daughter."

"Stop it!" Rhaina put out her hand and raged the power out of herself. Leaves flew. Branches snapped. Meshet flew backwards across the catwalk, some clinging to the vines and trees to keep from sailing over the edge.

"You have the power," Jane said from within her cocoon a hundred tics back. "But you don't yet have the control."

"What have you done to me?" Rhaina yelled. She slapped her hand through the air and clamped Jane's mouth shut.

"Rhaina," Ramiro said, stepping forward on the catwalk.

The meshet hung back, watching her with teeth bared and claws extended.

"Don't come near me, Ramiro."

"You can trust them," he said.

"They've...entered my head!" she said, gripping her hair. "They speak to me with their minds, they throw their emotions into my heart. Why should I trust them?"

"I trusted them," he said. "I hear them in my head. I feel their emotions in my heart. And they helped me to gain control."

The hatred burst through Rhaina's body, and she gripped the nearest branch for support. The emotion hadn't come from within her, though, but from somewhere outside of herself, from someone on the ground. A human. A broken, injured human....

"Tone," Rhaina said, tears rushing down her cheeks.

"I feel it too," Ramiro said. "But it hasn't overwhelmed me. My souls are in harmony. Yours are still scattered."

"My second soul was kidnapped!" Rhaina said, rounding on him again. She reached out to shove him back, and her fingertips touched his face for a fraction of a second. It was enough for her to contact his spirit, to see all the way through to his deepest emotions, most intimate thoughts and private feelings. He cared for her. He hated to see her hurting like this. Most impressive of all, though, was that he was being completely honest with her. He truly believed everything he said.

He also lacked a tenth of the power that flowed through Rhaina's spirit.

"Weakness," she said, stunned at the feeling. Instead of shoving him away, she looked into his caring, friendly eyes. "Where did I get this power? Not from the Lygmies."

"Not from the Lygmies," he said, taking her hand. "The power was in you already, through your second soul."

Panic.

Rhaina gasped as the emotion seized her.

"Don't!" Ramiro said, squeezing her hand to keep her facing him.

Death. True death. A death from which you could never return. It was coming for him.

"Jake." Rhaina yanked her hand away.

The jungle flashed before her eyes. That colonel's horribly disfigured face came into view. He laughed at her – he laughed at Jake. He brought his fist around and slammed it into Jake's chest.

Rhaina's legs slipped out from beneath her. She found herself face-down on the catwalk's hard floor.

"You don't have control," Ramiro said.

But she didn't need control, Rhaina thought, as the rage swelled within her.

71

Jake

jungle floor

So many warnings flashed before Jake's eyes that he shut them all off. He didn't have enough power to heal half the broken things in his body. He could feel the gears grinding to keep his body moving, bones and muscles operating on the tech's autopilot. The tech was still trying to get him clear of the Urkay's wrath, but Jake knew that would never happen.

He stood and braced himself against a tree. He couldn't take a deep breath without feeling his ribs trying to cave in. His right foot pointed out perpendicular to his left. Both his arms were bruised and bloody. The tech had numbed so much of his body to make repairs that he felt like he was floating on his feet.

"You make a stand?" the Urkay bellowed from behind him. "Or you run away again, and I chase you?"

His life had been good, Jake thought, staring through the trees. Funny that it would end in this jungle in the middle of nowhere, away from any people. He'd expected to go out in a flourish of gunfire in some hyper, light-saturated, nightclub somewhere, maybe fighting for a couple million's worth of antique pictures, or something equally ridiculous. Out here, no one would ever find his body, and that was kind of sad. He'd always hoped for a good picture and headline. Most everyone who knew he was in this jungle was either dead, too far away to ever find him again, or wrapped in a cocoon....

Rhaina, you made life good.

He should have stayed with her, he thought, and he chuckled at that – then winced until the tech pumped some more pain relievers into his bloodstream. All the time they'd lived together, worked together, conned together, neither had ever spoken the "M" word. It wasn't that either of them was opposed to the idea, they just never had the time or inclination to think about it. Or at least, he never did. He really couldn't say what Rhaina thought on the matter. He should have asked.

"Do you sleep?" the Urkay said.

Jake sighed, and the movement sent prickles of pain through his chest. His tech was running so low on resources it couldn't keep the pain away any longer.

Do or die, he thought, turning around to face the monster. He flashed his best smart-ass grin at the thing.

"Wondering when your momma's coming here to give you the lickin' of a lifetime," he said.

The Urkay's eyes narrowed.

"Of course, your momma's probably as ugly as you." Jake stepped across the muddy ground, careful not to slip in the running pools of water or trip over the exposed tree roots.

"You...insult me?"

"Would I do that?" Jake said with a laugh and a quick grip of his side to pressure against the pain. "I don't think you know me very well if that's what you think of me."

The Urkay's face contorted, and Jake saw the flash of his friend Sawn in the bulky features. Just as quickly, the eco-terrorist's face returned.

"You have no control," Jake said.

"I control." The Urkay stepped forward, pounding the mud between them into submission.

"You control nothing." He yanked a vine to steady himself, then kicked a pile of mud at the Urkay's rusted armor. "You're nothing more than a bully – a bully with multiple personalities. Who else have you got hidden in there?"

"I am one." The Urkay's head snapped back as his face contorted with rage. The features twisted again. The eyes shifted, the cheekbones raised, the lips stretched, and Rhaina looked back out of the thing's anguished face.

Jake stood there, stunned, staring at the thing. He thought back to the dungeon. The creature had killed – swallowed up! – Sawn, then Khonane. But Rhaina had been safe. She was hurt somehow, but she was safe. He and Cailin dragged her out of that lair. They'd been kidnapped by meshet, then....

The realization hit him harder than Urkay's punches. The meshet had stolen her from him. Ramiro had helped them, had been brainwashed by those Lygmies who lived in the trees with their pet meshet. The man had actually believed the meshet wouldn't hurt Rhaina. And, when Jake wouldn't go along with their psychotic plans, they dumped his body in the swamp...and fed Rhaina to this monster.

Her face disappeared again into the folds of the Urkay's slimy skin, replaced by that deranged eco-terrorist again.

"Now I squash you," the Urkay said with a grin.

Rhaina, Jake thought. Just her name stung him now – regret. Sadness.

Resolve.

He blinked and twisted his eyes to the right. Warnings flashed before his eyes, but he shut them all off. Fighting Mode took over his tech's functions, and the world ground to a halt around him. Thousands of glittering rain drops fell between him and his Urkay opponent.

The creature started to step forward, and Jake darted to the left. His hands gripped a stone from the mud. The targeting sights lined up the shot automatically, and he flung the fist-sized rock at the Urkay's temple, then slipped aside without waiting to see it hit the mark. He found a second rock, then a third and a fourth.

The Urkay swung wildly at him as he circled the thing, its eyes wide and bloodied and a booming laugh escaping its throat.

A final warning blinked red in the corner of Jake's vision: his batteries were almost out.

He lunged through the air and landed on the creature's armored back. He reached one arm around the thing's neck and squeezed tight, cutting off its air.

The Urkay pounded its fists across Jake's back, each blow crushing his body and dropping his battery levels by whole percentages.

>7%

Another blow.

>6%

Again, this time to his head.

>5%

Jake thrust his fist into the creature's eye, shattering the membrane and forcing his way through the tissues beneath.

The Urkay roared its pain.

The metal flashed through the glittering rain. The rusted sword swung at Jake, but with one arm holding him in place and the other buried in the creature's eye socket, he couldn't move quickly enough.

The blade sliced his back.

>2%

The creature gripped him by the scruff of his neck.

>1%

It yanked him off and tossed him through the air.

The batteries died. The world flew back into normal speed. Rain slashed Jake's body as the sudden pain of his injuries sent him into shock. He fell in the mud with a pained grunt.

The Urkay came at him again, and Jake had enough time to see the thing's bloodied eye had already grown back. The Urkay grinned and reared back for a kick.

Jake never felt the blow as the world turned black around him.

72

Rhaina

jungle canopy

Rhaina felt the loss in her spirit.

"Jake," she said as she ran along the catwalk. She was already too late. For whatever reason, he'd turned to fight instead of trying to keep himself alive. He'd thrown himself at the creature, trying to defeat a thing he couldn't even injure.

She stopped running and looked down. She was directly above the Urkay. Partomes stood just outside the thing's sight, watching Jake's body get pummeled with each brutal strike.

"No!" Ramiro said.

Rhaina looked around, but he was nowhere to be seen. Instead, Cailin had caught up with her, trailed by dozens of invisible meshet. She felt the animals in the trees, on the catwalk, and even climbing around beneath her to watch the Urkay from a safe distance.

"Ramiro said to tell you," Cailin said. "You're too valuable – to the meshet. He said – well, he said you shouldn't do something stupid."

"I'm doing this," Rhaina said.

"The meshet really brainwashed him, didn't they?"

Rhaina smiled. Finally, someone was on her side. "I need to get down there."

Cailin slipped the blow-gun from its holster, snapped a sheerwire spool into place, and aimed at the trees above Rhaina. The dart shot from the gun and lodged itself deep into a trunk. A metallic snap resounded from the tree as the exploding spikes secured it. Cailin handed the gun and belt clippings to Rhaina, then a pair of gloves from her back pocket.

"Do not follow me," Rhaina said as she took the weapon. She secured it to the belt and around her waist, then slipped on the gloves.

Cailin said nothing, but Rhaina knew better than to assume that was a yes.

The meshet stirred in the trees around them as Rhaina slipped over the catwalk's railing vine. She gripped the sheerwire and dropped into the trees. Falling through the branches and leaves, she left the protection of the meshets' invisible umbrella. Rain slapped harder at her face than the foliage did. Then, in a spray of water and leaves, she left the canopy and was dropping through open air.

She knew what to expect, but the scene on the ground still shocked her. Several dozen partomes stood around the trees, chanting and egging on the Urkay who was kicking Jake's broken body through the trampled and muddy underbrush.

The instant rage overwhelmed her, and she wished – she demanded! – that the creature leave him alone.

The Urkay flew backwards like something had punched it in the stomach.

Rhaina dropped to the ground with a yell, and the partome sprang at her.

Meshet materialized all around, clinging to the trees, crouching on the ground, and even leaping through the air. The trampled clearing filled with the screams of savage, fighting animals. Blood flew on the air, mixing with the rain, mud, and falling leaves.

Jane's voice burst into Rhaina's mind, drowning out all other noises: "This is foolish," she said. "Think of your potential. We've not yet trained you!"

Rhaina ignored Jane's pleading words and strode forward, untouched by any of the creatures around her.

The Urkay jumped back to his feet, sword drawn and blood streaming from his distorted, Colonel Walraven features.

"A mouse!" it said with a laugh. "Come to me, mouse."

Rhaina smiled as she called to her second soul.

* * *

Geminai and Khonane pounded against the door to the Urkay's black mind. The strengthened bond of their now-spoken love had made them more powerful by a hundred-fold, but it still wasn't enough to overcome the hatred and malevolence driving the creature forward. Colonel Walraven and Mr. Rosh had barricaded themselves inside the Urkay's mind, and they refused to relinquish any control.

The brief flashes of battle had shown the Urkay doing terrible, evil things. It had reveled in the pain of chopping off that poor man's hand, and then it had feasted on the power needed to fight Jake and his over-tech'd body.

But something had changed a moment ago, something that actually seemed to make a difference in the way the creature acted. For the first time since trying to break through to the creature's mind, it seemed genuinely worried about something.

"I hear meshet," Khonane said, throwing another shoulder against the dark door.

"And partome," Geminai said. She shoved with all her spiritual strength, but the door to the creature's mind didn't even creak. "They're fighting."

"There must be a lot of them to make the Urkay scared."

Geminai staggered back with a gasp. Something powerful had touched her, tried to contact her, tried to take control.

Khonane reached out to steady her.

The power shoved its way through the Urkay's black hide. Geminai screamed. She felt the power tugging at her, trying to make a connection.

"What is it?" Khonane asked.

"It hurts," Geminai cried. She clawed at her chest, trying to dig out the prickling that told her something was trying to make a connection with her spiritual cord. She thought of the Sea of Souls and of the ravenous Nomads hungering for her, and she panicked. Running from the Urkay's mind, she tried to dive out of the creature's impenetrable hide.

"Stop it," Khonane said, trying to grab her arms. "Stop it! Rhaina!"

At the sound of that name, the presence swept into Geminai's soul. She dropped to her knees with a gasp as the spiritual bond snapped tight to her human...and to the thousands, the millions, of meshet moving through the forests of Udo. Rhaina's newest memories poured back into Geminai: the torture of the Urkay stealing Geminai from her; Jake rescuing her from the Urkay's flooding dungeon; the party of meshet – and their Lygme children – meeting in the trees to decide her fate. And the cocoon. Rhaina's time in the meshet cocoon where Jane led her through the Awakening rituals to become more than she'd ever dreamed possible. To become a spirit without bounds. And now Geminai and Rhaina were once again tethered, reunited in their spiritual bodies.

"Rhaina?" Khonane squinted through the darkness like she was some kind of freak, backing away and putting his hand before his face.

Shafts of light exploded from Geminai's spiritual body, golden beams pulsating through the Urkay's black chasm. The light exposed the decay surrounding them, the decomposing tendrils on the sides of the Urkay's inner body, the barricaded walls and doors leading to hidden portions of its psyche.

"Hello, you," Rhaina whispered.

Geminai shut her eyes and smiled, golden tears streaming down her face. Her human had returned. The world was finally good again.

And then Rhaina felt the change within her Geminai, the scent of another upon her second soul. The scent of bonding.

"Khonane," she said.

He stood before Geminai, diminished in her radiating presence. He lowered his hand and squinted into the blinding light.

"Rhaina? Is that really you?"

"Oh, Khonane," she said through her Geminai's saddened voice. "What did you do?"

Before he could respond, sheer joy flooded through the Urkay's body. Geminai looked past Khonane to the stone door blocking the Urkay's central point of control. Colonel Walraven and Mr. Rosh had barricaded themselves inside, fueling the Urkay's rage and guiding his vendetta. Just on the other side of that room, in the physical world of the rain-filled jungle, Jake lay broken and bleeding in the trampled mud.

The revulsion coursed through Geminai's spirit. The Urkay body had done something horrible, and the elation surged through its every fiber – trying to infect Geminai, trying to infect Rhaina.

"This ends now," Rhaina declared.

She and Geminai burst from the confines of the Urkay's body, binding their spiritual cords to the thousands of meshet within the forest. They channeled the combined energy into one pounding force that blew apart the rage and hatred guarding the Urkay's primal control. Stones and metal and living tissue erupted in flames around the blown-apart door, spewing smoke and embers across the forms of Colonel Walraven and Mr. Rosh.

Geminai strode through the destruction and into the ruined room that looked out on the world around the Urkay – the world of the creature's mind, its senses, and its desires. The eye holes showed the jungle, the fighting partome and meshet, the rain pouring into the mud and mixing with Jake's blood.

"What the hell are you?" Mr. Rosh demanded.

Rhaina reached out with one glowing hand, gripped the man around the neck, and twisted. The neck snapped. The man's spirit collapsed to the floor. She turned to Colonel Walraven.

"Geminai," the colonel said, rubbing a hand across his cheek. "I told that lunatic Mr. Rosh he could never keep you out, but he wouldn't listen to me. He wouldn't listen to reason."

"Shut up," Rhaina said, stepping forward. She peered out of the Urkay's eyes and watched Jake lying on the ground. She reached out with her spirit, but she got nothing back from him. They'd killed him.

"I told him not to do it," Colonel Walraven blustered. "But there was no stopping him. You saw him. He was a madman."

"May I kill that guy?" Khonane said from the other side of the room.

"Kill me?" Colonel Walraven said with a nervous laugh. "Geminai – Rhaina! You wouldn't want to do that. I've been trying to help you – to stop this lunatic!" He gestured at Mr. Rosh's still body on the floor between them, the neck cocked at a right angle.

"Run," Rhaina whispered.

"What?" the colonel asked.

"Run." She looked him in the eye. "Now. Fast."

In a flash, his spirit soared through the Urkay's open eye, and he was gone.

"You let him go? Why?" Khonane said.

Rhaina dropped her gaze, stepped up to Khonane, and took his hand. "I can't help you," she said. "Your body is gone."

"I know," he said with a shrug. "This is death, but I'm here with you. This is all I need."

"But I'm not here. I'm still alive." She looked up, stroked her hand through his mussed hair, and smiled. "You really loved me, didn't you?"

"I have always loved you."

She sighed, leaned forward, and gave him a soft kiss. "I'm glad our spirits could find the courage to be honest with each other, even if we never could."

"So what happens now?"

She put a finger to his lips. "You're safe inside this shell, inside this Urkay. But out there, you'd be nothing more than food for the Soul Hunters."

"I have you."

"It's not enough." She put her hand across his eyes to shut the lids, reached up and kissed him one last time. "I love you," she whispered.

She felt his spirit die beneath her. He slumped forward, and she caught him, gently lowered him to the floor. She held his fading spirit, rocking him back and forth in the gloomy chamber. She shut her eyes to the pain of her decision, but she had done the right thing. She knew it was the right thing. He couldn't stay in this plain of existence. He had to be forced away, forced to move on for his own safety or he would be a soul with no person, a spirit wandering aimlessly in and out of the Sea of Souls.

But that didn't make the pain any easier.

She kissed his lifeless cheek and shut her eyes.

* * *

Tone stumbled through the forest. The sounds of fighting had stopped suddenly, moments ago, but that didn't distract him from his goal: he would catch that evil little pouncer, and he would make the creature pay for the pain he had caused.

Something gripped Tone's chest. It flung him backwards to the ground and slammed into his body, nearly arresting his heart in mid beat.

The presence flooded through Tone. The man's spirit slipped into Tone's skin, inhabiting Tone's arms, legs and head. The sweet scent of sweat and fear invaded his nostrils, and Tone heard the man's breathing from within his soul.

"Colonel?" Tone said, sitting up in the mud.

There was no physical response, no change in Tone's body, and certainly nothing as dramatic as when the spirit had first thrown him to the ground. But Tone felt the immense satisfaction that the spirit had been recognized for what it was, his old buddy from the Resurrected Mother organization.

"You never wanted to help anyone else, did you?" Tone called.

An upswelling of pride.

Tone clambered up beside a tree, rain pouring over the downturned leaves and running down his head, neck, and back. He shivered, as much from the spirit now residing within him as from the cool rain.

"You would have turned your back on everything we ever stood for – for our ideals!" He tore at his shirt with his good, right hand, and beat at the air around him with the stump of his left. "Get out of me. Get out!"

He clawed and tore and raged at the spirit, all the while hearing the echoes of laughter reverberate through his ears. The colonel was enjoying the show, and that infuriated Tone even more. He turned to flail against the nearest tree, but something else, something as powerful as the gods, held him still.

Tone stood against his will, desperately fighting to regain control of himself. For a fleeting moment, he thought he might have actually died, but then he felt the fear of Colonel Walraven's spirit within him, and he knew even his death would not have terrified his old friend so much.

The rain stopped falling. The trees shown golden around him. And something rose behind him, throwing Tone's shadow across the wet branches and leaves before him. Sparkles of golden light reflected off the glistening branches. The air crackled with the electricity of the power standing behind him, holding him still.

A hand punched through the Tone's chest, shoving neck-first the thrashing spirit of Colonel Walraven out of his body and into the bright glow.

An icy wind passed through Tone, and a woman – Rhaina – stepped through his body, first an arm, then a leg, her head, the other leg, all the while shoving the colonel out before her. She glowed brilliant white. Her hair waved behind her like she floated through a wind that howled around her alone. She turned to look at Tone, and fire flared through her eyes.

"An angel?" he whispered.

She smiled, and a shiver arched down Tone's body.

"I'm sorry he bothered you," she said, tilting her golden head to the colonel still struggling in her locked grip.

"Thank you," Tone said. That seemed the most inadequate thing he could have said, but anything more would have sounded stupid. How do you talk to an angel?

She turned and looked into his eyes. Tone had to look away, had to stop himself from falling into the blazing beauty of her face, her eyes, her silently blowing hair. That's when he noticed he had control of his own body again. He didn't know when she'd let him go, but he was glad.

"You're chasing that little pouncer, aren't you?" she asked.

Tone nodded.

The angel Rhaina smiled a wicked grin, then vanished with the struggling Colonel still in her grip.

The rain dumped back on Tone, and he ducked beneath an overhanging branch, cradling the stump of his left arm and staring through the darkening forest. The colonel was a ghost? That Rhaina woman was a ghost? And a Lygme god out of some horror of a legend had been rampaging through the forest? If his cauterized arm didn't hurt so bad, he would have thought it all a nightmare brought on by some bad rations back at the lunar base.

He missed that old place. He and the colonel had done some real good back there, long ago, before this chaotic dream of riches seemed to take hold of him and poison his soul. Good work. Helping the Earth to survive the industries polluting the rivers and soil, killing trees by the millions. It felt good to see all the things they'd done back then, when they'd first started. Before the politicians wised up to the Earth's predicament. Before they enacted the Worldwide Environmental Restrictions and put some real teeth into the punishments. An activist should never have to outlive his own cause.

Tone shivered.

With a crack and a blinding glow, the rain stopped again, and the Rhaina ghost appeared before him. She held the colonel's arm with her right hand and had Silny by the scruff of the neck in the other hand. The Pouncer hissed and pawed at the air with his extended claws, spitting obscenities every few breaths.

"They've tormented you these past weeks," Rhaina said.

Tone nodded.

She swung her right hand around and shoved the colonel's hand into the Pouncer's wide-open mouth. The animal jerked and shuddered, but Rhaina kept pushing, stuffing the colonel's arm in, then his shoulder. The colonel twisted his head away, but Rhaina shoved that in too, then his other arm, his torso, legs, and feet. She dropped Silny to the ground.

The Pouncer thrashed and clawed, scratched at his neck and mouth, and he leaned over to gag like he was hacking a hairball. Nothing came out.

"They're all yours now," Rhaina said. "Your pets, to do with as you please."

She disappeared, the brilliant glow vanishing from the forest and leaving Tone standing there, staring at the agonizing Pouncer on the ground before him. The rain poured back over them both. Tone knelt, watching the animal roll through the mud as it tried to get the colonel's ghost back out.

"Tell me," Tone said with a grin and a cock of his head. "Tell me...about that gem again. And about all the good we could do with that money."

Silny spit a mouthful of mud, shook the water from his ears, and started biting at his fur.

* * *

Rhaina sighed as she retreated back inside her physical self. So many decisions. So many choices. She hated making them all – *Khonane, I am so sorry,* she whispered. One more, though, and this one no longer in her control. She knelt in the mud beside Jake's dead body, the meshet and partome fighting all around her. Bones broke, blood flew through the rain, animals died on each side. It was their millennia-old civil war, but she didn't care. She took Jake's bloodied and broken head and cradled it in her lap, stroking the wet, sticky hair.

Geminai grieved within her, grieved for her own loss, for the loss of Khonane. Soul mate? Maybe. Now they would never know.

And what of Jake? They'd loved each other back then, on Earth, pulling jobs and getting rich and living the good life in each other's company. It wasn't so much that they drifted apart, but he said he had a bead on the job of a lifetime, "The Job," the one that would set them up for life. And then he disappeared. Now she knew why. This was the job, this gem in the middle of a Lygme jungle. This job had killed so many people, had nearly stolen her Geminai from her.... And for what? A Lygme civil war that had been raging forever? So long that neither side even cared anymore why it was being fought. It just had to go on.

Like the bloodshed around her.

Like the Lygmies killing each other, the meshet-Lygmies, the partome-Lygmies, the young Lygmies who looked so much like little humans that nobody had ever thought they were anything other than the real things, the grownups running the show down here on their planet. But they were just the children.

Don't try, Jane whispered to her soul, and Rhaina knew what the metamorphosing Lygme feared. Unity. Peace.

It cannot happen, Jane said. *You cannot bring it about; you cannot stop the war. It must go on.*

And Rhaina burned in anger at the injustice of it all. At the Lygmies who had died. At the humans who had died in this chess game the Lygmies called their life. At Jake's death, his broken body lying here before her in the mud.

"No," she said. She reached out and touched Geminai.

Do not do this, Jane pleaded.

Geminai grabbed hold of a Lygme spirit, catching the creature's attention in mid-fight. She caught another, then a fourth, fifth, sixth. She bound the struggling spirits with the vision she held in her mind, a vision of unity from long ago, from the last time the Lygmies united in the face of a common enemy. The last time the Urkay had freely roamed the land.

It cannot be done, Jane said. *You will die.*

Rhaina's spiritual web stretched through the forest and caught up every last Lygme, whether meshet or partome. She found the common bond between them all, the spiritual bond that made them all one species. Diverged eons ago by the whim of evolution, these creatures retained so much of each other there was almost nothing different between them spiritually. The freedom of the air called the meshet to flight while the beauty of the sea held the partome entranced in its depths.

The Lygmies realized what she intended.

The forest grew silent.

Rhaina focused her thoughts and forced her will out to the hundreds of Lygmies surrounding her. They fought back, stiffening their resolve to never work together.

"You will," Rhaina said.

We will not, Jane replied.

Rhaina stood up, spread her arms, and encircled the forest with her spirit.

The Lygmies resisted. They turned and faced her on the forest floor, thousands of eyes and hungry teeth threatening to strike swiftly and without mercy if she did not desist.

"You will do this," Rhaina yelled, turning to face them all in turn, the rain running down her face and body, her feet squishing through the mud.

A low growl built in the trees, on the ground, and in the air as the Lygmies focused their hatred and rebelliousness on Rhaina.

A voice whispered through the spirits. It carried on the wind, a lilt to the attitudes if not the spoken words.

The cocoons, Ramiro said.

Every Lygme tensed.

Geminai wrapped her spirit around the cocoons.

"You will do this thing!" Rhaina yelled, and she forced the image into their minds – that she might take every last cocoon.

As one, the Lygmies lunged.

Geminai gripped the cocoons.

Rhaina enfolded herself within the spiritual union of the Lygme children, the meshet, and the partomes. She dropped to her knees and gripped Jake's dead body –

– and they all vanished from the forest.

73

Jake

location unknown

Jake drifted. Voices came and went.

The world revolved black and green. His tech winked around him, but then disappeared.

"Well?" a woman said. She sounded familiar, but so far away, like she stood at the other end of a long, dark tunnal and spoke into a weak microphone.

"Ya ya," a second voice said, this one much closer. This voice practically roared in Jake's ears. "He live. He been bamboozled somethin' jackin' wild, though. He need to rest."

"Do it," the woman said.

The voices continued, but they drifted away, back into their dream land.

74

Jake

He first heard the heart monitor's increased, rhythmic chirping. It hadn't been a dream after all. He lived. His body ached, and he told the tech to release a short burst of pain killers. He felt better in seconds, and he took a deep breath.

The bed rocked.

Jake opened his eyes.

A meshet sat balanced on the railing at the end of the bed, its orange fur bristling and its eyes flicking over Jake's prone body. It licked its chops, the orange tongue wiping back the whiskers from around its mouth.

Jake heard a low growl from beside his head. A second meshet leaned into his field of vision and stared into Jake's eyes.

Jake wondered if this was a nightmare. How long had it been? The tech flashed his internal clock, and Jake saw he'd lost a week since his time in the jungle fighting the Urkay.

"Rhaina," he mumbled. Had she made it out?

The meshet hovering by his head disappeared. Vanished was more like it as the thing's fur rippled colors until it blended into the room's muted grays and browns. A door opened and shut.

Jake looked back at the meshet at the end of the bed. The thing cocked its head and stared back at him in silence. They sat that way for several seconds, each waiting for the other to make a move.

Jake didn't feel confident about the situation. How many more were there? There could be dozens of the things hiding around the room, blending in with the walls, the computers, the curtains. Better to stay in the bed and wait for a clear sign to do...something. Whenever his brain came up with a plan that incorporated the fact he didn't know where he was, where his weapons were, or even if he would be able to go anywhere once he left this room.

The door opened and closed again.

A woman came into the room and spoke Lygmese. She told the meshet – "Jane" – to get off the bed. With a gentle lunge, the Jane meshet leaped to the back of the poofy chair in the corner, then turned and continued staring at Jake.

Rhaina stood beside the bed and smiled.

"Good morning," she said.

Jake didn't have to think about it. He reached up and pulled her down to the bed.

* * *

When Jake woke up next, the room was distinctly darker, the meshet was no longer hovering in the corner, and Rhaina was laying beside him, lightly touching his hair. He had his tech run a quick diagnostic and found his body completely healed. He still felt a little tired, but he couldn't remember ever being happier.

"Good evening," Rhaina said.

"It's a great evening," Jake said with a smile.

"You going to fall asleep on me again?"

"Don't you think you should cut me some slack?"

Rhaina blinked, then glanced down at his bare chest and ran her cool fingers over his skin. "You're right, Jake," she said. "You're the man of the hour."

"How did we get here?" he asked, glancing around the room. He knew the room this time; a recovery room in 2 Glorious's refab shop. It was several thousand kilotics – and an entire continent – away from the temple in the jungle.

"A coordinated effort," Rhaina whispered. "I came here with you and a few Lygmies; Cailin and Ramiro were brought up later by some other Lygmies."

"And the meshet," he said, looking back in the corner. It was still empty. Well, it looked empty. He really couldn't be sure the meshet wasn't still hiding there, blending in with the dark wallpaper. "They're really adult Lygmies?"

"Yeah. The partomes, too. Just...another kind of Lygme, one more branch on their evolutionary tree." She rolled off the bed and stood up.

"What's wrong?" Jake sat up and reached out to her. She let him take her hand, but she kept her distance.

"I have to go," she said.

"But...where? Why?"

She looked at him and grinned. "I have a job," she said. "I leave on the midnight shuttle."

"But I just woke up." He tugged at her arm, and she came closer to the bed. "Besides, I thought maybe I could make it up to you. You know, for being gone. I know you were worried, and it was wrong, to leave for as long as I did. But...." He slid her hand down his chest and under the covers. "I could make it up to you."

"Jake, I cannot stay." She smiled but withdrew her hand.

With a deep sigh, he reached up and kissed her forehead. She was about to cry, and he didn't know why. Something more was going on with her, and nothing would keep her here anymore. For whatever reason, she was determined to leave, and he had to let her go. "Will you call?"

"When I can," she whispered.

"Then I won't keep you." He kissed her again, this time on the lips. "I love you."

She brushed her fingers through his hair, smoothing it around his ears. She stood up and walked from the room. The door swung shut and latched into place, leaving Jake in silence.

* * *

At the sound of the latch clicking into place, Rhaina turned back to the door and leaned against the fake wood. She shut her eyes. She could still see through the door. She could see Jake sitting in the bed and picking at the covers, fidgeting with nothing in particular until he finally grabbed the magazine on the table and started paging through it. The God's Ear gem glowed brilliant brown from inside the closet, from inside the left pocket of his pants.

She opened her eyes and stared at the door, trying to focus her vision on one reality, the physical reality. Her Geminai stayed still at her side as she struggled to keep control of her spiritual self.

This is the worst time for you to leave.

Rhaina didn't even turn. She didn't have to. Jane's spirit glowed fiery red behind her, impossible to miss.

You don't have control, she spoke into Rhaina's mind.

"I'm not staying."

"Of course not," Cailin said.

Rhaina jerked around and stared at Cailin. Now that she'd turned, she could see the woman's spirit clearly standing beside her. Rhaina hadn't looked before.

I can teach you control, Jane said.

"Rhaina, is this overgrown Lygme bothering you?" Cailin said, pointing at Jane.

"No," Rhaina said as she started down the hallway. "Let's go."

"Ramiro decided to stay."

"I'm happy for him." Rhaina looked back over her shoulder to see the meshet, Jane, still standing in the hallway.

Running away will not help, Jane continued.

Rhaina ignored her and turned around, leaving the Lygmies and their cursed homeworld for good. Never to return.

75

Jake

Jake stood by the bed and watched himself in the mirror as he buttoned the dark green shirt. It was a new shirt that Rhaina had left for him. Long-sleeved with a tight cut around the shoulders and neck. It looked good on him.

He pulled the black pants off the hanger in the closet and a weight yanked them from his grip. The pants clunked to the floor.

He reached down and picked them up again. There was something heavy in the front pocket. He unzipped the fasten, reached inside, and pulled out a large stone.

The God's Ear gem gleamed in his hand, its brown angles reflecting lights across the room and into his eyes. He grinned. He had no idea how Rhaina had gotten this thing back from the Urkay, but she had done it.

2 Glorious spent the night telling Jake all the rumors and stories that were flying through town. How a woman had suddenly appeared in the city center surrounded by packs of meshet and partomes. Giant cocoons had hung suspended from the building rafters and doorways until the animals rounded up the cocoons and strung them from trees. They hatched several days later, adding another dozen animals to the city's population. The locals were not happy, and they were spreading

stories of the woman being some kind of sorceress or maybe even a demon.

Any woman who could accomplish all that could certainly sneak a priceless gem into his pants. Of course, now he had to figure out how to get it off the planet.

He smiled as he shoved the gem back into the pocket. This would be fun.

H. Dean Fisher
*Photo by: John
Kilker at
JohnJKilker.com*

H. Dean Fisher is author of the fantastic, the scientifically fictional, and the macabre. He has been writing since he was 5: first comic books, then short stories, and now novels. He currently teaches in a mass communication department at a private university in Pennsylvania.

Website: www.HDeanFisher.com - Sign up for the monthly newsletter.
Facebook: www.facebook.com/SeventhBattlePublishing
Twitter: @HDeanFisher1
Instagram: HDeanFisher

Books by H. Dean Fisher

MEDUSA: RISE OF A GODDESS

(Forthcoming 2022)

Medusa: The monster from legend, with snakes for hair and a gaze that turns humans to stone. Cursed by Athena for the crime of being raped, she was destined to be slain by Perseus. Except...she never died. The stories got it wrong.

At the dawn of creation, the girl Medusa lives with her family on the Eastern Edge of the World, but she yearns for more. Fascinated by the newly-created humans, she leaves home to see it all for herself, the farms, the cities, and the temples. Little does she know that a sex-crazed God has been lusting after her for decades. He intends her for Himself, and His obsession will change the course of her life for millennia.

In modern New York City, Chloe finally embraces her true self: After years of repressing it, she's willing to admit her own bisexual nature. Her religiously-conservative husband, however, is not, and Chloe flees the abuse that follows. What she doesn't know is that a creature from legend, a myth come to life – Medusa herself – has been hiding in plain sight, and they are about to come face-to-face.

One woman's deity cursed her for being true to herself. The other woman's deity won't allow her to become her true self. Together, they might have the strength to overcome, and to embrace the divine.

THE INITIATE: THE TALES OF ZHAVA BOOK 1

Zhava's life was planned for her: She was promised in marriage to a respectable trader's son across the mountains. But as her father negotiated the bride-price, the King's guards showed up, paid him more than he asked, and took her away. As one blessed by the Gods, Zhava can control the wind and small rocks - and most impressive of all, fire. Now an Initiate at the King's training center, Zhava must study the kingdom's holy book, learn to fight with a sword, and hardest of all, take firm control of her Gods-given Abilities.

Not all is safe for her and the other trainees, however. Students and even soldiers are vanishing in the night, stolen away by a mighty creature out of legend. Worst of all, the creature is controlled by a shadowy figure who quotes an evil God and seems determined to kill anyone loyal to the King - especially those blessed with Abilities such as Zhava's.

7,000 years ago, when the Gods bestowed their gifts, one girl received more than she ever dreamed.

THE NOVICE: THE TALES OF ZHAVA BOOK 2

Zhava is doing well in her new life: she has many friends, she's learning to use her magical abilities, and she's been promoted to Novice rank. But when everything seems to be going her way, tragedy strikes: her parents are kidnapped and sold into slavery – and her former fiancé is behind it. Transferred to the command of the King's guard, Zhava and her friends must retake the farmstead and rescue her family.

But the kidnapping is not that simple. High Priest Viekoosh, follower of an evil God, is manipulating things behind the scenes. He's gathering an army of cult followers in the desert to start a war between the kingdoms, and he's employed a pair of mercenaries to capture Zhava: a woman who wields water with as much force as Zhava controls fire, and a powerful giant almost impervious to magic.

With time running out to rescue her parents, and her friends in danger from mercenary thugs, Zhava must learn to balance sword with fire, security with danger…and her mission to rescue her family against the lives of her friends.

A REVELATION OF OUR SAVIOR: WITH TRANSLATION AND COMMENTARY BY DR. MICHEL S. CURLLEN

Hidden in the forests of Romania, buried deep underground, a treasure house of secret documents has been kept out of sight for millennia.

When a team of researchers accidentally discovers the documents, warnings are whispered. People vanish. The camp suffers a midnight attack. And a secret order of religious zealots will stop at nothing to keep the truth from being revealed to the world. But what is that truth?

Dr. Michel S. Curllen is the only person to survive the tragedy and escape with the secret documents. Now, in his own words, he describes the harrowing account of the most significant discovery of ancient artifacts to happen in over 75 years – and you can read one of those documents for yourself: The Revelation of Simon, a follower of the Christ. Painstakingly translated by Dr. Curllen, including an in-depth analysis of the Revelation, you can decide for yourself what it was that was so dangerous that people had to die, and Dr. Curllen had to suffer so much.

Hidden for 2,000 years. Protected by a secret order. Read what was never meant to be seen again.